BEYOND THE

HIGHLAND

MIST

KAREN MARIE MONING

A Dell Book

BEYOND THE HIGHLAND MIST
A Dell Book

PUBLISHING HISTORY
Dell mass market edition / March 1999
Dell mass market reissue / June 2004

Published by
Bantam Dell
A Division of Random House, Inc.
New York, New York

ISBN 0-440-24235-5

Manufactured in the United States of America
Published simultaneously in Canada

OPM 10 9 8 7 6 5 4 3 2 1

Praise for the novels of

Karen Marie Moning

the dark highlander

"Darker, sexier, and more serious than Moning's previous time-travel romances . . . this wild, imaginative romp takes readers on an exhilarating ride through time and space."
—*Publishers Weekly* (starred review)

"Pulsing with sexual tension, Moning delivers a tale romance fans will be talking about for a long time."
—*The Oakland Press*

"*The Dark Highlander* is dynamite, dramatic, and utterly riveting. Ms. Moning takes the classic plot of good vs. evil . . . and gives it a new twist."
—*Romantic Times*

kiss of the highlander

"Moning's snappy prose, quick wit and charismatic characters will enchant."
—*Publishers Weekly*

"Moning is quickly building a reputation for writing poignant time travels with memorable characters. This may be the first book I've read by her, but it certainly won't be my last. She delivers compelling stories with passionate characters readers will find enchanting."
—*The Oakland Press*

For my sister, Elizabeth, with love.
You are my sunshine . . .

Special thanks to—
My mother and father;
Rick Shomo;
Carrie Edwards and Jeanne Meyer;
and my agent Deidre Knight.
I couldn't have done it without you.

BELTANE

(Spring)

You spotted snakes with double tongue
Thorny hedgehogs be not seen;
Newts and blind worms, do no wrong
Come not near our fairy queen.

SHAKESPEARE, *A Midsummer Night's Dream*

Prologue

SCOTLAND
1 FEBRUARY 1513

THE FRAGRANCE OF JASMINE AND SANDALWOOD DRIFTED through the rowan trees. Above dew-drenched branches, a lone gull ghosted a bank of mist and soared to kiss the dawn over the white sands of Morar. The turquoise tide shimmered in shades of mermaid tails against the alabaster shore.

The elegant royal court of the Tuatha De Danaan dappled the stretch of lush greenery. Pillowed chaises in brilliant scarlet and lemon adorned the grassy knoll, scattered in a half-moon about the outdoor dais.

"They say he is even more beautiful than you," the Queen remarked to the man sprawled indolently at the foot of her dais.

"Impossible." His mocking laughter tinkled like cut-crystal chimes on a fae wind.

"They say his manhood at half-mast would make a stallion

envious." The Queen slanted a glance beneath half-lowered lids at her rapt courtiers.

"More likely a mouse," sneered the man at her feet. Elegant fingers demonstrated a puny space of air, and titters sliced the mist.

"They say at full-mast he steals a woman's mind from her body. Claims her soul." The Queen dropped fringed lashes to shield eyes alight with the iridescent fire of mischievous intent. *How easily my men are provoked!*

The man rolled his eyes and disdain etched his arrogant profile. He crossed his legs at the ankles and gazed out across the sea.

But the Queen wasn't fooled. The man at her feet was vainglorious, and not as impervious to her provocation as he feigned.

"Quit baiting him, my Queen," King Finnbheara admonished. "You know how the fool gets when his ego is wounded." He patted her arm soothingly. "You've teased him enough."

The Queen's eyes narrowed thoughtfully. She briefly considered forgoing this vein of revenge. A calculating look at her men dashed that thought, as she recalled what she'd overheard them discussing late last evening in excruciating detail.

The things they'd said were unforgivable. The Queen was not a woman to be compared with another woman and found lacking. Her lip tightened imperceptibly. Her exquisitely delicate hand curled into a fist. She carefully selected her next words.

"But I have found him to be all that they say," the Queen purred.

In the silence that followed, the statement lingered, unacknowledged, for the cut was too cruel to dignify. The

King at her side and the man at her feet shifted restlessly. She was beginning to think she hadn't made her point quite painfully clear enough when, in unison, they rose to her bait. "Who is this man?"

Queen Aoibheal of the Fairy disguised a satisfied smile with a delicate yawn, and drank deeply of her men's jealousy. "They call him the Hawk."

CHAPTER 1

SCOTLAND
1 APRIL 1513

SIDHEACH JAMES LYON DOUGLAS, THIRD EARL OF DALKEITH, stalked across the floor. Droplets of water trickled from his wet hair down his broad chest, and gathered into a single rivulet between the double ridges of muscle in his abdomen. Moonlight shimmered through the open window, casting a silvery glow to his bronze skin, creating the illusion that he was sculpted of molten steel.

The tub behind him had grown cold and been forgotten. The woman on the bed was also cold and forgotten. She knew it.

And she didn't like it one bit.

Too beautiful for me, Esmerelda thought. But by the saints, the man was a poison draught, another long cool swallow of his body the only cure for the toxin. She thought about the things she had done to win him, to share his bed, and—God forgive her—the things she would do to stay there.

She almost hated him for it. She knew she hated herself for it. *He should be mine,* she thought. She watched him stalk across the spacious room to the window which opened between fluted granite columns that met in a high arch twenty feet above her head. Esmerelda sneered at him behind his back. Foolish—such large unprotected openings in a keep—or arrogant. So what if one could lie in the massive goosedown bed and gaze through the rosy arch at a velvety sky pierced by glittering stars?

She'd caught him gazing that way tonight as he'd slammed into her, exciting that bottomless hunger in her blood with the rock-hard kind of maleness only he possessed. She'd whimpered beneath him in the greatest ecstasy she'd ever experienced and he'd been looking out the window—as if no one else was there with him.

Had he been counting the stars?

Silently reciting bawdy dittys to prevent himself from toppling over and falling asleep?

She'd lost him.

No, Esmerelda vowed, she would *never* lose him.

"Hawk?"

"Hmmm?"

She smoothed the lavender silk sheet through her trembling fingers. "Come back to bed, Hawk."

"I'm restless tonight, sweet." He toyed with the stem of a large pale blue blossom. A half hour earlier he'd swept the dewy petals along her silken skin.

Esmerelda flinched at his open admission that he still had energy to spare. Sleepily sated, she could see that his body still thrummed from head to toe with restless vigor. What kind of woman would it take—or how many—to leave that man drowsing in fascinated satisfaction?

More woman than she, and ye gods, how that offended her.

Had her sister left him more sated? Her sister who had warmed his bed until Zeldie had found a way to take her place?

"Am I better than my sister?" The words were out before she could prevent them. She bit her lip, anxiously awaiting his answer.

Her words dragged his smoky gaze from the starry night, across the wide expanse of the bedchamber, to rest on the sultry, raven-haired Gypsy. "Esmerelda," he chided gently.

"Am I?" Her husky contralto soared to a shrewish pitch.

He sighed. "We've had this discussion before—"

"And you never answer me."

"Stop comparing yourself, sweet. You know it's foolish . . ."

"How can I not when you can compare me to a hundred, nay a thousand, even my own sister?" Shapely brows puckered in a scowl above her flashing eyes.

His laughter rolled. "And how many do you compare me to, lovely Esmerelda?"

"My sister couldn't have been as good as me. She was nearly a *virgin*." She spit out the word with distaste. Life was too unpredictable for virginity to be a prized possession among her people. Lust, in all its facets, was a healthy aspect of the Rom culture.

He raised a hand in warning. "Stop. Now."

But she couldn't. The poison words of accusation tumbled out fast and furious at the only man who had ever made her pagan blood sing, and his boredom between her thighs had been chiseled in granite upon his perfect face this very eve. In truth, for many evenings now.

He suffered her rage in silence, and when at last her tongue rested, he turned back to his window. The howl of a solitary wolf ruptured the night and she felt an answering cry well up within her. She knew the Hawk's silence was his farewell. Stinging with rejection and humiliation, she lay trembling in his bed—the bed she knew she would never be asked to enter again.

She would kill for him.

Which is precisely what she meant to do moments later when she rushed him with the silver dirk she'd slipped from the table by the bed. Esmerelda might have been able to leave without swearing an oath of vengeance, if he had looked surprised. Momentarily alarmed. *Sorry,* even.

But he exhibited none of these emotions. His perfect face lit up with laughter as he spun effortlessly, caught her arm and sent the dirk hurtling through the open window.

He laughed.

And she cursed him. And all his begotten and any subsequent misbegotten.

When he shushed her with kisses, she cursed through gritted teeth, even as her traitorous body melted for his touch. No man should be so beautiful. No man should be so untouchable. And so damned fearless.

No man should be able to forsake Esmerelda. He was done with her, but she wasn't done with him. She would never be done with him.

*   *   *

"It wasn't your fault, Hawk," Grimm offered. They sat upon the cobbled terrace of Dalkeith sipping port and smoking imported tobacco in purely male contentment.

Sidheach James Lyon Douglas rubbed his perfect jaw

with a perfect hand, irritated by the perfect shadow of stubble that always appeared just a few hours after shaving.

"I just don't understand, Grimm. I thought she'd found pleasure with me. Why would she seek to kill me?"

Grimm arched a brow. "Just what do you *do* to the lasses in bed, Hawk?"

"I give them what they want. Fantasy. My willing flesh and blood to serve their every whim."

"And how do you know what a woman's fantasies are?" Grimm wondered aloud.

The Earl of Dalkeith laughed softly, a heady, confident rumble of a purr that he knew drove women wild. "Ah, Grimm, you just have to listen with your whole body. In her eyes she tells you, whether she knows it or not. In her soft cries she guides you. In the subtle turnings of her body, you know if she wants you in front or behind her lush curves. With gentleness or with power; if she desires a tender lover or seeks a beast. If she likes her lips kissed, or savagely devoured. If she likes her breasts—"

"I get the picture," Grimm interrupted, swallowing hard. He shifted in his chair and uncrossed his legs. Recrossed them and tugged at his kilt. Uncrossed them again and sighed. "And Esmerelda? Did you understand her fantasies?"

"Only too well. One of them included being Lady Hawk."

"She had to know it couldn't be, Hawk. Everyone knows you've been as good as wed since King James decreed your betrothal."

"As good as *dead*. And I don't want to talk about it."

"The time draws near, Hawk. You're not only going to have to talk about it, you're going to have to do something about it—like go collect your bride. Time is running out. Or don't you care?"

Hawk slanted a savage look Grimm's way.

"Just making sure, that's all. There's scarce a fortnight left, remember?"

Hawk stared out into the crystalline night, heavy with glowing stars. "How could I forget?"

"You really think James would carry out his threats if you don't wed the Comyn lass?"

"Absolutely," Hawk said flatly.

"I just don't understand why he hates you so much."

A sardonic smile flitted across the Hawk's face. He knew why James hated him. Thirty years ago Hawk's parents had humiliated James to the seat of his vain soul. Since the Hawk's father had died before James could avenge himself, the king had turned on Hawk in his father's stead.

For fifteen long years James had controlled every minute of the Hawk's life. Days before his pledge of service was to expire, James contrived a plan to affect every future moment of it. By the king's decree, the Hawk was being forced to wed a lass he didn't know and didn't want. A reclusive spinster who was rumored to be quite hideous and unquestionably mad. It was King James's twisted idea of a lifetime sentence. "Who fathoms the minds of kings, my friend?" Hawk evaded, pointedly putting an end to the topic.

The two men passed a time in silence, both brooding for different reasons as they stared into the velvety sky. An owl hooted softly from the gardens. Crickets rubbed their legs in sweet concerto, offering twilight tribute to Dalkeith. Stars pulsed and shimmered against the night's blue-black canopy.

"Look. One falls. There, Hawk. What do you make of it?" Grimm pointed at a white speck plummeting from the heavens, leaving a milky tail glowing in its wake.

"Esmerelda says if you make a wish upon such a falling star 'twill be granted."

"Did you wish just now?"

"Tinker talk," Hawk scoffed. "Foolish romantic nonsense for dreamy-eyed lasses." Of course he'd wished. Every time he'd seen a falling star lately. Always the same wish. After all, the time *was* nearing.

"Well, I'm trying it," Grimm grumbled, not to be swayed by Hawk's mockery. "I wish . . ."

"Yield, Grimm. What's your wish?" Hawk asked curiously.

"None of your concern. You don't believe."

"I? The eternal romantic who enchants legions with his poetry and seduction—not a believer in all those lovely female things?"

Grimm shot his friend a warning look. "Careful, Hawk. Mock them at your own risk. You may just really make a lass angry one day. And you *won't* know how to deal with it. For the time being, they still fall for your perfect smiles—"

"You mean like this one." Hawk arched a brow and flashed a smile, complete with sleepily hooded eyes that spoke volumes about how the lass receiving it was the only true beauty in his heart, a heart which had room for only one—whoever happened to be in the Hawk's arms at the moment.

Grimm shook his head in mock disgust. "You practice it. You must. Come on, admit it."

"Of course I do. It works. Wouldn't you practice it?"

"Womanizer."

"Uh-hmm," Hawk agreed.

"Do you even remember their names?"

"All five thousand of them." Hawk hid his grin behind a swallow of port.

"Blackguard. Libertine."

"Rogue. Roué. Cad. Ah, here's a good one: 'voluptuary,' " Hawk supplied helpfully.

"Why don't they see through you?"

Hawk shrugged a shoulder. "They like what they get from me. There are a lot of hungry lasses out there. I couldn't, in good conscience, turn them away. 'Twould trouble my head."

"I think I know exactly which head of yours would be troubled," Grimm said dryly. "The very one that's going to get you in big trouble one day."

"What did you wish for, Grimm?" Hawk ignored the warning with the devil-may-care attitude that was his wont where the lasses were concerned.

A slow smile slid over Grimm's face. "A lass who doesn't want you. A lovely, nay, an earth-shatteringly beautiful one, with wit and wisdom to boot. One with a perfect face and a perfect body, and a perfect 'no' on her perfect lips for you, my oh-so-perfect friend. And I also wished to be allowed to watch the battle."

Hawk smiled smugly. "It will *never* happen."

* * *

The wind gusting sweetly through the pines carried a disembodied voice that drifted on a breeze of jasmine and sandalwood. Then it spoke in laughing words neither man heard. *"I think that can be arranged."*

CHAPTER 2

THE MYSTICAL ISLE OF MORAR WAS CLOAKED IN EVENTIDE,
the silica sands glistening silver beneath King Finnbheara's
boots as he paced, impatiently awaiting the court fool's
return.

The Queen and her favorite courtiers were merrily cele-
brating the Beltane in a remote Highland village. Watching
his elfin Aoibheal dance and flirt with the mortal Highlanders had goaded his slumbering jealousy into wakeful
wrath. He'd fled the Beltane fires before he could succumb
to his desire to annihilate the entire village. He was too angry with mortals to trust himself around them at the moment. The mere thought of his Queen with a mortal man
filled him with fury.

As the fairy Queen had her favorites among their courtiers, so did the fairy King; the wily court fool was his long-
time companion in cups and spades. He'd dispatched the
fool to study the mortal Hawk, to gather information so he

might concoct a fitting revenge for the man who'd dared
trespass on fairy territory.

"His manhood at half-mast would make a stallion envious. . . . he claims a woman's soul." King Finnbheara
mocked his Queen's words in scathing falsetto, then spit
irritably.

"I'm afraid it's true," the fool said flatly as he appeared
in the shade of a rowan tree.

"Really?" King Finnbheara grimaced. He'd convinced
himself Aoibheal had embellished a bit—after all, the man
was mortal.

The fool scowled. "I spent three days in Edinburgh. The
man's a living legend. The women clamor over him. They
speak his name as if it's some mystic incantation guaranteed to bestow eternal ecstasy."

"Did you see him? With your own eyes? Is he beautiful?" the King asked quickly.

The fool nodded and his mouth twisted bitterly. "He's
flawless. He's taller than me—"

"You're well over six feet in that glamour!" the King
objected

"He stands almost a hand taller. He has raven hair worn
in a sleek tail; smoldering black eyes; the chiseled perfection of a young god and the body of Viking warrior. It's revolting. May I maim him, my liege? Disfigure his perfect
countenance?"

King Finnbheara pondered this information. He felt sick
in the pit of his stomach at the thought of this dark mortal
touching his Queen's fair limbs, bringing her incomparable
pleasure. *Claiming her soul.*

"I will kill him for you," the fool offered hopefully.

King Finnbheara gestured impatiently. "Fool! And break

the Compact between our races? No. There must be another way."

The fool shrugged. "Perhaps we should sit back and do nothing. The Hawk is about to come to harm at his own race's hand."

"Tell me more," Finnbheara ordered, his interest piqued.

"I discovered that the Hawk is to be wed in a few days. He is affianced by his mortal king's decree. Destruction is about to befall him. You see, my liege, King James has ordered the Hawk to wed a woman named Janet Comyn. The king has made it clear that if the Hawk doesn't wed this woman, he will destroy both the Douglas and Comyn clans."

"So? What's your point?" Finnbheara asked impatiently.

"Janet Comyn is dead. She died today."

Finnbheara tensed instantly. "Did you harm her, fool?"

"No, my liege!" The fool gave him a wounded look. "She died by her father's hand. I no more put the idea in his head than a key to her tower in his sporran."

"Does that mean you did or you didn't put the idea in his head?" the King asked suspiciously.

"Come now, my liege," the fool pouted, "think you I would resort to such trickery and jeopardize us all?"

Finnbheara templed his fingers and studied the fool. Unpredictable, cunning, and careless, the jester had not yet been foolish enough to risk their race. "Go on."

The fool cocked his head and his smile gleamed in the half-light. "It's simple. The wedding can't take place now. King James is going to destroy the Douglas. Oh, the Comyn too," he added irreverently.

"Ah!" Finnbheara debated a pensive moment. He didn't have to lift a finger and the Hawk would soon die.

But it wasn't enough, he seethed. Finnbheara wanted his

own hand in the Hawk's destruction. He had suffered personal insult, and he wanted an intimately personal revenge. No mortal man cuckolded the King of the Fairy, without divine retribution—and how divine it would feel to destroy the Hawk.

The glimmer of an idea began to take shape in his mind. As he considered it, King Finnbheara felt more vital than he had in centuries.

The fool didn't miss the smug smile that teased the King's lips.

"You're thinking something wicked. What are you planning, my liege?" the fool asked.

"Silence," King Finnbheara commanded. He rubbed his jaw thoughtfully as he sifted through his options, carefully refining his scheme.

If time passed while Finnbheara plotted, neither fairy noticed; time meant little to the race of beings who could move about in it at will. The first flames of dawn painted the sky above the sea when the King spoke again:

"Has the Hawk ever loved?"

"Loved?" the fool echoed blankly.

"You know, that emotion for which mortals compose sonnets, fight wars, erect monuments," the King said dryly.

The fool reflected a moment. "I would say no, my King. The Hawk has never wooed a woman he didn't win, nor does it appear he ever desired any special woman over another."

"A woman has never denied him?" King Finnbheara asked with a trace of incredulity.

"Not that I could find. I don't think the woman lives and breathes in the sixteenth century who *could* deny him. I'm telling you, the man's a legend. Women swoon over him."

The King smiled avariciously. "I have another errand for you, fool."

"Anything, my liege. Let me kill him."

"No! There will be no blood spilled by our hand. Listen to me carefully. Go now through the centuries. Go forward—women are more independent and self-possessed there. Find me a woman who is irresistible, exquisite, intelligent, strong; one who knows her own mind. Bid you well, she must be a woman who won't lose her wits being tossed through time, she must be adaptable to strange events. It wouldn't do to bring her to him and have her brain addled. She must believe in a bit of magic."

The fool nodded. "Too true. Remember that tax accountant we took back to the twelfth century? She turned into a raving lunatic."

"Exactly. The woman you find must be somewhat inured to the unusual so she can accept time travel without coming undone." Finnbheara mulled this over a moment. "I have it! Look in Salem, where they still believe in witches, or perhaps New Orleans, where the ancient magic sizzles in the air."

"Perfect places!" the fool enthused.

"But most important, fool, you must find me a woman who harbors a special hatred for beautiful, womanizing men; a woman guaranteed to make that mortal's life a living hell."

The fool smiled fiendishly. "May I embellish on your plan?"

"You're a crucial part of it," the King said with sinister promise.

＊　　＊　　＊

Adrienne de Simone shivered, although it was an unusually warm May evening in Seattle. She pulled a sweater over her head and tugged the French doors closed. She stared out through the glass and watched night descend over the gardens that tumbled in wild disarray beyond the walk.

In the fading light she surveyed the stone wall that protected her house at 93 Coattail Lane, then turned her methodical scrutiny to the shadows beneath the stately oaks, seeking any irregular movement. She took a deep breath and ordered herself to relax. The guard dogs that patrolled the grounds were quiet—things must be safe, she assured herself firmly.

Inexplicably tense, she entered the code on the alarm pad that would activate the motion detectors strategically mounted throughout the one-acre lawn. Any nonrandom motion over one hundred pounds in mass and three feet in height would trigger the detectors, although the shrill warning would not summon the police or any law enforcement agency.

Adrienne would run for her gun before she'd run for a phone. She'd summon the devil himself before she'd dream of calling the police. Although six months had passed, Adrienne still felt as if she couldn't get far enough from New Orleans, not even if she moved across an ocean or two, which she couldn't do anyway; the percentage of fugitives apprehended while trying to leave the country was shockingly high.

Was that what she really was? she marveled. It never failed to astonish her, even after all these months. How could she—Adrienne de Simone—be a fugitive? She'd always been an honest, law-abiding citizen. All she'd ever asked of life was a home and a place to belong; someone to love and someone who loved her; children someday—children she would never abandon to an orphanage.

She'd found all of that in Eberhard Darrow Garrett, the toast of New Orleans society, or so she'd thought.

Adrienne snorted as she surveyed the lawn a final time then dropped the drapes across the doors. A few years ago the world had seemed like such a different place; a wonderful place, full of promise, excitement, and endless possibility.

Armed only with her irrepressible spirit and three hundred dollars cash, Adrienne Doe had invented a last name for herself and fled the orphanage on the day she'd turned eighteen. She'd been thrilled to discover student loans for which practically anyone could qualify, even an unsecured risk like an orphan. She'd taken a job as a waitress, enrolled in college, and embarked on her quest to make something of herself. Just what, she wasn't sure, but she'd always had a feeling that something special was waiting around the next corner for her.

She'd been twenty, a sophomore at the university, when that special thing had happened. Working at the Blind Lemon, an elegant restaurant and bar, Adrienne had caught the eye, the heart, and the engagement ring of the darkly handsome, wealthy Eberhard Darrow Garrett, the bachelor of the decade. It had been the perfect fairy tale. She'd walked around for months on clouds of happiness.

When the clouds had started to melt beneath her feet, she'd refused to look too closely, refused to acknowledge that the fairy-tale prince might be a prince of darker things.

Adrienne squeezed her eyes shut wishing she could blink some of her bad memories out of existence. How gullible she'd been! How many excuses she'd made—for him, for herself—until she'd finally had to run.

A tiny meow coaxed her back to the present and she smiled down at the one good thing that had come of it all; her kitten, Moonshadow, a precocious stray she'd found outside a gas station on her way north. Moonie rubbed her ankles and purred enthusiastically. Adrienne scooped up the furry little creature, hugging her close. Unconditional love, such was the gift Moonie gave. Love without reservation or subterfuge—pure affection with no darker sides.

Adrienne hummed lightly as she rubbed Moonie's ears, then broke off abruptly as a faint scratching sound drew her attention to the windows again.

Perfectly still, she clutched Moonie and waited, holding her breath.

But there was only silence.

It must have been a twig scratching at the roof, she decided. But, hadn't she cut all the trees back from the house when she'd moved in?

Adrienne sighed, shook her head, and ordered her muscles to relax. She had nearly succeeded when overhead a floorboard creaked. Tension reclaimed her instantly. She dropped Moonie on a stuffed chair and eyed the ceiling intently as the creaking sound repeated.

Perhaps it was just the house settling.

She really had to get over this skittishness.

How much time had to pass until she stopped being afraid that she would turn around and see Eberhard standing there with his faintly mocking smile and gleaming gun?

Eberhard was dead. She was safe, she knew she was.

So why did she feel so horridly vulnerable? For the past few days she'd had the suffocating sensation that someone was spying on her. No matter how hard she tried to reassure herself that anyone who might wish her harm was either dead—or didn't know she was alive—she was still consumed by a morbid unease. Every instinct she possessed warned her that something was wrong—or about to go terribly wrong. Having grown up in the City of Spooks— the sultry, superstitious, magical New Orleans—Adrienne had learned to listen to her instincts. They were almost always right on target.

Her instincts had even been right about Eberhard. She'd had a bad feeling about him from the beginning, but she'd convinced herself it was her own insecurity. Eberhard was the catch of New Orleans; naturally, a woman might feel a little unsettled by such a man.

Only much later did she understand that she'd been lonely for so long, and had wanted the fairy tale so badly, that she'd tried to force reality to reflect her desires, instead of the other way around. She'd told herself so many white lies before finally facing the truth that Eberhard wasn't the man she'd thought he was. She'd been such a fool.

Adrienne breathed deeply of the spring air that breezed gently in the window behind her, then flinched and spun abruptly. She eyed the fluttering drapes warily. Hadn't she closed that window? She was sure of it. She'd closed all of them, just before closing the French doors. Adrienne edged cautiously to the window, shut it quickly, and locked it.

It was nerves, nothing more. No face peered in the window at her, no dogs barked, no alarms sounded. What was the use of taking so many precautions if she couldn't relax? There couldn't *possibly* be anyone out there.

Adrienne forced herself to turn away from the window. As she padded across the room her foot encountered a small object and sent it skidding across the faded Oushak rug, where it clunked to a rest against the wall.

Adrienne glanced at it and flinched. It was a piece from Eberhard's chess set, the one she'd swiped from his house in New Orleans the night she'd fled. She'd forgotten all about it after she'd moved in. She'd tossed it in a box—one of those piled in the corner that she'd never gotten around to unpacking. Perhaps Moonie had dragged the pieces out, she mused, there were several of them scattered across the rug.

She retrieved the piece she'd kicked and rolled it gingerly between her fingers. Waves of emotion flooded her; a sea of shame and anger and humiliation, capped with a relentless fear that she still wasn't safe.

A draft of air kissed the back of her neck and she stiffened, clutching the chess piece so tightly that the crown of the black queen dug cruelly into her palm. Logic insisted that the windows behind her were shut—she *knew* they were, still—instinct told her otherwise.

The rational Adrienne *knew* there was no one in her library but herself and a lightly snoring kitten. The irrational Adrienne teetered on the brink of terror.

Laughing nervously, she berated herself for being so jumpy, then cursed Eberhard for making her this way. She would *not* succumb to paranoia.

Dropping to her knees without sparing a backward glance, Adrienne scooped the scattered chess pieces into a pile. She didn't really like to touch them. A woman couldn't spend her childhood in New Orleans—much of it at the feet of a Creole storyteller who'd lived behind the orphanage—without becoming a bit superstitious. The set was ancient, an original Viking set; an old legend claimed it was cursed, and Adrienne's life had been cursed enough. The only reason she'd pilfered the set was in case she needed quick cash. Carved of walrus ivory and ebony, it would command an exorbitant price from a collector. Besides, hadn't she earned it, after all he'd put her through?

Adrienne muttered a colorful invective about beautiful men. It wasn't morally acceptable that someone as evil as Eberhard had been so nice to look at. Poetic justice demanded otherwise—shouldn't people's faces reflect their hearts? If

Eberhard had been as ugly on the outside as she'd belatedly discovered he was on the inside, she never would have ended up at the wrong end of a gun. Of course, Adrienne had learned the hard way that any end of a gun was the wrong end.

Eberhard Darrow Garrett was a beautiful, womanizing, deceitful man—and he'd ruined her life. Clutching the black queen tightly she made herself a firm promise. "I will never go out with a beautiful man again, so long as I live and breathe. I hate beautiful men. Hate them!"

*   *   *

Outside the French doors at 93 Coattail Lane, a man who lacked substance, a creature manmade devices could neither detect nor contain, heard her words and smiled. His choice was made with swift certainty—Adrienne de Simone was definitely the woman he'd been searching for.

CHAPTER 3

ADRIENNE HAD NO IDEA HOW SHE ENDED UP ON THE MAN'S lap. None.

One moment she was perfectly sane —perhaps a bit neurotic, but firmly convinced of her sanity nonetheless—and the next moment the ground disappeared beneath her feet and she was sucked down one of Alice's rabbit holes.

Her first thought was that she must be dreaming: a vivid, horrifying subconscious foray into a barbaric nightmare.

But that didn't make any sense; only moments before, she'd been petting Moonshadow or doing . . . something . . . what? She couldn't have just fallen asleep without even knowing it!

Maybe she'd stumbled and struck her head, and this hallucination was the dreamy result of a concussion.

Or maybe not, she worried as she looked around the cavernous smoky room filled with oddly dressed people speaking a mutilated version of the English tongue.

You've done it now, Adrienne, she mused soberly. *You've finally slipped over the edge, heels still kicking.* Adrienne struggled to focus her eyes, which felt strangely heavy. The man who clutched her was revolting. He was a belching beast with thick arms and a fat belly, and he smelled.

Only moments ago she'd been in her library, hadn't she?

A greasy hand squeezed her breast and she yelped aloud. Bewilderment was vanquished by embarrassed outrage when his hand deliberately grazed the crest of her nipple through her sweater. Even if this was a dream, she couldn't permit that kind of activity to pass without redress. She opened her mouth to deliver a scathing tongue lashing, but he beat her to the punch. His pink mouth in that tangled mass of hair expanded into a wide *O*. Dear *heaven* but the man hadn't even finished chewing, and no wonder—his few remaining teeth were stumpy and brown.

It was with revulsion that Adrienne wiped bits of chicken and spittle from her face when he roared, but it was with genuine alarm that she comprehended his words, through his thick brogue.

She was a godsend, he proclaimed to the room at large. She was a gift from the angels.

She would be married on the morrow.

Adrienne fainted. Her unconscious body spasmed once, then went limp. The black queen slipped from her hand, hit the floor, and was kicked under a table by a scuffed leather boot.

*   *   *

When Adrienne awoke, she lay still, her eyes squeezed tightly shut. Beneath her back she felt the lumpy down ticks piled thickly. It could be her own bed. She had purchased antique ticks and had them restitched to plump atop her waist-high Queen Anne bed. She was in love with old things, no dithering about it.

She sniffed cautiously. No odd scents from the banquet she'd dreamt. No hum of that thick brogue she'd imagined earlier.

But no traffic either.

She strained her ears, listening mightily. Had she ever heard such silence?

Adrienne drew a ragged breath and willed her heart to slow.

She tossed on the lumpy tick. Was this how insanity occurred? Started with a vague inkling of unease, a dreadful sense of being watched, then escalated rapidly into full blown madness, only to culminate in a nightmare where a smelly, hairy beast announced her impending nuptials?

Adrienne squeezed her eyes even more tightly shut, willing her return to sanity. The silhouette of a chess set loomed in her mind; battle-ready rooks and bitter queens etched in stark relief against the insides of her eyelids, and it seemed that there was something urgent she needed to remember. What had she been doing?

Her head hurt. It was a dull kind of ache, accompanied by the bitter taste of old pennies in the back of her throat. For a moment she struggled against it, but the throbbing intensified. The chess set danced elusively in shades of black and white, then dissolved into a distant nagging detail. It couldn't have been too important.

Adrienne had more pressing things to worry about— where in the blue blazes was she?

She kept her eyes closed and waited. A few moments more and she would hear the purr of a BMW tooling sleekly down Coattail Lane or her phone would peal angrily. . . .

A rooster did *not* just crow.

Another minute and she'd hear Moonie's questioning *mer-ooow*, and feel her tail swish past her face as she leapt up on the bed.

She did *not* hear the grate of squeaky hinges, the scrape of a door cut too long against a stone threshold.

"Milady, I know you're awake."

Her eyes sprang open to find a portly woman with silver-brown hair and rosy cheeks, wringing her hands as she stood at the foot of the bed. "Who are you?" Adrienne asked warily, refusing to look at any more of the room than the immediate spot that contained this latest apparition.

"Bah! Who am *I* she asks? The lass who pops out of no-where, lickety-split, like a witch if you please, is wishing to know who I am? Hmmph!"

With that, the woman placed a platter of peculiar-smelling food on a nearby table, and forced Adrienne up by plumping the pillows behind her back.

"I'm Talia. I've been sent to see to your care. Eat up. You'll never be strong enough to face wedding *him* if you doona be eating," she chided.

With those words and a full glimpse of the stone walls hung with vividly colored tapestries depicting hunts and orgies, Adrienne fainted again—this time, with relish.

✳   ✳   ✳

Adrienne awoke again to a score of maids bearing under-garments, stockings, and a wedding dress.

The women bathed her in scented water before a massive stone fireplace. While she huddled submerged in the deep wooden tub, Adrienne examined every inch of the room. How could a dream be so vivid, so rich with scent and touch and sound? The bathwater smelled of fresh heather and lilac. The maids chatted lightly as they bathed her. The stone fireplace was easily as tall as three men—it rose up to kiss the ceiling and sprawled along half the width of the east wall. It was bedecked with an array of artistic silverwork; delicately filigreed baskets, cunningly handcrafted roses that gleamed like molten silver, yet each petal distinct and looking somehow velvety. Above the great mantel, rough-hewn of honey oak, hung a hunt scene depicting a bloody victory.

Her study was cut short by the screech of the door. Shocked gasps and immediately hushed voices compelled her gaze over one bare shoulder, and she, too, gasped aloud. The villain with the matted rug upon his face! Her cheeks flamed with embarrassment and she sunk deeper into the tub.

"Milord, 'tis no place for you—" a maid began.

The slap ricocheted through the room, silencing the maid's protest and halting anyone else's before they even considered beginning. The great greasy beast from earlier in her nightmare sunk down on his haunches before the steaming tub, a leer on his face. Slitted blue eyes met steely gray as Adrienne held his rude stare levelly.

His eyes dropped from hers, searched the water line and probed below it. He grinned at the sight of her rosy nipples before she crossed her arms and hugged herself tightly.

"Methinks he doesn't do so badly for himself," the man murmured. Then, dragging his eyes from the water to her flushed face, he commanded, "From this moment forth, your name is Janet Comyn."

Adrienne shot him a haughty look. "My name," she snapped, "is Adrienne de Simone."

Crack!

She raised a hand to her cheek in disbelief. A maid cried out a muffled warning.

"Try it again," he counseled softly, and as soft as his words were, his blue eyes were dangerously hard.

Adrienne rubbed her stinging cheek in silence.

And his hand rose and fell again.

"Milady! We implore you!" A petite maid dropped to her knees beside the tub, placing a hand upon Adrienne's bare shoulder.

"That's right, give her counsel, Bess. You know what becomes of a lass foolish enough to deny me. Say it," he repeated to Adrienne. "Tell me your name is Janet Comyn."

When his beefy hand rose and fell again, it came down on Bess's face with fury. Adrienne screamed as he struck the maid repeatedly.

"Stop!" she cried.

"Say it!" he commanded as his hand rose and fell again. Bess sobbed as she crumpled to the floor, but the man went down after her, his hand now a fist.

"My name is Janet Comyn!" Adrienne cried, half rising from the tub.

The Comyn's fist halted in midair, and he sank back on his haunches, the light of victory gleaming in his eyes. Victory—and that disgusting slow perusal of her flesh.

Adrienne flushed under the sheer lechery of his pale eyes, and plunged her upper body back into the water.

"Nay, he doesn't get a bad bargain at all. You are much more comely than mine own Janet." His mouth twisted into a smile. "Would that I had leisure to taste such plump pillows myself, but you came just in the nick of time."

"Came where?"

"Came *from* where is my question," he countered. Adrienne realized in that instant that to underestimate this brutish man would be a grave mistake. For behind the slovenly manners and the unkempt appearance was steely mettle and rapier sharp wit. The flabby arm that had felled the blows couched muscle. The pale slitted eyes that wandered restlessly didn't miss a beat. He hadn't punished Bess in rage. He'd beat her in a cold, calculated act to get what he wanted from Adrienne.

She shook her head, her eyes wide with confusion. "Really, I haven't the faintest idea how I got here."

"You don't know where you came from?"

Bess was sobbing softly, and Adrienne's eyes darkened as she watched the maid curl into a ball and surreptitiously try to inch away from the Comyn. His hand shot out and fastened on the maid's ankle. Bess whimpered hopelessly.

"Oh nay, my pretty. I may need you yet." His eyes swept her shuddering form with a possessive leer. Adrienne gasped when he ripped Bess's gown and proceeded to shred it from her body. Adrienne's stomach churned in agony when she saw the great welts rising from the maid's pale flanks and thighs. Cruel, biting welts from a belt or a whip.

The other maids fled the room, leaving her alone with the weeping Bess and the madman.

"This is my world, Adrienne de Simone," he intoned, and Adrienne had a premonition that the words he was about to utter would be carved deeply into her mind for a long time to come. He stroked Bess's quivering thigh lightly. "My rules. My people. My will to command life or death. Yours and hers. 'Tis a simple thing I want of you. If you don't cooperate, she dies. Then another and still another. I will find the very core of that foolish compassion you wear like a shroud. It makes you so easy to use. But women are that way. Weak."

Adrienne sat hunched in silence, her labored breathing an accompaniment to Bess's weary sobs.

"Quiet, lass!" He slapped the maid's face, and she curled into a tighter ball, weeping into her hands to smother the sound.

One day I will kill him with my bare hands, Adrienne vowed silently.

"I don't know how you came to be here or who you are, and frankly, I don't care. I have a problem, and you're going to fix it. If you ever forget what I am about to tell you, if you ever slip, if you ever betray me, I will kill you after I've destroyed everything you care about."

"Where am I?" she asked tonelessly, reluctantly voicing one of the questions that had been bothering her. She was afraid that once she started asking questions, she might discover this really wasn't a dream after all.

"I don't care if you're mad," he chuckled appreciatively. "Fact is, I rather relish the thought that you might have bats flapping in your belfry. God knows, my Janet did. 'Tis no more or less than he deserves."

"Where am I?" she insisted.

"Janet had a difficult time remembering that, too."

"So, where am I?"

The Comyn studied her, then shrugged. "Scotland. Comyn keep—*my* keep."

Her heart stopped beating within her breast. It was not possible. Had she truly gone mad? Adrienne steeled her will to ask the next question—the obvious question, the terrifying question she'd been studiously avoiding since she'd first awoken. She'd learned that sometimes it was safer not to ask too many questions—the answers could be downright unnerving. Obtaining the answer to this question could tamper with her fragile grasp on reason; Adrienne had a suspicion that *where* she was wasn't quite the only

problem she had. Drawing a deep breath, she asked carefully, "What year is it?"

The Comyn guffawed. "You really are a wee bit daft,
aren't you lass?"

Adrienne glared at him in silence.

He shrugged again. " 'Tis fifteen hundred and thirteen."

"Oh," Adrienne said faintly. *Ohmygodohmygod,* she
wailed in the confines of her reeling mind. She took a deep,
slow breath, and told herself to start at the beginning of this
mystery; perhaps it could be unraveled. "And who exactly
are you?"

"For all intents and purposes, I am your father, lass.
That's the first of many things you must never forget."

A broken sob temporarily distracted Adrienne from her
problems. Poor abused Bess; Adrienne could not bear a person in pain, not if she could do something about it. This
man wanted something from her; maybe she could bargain
for something in exchange. "Let Bess go," she said.

"Do you pledge your fealty to me in this matter?" He had
the flat eyes of a snake, Adrienne realized. Like the python
in the Seattle zoo.

"Let her go from this keep. Give her her freedom," she
clarified.

"Nay, milady!" Bess shrieked, and the beast chuckled
warmly.

His eyes were thoughtful as he stroked Bess's leg. "Methinks, Janet Comyn, you don't understand much of this
world. Free her from me and you condemn her to death by
starvation, rape, or worse. Free her from my 'loving atten-
tions' and the next man may not be so loving. Your own husband may not be so loving."

Adrienne shivered violently as she struggled to tear

her gaze from the plump white hand stroking rhythmically. The source of Bess's pain was the same hand that fed her. "Protected" her. Bile rose in Adrienne's throat, almost choking her.

"Fortunately, he already thinks you're mad, so you may talk as you will after this day. But for this day from dawn till dusk, you will swear that you are Janet Comyn, only blood daughter of the mighty Red Comyn, sworn bride of Sidheach Douglas. You will see this day through as I tell you—"

"But what of the real Janet?" she couldn't help but ask.

Slap! How had the man managed to hit her before she could so much as blink? As he stood quivering with rage above her, he said, "The next blows won't be to your face, bitch, for the gown won't cover there. But there are ways to hit that hurt the most, and leave no mark. Don't push me."

Adrienne was silent and obedient through all the things he told her then. His message was plain. If she was silent and obedient, she would stay alive. Dream or no dream, the blows hurt here, and she had a feeling that dying might just hurt here too.

He told her things then. Hundreds of details he expected her to commit to memory. She did so with determination; it temporarily prevented her from contemplating the full extent of her apparent insanity. She repeated each detail, each name, each memory that was not hers. From careful observation of her "father," she was able to guess at many of the memories that had belonged to the woman whose identity she was now to assume.

And all the while a soft mantra hummed through the back of her mind. *This cannot be happening. This is not possible. This cannot be happening.* Yet in the forefront of her mind, realist that she was, she understood that the words *can't* and *impossible* had no bearing when the impossible was indeed happening.

Unless she woke up soon from a nightmarish and vivid dream, she was in Scotland, the was year 1513, and she was indeed getting married.

CHAPTER 4

"SHE'S TALL AS JANET."

"Not many as tall as she."

"Hush! She *is* Janet! Else he'll have our heads on serving platters."

"What happened to Janet?" Adrienne asked softly. She wasn't surprised when the mouths of a half-dozen maids clamped shut and they turned their complete attention to dressing her in stalwart silence.

Adrienne rolled her eyes. If they wouldn't tell her a thing about Janet, perhaps they'd talk about her bridegroom.

"So, who is this man I am to wed?" *Sidhawk Douglas. What kind of name was Sidhawk anyway?*

The maids tittered like a covey of startled quail.

"Truth of it is, milady, we've only heard tales of him. This betrothal was commanded by King James himself."

"What are the tales?" Adrienne asked wryly.

"His exploits are legendary!"

"His conquests are legion. 'Tis rumored he's traveled the world accompanied by only the most beautiful lasses."

" 'Tis said there isna a comely lass in all of Scotia he hasna tumbled—"

"—in England, too!"

"—and he canna recall any of their names."

"He is said to have godlike beauty, and a practiced hand in the fine art of seduction."

"He is fabulously wealthy and rumors say his castle is luxurious beyond compare."

Adrienne blinked. "Wonderful. A materialistic, unfaithful, beautiful playboy of a self-indulged, inconsiderate man with a bad memory. And he's all mine. Dear sweet God, what have I done to deserve this?" she wondered aloud. *Twice,* she brooded privately.

Lisbelle looked at her curiously. "But the rumors tell he is a magnificent lover and most comely to look upon, milady. What could be wrong with that?"

Methinks you don't understand this world, Janet Comyn. Perhaps he was right. "Does he beat his women?"

"He doesn't keep them long enough, or so they say."

"Although, I hear tell one of his women tried to kill him recently. I can't imagine why," the maid added, genuinely puzzled. " 'Tis said he is more than generous with his mistresses when he's done with them."

"I can imagine why," Adrienne grumbled irritably, suddenly impatient with all the plucking, fastening, adorning, and arranging hands on her body. "Stop, stop." She lightly slapped Lisbelle's hands from her hair, which had been washed, combed mercilessly, and teased torturously for what felt like years.

"But milady, we must do something with this hair. 'Tis so straight! You must look your best—"

"Personally, I'd prefer to look like something the cat dragged in. Wet, bedraggled, and smelling like a ripe dungheap."

Gasps resounded. "Lass, he will be your husband, and you could do far worse," a stern voice cut across the room. Adrienne turned slowly and met the worldly-wise gaze of a woman with whom she felt an instant kinship. "You could have mine, for lack of a better example."

Adrienne sucked in a harsh breath. "The Laird Comyn?"

"Your *father*, my darling daughter," Lady Althea Comyn said with an acid smile. "Begone—all of you." She ushered the maids from the room with a regal hand, her eyes lingering overlong on Bess. "He'll kill the lass one day, he will," she said softly. She squeezed her eyes shut tightly for a long moment.

"He explained what you must do?"

Adrienne nodded.

"And you will do it?"

Again she nodded. The Lady Comyn expelled a sigh of relief.

"If there is aught a time I may repay the kindness—"

"It's not a kindness. It's to save my life."

"—you need only ask. For it saves mine own."

✳   ✳   ✳

Adrienne stood tall before the man of the cloth, fulfilling her part of the farce. "I am Janet Comyn," she proclaimed loudly. God's man paled visibly and clutched his Bible until his knuckles looked to split at the seams. *So he knows I'm not,* she mused. *What on earth is really going on here?*

She felt a presence near her left shoulder, and turned reluctantly to face the man she was to wed. Her eyes met the area slightly below his breastbone and every inch of it was encased in steel.

Adrienne started to rise and look her fiancé in the face, when she realized with horror that she wasn't kneeling. Beyond chagrined, she tipped her head back and swallowed a thousand frantic protests that clotted in her throat.

The giant stared back with an inscrutable expression, flames from flickering candles dancing in the bluest eyes she'd ever seen.

I can't marry him, she screamed silently. *I can't do it!*

Her eyes fled his countenance and chafed lightly across the audience in search of someone to save her from this debacle. Bess sat in the rear pew, eyes closed in supplication.

Adrienne flinched and closed her eyes in kind. *Please God, if I've gone mad, please make me sane again. And if I haven't gone mad and somehow this is really happening— I'm sorry I wasn't grateful for the twentieth century. I'm sorry I did what I did to Eberhard. I'm sorry for everything, and I promise I'll be a better person if you just GET ME OUT OF HERE!*

When she opened her eyes again she could have sworn the man of the cloth had a knowing and rather amused gleam in his eye.

"Help me," she mouthed silently.

Quickly, he lowered his eyes to the floor. He didn't raise them again.

In spite of herself, Adrienne dragged her reluctant gaze to the midsection of her bridegroom, then upward even farther, to his darkly handsome face.

He arched a brow at her as the flutists piped away, the rhythm increasing in gaiety and tempo.

She was rescued from the stress of his regard when a

ruckus erupted and she heard the furious voice of her "father" carrying to the rafters.

"What say you he couldna come himself?" Red Comyn shouted at the soldier.

" 'Twas a bit of a problem in North Uster. The Hawk had to ride out in haste, but he hasna forsaken his pledge. He does no dishonor to the clans." The soldier delivered his rehearsed message.

"He dishonors the troth by not being here!" Lord Comyn roared. Then he turned to the man at Adrienne's side. "And who are you, to come in his stead?"

"Grimm Roderick, Hawk's captain of the guard. I come to wed your daughter as his proxy—"

"A pox on proxy! How dare he not come to claim my daughter himself?"

"It's perfectly legal. The king will recognize it and the troth is thus fulfilled."

Adrienne couldn't prevent the joy that leapt into her face at his words. This man wasn't her husband!

"Am I so offensive then, lass?" he asked, smiling mockingly, not missing one ounce of her relief.

About as offensive as a platter of strawberries dipped in dark chocolate and topped with whipped cream, she thought wryly.

"I'd sooner marry a toad," Adrienne said.

His laughter teased a miserly smile from her lips.

"Then you're definitely out of luck, milady. For the Hawk is no toad for certain. I, lass, standing next to the Hawk, am truly a toad. Nay—a troll. Worse still, a horned and warty lizard. A—"

"I get the picture." *Dear heaven, deliver me from perfection.* "Where is he, then, my unwilling husband?"

"Managing the aftermath of a serious problem."

"And that might be?"

"A grave and terrible uprising."

"In North Uster?"

"Close." The man's lips twitched.

Adrienne was seized by a fit of urgency. No matter how she dragged her feet, this deed would be done. If she had to face the unknown, she'd like to tackle it now. Waiting only made it worse, and Lord Comyn's shouting combined with the wild cacophony of floundering flutists was flaying her nerves. *Mad, am I, Janet? Works for me.* Straightening to her full five and half feet, she sought the still bellowing form of her "father" and shouted into the melee.

"Oh, do shut up, Father, and let's be on with it! I've a wedding to be about and you're only delaying it. So what if he didn't come? Can't say that I blame him."

The chapel went deathly still. Adrienne could have sworn she felt the man beside her tremble with suppressed laughter, although she dared not meet his gaze again.

Whispers of "Mad Janet" rebounded through the chapel, and Adrienne felt a surge of relief. This fame for being mad could be useful. So long as she obeyed the Comyn's orders this one day, she could be as odd as a square ball bearing and no one would find it unseemly.

Adrienne had been worried that she wouldn't be able to remember all the details the Comyn had told her; that she would slip up and someone at her new husband's home would discover she was an impostor. Once she was un-cloaked as a charlatan, the Comyn would make good on his threat to kill her.

Suddenly that pressure vanished in a puff of smoke. In the here and now (if she was really here and now) she was crazy Janet Comyn. How could she be held accountable for anything she said or did that didn't make sense? Madness was a license to freedom.

A license to do and say anything she wanted—with no repercussions.

No Eberhard, no guns, no bad memories.

Maybe this place wasn't so bad after all.

CHAPTER 5

ADRIENNE HAD BEEN WANDERING THE GROUNDS OF DALKEITH
for several hours when she stumbled upon the smithy. After
a grueling two-day ride from Comyn Keep to her new
home— Dalkeith-Upon-the-Sea—by cantankerous steed,
she'd planned to collapse in the nearest soft bed, sleep for
days, and then when she woke up (if she was still here) find
a good bottle of Scotch and drink herself into oblivion. And
then check again to see if she was still here.

Not only hadn't she been able to find a soft bed in the ri-
otous castle, but there had been no Scotch, no sign of a husband, and everyone had summarily ignored her. Made it
awfully hard to feel at home. Grimm had made haste from
her company the moment they'd entered the pink granite
walls of the Douglas keep, although he'd seemed quite the
gentleman during the journey.

But she was no fool. She didn't have to be hit in the head
with a stick to figure out that she was definitely not a wanted

wife. Wed by proxy, no welcome, and no sign of a husband. Definitely not wanted.

Adrienne gave up her fruitless search for husband, bed, and bottle and went for a stroll to explore her new home.

And so it was quite by accident that she stumbled through the rowan trees and upon the forge at the edge of the forest. Upon the man, clad only in a kilt, pumping the bellows and shaping the steel of a horseshoe.

Adrienne had heard that her husband by proxy was too beautiful to be borne, but this man indeed rendered the magnificent Grimm a veritable toad.

There just wasn't this much raw man around in the twentieth century, she thought in helpless fascination as she watched him work. To see this kind of man in the twentieth century, a woman had to somehow gain entry to that inner sanctum of dumbbells and free weights, where the man was defining his body in homage to himself. But in this century such a man existed by simple force of nature.

His world demanded that he be strong to survive, to command, to endure.

When the smithy twisted and swooped to switch hammers, she saw a rivulet of sweat which had beaded at his brow run down his cheek, drop with a splatter to his chest, and trickle, oh, so slowly along the thick ridges of muscle in his abdomen. To his navel, to the top of his kilt, and lower still. She eyed his legs with fascination, waiting to see the drops of sweat reappear on those powerful calves, and wondering deliriously about every inch in between.

So intense was the shimmering heat from the forge, so strange her need, that Adrienne didn't realize he had stopped for several moments.

Until she raised her eyes from his chest to meet his dark, unsmiling eyes.

She gasped.

He crossed the distance and she knew she should run. Yet she also knew that she couldn't have run if her life depended on it. Something about his eyes. . . .

His hand was rough when it closed upon her jaw, forcing her head back to meet him eye to flashing silver eye.

"Is there a service I might perform for you, my fair queen? Perhaps you have something in need of a heated shaping and molding? Or perhaps I might reshape my steel lance in the heat of your forge, milady?"

Her eyes searched his face wildly. *Composure,* she commanded herself.

He shook her ruthlessly. "Do you seek my services?"

"It's the heat, nothing more," she croaked.

"Aye, 'tis most assuredly the *heat*, beauty." His eyes were devilish. "Come." He took her by the hand and started off at a fast pace.

"No!" She swatted at his arm.

"Come," he ordered, and she suffered the uncanny sensation that he was reaching inside her with those eyes and reordering her will to match his will. It terrified her.

"Release me!" she gasped.

His eyes searched deeper, and although she knew it was crazy, Adrienne felt as if she was fighting for something terribly important here. She knew she must not go with this man, but she couldn't begin to say why. She sensed danger, dark and primeval. Unnatural and ancient danger beyond her control. If he opened his cruelly beautiful mouth and said *come* one more time, she might do just that.

He opened his mouth. She braced herself for the command she knew would follow.

"Release my wife," commanded a deep voice behind them.

CHAPTER 6

SO THIS MAN AT THE FORGE WAS NOT HER HUSBAND. DEAR God in heaven, what was she going to find when she turned around? Dare she?

She turned slightly, as if a small sidewise peek might be safer. Might minimize the impact. Adrienne soon discovered just how wrong she was. *Nothing* could minimize *that* man's impact.

Valhalla on the right. Paradise regained on the left.

Stuck between a Godiva truffle and a chocolate éclair.

Between a rock and a very hard place. Two very hard places from the looks of it. *I hate beautiful men,* she mourned soulfully. *Hate them. Hate them. Hate them.* Yet to resist. . . .

Hands clasped her waist from behind as the smithy pulled her back against his sculpted body.

"Let go of me!" she cried, the strange fog lifting from her brain.

The smithy released her.

And that very big, beautiful man facing her—the legendary Hawk—was glaring like Odin preparing to zap her with a thunderbolt. She snorted.

"Don't glare at *me*. You didn't even bother to show up at our wedding." Adrienne started pacing. If she really was Janet, how would Janet have felt? How terrible to be wed away like a piece of property and then be treated so shabbily by the new in-laws! "I spend two miserable soggy days on the back of a nag and does it ever stop raining in this god-awful place? Two days it took us to get here! Gracious Grimm dumps me the minute we set foot on Dalkeith. *You* don't even bother to greet me. Nobody shows me to a room. Nobody offers me anything to eat. Or drink for that matter." She paused in her litany and leaned back against a tree, hands on her hips, one foot tapping. "And then, since I can't find anyplace to sleep that I'm not afraid doesn't belong to someone else, I go off wandering until you finally bother yourself enough to show up and now you glare at me? Well, I'll have you know—"

"Silence, lass."

"That I am *not* the kind of woman that one can push to the side and have her take it docilely. I know when I'm not wanted—"

"You're most assuredly wanted," the smithy purred.

"I don't need to be hit over the head with a ton of rocks—"

"I said be silent."

"And I didn't get even one wedding present!" she added, proud that she had thought of that. Yes, Janet would certainly have been offended.

"Silence!" Hawk roared.

"And I don't take orders! Ummmph!" Adrienne grunted as her husband lunged the distance separating them and

tumbled her to the ground. Once she hit the earth with what
felt like a small rhinoceros on top of her, he rolled her over
several times, locked in the curve of his arm. She could hear
the blacksmith cursing softly, then the sound of running
feet, as she struggled mightily against his steely embrace.

"Be still!" Hawk growled, his breath warm against her
ear. It took her a few moments to realize that he was holding
her almost protectively, as if shielding her with his body.
Adrienne raised her head to see his dark eyes scanning the
forest's edge intently.

"What are you doing?" she whispered, her heart hammering. From being tumbled so roughly, she assured herself, not from being cradled in this man's powerful arms.
She squirmed.

"Be still, I said."

She wriggled, partly to spite him and partly to get his leg
out from between her thighs, but she only succeeded in ending up with her tush pressed against his—oh dear—surely
he didn't walk around like *that* all the time! She jerked
sharply at the contact and heard a muffled thud, the sound
of bone hitting bone when her head struck his jaw with a
thwack. He cursed softly, then the rumble of his husky baritone laughter vibrated as his arms tightened around her.

"A wee hellcat, aren't you?" he said in her ear.

She struggled violently. "Let me go!"

But he didn't. He only eased his tight grip enough to turn
her around so that she was sprawled atop him, facing him.
Big, big mistake, she thought mournfully. It presented a
whole new array of problems, starting with her breasts being crushed against him, her leg caught between his, and
her palms splayed on his muscular chest. His white linen
shirt was open and pure male heat rose from his broad
chest. There was blood trickling down his arrogantly

curved lower lip, and for an insane moment she actually considered licking it off. In one swift, graceful motion he rolled her beneath him and she lost her breath. Her lips parted. She stared in mute fascination and knew in that terrifying instant the man she had married by proxy was about to kiss her and she was quite certain her life would never be the same again if he did.

She snarled. He smiled and lowered his head toward hers.

Just then the blacksmith burst back into the clearing. "Not a damned thing!" he spat. "Whoever it was is gone."

The Hawk jerked away in surprise and Adrienne seized the moment to push against him. She might just as well have tried to push the Sphinx across the sand and into the Nile.

It was only then that Adrienne saw the arrow still quivering in the tree that she had been, moments before, standing directly in front of, soundly berating her new husband. Her eyes widened as she gazed up at the Hawk questioningly. This was all too weird.

"Whom have you offended?" Her husband shook her smartly. "Who seeks to kill you?"

"How do you know it wasn't you they were after, that it wasn't just a bad shot?"

"Nobody wants to kill me, lass."

"From what I hear your last lover tried to do just that," she retorted nastily.

He paled ever so slightly beneath the flawless bronze of his skin.

The blacksmith laughed.

Her neck was getting sore from peering up at him. "Get off me," she growled at her husband.

She wasn't prepared when the Hawk's eyes darkened and he rolled over and pushed her from him.

"Though you persist in rejecting me, *wife,* I think you may need me," Hawk said softly.

"I don't think so," she retorted fiercely.

"I'll be here, should you reconsider."

"I'll take my chances. No one shot anything in my direction until you showed up. That makes two attempts that I know of on you, and none on me." She stood up, brushing her gown off. Dirt and nettles stuck to the heavy fabric. She tugged a few leaves from her hair and dusted off her rump until she became aware of an uncomfortable sensation. Slowly she raised her eyes from her clothing to find both men watching her with the intensity of wolves. Large, hungry wolves.

"What?" she snapped.

The blacksmith laughed again. The sound was deep, dark, and mysterious. "Methinks the lady doth not see how sweetly cruel beckons such beauty."

"Spare me," she said tiredly.

"Fair the dawn of yon lass's blush, rich and ripe and deeply lush." Her husband was not about to be outdone.

Adrienne stamped a foot and glared at them both. Where was her Shakespeare when she needed it? "For I have sworn thee fair and thought thee bright/, who art as black as hell, as dark as night," she muttered.

The smithy threw his head back and roared with laughter. Her husband's lips curved in an appreciative smile at her wit.

Hawk stood then and extended his hand. "Cry peace with me, lass."

Cry. The man could make an angel weep. But she was hungry. Thirsty. Tired. She took his hand, vowing fiercely to take nothing more. Ever.

As her husband guided her from the clearing the

smithy's voice followed on a jasmine-scented breeze, and she was surprised that her husband didn't react. Either he was not a possessive man, or he simply hadn't heard. For clearly she heard the smithy say, "Woman who renders all men as weak kittens to cream, I can take you places you've known only in your dreams."

"Nightmares," she grumbled, and heard him laugh softly behind her.

Her husband glanced at her curiously. "What?"

She sighed heavily. "Night's mare rides hard upon my heels. I must sleep soon."

He nodded. "And then we talk."

Sure. If I'm still in this godforsaken place when I wake up.

✳   ✳   ✳

Sidheach James Lyon Douglas worried his unshaven jaw with a callused hand. Anger? Perhaps. Disbelief, surely. Possessiveness. Where the hell did that come from?

Fury. Aye, that was it. Cold, dark fury was eating him from the inside out and the spirited Scotch was only aiding the ache.

He had stood and watched his new wife with starvation in his eyes. He had seen her suffer raw and primal hunger for a man—and it was not him. Unbelievable.

"Keep drinking like that and we'll never make Uster on the morrow," Grimm warned.

"I'm not going to Uster on the morrow. My wife could be with babe by the time I got back."

Grimm grinned. "She's in a full fury with you, you know."

"She's in a fury with *me*?"

"You were too drunk to wed her, much less bed her, and now you're in a tizzy because she looked on Adam agreeably."

"Agreeably? Give the lass a trencher and she would have slid it under him, licking her lips as she dined!"

"So?"

"She's my wife."

"Och, this one's getting too deep for me. You said you didn't care what became of her once the deed was done. You swore to honor the pact and you have. So why this foolish ire, Hawk?"

"My wife will not make a cuckold of me."

"I believe a husband can only be a cuckold if he cares. You don't care."

"Nobody *asked* me if I cared."

Grimm blinked, fascinated by the Hawk's behavior. "All the lasses look on Adam like that."

"She didn't even notice me. 'Tis Adam she wants. Who the bloody hell hired that blacksmith anyway?"

Grimm mused into his brew. "Wasn't Thomas the smithy?"

"Come to think of it, aye."

"Where'd Thomas go?"

"I don't know, Grimm. That's why I asked you."

"Well, somebody hired Adam."

"You didn't?"

"Nay. I thought you did, Hawk."

"Nay. Maybe he's Thomas's brother and Thomas was taken ill."

Grimm laughed. "Ugly Thomas his brother? Not a chance on that."

"Get rid of him."

"Adam?"

"Aye."

Silence.

Then, "By the saints, Hawk, you can't be serious! 'Tisna

like you to take away a man's livelihood because of the way
a lass looks at him . . ."

"This lass happens to be my wife."

"Aye—the very one you didn't want."

"I've changed my mind."

"Besides, he's been keeping Esmerelda quite content,
Hawk."

Sidheach sighed deeply. "There is that." He paused the
length of several jealous heartbeats. "Grimm?"

"Um?"

"Tell him to keep his clothes on while he works. And
that's an order."

*   *   *

But Hawk couldn't leave it alone. His mind became aware
of where his feet had taken him just as he entered the amber
rim of firelight beneath the rowan trees at Adam's forge.

"Welcome Lord Hawk of Dalkeith-Upon-the-Sea."

Hawk spun about to come nose to nose with the glistening blacksmith, who had somehow managed to get behind
him. Not many men could take the Hawk by surprise, and
for an instant Hawk was as fascinated as he was irritated
with the smithy.

"I didn't hire you. Who are you?"

"Adam," the smithy replied coolly.

"Adam what?"

The smithy pondered, then flashed a puckish smile.
"Adam Black."

"Who hired you?"

"I heard you were in need of a man to tend a forge."

"Stay away from my wife." Hawk was startled to hear the
words leave his lips. *By the saints, he sounded like a jealous
husband!* He had intended to push the question of who had

hired the smithy, but apparently he was no more in control
of his words than he had been of his feet; at least not where
his new wife was concerned.

Adam laughed wickedly. "I won't do a thing the lady
doesn't want me to do."

"You won't do a thing *I* don't want you to do."

"I heard the lady didn't want *you*."

"She will."

"And if she doesn't?"

"All the lasses want me."

"Funny. I have just the same problem."

"You're uncanny rude for a smithy. Who was your laird
before?"

"I have known no man worthy to call master."

"Funny, smithy. I have just the same problem."

The men stood nose to nose. Steel to steel.

"I can order you from my land," Hawk said tightly.

"Ah, but then you'd never know if she would choose you
or me, would you? And I suspect there is this deep kernel of
decency in you, a thing that cries out for old-fashioned
mores like fairness and chivalry, honor and justice. Foolish
Hawk. All the knights will soon be dead, as dust of dreams
passing on time's fickle fancy."

"You're insolent. And as of this moment, you're
unemployed."

"You're afraid," the smithy marveled.

"Afraid?" The Hawk echoed incredulously. This fool
smithy dared stand on his land and tell him that he, the legendary Hawk, was afraid? "I fear nothing. Certainly not
you."

"Yes you do. You saw how your wife looked at me.
You're afraid you won't be able to keep her hands off me."

A bitter, mocking smile curved Hawk's lip. He was not a

man given to self-deception. He *was* afraid he wouldn't be able to keep his wife away from the smithy. It galled him, incensed him, and yet the smithy was also right about his underlying decency. Decency that demanded, as Grimm had suspected, that he not deprive a man of his livelihood because of his own insecurity about his wife. The Hawk suffered the rare handicap of being noble, straight to the core. "Who are you, really?"

"A simple smithy."

Hawk studied him in the moonlight that dappled through the rowans. Nothing simple here. Something tugged at his mind, drifting on a scent of memory, but he couldn't pin it down. "I know you, don't I?"

"You do now. And soon, she will know me as well."

"Why do you provoke me?"

"You provoked me first when you pleased my queen." The words were spat as the smithy turned away sharply.

Hawk searched his memory for a queen he had pleased. No names came to mind; but they usually didn't. Still, the man had made his game clear. Somewhere, sometime, Hawk had turned a woman's head from this man. And the man was now to play the same game with him. With his wife. A part of him tried not to care, but from the moment he'd laid eyes on Mad Janet this day he'd known he was in trouble for the first time in his life. Deep, over his head, for had her flashing silver eyes coaxed him into quicksand, he would willingly have gone.

What do you say to a man whose woman you've taken? There was nothing to say to the smithy. "I had no intention to give offense," Hawk offered at last.

Adam spun around and his smile gleamed much too brightly. "Offense to defense, all's fair in lust. Do you still seek to send me hence?"

Hawk met his gaze for long moments. The smithy was right. Something in him cried out for justice. Fair battles fought on equal footing. If he couldn't hold a lass, if he lost her to another man . . . His pride blazed hot. If his wife left him, whether he had wanted her to begin with or not, and for a smithy at that, well, the legend of the Hawk would be sung to a vastly different tune.

But worse even than that, if he dismissed the smithy tonight, he would never know for certain if his wife would have chosen him over Adam Black. And it mattered. The doubt would torment him eternally. The image of her as she'd stood today, leaning against a tree, staring at the smithy—ah! That would give him nightmares even in Adam's absence.

He would allow the smithy to stay. And tonight the Hawk would seduce his wife. When he was completely convinced where her affections rested, well, maybe *then* he might dismiss the bastard.

Hawk waved a hand dispassionately. "As you will. I will not command your absence."

"As I will. I like that," Adam Black replied smugly.

✳   ✳   ✳

Hawk walked through the courtyard slowly, rubbing his head that still ached from a bout of drunkenness three nights past. The troth King James had commanded was satisfied. Hawk had wed the Comyn's daughter and thus fulfilled James's final decree. Dalkeith was safe once again.

The Hawk had high hopes that out of sight was truly out of mind, and that King James would forget about Dalkeith-Upon-the-Sea. All those years he'd done James's twisted bidding to the letter, only to have the king demand more of him, until by royal decree James had taken from the Hawk his last claim to freedom.

Why had it surprised him? For fifteen years the king had delighted in taking his choices away, whittling them down to the single choice of obeying his king or dying, along with his entire clan.

He recalled the day James had summoned him, only three days before his service was to end.

Hawk had presented himself, his curiosity piqued by the air of tense anticipation that pervaded the spacious throne room. Attributing it to yet another of James's schemes—and hoping it had naught to do with him or Dalkeith—Hawk approached the dais and knelt.

"We have arranged a marriage for you," James had announced when the room quieted.

Hawk stiffened. He could feel the eyes of the courtiers resting on him heavily; with amusement, with mockery and a touch of . . . pity?

"We have selected a most suitable"—James paused and laughed spitefully—"wife to grace the rest of your days at Dalkeith."

"Who?" Hawk allowed himself only the one word. To say more would have betrayed the angry denial simmering in his veins. He couldn't trust himself to speak when every ounce of him screamed defiance.

James smiled and motioned Red Comyn to approach the throne, and Hawk nearly roared with rage. Surely not the notorious Mad Janet! James wouldn't force him to wed the mad spinster Red Comyn kept in his far tower!

The corner of James's lip twisted upward in a crooked smile. "We have chosen Janet Comyn to be your bride, Hawk Douglas."

Soft laughter ripped through the court. James rubbed his hands together gleefully.

"No!" The word escaped Hawk in a burst of air; too late, he tried to suck it back in.

"No?" James echoed, his smile chilled instantly. "Did We just hear you refuse Our command?"

Hawk trained his eyes on the floor. He took a deep breath. "Nay, my king. I fear I did not express myself clearly." Hawk paused and swallowed hard. "What I meant was 'no, you've been too good to me already.' " The lie burned his lips and left the taste of charred pride on his tongue. But it kept Dalkeith safe.

James chuckled, grandly amused by the Hawk's quick capitulation as he enjoyed anything that showcased the extent of his kingly powers. The Hawk reflected bitterly that once again James held all the cards.

When James spoke again, his voice dripped venom. "Fail to wed the Comyn's daughter, Hawk Douglas, and We will wipe all trace of Douglas from Scotia. Not one drop of your bloodline will survive unless you do this thing."

It was the same threat James had always used to control Hawk Douglas, and the only one that could have been so ruthlessly effective, over and over again.

Hawk bowed his head to hide his anger.

He'd wanted to choose his own wife. Was that so much to ask? During his fifteen years of service the thought of choosing a woman of his own, of returning to Dalkeith and raising a family far from the corruption of James's court, had kept his dreams alive despite the king's efforts to sully and destroy them, one by one. Although the Hawk was no longer a man who believed in love, he did believe in family and clan, and the thought of spending the rest of his days with a fine woman, surrounded by children, appealed to him immensely.

He wanted to stroll the seaside and tell stories to his sons. He wanted lovely daughters and grandchildren. He wanted to fill the nursery at Dalkeith. *Och, the nursery,* the thought stung him; this new realization more bitter and painful than anything the king had ever done to him. *I can never fill the nursery now—not if my wife bears seeds of madness!*

There would be no wee ones—at least not legitimate ones—for the Hawk. How could he bear never holding a child of his own?

Hawk had never spoken of his desire for a family; he'd known that if James found out, he'd eradicate any hope of it. Well, somehow James had either found out or had decided that since he hadn't been able to have the wife he wanted, neither could the Hawk.

"Raise your head and look at Us, Hawk," James commanded.

Hawk raised his head slowly and fixed the king with lightless eyes.

James studied him then turned his brilliant gaze on Red Comyn and appended a final threat to ensure cooperation, "We will destroy the Comyn, too, should this decree be defied. Hear you what We say, Red Comyn? Don't fail Us."

Laird Comyn appeared oddly disturbed by James's command.

Kneeling before James's court, the Hawk subdued the last of his rebellious thoughts. He acknowledged the pitying stares of the soldiers with whom he'd served; the sympathy of Grimm's gaze; the complacent hatred and smug mockery of lesser lords who'd long resented the Hawk's success with women, and accepted the fact that he would marry Janet Comyn even if she was a toothless, ancient, deranged old crone. Hawk Douglas would always do whatever it took to keep Dalkeith and all her people safe.

The gossip mill had churned out endless stories of Janet Comyn, a crazed spinster, imprisoned because she was incurably mad.

As Hawk trod the cobbled walkway to the entrance of Dalkeith, he laughed aloud at the false image he'd created in his mind of Mad Janet. He realized that James had obviously known no more about her than anyone else, because James never would have bound the Hawk to such a woman had he known what she was truly like. She was too beautiful, too fiery. James had intended Hawk to suffer, and the only way a man would suffer around this woman was if he couldn't get his hands on her, if he couldn't taste her kisses and enjoy her sensual promise.

Hawk had expected nothing like the shimmering, silken creature of passionate temperament he'd found at the forge. He'd sent Grimm on the last day to wed the lass by proxy, fully intending to ignore her when she arrived. He'd made it clear that no one was to welcome her. Life would go on at Dalkeith as if nothing had changed. He'd decided that if she was half as mad as the gossips claimed, she probably wouldn't even be able to understand that she *was* married. He'd concluded he could surely find some way to deal with her, even if it meant confining her somewhere, far from Dalkeith. James had ordered him to wed, he had said nothing about sharing living quarters.

Then, he'd laid eyes upon "Mad" Janet Comyn. Like an impassioned goddess she'd flayed him with her words, evidencing wit handfasted to unearthly beauty. No lass he could recall had stirred in him the tight, clenching hunger he'd suffered when he'd caressed her with his eyes. While she'd been caressing that damned smithy with hers.

The gossips couldn't have been more wrong. Had the Hawk been left to choose a woman for himself, the qualities Janet possessed—independence, a quick mind, a luscious body, and a strong heart—were all qualities he would have sought.

Perhaps, Hawk mused, life might just take a turn for the better after all.

CHAPTER 7

ADRIENNE KNEW SHE WAS DREAMING. SHE WAS HOPELESSLY
mired in the same horrible nightmare she'd been having for
months; the one in which she fled down dark, deserted New
Orleans alleys trying to outrun death.

No matter how hard she tried to control the dream, she
never made it to safety. Inevitably, Eberhard cornered her in
the abandoned warehouse on Blue Magnolia Lane. Only
one thing differed significantly from the reality Adrienne
had lived through—in her nightmare she didn't make it to
the gun in time.

She awoke shaking and pale, with little beads of sweat
dappling her face.

And there was the Hawk; sitting on the end of her bed,
silently watching her.

Adrienne stared wide-eyed at him. In her sleepy confusion the Hawk's darkly beautiful face seemed to bear traces
of Eberhard's diabolic beauty, making her wonder what dif-

ference there was between the two men—if any. After a nightmare about one attractive deadly man, waking up to find another in such close proximity was just too much for her frazzled nerves. Although she still had virtually no memory of how she'd come to be in the sixteenth century, her other memories were regrettably intact. Adrienne de Simone remembered one thing with excruciating clarity—she did not trust and did not like beautiful men.

"You screamed," the Hawk informed her in his mellifluous voice.

Adrienne rolled her eyes. Could he do something besides purr every time he opened his perfect mouth? That voice could sweet-talk a blind nun out of her chastity.

"Go away," she mumbled.

He smiled. "I came but to see that you weren't the victim of another murder attempt."

"I told you it wasn't *me* they were after."

He sat carefully, seemingly caught in a mighty internal struggle. Her mind spun with unchecked remnants of her nightmare as a soft breeze wafted in the open window and kissed her skin. Ye gods, her skin! She plucked the silk sheet to her nearly bare breasts in a fit of pique. The dratted gown she'd found neatly placed on her bed—by someone who obviously had fewer inhibitions about clothing than she—scarcely qualified as sleepwear. The tiny sleeves had slipped down over her shoulders while the skirt of the gown had bunched up; yards of transparent fabric pooled in a filmy froth around her waist, barely covering her hips—and that only if she didn't move at all. Adrienne tugged firmly at the gown, trying to rearrange it without relinquishing her grip on the sheet.

Hawk groaned, and the husky sound made her every

nerve dance on end. She forced herself to meet his heated gaze levelly.

"Janet, I know we didn't exactly start this marriage under the best of circumstances."

"Adrienne. And one could definitely say that."

"No, my name is Sidheach. My brother is Adrian. But most call me Hawk."

"I meant me. Call me Adrienne." At his questioning look she added, "My middle name is Adrienne, and it's the one I prefer." A simple, tiny lie. She couldn't hope to keep answering to Janet, she was bound to slip eventually.

"Adrienne," he purred, putting the inflection on it as *Adry-EN*. "As I was saying"—he slid along the bed with such grace that she only realized he'd moved when he was much too close—"I fear we didn't get the best start, and I intend to remedy that."

"You can remedy it by removing yourself from my sight this instant. Now. Shoo." She clutched the sheet in a careful fist and waved her other hand dismissively. He watched it with fascination. When he didn't move, she tried to dismiss him again, but he snared her hand mid-wave.

"Beautiful hands," he murmured, turning it palm up and planting a lingering kiss in the sensitive center. "I feared Mad Janet was a most uncomely shrew. Now I know why the Comyn kept you hidden in his tower all those years. You are the true silver and gold in the Comyn treasure trove. His wealth has been depleted in full measure by the loss of you."

"Oh, get off it," she snapped, and he blinked in surprise. "Listen Sidhawk or Hawk or whoever you are, I'm not impressed. If we're going to be forced to suffer the same roof above our heads we need to get a few things straight. First"—she held up a hand, ticking off the fingers as she went—"I don't like you. Get used to that. Second, I didn't want to marry you, but I had no alternative—"

"You desire another." The purr deepened into a rumble of displeasure.

"Third," she continued without bothering to respond, "I don't find your manly wiles even remotely intriguing. You're not my type . . ."

"But Adam certainly is, eh?" His jaw clenched and his ebony eyes flashed.

"More so than you," she lied, thinking that if she could convince him she meant it, he might leave her alone.

"You won't have him. You are *my* wife, whether you like it or not. I will not be made a cuckold —"

"You have to *care* to be made a cuckold."

"Perhaps I could." Perhaps he already did and he didn't have the first inkling why.

"Well, I can't."

"Am I so displeasing then?"

"Yes."

He stared. Gazed about the room. Studied the rafters. No mysterious answer was hovering anywhere to be found.

"The lasses have always found me most comely," he said finally.

"Maybe that's part of your problem."

"Pardon?"

"I don't like your attitude."

"My attitude?" he echoed dumbly.

"Right. So get thee from my bed and from my sight and speak no more to me this night."

"You're the damnedest lass I've ever met."

"And you're the most shallow, incorrigible knave of a man I've ever had the displeasure of meeting."

"Where do you get all these ideas of me?" he wondered.

"We could start with you being too drunk to show up at your own wedding."

"Grimm told you? Grimm wouldn't have told you that!"

"A pox on male bonding." Adrienne rolled her eyes. "All he would tell me was that you were tending to an uprising. Of your stomach, I hadn't guessed. The maid who showed me to this room earlier had a fine time telling me. Went on and on about how you and three casks of wine and three women spent the week before our wedding trying to . . . you know"—Adrienne muttered an unintelligible word—"your brains out."

"To *what* my brains out?"

"You know." Adrienne rolled her eyes.

"I'm afraid I don't. What was that word again?"

Adrienne looked at him sharply. Was he teasing her? Were his eyes alight with mischief? That half-smile curving his beautiful mouth could absolutely melt the sheet she was clutching, not to mention her will. "Apparently one of them succeeded, because if you had any brains left you'd get out of my sight *now*," she snapped.

"It wasn't three." Hawk swallowed a laugh.

"No?"

"It was five."

Adrienne's jaw clenched. She held her fingers up again. "Fourth—this will be a marriage in name only. Period."

"Casks of wine, I meant."

"You are *not* funny."

His laughter rolled dangerous and heavy. "Enough. Now we're going to count the Hawk's rules." He held up his hand and began ticking fingers off. "First, you're my wife, thusly you'll obey me in all things. If I must command you to my bed, then so be it. Second"—his other hand rose and she flinched, half expecting to be hit, but he cupped her face

firmly and glared into her eyes—"you will stay away from
Adam. Third, you'll give all pretense of being delighted to
be married to me—both publicly and privately. Fourth,
fifth, and sixth, you'll stay away from Adam. Seventh"—he
yanked her from the bed and to her feet in one swift
motion—"you'll explain precisely what you find so displeasing about me, *after* I make love to you, and eighth,
we're going to have children. Many. Perhaps dozens. Perhaps I'll simply keep you fat with child from this moment
forth."

Adrienne's eyes grew wider and wider as he spoke. By
the time he got to the children part she was nearing a full
panic. She gathered her scattered wits and searched for the
most effective weapon. What could she say to keep this man
at bay? His ego. His gargantuan ego and manly pride. She
had to use it.

"Do what you will. I'll simply think on Adam." She stifled a yawn and studied her cuticles.

Hawk stepped back, dropping his hands from her body
as if burned. "You'll simply think on Adam!"

He rubbed his jaw, not quite believing what he'd heard
while he stared at the vision before him, half clad in a cloud
of transparent froth. Silver-blond hair tumbled around the
most beautiful face he had ever beheld. Her face was heart-
shaped, her jaw delicate yet surprisingly strong. Her lips
were full and velvety plum-rich, and she had spitting silver-
gray eyes. She was passion breathing, and she didn't seem
to have a clue about her own beauty. Or she didn't care. Lust
clenched a fist hard around him and squeezed. His ebony
eyes narrowed intently. She had creamy skin, beautiful
shoulders, a slim waist, sweet flare of hips and legs that
climbed all the way up to heaven. Her beauty branded him,
claimed him. The lass was sheer perfection. Although the

Hawk was not a superstitious man, the words of Grimm's wish on the falling star chose that moment to resurface in his mind. *What exactly had Grimm said?*

He'd wished for the Hawk to meet a woman with "wit and wisdom"; an intelligent woman.

"Can you do sums?" he snapped.

"I keep ledgers like a pro."

"Do you read and write?" he pushed.

"Three languages fluently, two reasonably well." It was the primary reason she could fake their brogue so well and convince them she *was* Mad Janet Comyn. Although some of the words and expressions she used might seem odd to them—they did expect her to be batty—she'd been a quick study at the Comyn keep, assimilating a burr with the ease of a child. She'd always had an ear for languages. Besides, she'd watched every episode of *The Highlander* ever made.

Hawk groaned. The second part of Grimm's wish had been that the woman be perfect of face and form. He need ask no questions on that score. She was a Venus, unadorned, who'd slipped into his world, and he had a nagging premonition that his world might never be the same again.

So, the first two requirements for which Grimm had wished were met. The woman possessed both brains and bewitching beauty.

It was the last requirement Grimm had specified that concerned Hawk the most: *A perfect "no" on her perfect lips . . .*

The woman didn't live and breathe who'd ever said no to the Hawk.

"Lass, I want you," he said in a raw, husky voice. "I will make the most incredible love to you you'll ever experience this side of Valhalla. I can take you beyond paradise, make you wish to never set your feet upon this ground again. Will you let me take you there? Do you want me?" He waited, but he was already certain of what was to come.

Her lips pursed in a luscious pucker as she said, "No."

* * *

"You've laid a *geis* upon me with your bloody wish, Grimm!" Laird Sidheach James Lyon Douglas was heard to howl to the starless heavens later that night. Beyond a circle of rowan trees Adam stoked a bank of embers and made a sound a shade too dark to be laughter.

* * *

Adrienne sat in the darkness on the edge of her bed for a long time after he'd left, and flinched at his husky howl that rose to touch the moon. A *geis*? A curse. Bah! She was the one cursed.

To him, she was just like all the rest, and the one thing Adrienne de Simone had learned was that where a man was concerned she couldn't tolerate being one of all the rest.

Guilty as the legions who'd fallen before her, she wanted this man called the Hawk. Wanted him with an unreasoning hunger that far surpassed her attraction to the smithy. There'd been something almost frightening about the smithy's eyes. Like Eberhard's. But the Hawk had beautiful dark eyes with flecks of gold dusting them beneath thick sooty lashes. Hawk's eyes hinted at pleasures untold, laughter, and if she wasn't imagining it, some kind of past pain held in careful check.

Right, she told herself caustically. *The pain of not having enough time to make love to* all *the beautiful women in the world. You know what he is. A womanizer. Don't do this to yourself again. Don't be a fool, Adrienne.*

But she couldn't shake the discomfort she'd felt each time she'd forced herself to say cruel and hateful things to him. That perhaps he didn't deserve them. That just because the Hawk was a dark and beautiful man like Eberhard didn't mean he was the same kind of man as Eberhard. She had a nagging feeling that she was being unfair to him, for no logical reason whatsoever.

Ah, but there is a logical explanation for how and why you've suddenly vaulted back from 1997 to 1513? She snorted derisively.

Adrienne had learned to examine facts and deal with reality, regardless of how irrational the immediate reality appeared to be. New Orleans born and raised, she understood that human logic couldn't explain everything. Sometimes there was a larger logic at work—something tantalizingly beyond her comprehension. Lately, Adrienne felt more surprised when things made sense than when they didn't—at least when things were odd she was on familiar territory. Despite its being highly illogical and utterly improbable, all five of her senses insisted that she wasn't exactly in Kansas anymore.

A dim memory teased the periphery of her mind. . . . What had she been doing just before she'd found herself on the Comyn's lap? The hours before were hazy, uncertain. She could recall the uneasy feeling of being watched . . . and what else? An odd scent, rich and spicy, that she smelled just before she'd . . . what? Adrienne pushed hard against a blanket of confusion and succeeded only in making her head throb.

She struggled with it a moment, then yielded to the pain. Adrienne muttered a fervent prayer that the larger logic behind this irrational reality treat her with more benevolence than whatever had thrown Eberhard her way.

Too bad she hadn't lost some of those really, really bad memories. But no, just a few strange hours; a short gap of time. Perhaps the shock of what had occurred was muting her memory for now. But surely as she adjusted to this new environment she would figure out just how she'd managed to travel through time. And figure out how to get back.

But then she wondered, did she really want to get back to what she'd left behind?

✳   ✳   ✳

In the morning, Adrienne splashed icy water on her face and assessed herself in the blurry polished silver disc hanging above the basin. Ah, the little luxuries. Hot water. Toothpaste. What did she pine for the most?

Coffee. Surely somewhere in the world someone was growing coffee in 1513. If her luscious husband was so anxious to please, perhaps he would find it for her —and quickly. She'd need a full carafe every morning if she continued to lose sleep like this.

By the time the Hawk had left her room last night she'd been shaking from head to toe. The lure of the smithy was but a dim echo of the pull the man called Hawk had on all her senses. Just being in his presence made her feel quivery inside and weak at the knees—far worse than Adam had. She snorted as she recalled the Hawk's rules. Four of them had been to stay away from the smithy. Well, that was one sure way to irritate him if she felt like it. After she got her coffee.

Adrienne rummaged through Janet's "trousseau" seeking something reasonably simple to wear. Donning a lemon-yellow gown (how did they make these brilliant fabrics in this age?), she accented it with a gold girdle at the waist and several gold arm cuffs she found. Soft leather slippers for her feet and a shake of her silvery mane and coffee assumed the priority of breathing.

*   *   *

"Coffee," she croaked when she'd finally managed to wind her way through the sprawling castle and find several people enjoying a leisurely breakfast. There were a dozen or so seated at the table, but the only ones Adrienne recognized were Grimm and Him, so she issued the word in their general direction hopefully.

Everyone at the table stared at her.

Adrienne stared back unblinkingly. She could be rude too.

"I think she said coffee," Grimm suggested after a long pause, "although I've heard more intelligible sounds from some of our falcons."

Adrienne rolled her eyes. Morning always lent a husky quality to her brandy-rich voice. "I need coffee," she explained patiently. "And my voice is always like this in the morning."

"A voice to cherish, smooth and complex as the finest malt Scotch," the Hawk purred. His eyes lingered on her face, then slid gently down to her toes. How in God's name could a mere look make her feel as if he'd peeled her gown from her body slowly and deliciously?

"Didn't that fellow from Ceylon leave a store of odd things in the buttery? And I'm Lydia Douglas, by the bye, this rapscallion's—"

"Mother—"

"Hush. You botched the wedding and you're making a fine mess of things now, so just hush."

Adrienne forgave him for almost everything at that moment, because he looked like a small boy as he blinked in silence. "My lady," she said, attempting a curtsy and hoping she'd addressed Hawk's mother correctly because she liked the woman instinctively, even if she had given birth to that overbearing womanizer.

"Lydia is fine, and if I may—Adrienne? Hawk told me it's your address of preference."

"Adrienne is wonderful. Coffee?"

Lydia laughed, obviously unabashed by this single-minded obsession. "I take it you're used to having the strong brew of a morn. My healer tells me it has rejuvenating properties and is a natural energizer."

"Yes." Adrienne nodded vehemently.

"The buttery, Hawk," Lydia encouraged her son.

"You're going to let me go?" he asked caustically.

"Since when do you listen to me?" Lydia asked with a twinkle in her eye. "Take your new wife to find her coffee. And Adrienne, if you need aught else, even a commiserating ear, do find me. I spend much of the day in my gardens. Anyone can point you the way."

"Thank you." Adrienne meant it from the bottom of her heart. How nice it was to have someone extend a friendly welcome! Someone not male and beautiful beyond endurance.

"Come." The Hawk extended a hand to her. Refusing to touch him, she said sweetly, "After you."

"Nay, lass, after you." He motioned. He'd follow the sweet curve of her hips past the horned minions of hell.

"I must insist," Adrienne demurred.

"As must I," he countered.

"Go," she snapped.

He folded his powerful arms across his chest and resolutely met her gaze.

"Oh, for God's sake, do we have to fight about this, too?"

"Not if you obey me, lass."

Behind them Lydia half laughed, half groaned. "Why don't the two of you just walk side by side," she said encouragingly.

"Fine," Adrienne snapped.

"Fine," the Hawk snarled.

* * *

Lydia laughed until tears twinkled in her merry green eyes. Finally—a lass worthy of her son.

CHAPTER 8

SIDE BY SIDE. SHE DIDN'T HAVE TO LOOK AT HIM. *THANK GOD for small favors.*

"And here we have the buttery," the Hawk said as he unlocked the door and pushed it open. Adrienne's spirits rose. Her nose twitched delicately. She could smell coffee beans, spices, teas, all manner of wonderful things. She practically vaulted into the room, the Hawk at her heels. As she was about to plunge a hand deep into the woven brown sack from which issued the most delicious aroma of sinfully dark coffee, the Hawk somehow managed to insinuate himself between Adrienne and her prize.

"It would seem you quite like your coffee," he observed, with too keen an interest for her liking.

"Yes." She shifted her weight from foot to foot, impatiently, but the man had a lot of body to block her way with. "Move, Hawk," she complained, and he laughed softly as he gripped her waist with his big hands, nearly circling it.

Adrienne froze as a scent even more compelling than her beloved coffee tantalized her nostrils. Scent of leather and man. Of power and sexual prowess. Of confidence and virility. Scent of everything she'd imagined in her dreams.

"Ah, my heart, there is a price—" he murmured.

"You have no heart," she informed his chest.

"True," he agreed. "You've thieved it. And last night I stood before you in agony whilst you ripped it asunder—"

"Oh give over—"

"You have odd sayings, my heart—"

"Your heart is a puny black walnut. Wizened. Shriveled." She refused to look up at him.

He laughed. "Lass, you will keep me amused long into my twilight years."

"Coffee," she muttered.

"The toll troll must be reckoned with."

"And just what does the toll troll wish?"

"This morn, 'tis simple. Other days it may not be. Today your coffee will cost you only a wee kiss."

"You think to dole out the coffee to me in return for kisses?" she exclaimed, disbelieving. And in spite of herself she tilted her head back and met his gaze. Well, almost. Her eyes snagged and held about three inches below his eyes on his perfectly sculpted, beautifully colored lips. A man's lips should not be so well formed and desirable. She forgot about coffee as she thought about tasting him, and her traitorous knees started to get all wobbly again.

"Go ahead," he encouraged.

The bastard. He knew she wanted to kiss him.

"I know you don't want to, lass, but you must if you want your coffee."

"And if I don't?"

"You don't get your coffee." He shrugged. "Really, 'tis a wee price to pay."

"I don't think this is quite what your mother had in mind."

He laughed, a dark, sensual purr, and she felt her nipples tighten. God in heaven, he was dangerous. "My mother is half responsible for me, so don't offer her up for sainthood yet, my heart."

"Quit 'my hearting' me. I have a name."

"Aye, and 'tis Adrienne Douglas. My *wife*. Be glad I seek only a boon for a boon and don't simply take what's mine by right."

She grabbed his hand quick as lightning and deposited the requisite kiss on it, then flung it back down. "My coffee," she demanded.

The Hawk's dark eyes simmered with impatient sensuality. "Obviously, lass, there is much I need to teach you about kissing."

"I know how to kiss!"

"Oh? Perhaps you should demonstrate again, for if that was your idea of a kiss, I'll have to demand a more generous boon." He smiled at her, his lower lip curving invitingly.

Adrienne closed her eyes to escape the sight of his perfect lips and realized the moment her lids fluttered shut that she'd made a serious tactical error. The Hawk cupped her face with his hands and backed her against the wall, trapping her with his powerful body. Adrienne's eyes sprang open instantly. "I did *not* close my eyes so you would kiss me!" she exclaimed, but her denial lost its force when she met his gaze. His intense ebony eyes scrambled her wits, making her ache to accept the pleasure he offered, but she knew she must not. Adrienne tried to free herself from his grip, but his hands on her face were firm. "Hawk! I don't think—"

"Yes, you do, lass, and entirely too much," he interrupted, his hooded gaze mocking. "So stop thinking for a moment, will you? Just feel." He kissed her swiftly, taking erotic advantage of her lips, which were still parted in mid-protest. Adrienne pushed at his chest, but he paid no heed to her resistance.

The Hawk buried his hands in her hair, tilting her head back to kiss her more deeply, his tongue exploring her mouth. His lips were demanding, his embrace possessive and strong, and when he leaned his hips against her body, he was insistently, undeniably male. He challenged her with his kiss, wordlessly demanding that she acknowledge the tension and heat that existed between them—a heat that was capable of incinerating a tender heart or welding two hearts into one. Desire shuddered through her so intensely that she moaned, confused and afraid. Adrienne knew it was dangerous to enjoy his touch, too risky to permit what could surely become addictive pleasure.

The Hawk's thumb played at the corner of her mouth, pressuring her to surrender completely to his mastery. Aroused, curious, helpless to resist, Adrienne yielded. The kiss he rewarded her with made her tremble; it was a kiss guaranteed to strip away her defenses.

And then where would she be? Vulnerable again—a fool for a beautiful man, again.

Hawk's hands slid from Adrienne's hair to cup her breasts, and the ensuing dampness between her thighs shocked her into awareness of her eroding control. Adrienne jerked, determined not to be just another one of this shameless womanizer's conquests. "Let me go! You said one kiss! This wasn't part of the bargain!"

The Hawk froze. He drew his head back, his strong hands still cupping her breasts, and searched her face intently, almost angrily. Whatever it was he looked for, she could tell he wasn't satisfied. Not satisfied at all.

He scrutinized her wide eyes a moment longer, then turned his broad back to her and scooped out a handful of coffee beans.

Adrienne rubbed irritably at her lips, as if she could brush away the lingering, unforgettable pleasure of his touch. As they exited the buttery and walked down the long corridor in silence, refusing to look at each other, the Hawk wrapped the beans in a cloth and tucked them in his sporran.

Just outside the Greathall he stopped and, as if tethered by a common leash, she halted in her tracks.

"Tell me you felt it," his low voice commanded, and still they didn't look at each other. She studied the floor for dust eddies while he studied the ceiling for cobwebs.

"Felt what?" She barely kept her voice from breaking. *A kiss to build a dream on, big beautiful man?*

He yanked her against his body; undeterred when she averted her face, he lowered his head and scattered kisses upon the high curves of her breasts where they pushed against the scooped neckline of her gown.

"Stop it!"

He raised his head, a snarl darkening his face. "Tell me you felt it too!"

The moment hovered, full of possibilities. It stretched into uncertainty and, in her fear, was lost.

"Me? I was thinking on Adam."

How could a man's eyes change from such burning intensity to such cold flat orbs in less than an instant? How could such an open face become so shuttered? A noble face become so savage?

"The next time you're foolish enough to say that after I touch you, I won't be responsible for my actions, lass."

Adrienne closed her eyes. *Hide it, hide it, don't let him see how he affects you.* "There won't be a next time you touch me."

"There will be a next time every day, Adrienne Douglas. You belong to me. And I can only be pushed so far. Adam can be sent away. Everyone can be sent away. Coffee can be sent away. I control everything you want. I can be very good to you if you're willing to try. The only thing I can't negotiate about is Adam. So be willing to try with me and all I ask is that you forgo Adam and never say his name to me. If you can grant me that wee boon, I will demand naught else but the price for your coffee each morn. And I promise you I won't make it too high."

The kiss was too high. Too dangerous in itself. "By what right—"

"By might. 'Tis simple enough."

"Brute force—"

"Don't bother trying to guilt me. Ask my mother. It doesn't work."

Well, well. No chivalry here, she noted. But all in all, the deal he offered was more reasonable than the myriad alternatives. He could demand *all* his husbandly prerogatives rather than one small kiss each morning. She could live through it. "A kiss each morning? That's all you seek in return for my not mentioning Adam to you? And I get my coffee every day?"

"Stay away from Adam. Don't let me find you near him. Don't say his name to me."

"For a kiss each morn?" She had to tie this down to the letter of his law.

"For a boon each morn."

"That's not fair! Just what's a boon?"

He laughed. "Who told you life was fair? Who misled you so sorely? And considering that we're wed and the alternative to my kind offer is sharing full conjugal privileges, what right have you to squabble over fair?"

"Well, you could pin it down a little for my peace of mind! Otherwise I'll wake up dreading things unknown."

His face darkened. "I seek to give her carnal pleasure and she 'dreads things unknown.' " Bitterly he turned away.

"I didn't mean it like that—" she started to say, hating the bitter lines set about his eyes. She had put them there. But for her own safety, she had to keep them there, so she broke off quickly.

He didn't hear her anyway, so caught up was he in his dark brood as he stalked away.

Much too late, as he faded out of sight around the corner, she recalled her coffee beans forlornly They were tucked in that pouch he wore around his hips. And he'd relocked the buttery.

*   *   *

A shower. That was it. What Adrienne wouldn't give for thirty minutes of steam rolling in thick clouds, a rich lather of Aveda soap, shampoos and body oils and a fluffy white towel to dry off with.

She paid careful attention to embellishing the finer nuances of her fantasy shower to keep her mind off Him while she located the gardens. She found them behind the castle; one had to cut through the kitchens to get there, or walk all the way around the castle—and all the way around was a long walk.

"Well, poke in a little more than your wee nose, I'll say. I'd like to be seeing all of our new lady," a voice beckoned from within the kitchen.

Adrienne stepped in curiously. The kitchen was unlike anything she'd imagined existed this far back in time. It was huge, well-designed, and spotless. The central focus of the room was a massive column fireplace that offered an opening on each side, quadrupling the cooking areas. A stone chimney climbed to a vent at the high ceiling. Upon closer inspection, she realized that the kitchen had been built as a freestanding addition to the castle proper, designed to be airy and well vented. Windows lined the two perimeter walls, counters of gleaming oak circled the entire area, and the floors were of palest gray quarry stone. No rotting foods here, no rodents or bugs, this kitchen vied with her own kitchen back home in the late twentieth century except it didn't have a dishwasher. Stairs descended to larders, pantries were cleverly nooked into alcoves, and beyond the open windows sprawled lush gardens. Upon the sills sat tiny jars of herbs and spices.

"You find our kitchen passing fair?"

Adrienne nodded, awestruck, and turned her attention to the smiling man. He was tall and tanned, with a lean body and forearms that were heavily corded with muscle either from wielding a sword or working with his hands. His dark hair and close-cropped beard were both streaked with silver, and when his clear gray eyes met hers, they sparkled with curiosity and welcome.

"The Hawk designed it himself. From his travels. Said he'd seen wonders to make life far more pleasant, and used them all to better Dalkeith, I'll say."

The laird of the castle had been in the kitchens?

"He cut the counters and built the cabinets himself. Likes to work with wood he does. Busies his hands he says. Though where he finds time is beyond me, I'll say." The man rolled his eyes and folded his hands behind his head, leaning his chair back into a puddle of sunshine that streamed in the window. "Name's Tavis, milady," he offered. "Pleased to be welcoming you."

"I'm Mad Janet," she blurted in response to his kindness.

"Don't know much about mad, but Lydia's taken a liking to you and that's one discriminating woman, I'll say."

Adrienne took another step into the kitchen; her eyes swept the room admiring the simple genius with which it had been designed. Everything tidy and easily accessible.

"Lydia is out back," Tavis encouraged. She's been expecting you for some time now, I'll say." He winked at her. "Don't let these Douglas overwhelm you, milady. Stubborn, opinionated people they are, but hearts of purest gold. You'll not find another like the Douglas in all of Scotia. Welcome, I'll say, and if you need anything, you've only to come find Tavis of the tannery." He flexed his strong hands. "I still make the softest hides this side of Uster. Perhaps on t'other side too." Pride gleamed in his smile as he shooed her toward the door.

Adrienne stepped into the sunshine and breathed as deeply as she could. Honeysuckle, a beloved scent from her earliest youth. Buttercups sprawled in golden beauty beneath the windows to her right and left. Lavender on the air, rugosa roses, and another earthy rich scent she struggled to identify. She heard the tinkling of water spilling into a basin. A fountain? Following the sound, Adrienne traipsed the stone walkways through towering bushes of rhododendrons, lush anemones, bluebells, and scattered forget-me-nots.

Stone paths shot off in several directions, but the tinkling sound of water drew Adrienne unerringly. The Lady Lydia sat upon the ledge of a stone fountain that rose in four tiers, high above her head. A full-size stone dolphin poised atop the fountain, caught in mid-leap, spouted water from its open snout.

"Magnificent," Adrienne breathed, and Lydia turned to greet her with a welcoming smile.

"My son is quite the inventor." Pride was evident in every gentle line of her face.

"He did this too?" Adrienne grimaced.

"Most of the unusual aspects of Dalkeith are of my son's making. When he traveled he sought the most advanced secrets of civilization to bring back to his people—"

"When he traveled the world seeking beautiful bed-mates," Adrienne interrupted acerbically, recalling the words of the Comyn maids.

Lydia cocked her head, an amused gleam in her eyes. "Is that what they say?"

"Is that what he did?"

"What say you ask him yourself? But think well on this, Adrienne. What would people who didn't know you well say of you?"

"Point taken," Adrienne conceded, hoping Lydia never discovered her colorful past.

"Mad Janet," Lydia observed softly. "You don't seem a bit mad to me. Why did the Comyn keep you locked in that tower?"

Adrienne recited the words he'd pounded into her the day of her wedding. "I was too beautiful to risk his own men seeing. So he said." She added her own words without thinking, "Truth is, I've never felt that way."

Lydia snorted. "Have you never seen a glass?"

"Of course I have. But I still never felt that way."

"Rather like the Hawk, I believe," Lydia remarked. "He told me once that he knew he was good-looking only because of the way women fussed over him. That if women hadn't made such a hubbub, he would have just considered himself reasonably neat and clean—"

"Reasonably neat and clean?" Adrienne said incredulously. "The man is flawless from head to toe! He makes David and the Greek gods and Pan seem all out of proportion. He is raw sex in a bottle, uncorked. And somebody should cork it! He's—*accck*! Bah!" Adrienne spluttered and stuttered as she belatedly realized her words. Lydia was laughing so hard, tears misted her eyes.

When Lydia was able to draw a breath, she gave a pleased sigh. "Well, that's a relief. I wasn't sure you weren't immune. He thinks you are. Don't worry. 'Twill be our wee secret, dear Adrienne, and do come sit beside me so I can tell you how glad I am that you're here. I'm only sorry I wasn't here to give you a proper welcome when you arrived. From what I've heard, they all botched things quite terribly."

Adrienne found herself wanting to rush headlong into the closest thing to mothering arms she'd ever known. Her hardened heart slipped on treacherously thin ice—dare she? Dare she not?

✷   ✷   ✷

Behind bushes of blood-red rhododendrons a shadow flinched. *I hate her! Hate her!* Esmerelda's hand trembled as she raised the tube, then steadied it sharply. She would dispatch the enemy, and end her torment. She puckered her

lips around the mouth of the tube, keeping level the tiny in-
strument of death. She drew a deep breath and forced a
sharp burst of air from tight lips. A tiny dart erupted from
the end of the hollow chute, as small as the stinger of a bee.
Esmerelda watched as the dart flew home to embed itself in
the pale flesh of Adrienne's neck. She smiled with satisfaction as Adrienne slapped briefly at the wound, as if shooing
away an irritating midge. Esmerelda squinted hard—she
could see the glistening tail of the dart shine in Adrienne's
neck as she spoke to Lydia. Done. The deed was done.

* * *

"Where is your husband, Lydia?" Adrienne slapped sharply
at her neck. "Midges? Already?"

"We have our share. 'Tis the reason for the nettings upon
the beds during this season. A bit of mint seems to keep
them away. I stuff some in my pockets and tuck a leaf or two
in my bodice." She offered a few leaves of her own and
Adrienne accepted them gratefully. "As to my husband . . ."
Her eyes grew dreamy. "That impossible man left me over
thirty years ago. He died right after Hawk was born."

"How?" Adrienne wiped the back of her hand across her
forehead. The sun was too hot suddenly.

" 'Twas in battle for the king, and in his dying he made a
pledge, or so King James said, of fifteen years of his son's
life in service to the Crown, in exchange for the king's protection of Dalkeith. In fact, Sidheach's service ended only
recently."

Adrienne wrinkled her brow in confusion. Lydia's bright
flowers suddenly melted into a dizzying wash of color.

Lydia explained patiently, "Dalkeith is a rich keep. There
was no man to protect us when my husband died. I was left

with a wee heir of two months. Whether my husband actually made the pledge or James just invented it, I'll never know. I doubt my Douglas would have pledged our son to King James in any manner, but one rarely wins an argument with a king. I wasn't ready to wed again, my grieving for my husband was deep. The king's men protected Dalkeith until I doffed my widow weeds. But James gave us his protection on the condition that the Hawk report to Edinburgh on his eighteenth birthday, for fifteen years of fealty. As he claimed my husband promised him."

"You don't believe your husband pledged the Hawk?" Adrienne asked, her vision growing cloudy. She blinked hard a moment and her vision cleared.

Lydia's lovely face grew pensive, and for a long moment it seemed she might not answer the question at all. Adrienne could see memories flitting across her brow, some good, some obviously painful. "My Douglas was the second offer of marriage I received, Adrienne."

"And the first?" Adrienne asked, trailing her fingertips in the cool, sweet water of the fountain and then dabbing a few droplets at her temples.

"King James."

"Ah! A man scorned."

"Decidedly scorned. And not a bit forgiving. King James had set his mind on me and was not to be dissuaded. It was in my sixteenth summer, and I was at court with your mother, Althea. We both received many offers of marriage that season, and James was one of my most ardent admirers. I didn't take him too seriously, he was, after all, the king. It was only later that I discovered just how serious he was. But it was too late. I had set my mind on the Douglas when I was but a wee lass. And the Douglas, well, let's just say it was short work persuading him." Her green eyes twinkled with fond remembrances.

"So the king hates the Hawk because you turned down his offer of marriage? That seems incredibly childish."

"He is. James was spoiled since the moment he was born. He was coddled and pampered and pandered to endlessly. By the time he was of age to marry, he had been doted on ceaselessly. He had never heard the word *no* in his entire life and had no intention of ever hearing it. He found it simply incomprehensible that a woman would choose to be a mere earl's wife when she could be queen of all Scotland."

Adrienne thought briefly about the royals in her time. How very much one had sacrificed to be princess and one day queen. Lydia had made a wise choice when she'd married for love.

"What truly undid him was that he was foolish enough to announce to his court that I was going to be his queen, even after I'd declined his marriage proposals on several occasions. I wed my Douglas the day following his 'proclamation,' although we didn't know the king had actually gone so far as to announce his intentions publicly until weeks later, when the news finally reached Dalkeith. My husband said we'd made a powerful enemy that day. But I think neither of us knew how truly vengeful he could be. I suspect there are many things about his service to James that Hawk will never speak of. 'Tis rumored James held threats of destroying Dalkeith over his head unless Hawk obeyed his every whim." Her voice slipped a confidential notch. "Hawk doesn't know it, but I sought audience with James, myself, shortly after I began to hear tales of his servitude. I begged him to relinquish his claim on my son." Lydia's eyes clouded. "He laughed and told me that if I had wed wisely the Hawk would have been the king's *son* instead of the king's servant."

Adrienne rubbed her neck and blinked hard. Her vision was blurring alarmingly and her head was pounding. "Public humiliation," she said thickly. "Never met the man who took it well."

"I believe 'tis also why King James ordered the Hawk to wed on his command," Lydia continued softly. "Just another subtle way of prolonging his revenge. I think he felt almost cheated by my husband's death, and I've often wondered what he might have done to us had my husband lived longer. What a bitter man he's become." Lydia shook her head. "I'm glad it was you, Adrienne. The king would hate it if he knew how lovely and how very *not*-mad you really are. You are exactly what the Hawk needs. No timid lass, or simpering addlepate, but a woman with true mettle and depth."

Adrienne flushed with pleasure. The added heat did alarming things to her head. "You said you wed again. Do you have other children?" she asked, trying desperately to hold on to the gist of the conversation.

The smile returned to Lydia's face. "Oh, aye. Adrian and Ilysse. They're in France with my sister, Elizabeth. In her last letter she warned me that Adrian is becoming an incorrigible rogue and she's just about given up on civilizing Ilysse." Lydia laughed. "Ilysse can be a bit high-spirited and unmanageable at times. You would like her."

Adrienne wasn't certain how to take that, so she didn't comment. Besides, she wasn't feeling at all well. Her vision was now double, her stomach a roiling agony, and her mouth felt dry as cotton swabs. She struggled to swallow. "Wallah hubbah hah?" she croaked.

"Adrienne?" Lydia gazed at her with concern. "Adrienne!"

She placed a hand against the younger woman's forehead. "You're burning up!"

Adrienne groaned as she pitched forward and collapsed on the cobbled walkway.

"Hawk!" Lydia screamed.

CHAPTER 9

"POISON." HAWK'S FACE WAS GRIM AND DARK. HE CAREFULLY studied the tiny dart the aged healer had laid upon the cloth.

"Callabron." The healer combed his fingers through his long white beard and lowered himself into a chair by Adrienne's side.

Hawk groaned. Callabron was not a gentle poison. A vicious and slow toxin, it would cause lingering pain for days before it ended in death by suffocation as the toxin slowly paralyzed the body from the outside in.

The Hawk knew there was no cure. He'd heard of the toxin during his service to King James. It was rumored to have claimed the lives of many royal siblings. When one sought to remove a future king, one took no chances with a poison that might fail. Hawk dropped his head in his hands and rubbed his sore and bleary eyes furiously. The intensity of the heat from the high flames wasn't helping. But the heat would help her, the healer had said. It might break the fever. Still . . . she would die.

Take me, just leave her unharmed! Hawk wished with all of his heart.

"We can ease her pain. There are things I can give her . . . ," the healer said softly.

"Who?" the Hawk raged, ignoring the old man. "Who would wish to do this? Why kill her? What has she done?"

The healer flinched and squeezed his eyes shut.

In the doorway, Lydia drew a labored breath. " 'Tis Callabron, then?"

"Aye. The skin has blackened around the opening, and those pale green lines streak out from it. 'Tis the deadly bite of Callabron."

"I won't lose her, Hawk," Lydia demanded.

Hawk raised his head slowly from his hands. "Mother." The word was a plea, hopelessness in and of itself. *Mother make it better.* But he knew she couldn't.

"Some say 'tis more humane to end the suffering in the early stages," the healer offered very softly, not meeting the Hawk's gaze.

"Enough!" the Hawk silenced him with a shout. "If all you can bring is gloom and doom, then get thee gone!"

Pride and indignation stiffened the healer's back. "Milord—"

"Nay! I'll have none of it! We'll not be killing her! She won't be dying!"

"Perhaps the Rom might know of some cure," Lydia suggested softly.

The healer sniffed disdainfully. "I assure you, milady, the *Rom* know nothing of the sort. If I tell you there is no cure, you may rest assured that none could heal her. That vagrant band of cutthroats, cheats, and lightfingers certainly couldn't—" The old healer broke off abruptly at the Hawk's dark look.

" 'Tis worth trying," the Hawk agreed with Lydia.

"Milord!" The healer protested vehemently. "The Rom are no more than shabby illusionists! They are—"

"Camping on my land," the Hawk cut him off sternly, "as they have for over thirty seasons, with my blessing, so guard your tongue well, old man. If you're so certain they know nothing, why should you care if they come?"

The healer sneered. "I just don't think wild dancing and chanting and nasty-smelling bits of mummified who-zits and what-zits would be good for my patient," he snapped.

The Hawk snorted. It was obvious the healer knew nothing of the truth about the Rom, the proud band of people who'd fled country after country seeking only the freedom to live as they chose. Like so many who dared to fight for what they believed, they were frequently misunderstood and feared. The gypsy tribe that camped at Dalkeith was a tight community of talented and wise people. Although arguably superstitious, the Hawk had found many of their "instincts" accurate.

But this healer, like so many others, was afraid of what was different and thus condemned it. Ignorance translated into fear, which quickly became persecution. The Hawk leveled a steely glare on the old man and growled, "Anything that might heal *my wife* would be good for her. I don't care if it's mummified toad brains. Or mummified *healer* brains for that matter."

The healer shut his mouth and signed a quick cross.

The Hawk rubbed his eyes and sighed. The Rom were as good a chance as any. He quickly bade a guard at the door to dispatch a messenger to the camp.

"I think you're making a big mistake, milord—"

"The only mistake being made in this room is you open-ing your mouth again," Hawk growled.

The healer rose furiously, his ancient joints popping protest. With pursed lips, he removed a stone jar sealed by wax and a tight stopper from inside his overtunic, close to his body. He placed it on the hearth, then with the audacity and temerity often acquired by those who have survived plague, famine, and war to reach an advanced old age, the healer dared to snip, "You might choose to use it when your Rom fail. For fail, they will," before fleeing the room in a flurry of creaking joints and thin flapping limbs.

Hawk shook his head and stared broodingly at the shiv-ering woman on the bed. His wife. His lovely, proud, tem-pestuous *dying* wife. He felt utterly helpless.

Lydia crossed the room and pulled her son's head into the comfort of her bosom. "Hawk, my sweet Hawk." She murmured those nonsensical sounds only a mother knows.

A long moment passed, then Hawk pulled his head back. If he could offer no comfort to his wife, he would accept no comfort from his mother. "Tell me again exactly what hap-pened in the gardens."

✳   ✳   ✳

"Come, sweet whore," Adam commanded, and Esmerelda came.

She was beyond redemption now. Esmerelda knew who Adam Black was even as she went to him. Her people had always known, and were accordingly cautious. Particularly when dealing with this one, for to incite his ire, or merely to become the focus of his attention, could be the cup of death for an entire nation. And although such phenomenal power instilled immense terror in Esmerelda's veins, so too was it an irresistible aphrodisiac.

What had brought him here? she wondered. It was her last coherent thought as he began to do those things to her body that turned her inside-out. His face was dark with passion above her, gilded in the amber glow of fire beneath the rowans. The scent of sandalwood and jasmine rose up from the steaming earth around them. It was wee morn when she was finally able to crawl from his forge.

Adam templed his fingers and considered his strategy as he watched the woman falter from his tent on weak legs.

"Fool!" The word came sharply, harsh and condemning.

Adam stiffened. "You called, my King?" he asked, addressing his unseen master.

"What have you done this time, Adam?"

"I was having my way with a gypsy girl, since you ask. What of it?"

"The beauty lies dying."

"Adrienne?" Adam was startled. "Nay. Not of my hand."

"Well, fix it!"

"Truly, my King, I had nothing to do with it."

"I don't care. Fix it. Our Queen would be furious should we jeopardize the Compact."

"I'll fix it. But who would seek to fell the beauty?"

"It's your game, fool. Run it more tightly. Already the Queen asks about you."

"She misses me?" Adam preened a moment.

Finnbheara snorted. "You may have pleased her in passing, but I am her King."

*   *   *

Adrienne was burning. Tethered to a stake, like an ancient witch trapped amidst a mountain of blazing timbers while the villagers gazed placidly on. *Help me!* she pleaded through parched lips as she convulsed in the billowing smoke. Choking, choking, and then she felt the hideous sensation of a thousand fire ants scurrying frantically to and fro just beneath the top layer of her skin.

She was unaware of the Hawk sponging her brow, bathing her body with cool cloths, and wrapping her in soft woolens. He pushed damp tendrils of hair from her brow and kissed it gently. Stoking the fire, he turned back quickly to discover her thrashing violently against the snug cocoon of blankets the healer had assured him might ease her fever.

Desperation engulfed him, more brutal and pounding than the fiercest Highland squall.

A primitive groan escaped his lips as the Hawk watched her scratch viciously at her flawless skin in a vain attempt to assuage the attack of whatever fierce beastie the fever had conjured to torment her with. She'd scratch herself raw if he didn't stop her, yet he couldn't bear to bind her hands as the healer had recommended. A vision of her straining against the bonds flickered through his mind's eyes, and he swallowed a bitter howl of impotent fury. How could he wage war against an unseen invader that had no known vulnerability? How could he defeat a poison that had no cure?

He paused only a heartbeat before ripping the shirt from his body and kicking off his boots. Clad only in his kilt, he eased onto the bed and wrapped himself around her, drawing her back against him tightly.

"Adrienne!" He cursed harshly as he cradled her in his arms. How could he feel such grief for a virtual stranger? From whence rose this feeling that they were to have had more time?

He leaned back against the wall, cradling her between his legs, his arms wrapped tightly around her while she thrashed and shuddered, his chin resting upon her head.

Deep in the night the fever peaked, and she talked, and cried silvery tears.

She would never know that he kissed them away, one by one.

She would never know that he listened with a heavy heart as she cried for a man he deemed not worth crying for, and that he wished with all his might that he had been the first man she'd loved.

Ever-hard Darrow Garrett. The bastard who'd broken his wife's heart.

What kind of self-respecting Scotsman was named Ever-hard?

In the wee hours of dawn, the Hawk fingered the smooth ebony of the chess piece Grimm had given him, even as Adrienne called for it in her delirium. He studied it and wondered why this game piece was so important to her that as she lay dying, she searched desperately for it in the inky corridors of her mind.

$$* \quad * \quad *$$

It was the commotion that woke him, dragging him from a deep and dreamless sleep. Refusing to open his eyes, he felt his surroundings with his senses first. Damn it, she still burned! Hotter, if possible. His wife of scant days dying in his arms. What had woken him? Was it the Rom, finally arrived?

"Let me pass!" The smithy's voice thundered from beyond the closed door, loud enough to rattle it. Hawk came fully awake. *That* man's voice made his body ready for battle.

"The Hawk will kill you, man," Grimm scoffed. "He doesn't like you to begin with, and he's not in a good temper."

Hawk nodded agreement with Grimm's words, and was glad he'd posted a half-guard outside the Green Lady's room. There was no telling what he might have done if he'd woken to find the arrogant blacksmith peering down at him in his present frame of mind.

"Fools! I said I can cure her," the smithy snapped.

Hawk stiffened instantly.

"A fool, I am?" Grimm's voice cracked with disbelief. "Nay, a fool is he who thinks there's a cure for such a poison as Callabron!"

"Dare you risk it, Grimm?" the smithy asked coolly.

"Let him pass," the Hawk ordered through the closed door.

He heard the sound of swords drawing away with a metallic slash as guards parted the crossed blades that had been barring entrance to the Green Lady's room, and then Adam was standing in the doorway, his big frame nearly filling it.

"If you came here thinking to play with me, Adam Black, get thee gone before I spill your blood and watch it run on my floor. 'Twould be a wee distraction, but it would make me feel better."

"Why do you hold her thusly? So close, as if so dear?"

Hawk tightened his arms around her. "She's dying."

"But you scarce know her, man."

"I have no reason for it that makes any sense. But I refuse to lose her."

"She's beautiful," Adam offered.

"I've known many beautiful lasses."

"She's more beautiful than the others?"

"She's more *something* than the others." Hawk brushed his cheek gently against her hair. "Why have you come here?"

"I heard it was Callabron. I can cure her."

"Think not to tempt me with impossibilities, smithy. Lure me not to false hope or you will lie dying beside her."

"Think not to tempt *me* with impossibilities, Lord Hawk," Adam echoed brightly. "Furthermore I speak truth about a cure."

Hawk studied the smithy a careful moment. "Why would you do this, if you can?"

"Totally self-serving, I assure you." Adam crossed to the bed and sat upon the edge. He extended his hand, then stopped in mid-reach at the look on Hawk's face. "I can't heal her without touching her, dread Hawk."

"You mock me."

"I mock everything. Don't take it so personally. Although in your particular case, it is meant rather personally. But in this, I do offer you truth. I have the cure."

Hawk snorted and tightened his arms protectively about his wife. "How does it come to pass that a simple smithy has such knowledge of an invaluable cure?"

"You waste time asking me questions while the lady lies dying."

"Give it to me then, smithy."

"Oh no. Not so easily— "

"Now who's wasting time? I want the cure. Give it to me and begone, *if* you really have it."

"A boon for a boon," Adam said flatly.

Hawk had known this was coming. The man wanted his wife. "You son of a bitch. What do you want?"

Adam grinned puckishly. "Your wife. I save her. I get her."

Hawk closed his eyes. He should have fired the bastard smithy when he'd had the chance. Where the hell were the Rom, anyway? They should have been at Dalkeith by now.

The smithy could heal his wife, or so he said.

The Rom may know nothing.

And all the smithy wanted in exchange for saving his wife's life was his wife.

Every fiber in his body screamed in defiance. Entrust this woman, bequeath her body and her lush bounty unto another man? Never. Hawk forced his eyes open and stared at the man called Adam. He was to allow this arrogant, beautiful bastard of a smithy to raise his body above his wife's and capture her moans of pleasure in his lips? The smithy's lips were even now curving in a cruel smile as he savored the war that waged within the Hawk.

Hawk schooled his face to impassive calm. Never betray the real feelings. Never let them see what you're thinking when it hurts the deepest. How well he'd learned that lesson from King James.

Yet—still—*anything* so that she might live. "A lass is not a boon to be granted. I will give her to you if—and only if—she wants you," he said finally. If she died he would lose her. If she lived, by price of saving her, he would lose her too. But then again, maybe not. Unable to defuse the rage which he knew must be blazing in his eyes, he closed them again.

"Done. *You will give her to me if she wants me.* Remember your words, Lord Hawk."

Hawk flinched.

When he opened his eyes again, Adam was holding out a hand to his wife's face. Sweat glistened in beads above her lips and on her forehead. The wound upon her neck was pussing green around its blackened mouth. "You touch her, smithy, no more than you must to cure her," the Hawk warned.

"For now. When she's cured, I touch her all she wants."

"*She* is the key word there."

Adam laid his palm against Adrienne's cheek, intently

studying the wound on her neck. "I need boiling water, compresses, and a dozen boiled linens."

"Bring me boiling water, compresses, and a dozen boiled linens," the Hawk roared at the closed door.

"And I need you out of this room."

"No." There was no more finality in death than in the Hawk's refusal.

"You leave or she dies," Adam murmured, as if he'd merely said "It's raining, had you noticed?"

Hawk didn't move a muscle.

"Sidheach James Lyon Douglas, have you a choice?" Adam wondered.

"You have all my names. How do you know so much about me?"

"I made it my business to know so much about you."

"How do I know you didn't shoot her yourself with some obscure poison that isn't even Callabron but mimics it, and now you're faking a cure—all so you can simply steal my wife?"

"Absolutely." Adam shrugged.

"What?" Hawk snarled.

Adam's eyes glittered like hard stones. "You *don't* know. You must make a choice. Can you save her at this point, Lord Hawk? I don't think so. What are your options? She's dying from something, that much is plain to see. You think it's Callabron, but you're not certain. Whatever it is, it is killing her. I say I can cure her and ask a boon for it. What choice do you have, really? They say you make hard decisions look easy. They say you're a man who would move a mountain without blinking, if he wanted that mountain moved. They say you have an unerring sense of justice, right and wrong, honor and compassion. They say, also"—Adam grimaced at this—"that you are passingly fair between the sheets, or so one woman said, and it offended me in great sum. In fact, they say entirely too much about you for my liking. I came here to hate you, Hawk. But I didn't come here to hate this woman you claim as your wife."

Adam and Hawk stared at each other with barely harnessed violence.

Adrienne cried out sharply and shuddered in Hawk's arms. Her body convulsed, then tensed as if pulled taut on a rack. Hawk swallowed hard. *What choice?* There was no choice, no choice at all.

"Cure her," he muttered through gritted teeth.

"You grant my boon?" the smithy asked.

"As we agreed. Only if she chooses you."

"You will place no restrictions upon any time she chooses to spend with me. I am wooing her from this day forth and you will not caution her from me. She is free to see me as she pleases."

"I am wooing her too."

"That is the game, Hawk," Adam said softly, and Hawk finally understood. The smithy didn't want his wife handed over freely. He wanted a contest, a battle for her favors. He wanted an open challenge, and intended to win.

"You will hate it when I take her from you, dread Hawk," the smithy promised. "Close the door when you leave."

CHAPTER 10

"HOW IS IT POSSIBLE THAT A MAN'S WORLD CAN BE TURNED inside out before he even has a chance to see it coming and try to stop it, Grimm?"

Hawk had started drinking the moment the door had shut on his wife and the smithy. He was trying with determination to get head-reeling, feet-stumbling, bellyaching drunk and was not succeeding.

"Do you believe he can cure her, Hawk?"

Hawk puzzled a moment. "Aye, Grimm. I do. There's something unnatural about Adam Black, and I mean to find out what it is."

"What do you suspect?"

"I don't know. Grimm, I want you to find out everything about the man you can. Talk to everyone on the estate until you get some answers. Where he came from, when he came here, who he's related to, what he does all day. I want to know about every breath he draws, every piss he takes."

"Understood, Hawk."

"Good."

They both turned to stare at the door to the Green Lady's room. It had been hours since the smithy had closed the door. Not a sound had escaped since.

"Who would try to kill her, Hawk?" Grimm puzzled. "Mad Janet was practically a recluse. According to the gossip at Comyn keep, fewer than five people ever saw her. How could a lass so far out of circulation offend anyone enough to invite murder?"

Hawk rubbed his head tiredly. His stomach was churning and the Scotch wasn't helping. On sudden impulse he rolled the bottle away from him, toward Grimm. "Don't let me have any more. I need a clear head. I can't think right now. He's touching her, Grimm. He could be bathing her, gazing upon her. I want to kill him."

"So do it, when he's done curing her," Grimm said easily.

"I can't!"

"Then I'll do it for you," Grimm said, ever faithful.

"Nay. We made a pact."

"You made a pact with him?" Grimm's eyes flared wide. "Damn it all to hell, man! You never break a pact. Why would you be so foolish to make a pact with a man you can't stand?"

"He can save my wife."

"When did you come to have such feeling for this Mad Janet you swore never to take to wife anyway?"

"Shut up, Grimm."

"What's the pact, Hawk?" Grimm persisted.

"He wants Adrienne."

"You gave him Adrienne?"

"Grimm, no more questions. Just find out anything and everything about this man called Adam Black."

"Be assured, I will."

✳   ✳   ✳

"You are flawless, beauty," the smithy said as his coal-black eyes raked over her nude body twisted in the damp sheets.

"Flawless lalless," Adrienne pooh-poohed dreamily. The heat was ebbing, slowly.

"Decidedly lawless."

He couldn't know. Not possibly. "What do you mean by that?" She struggled to form the words, and wasn't certain she even made a sound.

"Just that there must be something *criminal* about a woman so beautiful," he replied archly.

"Nothing criminal about me," she demurred distantly.

"Oh, beauty, I think there is much criminal about you."

"There is something just not normal about you, Adam," she mumbled as she tossed restlessly.

"No," he replied smugly, "there is certainly nothing normal about me. Give me your hand, beauty, I'll show you not normal."

And then there was cool water, frothy ocean upon powder-white sand. Whisper of gentle surf rushing over the beach, cool sand beneath her bare toes. No ants, no rack, no fire. Just peace in her most favorite haven in the world. The seaside at Maui where she'd vacationed with her girlfriends. Beautiful, blissful days they'd passed there with fresh-squeezed orange juice and endless summer jogs on the beach, bare feet slapping the edge of the tide.

And then the stranger images. Scent of jasmine and sandalwood. Snowflake sand dotted with fuchsia silk tents and butterflies upon every bough of every limb of every rowan. An improbable place. And she was lying in the cool sands and healed by tropical lapis waves.

"Beauty, my beauty. Want me. Feel me, hunger for me and I will slake your need."

"Hawk?"

Adam's anger was palpable in the air.

Adrienne forced her eyes open a slit, and gasped. If her body had obeyed, she would have shot straight up in bed. But it didn't obey. It lay flaccid and weak upon the bed while her temper shot up instead. "Get out of my room!" she yelled. At least her voice hadn't lost its vigor.

"I was just checking to make sure your forehead cooled." Adam grinned puckishly.

"You thickheaded oaf! I don't care why you're in here, just get out!"

Finally her body obeyed a little and she managed to get her fingers around a tumbler at the bedside. Too weak to throw it, she was at least able to slide it off the table. Glass crashed to the floor and shattered. The sound mollified her slightly.

"You were dying. I cured you," Adam reminded.

"Thank you. Now get out."

Adam blinked. "That's all? Thank you, now get out?"

"Don't think I'm so stupid that I don't realize you were touching my breasts!" she whispered fiercely. At the abashed look on his face she realized he had indeed thought she'd been unconscious. "So that and my thanks are all you'll be getting, smithy!" she growled. "I hate beautiful men. *Hate* them!"

"I know," Adam smiled with real pleasure and obeyed her dismissal.

Adrienne squeezed her eyes shut tightly but upon the pink-gray insides of her eyelids shadows arose. Images of being held between the Hawk's rock-hard thighs, wrapped in arms that were bands of steel. His voice murmuring her name over and over, calling her back, commanding her back. Demanding that she live. Whispering words of . . . what? What had he said?

*   *   *

"She lives, Lord Buzzard—"

"Hawk."

"Both birds of prey. What difference?"

"A buzzard is a scavenger. A hawk selects his kill as carefully as a falcon. Stalks it with the same unerring conviction. And fails as frequently—which is never."

"Never," Adam mused. "There are no absolutes, Lord Hawk."

"In that you're wrong. I choose, I adhere, I pursue, I commit, I attain. That—that, my errant friend—is an absolute."

Adam shook his head and studied the Hawk with apparent fascination. "A worthy adversary. The hunt begins. No cheating. No tricks. You may not forbid her from me. And I know that you tried to already. You will recant your rules."

Hawk inclined his dark head. "She chooses," he allowed tightly. "I will forbid her nothing."

Adam nodded, a satisfied nod as he plunged his hands deep in the pockets of his loose trousers and waited.

"Well? Get thee from my castle, smithy. You have your place, and it is without my walls."

"You might try a thank-you. She lives."

"I'm not certain you aren't the reason she almost died."

At that, Adam's brow creased thoughtfully. "No. But now that I think on it, I have work to do. I wonder . . . who would try to kill the beauty, if not me? And I didn't. Had I, she would be dead. No slow poison from my hand. Quick death or not at all."

"You're a strange man, smithy."

"But I will soon be most familiar to her."

"Pray the gods she is wiser than that," Grimm mumbled as Adam stalked off into the dim corridor. Night had fallen and the castle lamps were still largely unlit.

Hawk sighed heavily.

"What deal did you make with that devil?" Grimm asked in a voice scarcely audible.

"Think you he may be?"

"Something is not natural about that man and I intend to find out what."

"Good. Because he wants my wife, and she doesn't want me. And I saw her wanting him with a hurt in her eyes."

Grimm winced. "You are certain you don't want her just because she doesn't want you and he wants her?"

Hawk shook his head slowly. "Grimm, I have no words for what she makes me feel."

"You always have words."

"Not this time, which warns me truly that I'm in deep trouble and about to get deeper. Deep as I must to woo that lass. Think you I've been spelled?"

"If love can be bottled, or shot from Cupid's bow, my friend," Grimm whispered into the breeze that ruffled in Hawk's wake when he entered Adrienne's chamber.

*   *   *

In the weeks to come the Hawk would wonder many times why the Rom, whom he trusted and valued, and whom he had thought returned those feelings in kind, had never come to tend his wife during those terrible days. When he spoke to his guard, the man said that he'd delivered the message. Not only didn't the Rom come, they were conspicuously absent from Dalkeith. They made no trips to the castle to barter their goods. They spent no evenings weaving tales in the Greathall before a rapt and dazzled audience. Not one of the Rom approached Dalkeith-Upon-the-Sea; they kept to their fields, out past the rowans.

That fact nagged at Hawk's mind briefly, but was quickly lost in the thick of more weighty concerns. He promised himself he would resolve his questions with a trip to the gypsy camp once his wife was fully healed and matters with the strange smithy were resolved. But it was to be some time before he made the trip to the Rom camp; and by that time, things would be vastly changed.

*   *   *

Adrienne drifted up from healing slumber to find her husband watching her intently.

"I thought I'd lost you." The Hawk's face was dark, glistening in the firelight, and it was the first thing she saw when she opened her eyes. It took her several long moments to shake loose the cotton stuffing that had replaced her brain. With wakefulness came defiance. Just looking at that man made her temper rise.

"Can't lose something you don't have. Never had me to begin with, Lord Hawk," she mumbled.

"Yet," he corrected. "I haven't had you yet. At least not in the sense that I will have you. Beneath me. Bare, silky skin slippery with my loving. My kisses. My hunger." He traced the pad of his thumb along the curve of her lower lip and smiled.

"Never."

"Never say never. It only makes you feel more foolish when you end up taking it back. I wouldn't want you to feel too foolish, lass."

"Never," she said more firmly. "And I never say never

unless I'm absolutely one hundred percent certain I will
never change my mind."

"There are a lot of nevers in there, my heart. Be careful."

"Your heart is a wrinkled prune. And I mean every
blasted one of those nevers."

"Mean them as you will, lass. 'Twill only make it that
much more pleasurable to break you to my bit."

"I am not a mare to be broken to ride!"

"Ah, but there are many similarities, wouldn't you say?
You need a strong hand, Adrienne. A confident rider, one
not dismayed by your strong will. You need a man who can
handle your bucking and enjoy your run. I won't break you
to ride. Nay. I will break you to the feel of my hand and
mine alone. A mare broken to ride allows many riders, but a
wild horse broken to the bit of one hand—she loses none of
her fire, yet permits none but her true master to mount her."

"No man has ever been my master, and none ever will.
Get that straight in your head, Douglas." Adrienne gritted
her teeth as she struggled to pull herself upright. It was hard
trying to hold her ground in a conversation while lying flat
on her back feeling ridiculously weak, looking up at this
goliath of a man. "And as to mounting me. . . ."

To her chagrin and the Hawk's vast amusement, she
slipped back into healing slumber without completing the
thought.

Unknown to him, she more than completed it in
her dreams. *Never!* her dreaming-within-the-dream mind
seethed, even as she was drawn to the great black charger
with fire in his eyes.

CHAPTER 11

"IT'S NOT *ME* SOMEONE'S TRYING TO KILL," ADRIENNE repeated.

She was buried in mounds of plush pillows and woolen throws and felt helplessly swallowed by a mountain of feathers. Every time she moved the dratted bed moved with her. It was wearing her out, like being cocooned in a down straitjacket. "I want to get up, Hawk. *Now.*" Too bad her voice didn't come off sounding as firm as she'd intended. It would have—it should have—except being in a bed while trying to argue with this particular man scattered her thoughts like leaves to a windstorm, into a jumble of passionate images; bronzed skin against pale, ebony eyes and hot kisses.

The Hawk smiled, and she had to bite down the overwhelming urge just to smile blankly back, like some dim-witted idiot. He was beautiful when somber, but when he smiled she was in grave danger of forgetting that he was the enemy. And she must never forget that. So she put a lot of frustration to good use, and dredged up an impressive scowl.

His smile faded. "Lass, it's been you both times. When are you going to face the facts? You must be guarded. You'll get used to it. In time you'll scarce notice them." He gestured at the dozen brawny men standing outside the Green Lady's room.

She shot a withering glance at her "elite guard" as he called them. They stood legs wide, arms folded across thin broad chests. Implacable, stony faces, and all of them with physiques that would make Atlas consider shrugging half his weight over. *Where do they breed these kind of men? The Bonny and Braw Beefcake Farm?* She snorted her disgust. "What you don't understand is that if you're so busy protecting *me*, the assassin is going to get whoever they're really after. Because it's *not* me!"

"Do they call you 'Mad Janet' because you refuse to accept reality?" he wondered. "*Reality is* that someone wishes you dead. *Reality is* that I am only trying to protect you. *Reality is* that you are my wife and I will always keep you safe from harm." He was leaning closer as he spoke, punctuating the phrase *reality is* with a sharp stab at the air directly in front of her. Adrienne compensated by shrinking deeper into her haven of feathers each time he stabbed.

"It is my duty, my honor, and my pleasure," he continued. His eyes swept her upturned face and darkened with desire. "Reality . . . ah . . . *reality is* that you are exquisitely beautiful, my heart," he said in a voice suddenly roughened.

His voice conjured images of sweet cream blended with fine Scotch, tossed over melting ice cubes. Smooth and rough at the same time. It unnerved her, flatly shattering what little composure she'd been hugging tightly around her. When he wet his full lower lip with his tongue her mouth went dry as a desert. And his dark eyes flecked with gold were a smoldering promise of endless passion. His eyes that were locked on her lips and oh, but he was going to kiss her and she would do anything to prevent that!

"It's time you know the truth. I am *not* Mad Janet," she snapped, saying something, anything, whatever came to mind to keep his lips from claiming hers in that intoxicating pleasure. "And for the umpteenth time—I am not your blasted heart!"

He agreed instantly. "I didn't think you were. Mad, I mean. But you *are* my heart, whether you like it or not. By the bye, neither does Lydia. Think you're mad, that is. We both know you're intelligent and capable. Except when it comes to two things: your safety and me. You're completely unreasonable about both of those issues." He shrugged one of his muscled shoulders. "That's why I'm having this wee talk with you. To help you see things more clearly."

"Oooh! Those are the two things *you're* being so pigheaded about. I'm not in danger and I don't want you!"

He laughed. Damn the man, but he laughed. "You *are* in danger, and as to wanting me . . ." He moved closer. His weight settling on the down ticks beside her caused her to shift and roll alarmingly. Right into his arms. *How convenient,* she thought sardonically. Now she understood why they'd used all those down ticks in the olden days. And why they'd had so many children.

"You're right, I do want you—"

He froze. "You do?"

"—out of my room," she continued. "Out of my face and out of my life. Don't get in my space, *don't even breathe my air, okay*?"

"It's *my* air, by the bye, as laird, and all that. But I could be persuaded to share it with you, sweet wife."

He was smiling!

"And I am *not* your wife! Or at least, not the one you were supposed to get! I'm from the nineteen nineties—that's almost five hundred years in the future in case you can't add—and the Comyn killed his own daughter. How? I don't know, but I have my suspicions, and I haven't got the faintest idea how I ended up in his lap. But he had to marry someone to you—he said I was a godsend—so he used me when I popped in! And that's the long and the short of how I ended up getting stuck with you."

There. It was out. The truth. That should stop him from any further plans of seduction. No matter that if what Lydia had told her was true about King James, she'd just jeopardized the entire Douglas clan. Her words prevented his lips from reaching hers and that was the most imminent danger she could see. Not even the wrath of vengeful kings seemed quite as threatening. One more beautiful man, one more broken heart.

The Hawk sat motionless. He studied her a long moment in silence, as if digesting what she'd just said. Then a gentle smile chased the clouds from his eyes. "Grimm told me you wove outlandish tales. He said you had an epic imagination. Your father told Grimm how you begged to be allowed to be his bard, rather than his daughter. Lass, I have nothing against a good tale and will willingly listen, if you but take my counsel about your safety."

Adrienne blew out a frustrated breath that sent a strand of her silvery-blond hair brushing the Hawk's face. He kissed it as it slid gently across his mouth.

Flames uncoiled in her belly. She shut her eyes and gathered her composure from the fleeting corners of her soul. *I will not think about him kissing any part of me,* she told herself firmly.

"I am *not* Red Comyn's daughter," she sighed, squeezing her eyes more tightly shut. When was she going to figure out that closing her eyes didn't make anything go away? She opened her eyes. Oh dear heaven, but the man was magnificent. She pondered the thought with some pride that she could dislike him so intensely, yet still be so objective about his good looks. A sure sign of her maturity.

"Nay, it doesn't matter. You are my wife now. That's all that matters."

"Hawk—"

"Hush, lass."

Adrienne stilled, absorbed in the warmth of his hands on hers. When had he taken her hands in his? And why hadn't she pulled away instinctively? And why was the slow, sensual movement of his skin against hers so intoxicating?

"Adrienne . . . this Callabron. For it to work correctly it must enter the body through a primary vessel of blood." His fingers lightly skimmed the faint red mark that still puckered the translucent skin of her throat. "This was no near miss. This was perfect aim."

"Who would want to kill me?" She swallowed tightly. How could anyone want to? No one here knew her. But . . . what if someone wanted to kill Mad Janet, and didn't know she *wasn't* her?

"For that I have no answer, my heart. Yet. But until I do you will be guarded day and night. Every moment, every breath. I will not risk your life foolishly again."

"But I am not Janet Comyn," she tried again, stubbornly.

His ebony gaze searched her clear gray eyes intently. "Lass, I really don't care who you are, or have been, or need to think you'll be. I want you. In my life. In my arms. In my bed. If it makes you feel better to believe this . . . this thing about being from the future, then believe it if you must. But from this day on, you are first and foremost my wife, and I will keep you safe from anything that would hurt you. You need never fear again."

Adrienne raised her hands helplessly. "Fine. Guard me. So can I get up now?"

"No."

"When?" she asked plaintively.

"When I say so." He smiled disarmingly and ducked to steal a kiss. His face came smack up against both her hands. It took every ounce of her willpower not to cradle it with her palms and lead him to the kiss he sought with shaking hands.

He growled and gave her a long measuring look. "I should treat you like one of my falcons, wife."

"Let me get out of bed," she bartered prettily. *No way was she going to ask how he treated his falcons*.

He growled, lower in his throat, and left then. But the elite dozen stayed at her door.

After he was gone she remembered one thing he'd said most clearly. *You need never fear again*. The man was just too good to be true.

*   *   *

The days of healing were pure bliss. Lydia overrode the Hawk's objections and had a chaise carried out to the gardens for Adrienne. Although she was still heavily guarded, she was able to curl up in the golden sunshine like a sleepy, smug cat, which went a long way toward healing her. The rose-drenched days of conversation with Lydia, as they came to know one another through small talk and small silences, healed more than her exhausted body. Sipping tea (she would have preferred coffee, but that would have brought the Hawk and his boons into the picture) and sharing stories, occasionally Adrienne would shiver with the intense feeling that this was where she'd belonged all her life.

Love can *grow among the rocks and thorns of life,* she thought in one of those small silences that was comfortable as a favored, love-worn blanket. From the desolate barrens of her own life, somehow, she had come to be here, and here life was blessed—peaceful and perfect and simple.

Adrienne healed more quickly than anyone imagined possible. Tavis pointed out that she had the resilience of youth on her side, as he flexed and studied his time-gnarled hands. Not to mention an indomitable nature, he'd added. *You mean stubborn,* the Hawk had corrected him.

Lydia believed there might have been just a blush of love on her cheeks. *Ha!* Hawk had scoffed. *Love of the sunshine, perhaps.* And Lydia had almost laughed aloud at the seething look of jealousy Hawk had turned on the bright rays as he'd gazed out the kitchen windows.

Grimm offered the likelihood that she was so angry with the Hawk that she hurried her healing just to fight with him on equal footing. *Now there's a man who understands women,* Hawk had thought.

None of them knew that with the exception of missing her cat, Moonshadow, those days were the happiest she'd ever known.

While she lazed in the peace and sunshine, Adrienne enjoyed a blissful kind of ignorance. She would have been mortified had someone told her that she'd talked about Eberhard in her drugged stupor. She would not have understood if someone had told her she'd spoken of a black queen, for her waking mind hadn't remembered the chess piece yet.

She had no idea that while she and Lydia were passing sweet time, Grimm had been sent to, and was now on his way back from, Comyn keep, where he'd discovered shocking information about Mad Janet.

And she would have packed up a few things and run for her very life, if not her soul, had she known how obsessively determined the Hawk was to claim her as his wife, in *all* the aspects it entailed.

But she knew none of this. And so her time spent in the gardens of Dalkeith-Upon-the-Sea would be lovingly placed as a precious jewel into the treasure chest of her memory, where it would twinkle like a diamond amid the shadows.

CHAPTER 12

IT WASN'T MUCH FUN SNOOPING AROUND THE CASTLE WITH A dozen hard-boiled commandos trailing along behind her, but Adrienne managed. After a while she pretended they weren't there. Just as she pretended the Hawk was nothing more than an annoying gnat to be brushed away repeatedly.

Dalkeith Upon-the-Sea was as lovely a castle as she'd ever imagined when as a child she'd snuggled under a tent of blankets in bed with a pilfered flashlight, reading fairy tales long after lights out.

The rooms were spacious and airy, with brightly woven tapestries hung on the thick stone walls to smother any chill drafts that might seep through the cracks, although Adrienne hadn't been able to find so much as one crack in a wall—she'd peeped behind a few tapestries, just to see.

Historical curiosity, she'd told herself. Not that she was hunting for imperfections in either the castle or the castle's laird.

Hundreds of beautiful mullioned windows. Obviously the people who inhabited Dalkeith couldn't bear to be cooped up inside when there was so much lush landscape to be enjoyed outdoors in Scotland's mountains, vales, and seasides.

Adrienne sighed wistfully as she paused by a vaulted window to savor the view of the unceasing slate-silver waves crashing against the cliffs at the west end.

A woman could fall in love in a place like this. Tumble silken tresses over dainty satin slippers to land in a mass of ribbons and romance right at the perfect laird's perfect feet.

At that very moment, as if summoned by her wayward thoughts, the Hawk walked into her line of vision in the bailey below, leading one of the largest black chargers she'd ever seen. Adrienne started to turn away, but her feet would no more walk her away from the window than her eyes would avert themselves, and in spite of her best intentions to ignore him, she stood watching in helpless fascination.

With a fluid leap, the kilt-clad Scottish laird tossed himself onto the back of the snorting fiesty stallion.

And as he mounted, that lovely kilt went flying up, giving Adrienne a sinful glimpse of powerfully muscled thighs, beautifully dusted with a bit of silky black hair. She blinked a moment, refusing to ponder what else she thought she'd seen.

Surely they wore something under those kilts. Surely it was only her overactive imagination, absurdly overlaying the stallion's obvious masculinity upon the Hawk's body.

Yes. That was it, decidedly. She'd noticed the stallion's prominently displayed attributes in the periphery of her vision while she'd been looking at the Hawk's legs, and managed to muddle the two together, somehow. She certainly had *not* seen that the Hawk was, himself, hung like a stallion.

Her cheeks flushed with that thought. She turned sharply on her heel to squelch it firmly and sought the next unsurveyed room. She had decided to explore the castle that morning, in large part to keep her mind off that dratted man. It just figured that he'd have to walk by the one window she was looking out. *And* toss up his skirts to add fuel to the proverbial fire.

She forced her mind back to the lovely architecture of Dalkeith. She was on the second floor of the castle, and had already traipsed through dozens of guest rooms, including the chamber in which she'd spent her first night. Dalkeith was enormous. There must have been a hundred or more rooms, and many of them appeared as if they'd lain unused for decades. The wing she currently explored was the most recently renovated and frequently utilized. It was finished in light woods, polished to a fine gleam, and not a speck of dust could be seen. Thick woven mats covered the floors, no rushes or cold bare stones here. Bunches of fragrant herbs and dried flowers hung upside down from nearly every window ledge, scenting the corridors.

A shaft of sunlight drew Adrienne's attention to a closed door halfway down the corridor. Etched into the pale wood was an exquisitely detailed prancing horse, rearing elegantly, mane tossing in the wind. A single horn spiraled daintily from its equine brow. A unicorn?

Her hand on the door, she paused, suddenly suffering an odd premonition that this room might be better left alone. *Curiosity killed the cat. . . .*

When the door swung silently inward, she froze, a hand fluttering on the jamb.

Unbelievable. Simply incomprehensible. Her astonished gaze swept the room from floor to rafter, end to end and back again.

Who had done this?

The room appealed to every ounce of woman in her body. *Face it, Adrienne,* she told herself grimly, *this entire castle appeals to every ounce of woman in your body.* Not to mention the sexy, masculine laird of the keep himself.

This room was made for babies. Crafted with such loving hands that it was almost overwhelming. A cacophony of discordant emotions skittered through her before she shoved them away.

There were cradles of honey oak, curved and sanded smooth so not one splinter could work free and harm baby-soft skin. The east wall displayed high windows, too high for a toddler to risk harm, yet open to the golden glow of the morning sun. Wood floors were smothered with thick rugs to keep baby feet warm.

Brightly painted wooden soldiers dotted the shelves, and lovingly crafted dolls reclined on tiny beds. A miniature castle, replete with turrets, dry moat, and drawbridge was filled with tiny carved people; an honest-to-goodness medieval dollhouse!

Fluffy blankets dotted the cradles and beds. It was a huge room, this nursery. A room in which a child (or a dozen) could grow from baby to young teen before seeking a more adult room elsewhere. It was a room that would fill a child's world with love and security and pleasure for hours on end.

As if someone had created this room thinking like the child he or she used to be, and designed it with all the treasures that had given him or her such pleasure as a wee lad or lass.

But the thing about the room that struck her so hard was that it seemed to be waiting.

Open and warm and inviting, saying, *fill me with laughing babies and love.*

All was in readiness, the nursery was merely biding time—until the right woman would come along and breathe into it the sparkling life of children's songs and dreams and hopes.

A pang of such longing flashed through her that Adrienne wasn't even sure what it was. But it had everything to do with the orphan she'd been, and the cold place she'd grown up in—a place nothing at all like this lovely room; part of a lovely home, in a lovely land, with people who would lavish love upon their children.

Oh, to raise babies in a place like this.

Babies who would know who their mother and father were, unlike Adrienne. Babies who would never have to wonder why they hadn't been worth keeping.

Adrienne rubbed her eyes furiously and turned away. It was too much for her to deal with.

And she turned right into Lydia. "Lydia!" she gasped. But of course. Why should it surprise her to run smack into the wonderful mother of the wonderful man who'd probably built the wonderful nursery?

Lydia steadied her by the elbows. "I came to see if you were feeling all right, Adrienne. I thought it might be too soon for you to be up and about—"

"Who built this room?" Adrienne whispered.

Lydia ducked her head, and for a brief moment Adrienne had the absurd impression that Lydia was trying not to laugh. "The Hawk designed and crafted it himself," Lydia said, intently smoothing tiny crinkles from her gown.

Adrienne rolled her eyes, trying to convince her emotional barometer to stop registering vulnerability and rise to something safe, like anger.

"Why, dear Adrienne, don't you like it?" Lydia asked sweetly.

Adrienne turned back and swept the room with an irritated gaze. The nursery was bright and cheery and alive with the creator's own outpouring of emotion into his creation. She glanced back at Lydia. "When? Before or after the king's service?" It was terribly important that she know if he had built it at seventeen or eighteen, to please his mother perhaps, or recently, in hopes of his own children someday filling it.

"During. The king gave him a brief leave when he was twenty-nine. There was some trouble with the Highlanders in these parts, and the Hawk was permitted to return to fortify Dalkeith. When the feuding was resolved, he spent a measure of time working up here. He worked like a man possessed, and in truth, I had little idea what he was doing. The Hawk has always worked with wood, building and designing things. He wouldn't let any of us see it, and didn't talk much about it. After he returned to James, I came up to see what he'd been doing." Lydia's eyes misted briefly. "I'll tell you the truth, Adrienne, it made me cry. Because it told me that my son was thinking of children and how precious they were. It filled me with wonder, too, when I saw it completed. I think it would most any woman. Men don't usually see children like this. But the Hawk, he's a rare man. Like his father."

You don't have to sell me *on him,* Adrienne thought morosely. "I'm sorry, Lydia. I'm very tired. I need to go rest," she said stiffly, and turned for the door.

As she entered the corridor she could have sworn she heard Lydia laughing softly.

*   *   *

Hawk found Grimm waiting for him in the study, gazing out at the west cliffs through the open doors. He didn't miss the tiny whiteness at Grimm's knuckles on the hand that clenched the door frame, or the rigid line of his back.

"So?" Hawk asked impatiently. He would have gone to the Comyn keep to investigate his wife's past himself, but that would have meant leaving Adrienne alone with the damned smithy. No chance of that. Nor could he have taken her with him, so he'd sent Grimm to uncover what had happened to Janet Comyn.

Grimm turned slowly, kicked out a chair, and sat heavily before the fire.

Hawk sat as well, rested his feet upon the desk, and poured them both a brandy. Grimm accepted it gratefully.

"Well? What did she say?" The Hawk's grip tightened on his glass as he waited to hear who had done such terrible things to his wife that her mind had retreated into fantasy. The Hawk understood what was wrong with her. He'd seen battle-scarred men who had experienced such horrors that they had reacted in similar fashion. Too many barbaric and bloody losses made some soldiers spin a dream to replace the reality, and in time many came to believe the dream was true. As his wife had done. But, unfortunately, with his wife he had no idea what had caused her painful retreat into such an outlandish fancy that she couldn't even bear to be called by her real name. And whatever had happened to her had left her totally unwilling to trust any man, but especially him, it seemed.

The Hawk braced himself to listen, to channel his rage when it came so he could wield it as a cool and efficient weapon. He would slay her dragons, and then begin her healing. Her body was growing stronger day by day, and the Hawk knew Lydia's love had much to do with it. But he wanted *his* love to heal her deepest wounds. And the only way he could do that was to know and understand what she had suffered.

Grimm swallowed, fidgeted in his chair, tilted it at the sides like a lad, then got up and moved to the hearth to shift restlessly from foot to foot.

"Out with it, man!" The week Grimm had been gone had nearly driven the Hawk crazy imagining what this Everhard man must have done. Or even worse, perhaps the Laird Comyn himself was to blame for Adrienne's pain. Hawk dreaded that possibility, for then it would be clan war. A terrible thing to be sure, but to avenge his wife—he would do anything. "Who is this Ever-hard?" The question had been gnawing at his insides ever since the night he'd first heard the name emerge from her fevered lips.

Grimm sighed. "Nobody knew. Not one person had ever heard of him."

The Hawk cursed softly. *So, the Comyn was keeping secrets, was he?* "Talk," he commanded.

Grimm sighed. "She thinks she's from the future."

"I know Adrienne thinks that," Hawk said impatiently. "I sent you to discover what Lady Comyn had to say."

"That's who I meant," Grimm said flatly. "The Lady Comyn thinks Adrienne is from the future."

"What?" Hawk's dark brows winged incredulously. "What are you telling me, Grimm? Are you telling me the Lady Comyn claims Adrienne isn't her blood daughter?"

"Aye."

Hawk's boots hit the floor with a thump as the latent tension charging his veins became a living heat.

"Let me get this straight. Althea Comyn told you that Adrienne is *not* her daughter?"

"Aye."

Hawk froze. This was not what he had expected. In all

his imaginings he had never once considered that his wife's fantasy might be shared by her mother. "Then exactly who does Lady Comyn think the lass is? Who the hell have I married?" Hawk yelled.

"She doesn't know."

"Does she have any ideas?" Sarcasm laced the Hawk's question. "Talk to me, man!"

"There's not much I can tell you, Hawk. And what I know. . .well, it's damned odd, the lot of it. It sure as hell wasn't what I expected. Ah, I heard such tales, Hawk, to test a man's faith in the natural world. If what they claim is true, hell, I don't know what a man can believe in anymore."

"Lady Comyn shares her daughter's delusions," Hawk marveled.

"Nay, Hawk, not unless Althea Comyn and about a hundred other people do. Because that's how many saw her appear out of nowhere. I spoke with dozens, and they all told pretty much the same tale. The clan was sitting at banquet when all of the sudden a lass—Adrienne—appeared on the laird's lap, literally out of thin air. Some of the maids named her witch, but it was quickly hushed. It seemed the laird considered her a gift from the angels. The Lady Comyn said she saw something fall out of the oddly dressed woman's hand, and fought through the panic to get it. 'Twas the black queen she'd given me at the wedding, which I gave to you when we returned."

"I wondered why she'd sent that to me." Hawk rubbed his jaw thoughtfully.

"Lady Comyn said she thought it might become important later. She said that she thinks the chess piece is somehow bewitched."

"If so, that would be how she traveled through"—he broke off, unable to complete the thought. He'd seen many wonders in his life, and was not a man to completely discount the possibility of magic—what good Scotsman raised to believe in the wee folk would? But still. . .

"How she traveled through time," Grimm finished for him. The two men stared at each other.

Hawk shook his head. "Do you believe . . .?"

"Do you?"

They looked at each other. They looked at the fire.

"No,"they both scoffed at the same time, studying the fire intently.

"She doesn't seem quite usual though, does she?" Grimm finally said. "I mean, she's unnaturally bright. Beautiful. And witty, ah, the stories she told me on the way back here from the Comyn keep. She's strong for a lass. And she does have odd sayings. Sometimes—I don't know if you've noticed—her brogue seems to fade in and out."

Hawk snorted. He had noticed. Her brogue had virtually disappeared when she'd lain ill from the poison, and she'd spoken in an odd accent he'd never heard before.

Grimm continued, almost to himself, "A lass like that could keep a man—" He broke off and looked sharply at the Hawk. Cleared his throat. "Lady Comyn knows who her daughter was, Hawk. *Was* is the key word there. Several of the maids confirmed Lydia's story that the real Janet is dead. The gossip is that she's dead by her father's hand. He had to marry someone to you. Lady Comyn said their clan will never breathe a word of the truth."

"I guess not,"Hawk snorted. *If* any of this is true, and I'm not saying it is, the Comyn knows James would destroy us both for it." The Hawk pondered that bitter thought a long moment, then discarded it as an unnecessary concern. The Comyn would assuredly swear Adrienne was Janet, as would every last man of the Douglas, if word of this ever got to the king in Edinburgh, for the existence of both their clans depended upon it. The Hawk could count on at least that much fealty from the self-serving Comyn.

"What did the laird himself have to say, Grimm?"

"Not a word. He would neither confirm she was his daughter, nor deny it. But I spoke with the Comyn's priest, who told me the same story as Lady Comyn. By the way, he was lighting the fat white praying candles for the soul of the late Janet," he added grimly. "So if there are delusions at the Comyn keep, they are mass and uniformly detailed, my friend."

The Hawk crossed swiftly to his desk. He opened a carved wooden box and extracted the chess piece. He rolled it in his fingers, studying it carefully.

When he raised his eyes again they were blacker than midnight, deeper than a loch and just as unfathomable. "The Lady Comyn believes it brought her here?"

Grimm nodded.

"Then it could take her away?"

Grimm shrugged. "Lady Comyn said Adrienne didn't seem to remember it. Has she ever mentioned it to you?"

Hawk shook his head and looked thoughtfully, first at the black queen, then at his brightly burning fire.

Grimm met Hawk's gaze levelly, and Hawk knew there would never be words of reproach or even a whisper of the deed, if he chose to do it.

"Do you believe?" Grimm asked softly.

✳   ✳   ✳

The Hawk sat before the fire for a long time after Grimm left, alternating between belief and disbelief. Although he was a creative man, he was also a logical man. Time travel simply didn't fit into his understanding of the natural world.

He could believe in the banshee, who warned of pending death and destruction. He could even believe in the Druids as alchemists and practitioners of strange arts. He'd been raised on childhood warnings of the kelpie, who lived in deep lochs and lured unsuspecting and unruly children to their watery graves.

But traveling through time?

Besides, he told himself as he stuffed the chess piece into his sporran for later consideration, there were other more pressing problems to address. Like the smithy. And his willful wife, upon whose lips the smithy's name sat far too often.

The future would allow plenty of time to unravel all of Adrienne's secrets, and make sense of the mass delusions at the Comyn keep. But first, he had to truly make her his wife. Once that was accomplished, he could begin to worry about other details. Thus resolved, he stuffed away the unsettling news Grimm had brought him, much as he had stuffed away the chess piece.

Plans of just how he would seduce his lovely wife replaced all worries. With a dangerous smile and purpose in his stride, the Hawk went off in search of Adrienne.

CHAPTER 13

ADRIENNE WALKED RESTLESSLY, HER MIND WHIRLING. HER brief nap in the sunshine had done nothing to dispel her wayward thoughts. Thoughts like just how capable, not to mention how willing, the Hawk was of providing babies to fill that dratted nursery

Instinctively she avoided the north end of the bailey, unwilling to confront the smithy and those unnerving images still fermenting in her mind from when she'd been ill.

South she strayed, beckoned by the glimmer of sun off a glass roof and curiosity deep as a loch. These were no barbaric people, she mused. And if she didn't miss her guess, she was walking right toward a hothouse. How brilliant was the mind that had fashioned Dalkeith-Upon-the-Sea. It was impenetrable on the west end due to the cliffs, which presented a sheer, unscalable drop to the fierce ocean. Spreading north, south, and east, the keep itself was sealed behind monstrous walls, all of seventy to eighty feet high. How strange that the same mind which had designed Dalkeith as a stronghold had made it so beautiful. The complicated mind of a man who provided for the necessity of war, yet savored the times of peace.

Careful, getting intrigued are you?

When she reached the hothouse, Adrienne noticed that it was attached to a circular stone tower. During her many hours of surfing the Internet she'd been drawn time and time again to things medieval. The mews? Falcons. It was there they kept and trained falcons for hunting.

Drawn by the lure of animals and missing Moonshadow with an ache in her chest, Adrienne approached the gray stone broch. What had Hawk meant about treating her like one of his falcons? she wondered. Well, she'd just find out for herself, so she'd know what to avoid in the future.

Tall and completely circular, the broch had only one window, which was covered by a slatted shutter. Something about the dark, she remembered reading. Curious, she approached the heavy door and pushed it aside, closing it behind her lest any falcons be tempted to escape. She wouldn't give the Hawk any excuse to chastise her.

Slowly her eyes grew accustomed to the gloom and she was able to make out several empty perches in the dim light. Ah, not the mews, this must be the training broch. Adrienne tried to recall the way the trainers of yore had skilled their birds for the hunt.

The broch smelled of lavender and spice, the heavy musk from the attached hothouse permeating the stone walls. It was a peaceful place. Oh, how easily she could get used to never hearing the rush of traffic again; never having to look over her shoulder again; never seeing New Orleans again—an end to all the running and hiding and fear.

The walls of the broch were cool and clean to the touch,

nothing like the stone walls that had once held her prisoner in the gritty dirt of a New Orleans prison cell.

Adrienne shuddered. She'd never forget that night.

The fight had begun over—of all things—a trip to Acapulco. Adrienne hadn't wanted to go. Eberhard had insisted. "Fine, then come with me," she'd said. He was too busy, he couldn't take the time off, he'd replied.

"What good is all your money if you can't take the time to enjoy life?" Adrienne had asked.

Eberhard hadn't said a word, he'd simply fixed her with a disappointed look that made her feel like an awkward adolescent, a gauche and unwanted orphan.

"Well, why do you keep sending me on these vacations by myself?" Adrienne asked, trying to sound mature and cool, but her question ended on a plaintive note.

"How many times must I explain this to you? I'm trying to educate you, Adrienne. If you think for a moment that it will be easy for an orphan who has never been in society to be my wife, think again. My wife must be cultured, sophisticated, European—"

"Don't send me back to Paris," Adrienne had said hastily. "It rained for weeks, last time."

"Don't interrupt me again, Adrienne." His voice had been calm; too calm and carefully measured.

"Can't you come with me—just once?"

"Adrienne!"

Adrienne had stiffened, feeling foolish and wrong, even though she'd known she wasn't being unreasonable. Sometimes she had felt like he didn't want her around, but that didn't make sense—he was marrying her. He was preparing her to be his wife.

Still, she'd had doubts. . . .

After her last trip to Rio, she'd returned to hear from her

old friends at the Blind Lemon that Eberhard hadn't been seen in his offices all that much—but he *had* been seen in his flashy Porsche with an equally flashy brunette. A twinge of jealousy had speared her. "Besides, I hear you don't work *too* hard while I'm gone," she had muttered.

The fight had begun in earnest then, escalating until Eberhard did something that so astonished and terrified Adrienne that she fled blindly into the steamy New Orleans night.

He hit her. Hard. And, taking advantage of her stunned passivity—more than once.

Crying, she flung herself into the Mercedes that Eberhard leased for her. She stomped the accelerator and the car surged forward. She drove blindly, on autopilot, mascaratinted tears staining the cream silk suit Eberhard had chosen for her to wear that evening.

When the police pulled her over, claiming she'd been driving over one hundred miles an hour, she knew they were lying. They were Eberhard's friends. He'd probably called them the moment she'd left his house; he knew which route she always took home.

Adrienne stood outside her car with the policemen, her face bruised and swelling, her lip bleeding, weeping and apologizing in a voice that bordered on hysteria.

It didn't occur to her until much later that neither of the policemen had ever asked her what had happened to her face. They'd interrogated an obviously beaten woman without showing an ounce of concern.

When they'd cuffed her, taken her to the station, and called Eberhard, she wasn't surprised at all when they replaced the receiver, gazed at her sadly, and sent her to be locked up.

Three days she'd spent in that hellish place, just so Eberhard could make his point.

That was the night she'd realized how dangerous he really was.

In the cool of the broch, Adrienne hugged her arms around herself, trying desperately to exorcise the ghosts of a beautiful man named Eberhard Darrow Garrett and the foolish young woman who'd spent a lonely, sheltered life in an orphanage. Such easy prey she'd been. *Did you see little orphan Adri-Annie? Eberhard's little fool.* Where had she heard those sneering words? On Rupert's yacht, when they thought she'd gone below for more drinks. She shivered violently. *I'll never be a man's fool again.*

"Never," she vowed aloud. Adrienne shook her head to ebb the painful tide of memories.

The door opened, admitting a wide swath of brilliant sunlight. Then it closed again and blackness reigned absolute.

Adrienne froze, huddled in on herself, and forced her heart to slow. She'd been here before. Hiding, waiting, too terrified to draw a breath for fear of alerting the hunter to her exact location. How she'd run and hid! But there had been no sanctuary. Not until the streets of obscurity she'd finally found in Seattle, and there had been an eternity of murky hell down every winding backroad between New Orleans and the haven of the Pacific Northwest.

Bitter memories threatened to engulf her when a husky croon broke the silence.

The Hawk? Singing? A lullaby?

The Gaelic words tumbled husky and deep—why hadn't she suspected he would have a voice like rich butterscotch? He purred when he talked; he could seduce the Mother Abbess of Sacred Heart when he sang.

"Curious, were you? I see you came of your own accord." His brogue rolled through the broch when he finished the refrain.

"Came where?" she asked defiantly.

"To be trained to my hand." His voice sounded amused, and she heard the rustle of his kilt as he moved in the inky darkness.

She would not dignify it with a response.

A long pause, another rustle, then, "Know you what qualities a falconer must possess, my heart?"

"What?" she grumbled in spite of herself, moving slowly backward. She stretched out her hands like little makeshift antennae in the darkness.

" 'Tis an exacting position. Few men can be quality falconers. Few possess the temperament. A falconer must be a man of infinite patience, acute hearing, and uncanny vision. Possessed of a daring spirit, and a gentle yet forceful hand. He must be constantly attuned to his ladybird. Know you why?"

"Why?" she whispered.

"Because falcons are very sensitive and excitable creatures, my heart. They are known to suffer from headaches and all manner of human ailments, so sensitive are they. Their extreme sensitivity makes them the finest and most successful huntresses of all time, yet can make them most demanding as well. And the haggard . . . ah, my sweet haggard, she is the purest challenge of all. And by far the most rewarding."

She would not ask what a haggard was.

" 'What is a haggard,' you ask, deep in that stubborn, silent soul of yours, my heart?" He laughed richly and it echoed off the stone walls of the suddenly balmy broch.

"Quit 'my hearting' me," she muttered as she moved

back oh so cautiously. She had to find a wall. The broch was round, so a wall would guarantee a door at some point. She may as well have been blind in the abysmal blackness.

She heard his footfalls upon the stone floor. Dear heavens, how could he see her? But he was heading straight for her! She backed away slowly, stealthily.

"I am no stranger to the darkness, lass," he warned. "I will find you. I am the finest of falconers."

She said nothing, made no sound.

"A haggard is a wild, mature falcon," he continued, a hint of a smile in his voice. "Usually a falconer is reluctant to assume the challenge of training one, but sometimes, upon a truly rare moon like the harvest moon we had last eve, the falconer espies a bird of such brilliance, such magnificence, that he casts all caution aside and traps the haggard, vowing to bind her to him. Vowing to make her forget all her wild free past—whether in darkness or in light—and give herself freely only to her future with her falconer."

She must *not* answer him; he'd follow her voice.

"My sweet falcon, shall I tell you how I will tame her?"

Silence, absolute. They were circling in the darkness like wary animals.

"First I seel my lady, which is to deprive her of vision, with a black silken hood."

Adrienne smothered an indignant gasp in her shaking hand. The folds of her gown rustled as she sidestepped quickly.

"Then I blunt her talons."

A pebble skittered across the floor a mere yard away. She backstepped, clutching her skirts to keep them still.

"I fasten jesses and dainty bells to her ankles so that I can be aware of her every movement, for I am in the dark too."

She drew a labored breath—almost a pant—then cursed herself for slipping, knowing he would track her traitorous gasp. She knew his strategy was to keep talking until he provoked her into revealing herself. *And then what?* she couldn't help but wonder. Would the Hawk make love to her here and now in the darkness of the broch? A shiver coursed through her, and she wasn't certain it was fear. Not certain at all.

"Then a leash to tether her to her perch until I no longer need leash her. Until she becomes leashed of her own free will. And the best part—the long, slow process of binding her to me. I sing to her, the same sweet song until she grows accustomed to the sound of my voice and mine alone. . . ."

And his butterscotch rich voice began that same husky croon of a lullaby, melting her will.

Adrienne stepped slowly backward; she actually felt the breeze of him passing by her, mere inches away. Where was that wall?

She almost screamed when he found her in the blackness, struggled a long moment against his iron grip. His breath fanned her face and she struggled in his grasp. "Be still, sweet falcon. I will not harm you. Not ever," he whispered huskily.

Adrienne felt the heat of his thighs burning through her thin silk morning gown. She was enveloped in the heady scent of musk and man. *Oh beautiful man, why couldn't I have known you before my last illusion was shattered? Why couldn't I have met you when I still believed?* she mourned. She fought against his arms, which embraced her, cradled her.

"Let me go!"

Hawk ignored her protests, drawing her closer into the steel of his embrace. "Aye, I'll simply have to have you seeled. Or perhaps I should bind your hands and hood your eyes with silk, and lay you across my bed, stripped bare and laid wide open to pure sensation until you become accustomed to my touch. Would that tame you, sweet falcon? Could you grow to love my touch? Crave it as I crave you?"

Adrienne swallowed convulsively.

"A falcon must be wooed with relentless and rough love. By taking away her light, by seeling her, she learns to understand with all her other senses. Senses that don't lie. The falcon is a wise creature, she believes only what she can feel, what she can hold in her talon or her beak. Touch, scent, hearing. By slowly being given back her sight and freedom, she is bound to the hand that restores these things to her. If she fails to trust in her master and doesn't grant him absolute loyalty by the end of her training—she seeks to flee at every opportunity." He paused, his lips a scant breath from hers. "None of my falcons have ever flown my hand without returning," he warned.

"I am not a stupid bird—"

"Nay, not stupid, but the finest. A falcon is the only other bird that can match a hawk for flight, accuracy, and speed. Not to mention strength of heart."

She'd been lost to him the moment he'd started singing. And she didn't protest further when his lips brushed hers lightly. Nor did she protest in the next instant, when Hawk's hands on her body turned hard, hot and demanding. Coaxing. Claiming.

"Would you soar for me, sweet falcon? I'll take you higher than you've ever been. I'll teach you to bank heights you've only dreamed existed," he promised as he scattered kisses across her jaw, her nose, her eyelids. His hands cradled her jaw in the darkness, feeling every curve, every plane and silken hollow of her face and neck with his hands, memorizing the nuances.

"Feel me, lass. Feel what you do to me!" He pressed his body against hers and rocked his hips, making sure she felt the swollen manhood that rose beneath his kilt and teased the inside of her thigh.

And there was the wall; it had been just behind her back all the time. Cool stone to her back and the inferno of the Hawk searing her through the front of her gown. She raised her hands to pummel him, but he caught and pinned them above her head against the wall. His strong fingers splayed her grip, twined with and teased her hands. Palm to palm, flat against the stone.

"My sweet falcon," he breathed against her neck. "Fight me as you will, it will come to naught. I have set my mind on you, and this is your first time to be seeled. In this blackness you will come to know my hands as they touch every silken inch of your body. I will not take from you any more than that. Just that you suffer my touch, you needn't even see my face. I will be patient while you grow gentled to my hands."

His hands were liquid fire, sliding her gown up and over her thighs and oh! She hadn't had the faintest idea where to look for undergarments this morning. His hands, his strong, beautiful hands were kneading her thighs, pushing them gently apart to slip the heat of his muscled leg between them. He purred, a rich husky growl of masculine triumph, when he felt the betraying wetness between her thighs. Adrienne flushed furiously; despite her intentions her hands fluttered up to rest upon his shoulders, then slid deep into his soft, thick hair. Her knees, already weak, went limp when he eased the bodice of her gown aside and dropped his head to her breasts, licking and grazing the swollen peaks with his tongue, then his teeth.

She scarcely noticed when he pushed his kilt up; but she definitely noticed when his hard, hot, heavy arousal rose against her thigh. Adrienne made a throaty sound: half whimper, half plea. How had he done this to her? Merely by touching her, the Hawk had somehow managed to unravel every ounce of resistance she'd so painstakingly woven into the cloak of aloofness she wore.

It had never been like this with Eberhard! Her mind fled her body and she clung to the hand that had seeled her. The hand that had denied her sight she tasted with her lips—turned her head to catch his finger with her tongue. Adrienne almost screamed when he took that same finger and placed it inside the slick heat between her legs. "Fly for me, sweet falcon," he urged, cupping one of her heavy breasts with his hand and licking its puckered crest. He teased her mercilessly, nipping her gently, touching her everywhere.

His lips returned to claim hers with desperation sired of a hunger too long denied. A hunger that might never relent. His kiss was long, hard, and punishing, and she reveled in his unspoken demands. A whimper escaped her when the pad of his thumb found the tiny nub of heat nestled between her folds, and Adrienne's head dropped back as a burgeoning wave cast her up and up. Yielding to his fingers, his tongue and lips, she sacrificed the last vestige of her restraint.

"Adrienne," he whispered hoarsely, "you're so beautiful, so sweet. Want me, lass. Need me like I need you."

She felt the heat of a place with no name she'd ever been taught—luring her deeper.

Adrienne struggled to say the words she knew must be said. The one word that she knew would free her. This

legendary seducer of women—oh, how easy it was to
understand just how legions had fallen before him! He was
so good at it. He almost had her believing that it was for her
and only her that he hungered. Almost a fool again.

But that was why they called them rogues. Lotharios.
Don Juans. They applied the same skill and relentless determination to seduction that they applied to the art of war—to
conquests of any sort.

Resurrecting the tatters of her defenses, she steeled her
will against his advances.

The Hawk was lost. Lost as he'd been since the moment
he'd laid eyes upon the bewitching lass. No matter her
strange fancies risen from some secret and terrible past. He
would discover a way to erase all her fears. The things
Grimm had told him signified nothing. With love he could
overcome any obstacle in time. His lady hawk she would
be, for now and always. He treasured her yielding to his
hands, savored like the rarest delicacy the sweet honey of
her lips, trembled at the thought that she would one day feel
for him as he felt for her. With her it would never be like it
had been before, empty and hollow.

Nay, with this lass he would mate for life. She had no eye
for the beauty the other women had so adored. This lass
possessed secrets of her own. Horrors of her own. Depth of
her own. All in all, a rare lass indeed. He was sinking, sinking into her depths . . . the kiss deepened ferociously and he
felt her teeth graze his lower lip. It maddened him beyond
control.

"Oh!" she breathed, as he nipped her silken neck.

Emboldened by his success, he breathed the first tenta-
tive words. He needed to tell her; needed her to understand
that this was no game. That he had never in his life felt this
way, and never would again. She was the one he'd been

waiting for all these years—the one that completed his heart. "Ari, my heart, my love, I—"

"Oh, hush, Adam! No need for words." She pressed her lips to his to silence him.

Hawk froze, rigid as an arctic glacier and every bit as chill.

His lips went still against hers, and Adrienne's heart screamed in agony. But how much worse would it scream if she became a fool again?

His hands dug cruelly into her sides. They would leave bruises that would last for days. Slowly, very slowly, one by one, his fingers unclenched.

She had said *his* name!

"The next time you say Adam's name, lass, is the time I stop asking for what I already own and start taking. You seem to forget that you belong to me. There is no need for me to seduce you when I could simply take you to my bed. The choice is yours, Adrienne. I bid you—choose wisely."

Hawk left the broch without another word, leaving Adrienne alone in the darkness.

CHAPTER 14

ADRIENNE SHOULD HAVE WORKED UP AN APPETITE. SHE'D spent the rest of the day after the falcon incident wandering every inch of the bailey. *Was this day ever going to end?* she wondered. She must have walked twenty miles, so she should have burned off some of her pent-up frustration. Even her elite guard had looked a little peaked when she'd finally consented to return to the castle proper and brave encountering the Hawk.

Dinner offered fluffy potato soup, thick with melting cheese and spiced with five peppers; a delicate white fish steamed above a fire in oiled olive leaves, garnished with buttery crab; asparagus seared to perfection; plump sausages and crisp breads; puddings and fruits; lemony tarts and blueberry pie. Adrienne couldn't eat a morsel.

Dinner was awful.

If she glanced up one more time and caught the look of

death the Hawk had fixed on her, she would have to stuff a fist in her mouth to keep from screaming.

Adrienne sighed deeply as she spooned at the soup everyone else seemed to be relishing. She pushed it, poked at it, smashed the fluffy stuff. She was busily rearranging her asparagus into neat little rows when the Hawk finally spoke.

"If you're going to play with your food, Adrienne, you might give it to someone who's truly hungry."

"Like you, my lord?" Adrienne smiled sweetly at the Hawk's plate, which was also laden with untouched food.

His mouth tightened in a grim line.

"Is the food not to your liking, Adrienne, dear?" Lydia asked.

"It's wonderful. I guess I still don't have my appetite back—" she started.

Lydia sprang to her feet. "Perhaps you should still be resting, Adrienne," she exclaimed, shooting an accusing look at her son. The Hawk rolled his eyes, refusing to get involved.

"Oh, no, Lydia," Adrienne protested quickly. "I am totally recovered." No way she was going back to the Green Lady's room and playing invalid. Too many strange memories there. Tonight she planned to find a new room to sleep in; there certainly wasn't a shortage in this massive castle. She was rather looking forward to exploring the place further and selecting a room of her own. "Really, I'm fine. I just ate too much at lunch."

"You didn't eat lunch," Hawk said flatly.

"Oh, and who are you to know?" she shot back. "Maybe I ate in the kitchen."

"No you didn't," Tavis added helpfully. "I was in the

kitchen all day, I'll say. Plumb forgot to eat is what you did, milady. A time or two I've done the same myself, I'll say, and the hungrier I get, the less I feel like eating. So you better be eating, milady. You'll be needing your strength back and I'll say that again!" An emphatic nod of his cheerful head punctuated his decree.

Adrienne stared at her plate, a mutinous flush coloring her cheeks.

Lydia glared at Tavis as she came to stand protectively beside Adrienne's chair.

"I find I'm not all that hungry myself," Lydia said. "What say you and I go for a walk in the gardens—"

"With the brute force trailing behind?" Adrienne muttered, glancing at Hawk beneath lowered lashes.

"—while my son gets some beans from the buttery and brews us a fine cup of coffee for our return," Lydia continued, dangling the bribe as if she hadn't been interrupted.

Adrienne sprang to her feet. Anything to escape his eyes, and coffee to boot.

Betrayal shone in the Hawk's eyes now.

Lydia took Adrienne by the hand and started to lead her to the gardens.

"I'll brew the coffee, Mother," Hawk said to their backs. "But see to it that Maery has Adrienne's things moved to the Peacock Room."

Lydia stopped. The hand holding Adrienne's tightened almost imperceptibly. "Are you quite certain, Hawk?" she asked stiffly.

"You heard her. She is completely recovered. She is my wife. Where best to guard her?"

"Very well."

"Where's the Peacock Room?" Adrienne spun on her heel to face him.

"On the third floor."

"Will I have it to myself?"

"As much of it as I don't use. 'Tis the laird's chambers."

"I am *not* sleeping with you—"

"I don't recall *asking* you to—"

"You oversized, arrogant, conceited jackass—"

"Really, Adrienne, my son is none of those things," Lydia chastened.

"No reflection on you, Lydia. I really like you," Adrienne said politely. Politeness decamped abruptly as she glared at the Hawk. "But I'm not sharing your bed!"

"Not quite the topic to be bandying about over the dinner table, I'll say," Tavis offered, scratching his head, a flush stealing over his cheeks.

Hawk laughed and the dark rumble vibrated through her body, leaving her nipples erect and her heart hammering.

"Wife, you will share my room this eve if I must have you tied and carried there. Either you can suffer that humiliation or you can come willingly upon your own two feet. I'm not much concerned with how you get there. *Just get there.*"

Mutiny rose up in her breast, threatening to steal her very senses. Dimly she heard the door behind her open and shut and caught the scent of a cloying perfume that turned her stomach. Whatever the scent was, it reminded her of the orphanage; of attics and mothballs and days the nuns had made her scrub the floors and dust the heavy dark furniture.

"Lover!" came the cry of feminine delight from behind her.

Lydia's hand tightened painfully on hers. "Olivia Dumont," she muttered almost beneath her breath. "Dear heavens! I doubt I'll see this day through sane."

"Olivia?" Adrienne echoed, her eyes flying to the Hawk's.

Olivia, the Hawk thought gloomily. This day was rapidly running the gamut from bad to worse. He refused to meet Adrienne's questioning gaze. How dare she call him Adam in the midst of their lovemaking and then ask questions about another woman? She had no right. Not after she'd said *his* name.

Fury consumed him every time he thought about it.

Adam.

Images of his hands ripping apart the smithy flesh from bone comforted him for a moment.

Then desolation overwhelmed him. Now he had two problems: How was he going to make Adrienne want him? And what was he going to do with Olivia?

Fix Olivia up with the smithy?

That brought a grin to his face, the first in a while.

And naturally, Adrienne misunderstood it, thinking his smile was meant for Olivia, as did Olivia. As, it appeared, did his mother from the scowl on her face. Grimm cursed softly beneath his breath. Tavis shook his head, muttered a heated oath, and stalked from the heavily laden dinner table.

"Olivia." Hawk inclined his head. "What brings you to Dalkeith?"

"Why, Hawk," Olivia purred, "need you ask? I've missed you at court. You've been away from my . . . side . . . for far too long. I surmised I'd simply have to come collect you myself if I wanted you. So," she finished with a flutter of lashes and a blatant come-hither look, "here I am."

Hawk realized belatedly what a stupid question he'd asked as Adrienne fixed Olivia with a chilling gaze. Hawk knew from experience that Olivia could answer any question—no matter how innocent—with a loaded innuendo, but he'd shut the unpleasant memory of her antics from his mind the moment he'd returned to Dalkeith. It occurred to him that he would do well to resurrect those memories quickly. It would be unwise to forget Olivia's penchant for troublemaking; the asp was in his nest now.

Olivia's breath caught audibly as she stared at Adrienne.

"Greetings, Olivia. Have you come to speak with my *husband*?"

Momentarily free of Adrienne's wrathful gaze, the Hawk preened. *Husband*, she'd said. And she'd said it possessively. Perhaps there was hope after all.

"We've spoken quite the common language in the past," Olivia drawled. "A sort of wordless communication, if you catch my drift. Just the kind of talk the Hawk likes the best."

"Put *her* in the Peacock Room then," Adrienne spat over her shoulder as she tugged Lydia out the door and slammed it behind her.

CHAPTER 15

"THE KING MAY HAVE RELEASED YOU FROM HIS SERVICE, BUT I would never dream of releasing you from mine. You've serviced me so well in the past, I swear, I'm quite spoiled." Olivia wriggled closer on the low stone bench in the courtyard resting the curve of her ripe hip against the Hawk's muscular thigh.

Lydia had returned alone to the house a scant quarter hour after she and Adrienne had left, shooting a smug smile at her son where he reclined at the great table with the infernal Olivia. Coffee forgotten, the Hawk had quickly steered Olivia to the gardens to see what his wife might be up to. When his mother looked at him like *that*, well, the woman had a mind like a well-oiled catapult, deadly in the attack.

So he had strolled Olivia through the vast gardens at a breathless pace, his eyes peeled for the guards trailing his wife. Nothing. Time and time again his eyes had been drawn northward, to the flickering rim of firelight at the edge of the rowans.

"May I assume we'll entertain each other tonight as we used to, Hawk?" Olivia's warm breath fanned his cheek.

Hawk sighed inaudibly. "Olivia, I'm a married man, now."

Olivia's laugh tinkled just a bit too brightly, reminding Hawk that she was a woman who delighted in stealing another woman's man. The more difficult the man was to obtain, the happier Olivia was. Hawk was well acquainted with her peculiar game; she enjoyed hurting other women, crushing their dreams, breaking their hearts. Hawk suspected it was a revenge of sorts; that once a woman had taken her man, and she'd never gotten over it—had become a bitter, destructive woman instead. Once he'd finally understood, he'd felt almost sorry for her. Almost.

"She's Mad Janet, Hawk," Olivia said dryly.

"Her name is—" He broke off abruptly. He mustn't give Olivia any ammunition. He took a careful breath and rephrased. "Her middle name is Adrienne, 'tis the one she prefers." He added coolly, "You may call her Lady Douglas."

Olivia's brow rose derisively. "I shan't call her lady anything. The whole country knows she's mad as a rabid hound. I hadn't heard, however, that she was bearable to the eye."

Hawk snorted. "Bearable? My wife is exquisite by any standards."

Olivia laughed shakily, then her voice firmed sarcastically. "Well, and lah-de-dah! Could it be that the legendary Hawk thinks he's in love? The roué of endless women thinks he might stop with this one? Oh, do give it up, *mon chéri*. It's nauseating. I know what kind of man you are. There's no point in affecting elevated sensibilities we both know you don't possess."

Hawk's voice was icy when he spoke. "Contrary to your expectations, I am not the man I was at James's court. You don't know anything about me—other than the illusions you've chosen to believe in." He paused a heavy moment to lend emphasis to his next words. "Olivia, there is no king here to order me to accommodate you, and I'm never going back to James's court. It's over. It's all over." The moment the words were said, Hawk's heart soared. He was *free*.

"That's all it was? You *accommodated* me?" Olivia demanded.

"You knew that." Hawk snorted derisively. "I turned you away a dozen times before you went to James. Did you convince yourself that I'd had a change of heart? You know exactly what happened. It was *you* who petitioned the king to make me—" Hawk broke off abruptly, catching the glint of a silvery-blond mane in the moonlight a few yards from where they sat.

Adrienne approached, her arm tucked in the crook of Adam's elbow, a splendid crimson cape thrown over her shoulders, the silk billowing sensually in the gentle evening breeze.

"Olivia." Adrienne inclined her head.

Olivia snorted lightly and possessively grasped the Hawk's muscled arm.

"Join us," the Hawk said quickly, ignoring the sudden pinch of Olivia's nails.

The thought of Adrienne walking off into the darkness with Adam did dangerous things to his head. Hawk frowned as he realized that it was likely as dangerous for Adrienne to be exposed to anything Olivia might say or do.

He certainly didn't want the conversation to continue where it had broken off—not in front of Adrienne—without an explanation from him. He knew he had to gain control, but he had no experience with this type of situation. He'd never had an ex-mistress try to provoke trouble with his wife because he'd never had a wife before, and he'd certainly never been entangled in an encounter so rife with hazardous potential. His concern that Olivia might say or do something to hurt Adrienne unbalanced his customary logic.

Fortunately and unfortunately—depending on how he viewed it—Adrienne declined his offer. Relieved, Hawk resolved to pack Olivia off at the earliest moment possible then reclaim his wife from the smithy and have a good long talk with her.

"We wouldn't wish to disturb your cozy *tête-à-tête*," Adrienne demurred. "*Bouche-à-bouche* is more like it," she muttered half under her breath.

"What did you just say?" Olivia asked sweetly. *"Tu parles français?"*

"No," Adrienne replied flatly.

Olivia laughed airily and studied her. "You seem to be a woman of no few secrets, Janet Comyn. Perhaps you and I should have our own *tête-à-tête* and exchange a few of those intimacies. After all"—her gaze wandered possessively over the Hawk—"we share much in common. I'm sure you'd be fascinated to hear of the Hawk's time at James's court. He was quite the man about—"

"That would be lovely," Adrienne interrupted her smoothly, terminating the flow of Olivia's poisonous words. Her insides were already in a turmoil; if she heard much more, she'd either scream or cry—she didn't know which, but she did know it wouldn't be at all ladylike. "Some other time, however, Olivia. I quite have my hands full right now." She wrapped her hands around Adam's bicep, imitating

Olivia's clutch on the Hawk. Pressing closer to Adam, she
let him steer her away.

"Smithy!" Hawk finally found his voice. He'd listened to
the women's conversation in frozen horror, struggling to
conceive an entree into the risky repartee; but once again
Adrienne had unwittingly spared him by silencing Olivia
before the Hawk had resorted to stuffing his sporran into
her scheming, lying mouth.

Adam paused mid-stride and moved closer to Adrienne.
Her crimson cape flickered in the soft breeze and Hawk felt
as if it was taunting him. Where the hell had she gotten that
cape?

"My lord?" Adam smiled sardonically. His large, tanned
hand rose to cover Adrienne's where it rested on his arm.

"There are ninety-two horses I'm going to need shoes
for. That's three hundred and sixty-eight shoes. Get on it.
This minute."

"Certainly, my lord." Adam smiled gamely. "Heating up
a forge is *just* what I had in mind."

Hawk's hands clenched into fists at his sides.

"Ninety-two! Hawk!" Olivia fanned her breasts. Her
greedy attention had passed to the smithy and she was speculatively looking Adam over. Hawk watched as her tongue
darted out to moisten her lips. "I knew you were wealthy,
but that's a lot of prime flesh," she drawled, her eyes moving
up and down, surveying the smithy from head to toe. She
dragged her gaze away from Adam. "Perhaps you might
spare a stud for me?" She looked sidewise at the Hawk beneath fluttery lashes.

"Definitely." Hawk sighed as he watched his wife's retreating form. "What do you think of our smithy, Olivia?"
he asked cautiously.

*   *   *

What was she doing? Had she lost her mind? When Lydia had proposed that she seek out Adam and stroll the gardens with him, it had seemed like a good idea, although now Adrienne hadn't the faintest idea why.

Because Hawk made her angry, that's why. He'd dared think she was so stupid that he could pursue her and invite his mistress to visit all in the same day.

Once before she'd been just that stupid. Once, she might have convinced herself that Olivia was a troublemaking trespasser and that the Hawk was full of pristine intentions. Yes, once she would have believed that Eberhard really *was* going to the bathroom, leaving her in the main room of the party, while in fact he was stealing a quickie in the pool-house with a voluptuous socialite.

But she wasn't that woman anymore. She never would be again.

Hawk, the legendary seducer of women, had spent the afternoon trying to convince her that she was the only one he desired, but by dinner a new woman had appeared. An old flame. And he smiled at her. He strolled in the gardens with her. He forgot Adrienne's coffee for her. He was just one of those men who paid attention to whichever woman was in his face and willing.

Olivia was certainly willing.

And just why do you care, Adrienne?

I don't care. I just don't like being treated like a fool!

"The Hawk makes a fool of you," Adam said softly.

Adrienne smothered a gasp. The man seemed to read her very mind. Or it was so true that anyone could see it, even the smithy?

"You deserve far better, Beauty. I would gift you with

anything you desired. Silks for your perfect body. All the coffee beans on Jamaica's Blue Mountain. Yet he gifts you with nothing."

"It doesn't matter. Means nothing to me." Adrienne shivered slightly within the cape Adam had draped about her shoulders.

"It should. You're the most exquisite woman I've encountered, winsome Beauty. I would give you everything. Anything. Name it. Command me. I will make it yours."

"Fidelity?" Adrienne shot back at the blacksmith. Somehow they had reached the forge, although Adrienne had no memory of having walked that far. Her feet felt oddly light and her head swam.

"Forever," the smithy purred, "and beyond."

"Truly?" Adrienne asked, then kicked herself. Why ask? Men lie. Words proved nothing. Eberhard Darrow Garrett had given her all the right words.

"Some men lie. But then some men are incapable of it. Do you lie, sweet Beauty? If I asked you for fidelity and pledged mine in return, would you give it? Could I trust your words?"

Of course, she thought. She had no problem with fidelity.

"I suspected as much," Adam said. "You're one of a kind, Beauty."

Was she answering him? She hadn't thought she was. Adrienne felt light-headed. "Where are the guards?" she murmured.

"You are in my realm. I am all the protection you will ever need."

"Who are you?" Adrienne asked.

Adam laughed at her question. "Come into my world, Beauty. Let me show you marvels to exceed your wildest dreams."

Adrienne turned a dreamy eye toward Dalkeith, but all she saw was a strange shimmer at the forest's edge—no lights of the castle. The sound of surf filled her ears, but that couldn't be. The ocean was at the west end of the bailey and she was at the north. Why couldn't she see the castle? "Where is the castle, Adam? Why can't I see Dalkeith any- more?" Her vision blurred and she was assailed by the un- canny sensation that somehow she was no longer even in Scotland. Wherever she was, it didn't feel like a good place to be.

"The veil grows thin," Adam purred. "Morar awaits you, lovely one."

She was lying beside him in cool sand with no under- standing of how she'd managed to get there. Her mind was impossibly muddled. A sense of danger, inimical and an- cient, gripped the pit of her stomach. This man . . . some- thing about this man wasn't quite right.

"Who are you, really, Adam Black?" she insisted. Merely forming the words was a challenge, her tongue felt thick, her muscles rubbery.

Adam grinned. "You're closer than you think, Beauty."

"Who?" she insisted, fighting to retain control of her senses. The rich, dark scent of jasmine and sandalwood be- fuddled her mind.

"I am the *sin siriche du*, Beauty. I am the one for you."

"Are you from the twentieth century too?" she asked dizzily. "What's wrong with me? Why do I feel so strange?"

"Hush, Adrienne. Let me love you as you deserve. You are the only one for me . . ." Too late he realized his error.

The only one. The only one. Hawk had tried to make her believe the same thing. How was the smithy different? Judging from the feel of his hard arousal pressed against her thigh, not very. Just like Eberhard. Just like the Hawk.

Not again! Adrienne fought to steady her voice, to clear her head. "Release me, Adam."

"Never." Adam's powerful hands gripped her body. She could feel them unfasten her cape and slide over her breasts. Guiding her down to the silky sand, he rose above her, his face gilded amber by the fire. Sweat beaded at his brow and glistened just above his cruel and beautiful lips.

Adrienne puzzled at the illogic of sand beneath her body. She could see the red-gold glow of the fire. Where was she? On a beach or at the forge? She concluded foggily that it didn't matter, if he would only let her go. "Release me!" Her cry took all the strength she possessed.

Release her if she asks, fool, a shadow of a voice commanded.

Suddenly the night was still. The sound of surf faded into the chirping of crickets.

Adam's grip tightened painfully on Adrienne's shoulders.

Release her, Adam. She chooses was the bargain struck. Honor the pact—

But King Finnbheara—he dishonors us!

Fool! If you have not honor, you shall not roam freely in the future!

A bitter gust of breeze carried a furious sigh from Adam, and then she was standing nose to nose with the Hawk. His face was dark with fury.

The silken cape upon Adrienne's shoulders fluttered wildly, a flame of brilliant crimson.

"Where have you been?" Hawk demanded.

"Adam and I—" Adrienne began, then looked around. Adam was nowhere to be seen. Her mind was sharp and clear again; that dreamy fog was an unsavory and incomplete memory. She stood by the fire at the forge, but the flames had deteriorated to cold embers and the night was growing blacker by the minute. "I was just walking," she amended hastily, and ducked her head to avoid his penetrating gaze.

"Adrienne." Hawk groaned, gazing down at the pale cascade of hair that shielded her face from him. "Look at me." He reached for her chin, but she turned away.

"Stop it."

"Look at me," he repeated relentlessly.

"Don't," she pleaded. But he didn't listen. He gripped her waist and pulled her against the hard, male length of him.

Adrienne looked up, despite her best intentions, into eyes of midnight and the chiseled face of a warrior. His bronzed, hard Viking's body promised cataclysmic passion.

"Lass, tell me it's not him. Say it. Give me the words. Even if you can't feel for me yet, tell me you have no real feeling for him and I will overlook all that has transpired." Groaning, he dropped his silky dark head forward against her, as if reveling in simply being close.

The clean, spicy scent of his hair, black as sin, stirred her senses in ways she couldn't comprehend.

"I feel for Adam." Her tongue felt thick. Even her body tried to defy her around this man. She forced herself to say cruel words to hurt him, and it hurt *her* to do it.

"Where did you get this cape?" he asked evenly, his hands sliding over the rippling fabric.

"Adam." Perhaps he hadn't heard her. He hadn't even so much as flinched.

Deftly, he unfastened the silver brooch at her neck with steady hands. No, she mused, he definitely hadn't heard her. Maybe she'd mumbled inaudibly.

Easily he slid the cape from her body. Gracefully, even.

She stood frozen in shock as his strong, bronzed hands shredded the cape into tatters. The expression on his face was hard and cold. Oh, he'd definitely heard her. How could she remain untouched by the barbaric and beautiful mael-strom of masculine fury that he was in his . . . jealousy?

Yes, jealousy.

Same as she'd felt about Olivia.

Dear God, what was happening to her?

CHAPTER 16

"WHY DID YOU DO THAT?" SHE GASPED WHEN SHE WAS ABLE to speak.

Hawk placed a finger beneath her chin and tilted her head back, forcing her to meet his flinty gaze.

"I will tear from you anything Adam gives you. Remember that. If I find his body draped over yours, he will suffer the same fate." His eyes drifted meaningfully over a scrap of crimson silk stuck on the bark of tree, flapping like a dead thing in the breeze.

"Why?"

"Because I want you."

"You don't even know me!"

His mouth curved in a beautiful smile. "Oh, sweet lass, I know everything about you. I know you're a complex woman, full of dualities; you're innocent, yet tough; intelligent"—He cocked a teasing brow—"but lacking a smidge of common sense."

"I am not!" Adrienne scowled her protest.

He laughed huskily. "You have a wonderful sense of humor and you laugh often, but sometimes you're melancholy." He crowded her with his body and gazed down at her with heavy, hooded eyes. Adrienne tossed her head, trying vainly to dislodge his finger from beneath her chin and escape his penetrating gaze.

He cupped her face firmly with both hands. "You're a willful woman, and I'd like to be the focus of such a willful woman's desire. I'd like to have you yield your trust and loyalty to me as steadfastly as you withhold it. I'm a mature man, Adrienne. I will be patient while I woo you—but woo you, I will."

Adrienne swallowed hard. Damn him for his words!

Not only will I woo you, lass—I will win you completely, the Hawk added in the privacy of his heart. But he couldn't say that aloud, not yet. Not when she was staring at him, her lower lip trembling ever so slightly, but enough. Enough to give him hope. "I'm going to teach you that one lifetime isn't long enough for all the pleasure I can bring you, lass," he promised.

Adrienne closed her eyes, willing the image of him to hell and beyond. "Where's Olivia?" she asked, eyes closed.

"Fallen over a cliff, if the gods are smiling," Hawk replied dryly.

Adrienne opened her eyes and crinkled her nose, peering at him. Did she see the hint of a smile in his dark gaze? A passionate Hawk was deadly, but she was on guard against passion. A teasing Hawk might slip right through her defenses.

"Or if I'm really lucky and the gods are forgiving, she wandered into Adam's arms and he's been struck by the same thunderbolt that hit me when I saw you. Wouldn't that solve my problems?"

The corner of her mouth twitched.

"Oh, nay. I have it. She wandered into the forest and the fae mistook her for one of their own—the wicked banshee—and she is never to return."

Adrienne laughed and was immediately rewarded with one of the Hawk's devastating smiles.

He was melting her, disarming her defenses. And it felt good.

More seriously he said, "I instructed the guards to see to Olivia's return journey the moment her horses are rested enough to make the ride."

Adrienne's spirit elevated at his words.

"Adrienne." He sighed her name like a rich port, complex and sweet. "It's only you—"

"Stop!"

Abruptly his mood changed, lightened like quicksilver. "I want to take you somewhere. Come, lass. Give me this night to show you who I really am. That's all I ask."

Adrienne's mind shrieked a resounding no . . . but perhaps it wasn't too dangerous. *Let me show you who I really am . . .* how intriguing.

You mean besides beautiful beyond bearing?

But what harm could there be in conversation?

"What harm could there be in conversation, Adrienne?"

Adrienne blinked. He must have plucked the words right out of her mind.

"Look, Adrienne, the moon comes out, peeping from behind the rowans." The Hawk pointed, and her eyes followed. Down the muscled curve of his arm, over his strong hand to the shining moon beyond.

"Cool silver orb that guides the night's slumber," Hawk

mused softly. "I wager you sleep little on such nights as this, lass, when a storm hovers, threatening to break through the fragile night. Do you feel it? As if the very air is charged with tension? A storm threatening has always stirred a restlessness in me."

Adrienne could feel herself weakening with each word, beguiled by his enchanting brogue.

" 'Tis a restlessness I feel in you as well. Walk with me, Adrienne. You'll never sleep if you return to the castle now."

The Hawk stood, hand outstretched, gazing down at her with promises in his eyes. Not touching her, just waiting for her to choose, to commit—if only to walking with him. His breath was shallow and expectant. Her fingers twitched hesitantly beneath the heat of his smiling eyes—eyes with tiny lines at the outer corners. Eberhard hadn't had any wrinkles. She could never trust a man without a few wrinkles about his eyes. He hadn't lived and laughed enough if he didn't have a few faint creases. How had she failed to notice the fine lines of life on the Hawk's face?

"Give yourself this moment, lass," he breathed huskily. "Try."

Adrienne's hand slipped like a whisper into his and she felt him jerk at their contact. His ebony eyes flared, and she felt the exquisite sensation of his strong fingers closing over hers. He swayed forward and she felt the brush of his lips skim her cheek, an unspoken thank-you for the chance that pushed no further.

"I used to walk here when I was a boy. . . ." He took her hand and steered her westward, away from the circle of rowans and the forest's edge.

Tell her about yourself, he thought. About the boy you used to be before you went away. About who you couldn't wait to be when you got back. But most especially—make her love you before she discovers who you were in between. Love still might not be enough to make her understand, but then at least there's a chance.

They talked and strolled while the Hawk wove his wild tales of boyhood impetuosity and bravery and she laughed into the gentle breeze. They sat atop the cliff's edge and tossed pebbles down into the surf, the crisp salt air tangling her silvery-blond mane with his raven silk. He showed her where he'd hung a hammock, just over the edge and down a man's length, and he made her laugh at how he used to hide there from Lydia. Lying on his back, his arms folded behind his head he would watch the sea and dream while his mother searched the bailey for hours, her lilting voice demanding he return.

Adrienne told him about the nuns and the sultry streets of New Orleans, even got him to say it like the locals did a time or two. N'Awlins. And he listened without chiding her for believing such fantasy. Whether he believed she was weaving tall tales or he somehow placed it all in the context of the sixteenth century, she didn't know. All she did know was that he listened to her like a man had never listened before. So she told him about Marie Leveau the voodoo queen and Jean Laffite the famous pirate, and the great plantations that once stood with their magnificent sprawling houses and the scents and sounds of Bourbon Street. When she spoke of the jazz, the lover's croon of a deep sax, the trumpeting blare of the brass horns, her eyes grew deep with mystery and sensual arousal, and he found he could almost believe she *was* from another time. Surely from another land.

"Kiss me, lass."

"I . . . shouldn't."

Her breathless, husky murmur enchanted him. "Is it so bad then?"

Adrienne drew a deep breath. She stood up, moved away from him, and tipped her head back to study the sky. The night had cleared; the cloud cover had furled out to sea and the storm had passed without breaking. The sound of the surf ebbed and flowed below them in unfaltering rhythm. Stars pierced the mantle of night and Adrienne tried to locate the Big Dipper when suddenly a small, bright star seemed to shiver, then plummeted from the sky.

"Look!" she said excitedly. "A falling star!"

Hawk surged to his feet. "Whatever you do, don't wish, lass."

She turned a pure, glowing smile his way, and it dazzled him so completely that for a moment he couldn't think. "Why ever not, Hawk?"

"They come true," he finally managed.

Her gaze fled back to the falling star. Adrienne held her breath and wished with all her might. *Please let something very good happen to me soon. Please!* Unable to say the words even beneath her breath, she willed her vision to the stars.

He sighed. "What did you wish?"

"You can't tell," Adrienne informed him pertly. "It's against the rules."

Hawk cocked a questioning brow. "What rules, lass?"

"You know—the wishing-on-a-star rules," she informed him in a tone that said *everybody* knew those rules. "So what did *you* wish that came true?"

Hawk snorted. "You just told me I'm not allowed to tell."

Adrienne rolled her eyes and made an impatient sound. "That's only *until* they come true. Then you can tell anyone you want." Her eyes blazed with curiosity. "So—out with it." She pushed lightly at his chest.

Hawk stared at Adrienne with fascination. Over the space

of this wishing-on-a-star conversation, his wife seemed to have slid backward over the years. In her unfettered gaze, Hawk could clearly discern the trusting child she had once been.

"It's not what I wished, rather what a friend of mine wished upon me," Hawk said softly.

"And that was?" Adrienne urged.

Hawk almost laughed aloud; he half thought she might box his ears if he didn't answer her quickly enough for her liking. "Kiss me, Adrienne," he said huskily, "prove to me it's not true. That a friend can't curse you with a wish upon a falling star."

"Come on, Hawk, tell me what his wish was!" Laughter lilted on her lush, pouty lips, and he wanted to kiss her until she made all his private wishes come true.

"Will you kiss me, then?" he bartered.

"Oh! Everything's a deal isn't it?"

Hawk shrugged. "Tit for tat, lass. 'Tis the way of this world. If a villein has beans and no meat, he finds someone with meat and no beans. I'm merely offering you a mutually satisfying trade."

"Do I get coffee too?" she asked shrewdly. "Tomorrow morning? For the kiss tonight? Toll troll paid in advance?"

"Och, wee lassie, who taught you to drive such a hard bargain?" But if he had his way, he'd coax enough sweet kisses from her tonight that he'd need only roll over in the morning to kiss her again. In his bed.

"Was that a yes, Hawk?"

"Cease and desist, lass! Shoot me another one of those beguiling looks and I'll be giving you my buttery with the coffee and perhaps toss in a few horses."

"I have your word, then?"

"You have my word and my pledge."

"Deal." Adrienne sealed their bargain hastily. Answers, coffee, and the excuse for a kiss. How could she ask for more? "My answer first," she demanded.

Hawk's great dark head fell forward, his mouth to her ear. Shivers slid up her back when his breath fanned her neck. "What? I can't hear you?" she said, as he mumbled something indistinct.

"It's really too foolish to bear repeating. . . ."

"A deal's a deal, Hawk!" she complained, shivering violently as his lips grazed her neck again and again.

Hawk groaned. "He wished for me the perfect wife. That my wife would be all that I ever dared dream of . . . all I ever hoped for. And then he wished that she would refuse to love me. Refuse to touch me. Refuse to share my bed."

"Why would a friend wish such a thing?" she asked indignantly.

"Why would a wife do such a thing?" he countered smoothly against the tender lobe of her ear.

She felt the tip of his tongue against her skin, and wondered why herself. Why would a wife say no to this impossibly beautiful, intriguing man?

Her pulse quickened; she turned her head and stared straight into burnished ebony eyes of unfathomable depths. Bewildered by the flush and quiver of emotion, she touched a finger to his perfectly sculpted lips. Her mind cried out to identify this new feeling, to control it, but her body demanded that she know him in a sense that had nothing to do with reason or logic.

"Let me love you, lass. I won't take anything you don't wish to give." His eyes lingered on her face, a seductive visual caress that heated her blood, and she wondered what might have been—if she'd only met him when she'd still believed in happily ever after. What would it feel like to let him run his beautiful strong hands all over her shaking body, to be kissed and teased and finally completed with the raw, pulsing steel of his hunger. Her senses were overwhelmed by the Hawk; the spicy, male scent of him, the silky feel of his hair, the rock-hard press of his body against hers.

I'll stop him in just a moment, she promised herself as he scattered kisses along her jaw. *One kiss on his lips was the deal,* she reminded herself.

Her conscience momentarily assuaged, she permitted the glorious rasp of his callused palms against her skin, the whisper of his shadow beard against her neck.

Suddenly she was doing more than permitting. Her arms crept up to circle his neck. She buried her fingers in his silky dark hair, then slid them down his neck to his powerful shoulders, tracing the contours of each sculpted muscle.

Adrienne drew a shaky, bewildered breath. She couldn't get enough oxygen in her lungs, but that ceased to matter as Hawk replaced her need for air with a need for his lips, a need for his tongue, a need for his need of her.

"I am the one, lass," he warned her softly. "It all stops here. With me. The best and last. Oh, definitely your last."

My last, she reluctantly acknowledged, for she doubted that any other man could match this one.

In that breathless moment, the past blurred into utter insignificance. It was as if Eberhard had never touched her, as if the twentieth century had never existed. As if all her life she had been heading toward this moment. This man. This magic.

Hawk traced kisses across her jaw, over every inch of her face; her nose, her eyelids as they fluttered closed, her brows, and then he stopped, his sensual lips hovering a flicker of a tongue away from hers. Would she? Dare she?

Adrienne's tongue flickered out and she tasted the man

she'd wanted since the moment she'd laid fascinated eyes
on him. "Oh my," she whispered. She wanted him, wanted
this, more than she'd ever wanted anything in her life. A
husky sound rumbled deep in his throat; he splayed his
hand at the base of her neck and arched her head back to re-
ceive his kisses. The pink tip of his tongue circled her lips,
tasted every corner, every fullness, teased her senseless;
until it was too much for her, and her lips relaxed beneath
his, molded to his, opened for him as her whole body
seemed to be opening and crying for him. She was the bud
of a rose, unfurling to the golden heat of the sun. "Magnificent," she whispered, unaware that she'd spoken her
thoughts aloud.

But the Hawk wasn't unaware—he heard her one word
and desire slammed through him so savagely that he shuddered. Hot and hard, ruthlessly, the Hawk moved his mouth
over hers. He slanted across her lips with a relentless
hunger that caused stars to shimmer behind her shut eyes.

Adrienne's eyes flew open for the sheer pleasure of looking at him and she saw that he was looking directly into
them with such a smoldering promise of passion that she
whimpered against his mouth.

Hundreds of feet below, nature conspired with the raw,
unquenchable mystery of passion in its rhythm; the sensual
tempo of the waves as billions of gallons of water came in
with a fury, then eased out. Wave after wave of sensation
crashed over Adrienne; she was adrift in a sea of such passion that she literally felt herself being reshaped, molded to
this man's touch, just as the rocks below her were molded
by the ocean's relentless caress.

The Hawk's tongue was hot silk, exploring her mouth,
teasing her tongue. "Oh," she whispered, "I never knew. . . ."

"Is kissing me so bad, then, lass?"

"It's not the kissing that's bad . . ." Her words were lost in a soft moan as she tipped her head back for more kisses.

"What's bad, my heart?" Hawk nipped her neck, gently.

"Oooh! . . . you!"

"Me? I'm bad?" He wouldn't let her answer for a long moment while he nibbled at her lower lip, teased it, sucked it into his mouth, then slowly released it.

Adrienne drew a shaky breath. "Well . . . I mean . . . you *are* a man . . ."

"Yes," he encouraged.

"And very beautiful at that. . . ."

"Mmm . . . yes?"

"And I hate beautiful men. . . ." Her hands moved over his shoulders, his broad muscled back, and tapered down over his tight waist to his muscular buttocks. She was shocked at her own daring, thrilled by the groan of pleasure she coaxed from him.

"I can tell. Hate me just like *that*, lass. Hate me like that again. Hate me all you need to hate me."

In one fluid motion, the Hawk tumbled her gently to the ground and stretched his hard body over hers. Adrienne was amazed; she'd never been this intimate with Eberhard, never experienced anything like it before, this heady feeling of lying beneath a man. How tantalizing it was: the thrust of her breasts against his broad chest; the possessive way he snared and kept one of her legs between his; the ridge of his enormous cock against the curve of her thigh. When he shifted his weight so that rigid muscle rode rock-hard between her legs, the heat simmering between them flared, causing muscles to clench inside her she hadn't known she possessed. He rotated his hips, rubbing in slow erotic circles against her. She felt light-headed, disoriented by the sensations he evoked. She arched against him, wrapping a leg over him to pull him closer—to trap the heated man of him snug in the ache between her thighs.

He tugged gently at the bodice of her gown and slid it down over her shoulders, baring her breasts for his attentive expertise. "Beautiful," he murmured, his fingers teasing the puckered crests. When he circled the rosy peaks with his tongue, tendrils of fire radiated through her body, culminating in exquisite heat in her belly, and lower still.

"Oh my God!" Adrienne tossed her head in the fragrant grass and threaded her fingers possessively through his dark mane.

Hawk groaned, his hot breath fanning her breast. "How do you do this to me, lass?" She was all he'd ever dreamed he might one day have, then counseled himself sternly to give up the dreaming as a foolish lad's fancy.

But now he felt very much like that foolish lad again.

He almost laughed at the rightness of it. After all the women he'd had, he *loved* this one. The full enormity of his realization astounded and delighted him; he lowered his lips to hers, demanding wordlessly that she love him back. He put every ounce of longing, every shred of roguish seduction at his disposal into that silent plea—he kissed her so deeply, he no longer knew where he ended and she began. Her hips yielded when he thrust against her and rose hungrily to find his when he drew back. Primitive sounds escaped her lips, which were swollen and plum-colored from his fierce kisses.

"Love me, Adrienne," he commanded roughly. "Love me!"

Her only reply was a throaty moan.

"Tell me you want me, lass," he demanded hungrily against her lips.

"Please . . . ," came her choked reply as she squeezed her eyes tightly shut. *I'll stop him in just a minute. It will be easier if I don't look at him.*

"Do you want me, Adrienne?" Hawk asked, pulling back from their kiss. Her plea wasn't enough of an answer; he had to hear her say the words. That even with her eyes closed, she knew it was *him* on top of her, *him* kissing her.

But she didn't answer, and her eyes remained shut.

Hawk groaned and kissed her again anyway, losing himself for a moment in the texture and taste of her sweet lips. But doubt hammered at him. He was aware that if he didn't push the issue, he might yet carry her to his bed tonight in her sensual, drunken arousal. But he didn't want Adrienne incoherent. He wanted her wide-awake, fully aware and asking him to touch her. He wanted her to meet his gaze levelly with honest, unabashed hunger, and say the words. Hawk tore his mouth from hers, panting hard.

"Open your eyes, Adrienne." He forced himself to lie still, his hips rigid against the seductive arch of her body.

A wordless moment of shallow breaths passed, their lips inches apart.

"Look at me. Say my name. Now," Hawk commanded.

Adrienne's eyes opened just a sliver. *Don't make me acknowledge this . . . don't ask so much!* they pleaded. And again, her body quested upward, begging him to move atop her, to seduce her in her drunken arousal so that tomorrow she could pretend it hadn't been her choice.

"Look at me and say my name." His voice broke harshly on the words. His beautiful, chiseled mouth hovered only a whisper away from hers.

Adrienne stared up at him mutely. Tears stung her eyes, threatening to spill down her cheeks.

"Why can't you do it?" he demanded, his brogue rough

velvet over broken glass. "Is it so impossible? Sidheach. That's all you have to say. Or James, even Lyon. Laird Douglas would do!" Anything but Adam.

Adrienne stared, revulsion at her own weakness choking her. She'd learned nothing! One more inch, one scant movement, and she would be lost as never before. *Where the body goes . . . the heart will follow . . . say his name and kiss him again, then you can just kiss your soul goodbye. This man has the power to destroy you in ways Eberhard never could.*

"What will it take to make you forget him?"

And he thought it was Adam, but it wasn't Adam. It was Eberhard. And there would be nothing left of her this time if she played the fool again.

"Say my name, lass, for the love of God!" Hawk roared. He was shaking with a mixture of barely restrained passion and disbelief that she could respond to him so erotically, so completely, yet still withhold his name. "If there is any chance for me at all, Adrienne, call out to me! If you can't even say my name, then I stand no chance of ever gaining your love!"

His last plea was the agonized cry of a wounded animal; it laid open her heart.

A pulse throbbed in his neck and she raised her hand to place trembling fingers against it. Harder and harder she steeled her heart, until it was safe again behind a glacier of remembrance and regret.

He pushed her hand away.

"Say it." He forced his demand through gritted teeth.

"Now isn't this just *sooo* touching. I'll help her." Olivia's voice dripped venom. "Just call him the king's whore," she purred. "That's all *we* ever called him."

*   *   *

The storm raging in him stilled at precisely that moment.

"Is it true?" Adrienne finally whispered, her eyes wide and deep with hurt. Hurt and something else. Hawk saw the unspoken cry in her slate depths. He wanted to deny it, to explain the nightmare away. But he would not lie to this lass. She would have to take him in full truth or not at all; when she accepted him, if he even had any chance left, she would possess him entirely. Bitterness welled up, cloaking him in a despair so complete he almost cried aloud with the agony of it.

"I was called the king's whore," he replied stiffly.

Shadows leapt and flickered in her opalescent silver eyes. Darkness he had vowed to ease, he had fed with his own hands.

He rolled from her and rose slowly, then walked away into the night as silent as a wolf, leaving her on the edge of a precipice with his vengeful ex-mistress. He hoped she'd simply push the spiteful Olivia over the edge, but he knew it was not going to be that easy. For if he judged rightly, his wife would be in Adam's bed in no time now.

She was lost to him.

Better that he had never met this lass so that he might never have known the sweet rush of emotion, the absolving passion, the freeing wings of what love might have been.

He wandered that night, lost in memories of that time when he had been commanded by his king. All for Dalkeith and his mother, for Ilysse and Adrian. Aye, and fair Scotia from time to time when his king had been wildly foolish. Nay, there had never really been any choice.

Hawk's eyes searched the night sky for yet another

falling star. He intended to wish upon every one for the rest of his life if necessary. Surely ten thousand wishes could undo one. But the cloud cover had returned and there wasn't one flicker of a star to be seen in the absolute darkness that surrounded him.

CHAPTER 17

"OH MY DEAR, I THOUGHT YOU KNEW!" OLIVIA GUSHED.

"Go to hell," Adrienne said softly as she forced herself to her feet.

"I'm trying to help you—"

"No you're not. The only person you're trying to help is yourself—to a heaping helping of my husband."

"Ah, yes. Your precious husband. Have you no curiosity about his time at court?" Olivia purred invitingly.

"Do you really think I'm stupid enough to believe you would tell me any truth about him? A woman like you?"

Olivia stopped midsentence, her mouth hanging slightly ajar. "And just what is that supposed to mean?"

Adrienne's slate-gray eyes coolly met Olivia's heavily kohled ovals. "Just that you're the kind of woman who measures her success by the men she beds and the women she bites and one day soon, and not too far off from the look of you, you're going to be nothing but a plump, unwanted old woman with no friends. And then how are you going to pass the time?" Olivia might have taken her in years ago, but not much fooled her anymore.

"How dare you, you *petite salope*!" Olivia spit out. "I was only offering my help—"

"By following us, spying on us, and then bringing up his past? His past is gone, Olivia." Adrienne wasn't aware she was defending him until she heard herself doing it. "Some people learn from their past, grow better and wiser. My Hawk has done that. You're just angry because you know he's not the man he used to be. If he was, he would have stayed in the gardens with you instead of spending the evening talking with me."

"Talking? He and I used to . . . talk . . . like that too. He's just temporarily inflamed with a new body. He'll get over it. And when he does, he'll come back to my bed."

"You're wrong," Adrienne said calmly. "And you know it. That's what really upsets you."

"Old dogs do not learn new tricks, sweet young fool," Olivia sneered.

Adrienne flashed a saccharin smile at the older woman. "Perhaps not. But sometimes dogs give up their old tricks *entirely*."

"You speak like a woman in love. Yet you wouldn't say his name," Olivia declared, arching a penciled brow.

Adrienne's smile faded. "I speak for both myself and my husband when I suggest you leave Dalkeith at first light, whether the horses are rested or not. You are no longer welcome here. Don't ever come back."

*   *   *

I sure can pick 'em, can't I? she brooded as she picked her way through the garden.

Just as with Eberhard, the boat-deck-tanned playboy elite who'd manipulated her so flawlessly, she'd been a fool for a beautiful illusion. The real beauty had to come from inside. A man called the king's whore . . . well, what kind of beauty was there in that?

Worse yet was the thought of what she'd been about to do, would have willingly done with the Hawk, if Olivia hadn't come along. His pleas had virtually undone her defenses, and she knew full well that had Olivia not interrupted them, she would even now be lying beneath his magnificent body, just another one of the king's whore's conquests.

Maybe it's not like that, Adrienne. Maybe you don't know the whole story, a small voice in her heart pointed out.

Maybe I don't want to know the whole story, she seethed. She clenched her hands until she felt the painful tear of nails in the soft flesh of her palms. *I want to go home,* she mourned like a lost child. *I want Moonie.*

That's the only thing that's worth wanting back there, she thought.

She blew out a frustrated breath.

"Adrienne." His voice came out of the shadows of the lower bailey so softly that she thought at first she must have imagined it.

She whirled to meet his gaze. Moonlight fell in wide shafts through the trees, casting a silver bar across his chiseled face.

"Leave me alone, Hawk."

"What did Olivia tell you?" The words sounded as though they were ripped from him against his will.

"Why don't you go ask her? It seems the two of you

communicated quite well in the past. A sort of 'wordless communication,' if I recall."

"Lass, don't," he groaned.

"Why not? Does the truth hurt?"

"Adrienne, it wasn't like that. It wasn't . . ." His voice trailed off and he sighed.

"It wasn't what?" she said icily. Adrienne waited. Would he explain? The word *whore* could have a variety of meanings, none of them savory. She knew he'd been with beautiful women, and a lot of them from what the Comyn maids had told her, but just how many? A thousand? Ten thousand?

When the Hawk didn't reply, Adrienne pushed. "Are you Olivia's lover?"

"No, lass!"

"Were you?" Adrienne forced herself to ask.

Hawk sighed. "It's true, but it was a long time ago, and you don't know the circumstances—"

Adrienne glared. "I don't want to know the circumstances under which you would be with a woman like her! If you had any discrimination at all, you would never . . . You men are all the same!"

Hawk's brogue thickened measurably. "Give me a chance, Adrienne. Hear me out. 'Tisna fair to be hating me for things other men may have done to you. One more chance—that's all I'm asking of you, lass."

"I've given you too many chances! Leave me alone, Hawk Douglas. Just leave me alone!" Adrienne spun around and raced for the castle before she could humiliate herself by bursting into tears.

*   *   *

She dreamed of the Hawk and the promise she had glimpsed in his eyes. The hope. If he knew her past, would he still want *her*? Adrienne's slumbering psyche struggled mightily with the lot of it. Dare she let herself love him? Dare she not? Her heart was still too bruised. Her mind recoiled from any possibility of further shame and regret. But the temptation to fall grew harder to resist every day. If only she were home in her cocoon of solitude. Safe again, but so lonely . . .

Dreaming within a dream, she finally remembered how she'd come to be there, and understood how she might get back home. The way to escape the Hawk and all his infinite promises of passion and pain.

She was awakened by the impact of the memory. Disentangling herself from the silken sheets, she crossed the room and peered out into the inky night.

Eberhard's chess set.

She could finally recall with perfect clarity what she'd been doing moments before she'd been catapulted through time to land on the Comyn's lap.

She'd been in her library, picking up the pieces of Eberhard's chess set.

That dratted chess set really *was* cursed. When she'd swiped it from Eberhard's house, she'd been careful not to touch the pieces. Eberhard had often joked about the curse, but Adrienne preferred to give legends, curses, and myths a wide berth. After she'd pilfered the set, she had left it packed, intending to unpack it only if she needed to sell it.

She knew she'd had the black queen in her hand when she'd appeared on Red Comyn's lap, but where had it gone from there? She certainly didn't have it now. Had one of the maids taken it? Would she have to confront the despicable Red Comyn to get it back?

She shook her head dejectedly. It had to be *somewhere* at the Comyn keep, and wherever it was she had to make an effort to find it. It could take her home.

Could she find her way back to the Comyn keep?

Of course, she assured herself. After traveling scrubby backroads for two thousand miles, Adrienne de Simone could find her way anywhere. But quickly, while she was still under cover of the night. And before her resolve weakened.

*   *   *

Thirty minutes later she was ready. Tiptoeing through the kitchen, she'd found an oiled sack and filled it with crusty breads and cheeses and a few apples. Tavis snored in his chair by the door, his hand furled about a half-full glass of—she sniffed cautiously—pure grain alcohol from the smell of it. After a quick stop in the Green Lady's room where she'd left the boots Lydia had given her, she'd be ready to go.

Slipping from the kitchen, she moved quickly down the short corridor and pushed open the door to the Green Lady's room. Her eyes flared with dismay. There the Hawk slept, a white linen sheet wrapped around his legs, his torso bare to the dawn's caress. His dark head tossed against the white pillows, and he slept alone—grasping in his arms the dress she'd worn that day she'd taken the dart.

They called him the king's whore, she reminded herself. Perhaps there was actually a royal appointment to such a post. Or perhaps he was simply so nondiscriminating that he'd earned the title all by himself. Regardless, she would never again be one of many.

Adrienne spied her boots on the wooden chest at the foot of the bed. Eyes carefully averted from her sleeping husband, she slipped them from the burnished pine lid and skittered back toward the door on kitten paws, closing it gently behind her.

And now the difficult part. Guards were posted all over the castle. She would have to flee through the gardens, down the eternal bridge to the gatehouse, and through the east tower. She'd run from worse things, through worse climes before. She would manage somehow. She always did when it came to running.

*   *   *

Hawk slitted one eye open and watched her leave. He muttered darkly and shifted his body, folding his muscular arms behind his head. He stared at the door a long moment.

She was leaving him?

Never. Not so long as he lived and breathed, and he had a hell of a lot more fight in him than she must think.

He moved to his feet and grabbed his kilt, knotting it loosely at his waist.

So that's the way it was going to be, he mused bitterly. The first sign of something less than savory in his past, and she would run. He hadn't pegged her as the skittish type. He'd thought there was a lass of fiery mettle beneath her silken exterior, but one breath of his sordid past and she was ready to leave him. After the pleasure she'd so obviously experienced in his arms, still—to walk away.

Well, where the hell did she think he'd learned how to give pleasure?

Oh, nay. The next time his wife lay in his arms, and there would be a next time, he would take one of the gypsy potions to make him detached. Then he would truly show her the benefits she reaped from the past she eschewed so violently.

He was offering her his love, freely and openly. He, who had never offered anything more than physical pleasure for a short time to any lass, was offering this woman his life.

And still she would not accept him.

And she didn't even know the first bloody thing about what it meant to be the king's whore. Olivia had been about to tell her, there in the gardens. Olivia, who had ruthlessly exploited the Hawk's servitude to the king by petitioning James to command the Hawk to grant her those carnal favors he'd previously denied her. Olivia, who had given James a whole new way to humiliate the Hawk. The memory of it shamed and enraged him. He banished such thoughts and the blinding anger they generated with a firm flexing of his formidable will.

Adrienne was his immediate problem. Hawk snorted. Was she running off to discover the world in her smithy's arms?

Aye. He was sure she was.

At that moment Grimm pushed the door open and ducked his head in, a silent question in his eyes.

"Is she headed north?" Hawk's face was bitter.

"Nay," Grimm puzzled. " 'Tis what I expected too, but she goes east."

"To the gatehouse? Alone?"

"Aye. Carrying only a wee pack."

"He must be meeting her there," Hawk mused. "The guard is following?"

"Aye, at a distance. Until you give your command."

Hawk turned his back and studied the dying embers. His command. Should he let her go? Could he? And if she joined with Adam how would he keep himself from killing the smithy with his bare hands? No. Better to stop her before he had to know with absolute certainty her betrayal. "What have you learned of Adam?" Hawk kicked at the hearth.

"Nothing, Hawk. 'Tis as if he blew in on a fae breeze and

put down roots. It's the oddest thing. No one knows from whence he came. I think Esmerelda is our best bet for information, as she warms his bed. But I haven't been able to track her down just yet." Grimm rubbed his jaw thoughtfully. "Seems Esmerelda's people have moved their camp away from the north rowans to the far east pastures."

Hawk spun on his heel, his dark eyes searching Grimm's intently. "The Rom never move camp. They always stay in the north pastures through the summer."

"Not this summer." Grimm shrugged. "Verily odd. Said even the Samhain would be celebrated at a new site this harvest."

"Strange." Hawk pondered this new oddity. But he spared only a moment to consider the Gypsy tribe that camped Dalkeith—there were more important issues to attend to. His wife was leaving him. "Stop her at the gatehouse, Grimm. I'll be there shortly."

∗   ∗   ∗

Adrienne knew she was being followed.

Escaping the castle was as hard as trying to break out of a prison. She had less chance of evading the guards than she had of wishing herself back to the twentieth century. This time she didn't even have a gun.

Like the night Eberhard had died—a night she'd promised herself never to think of again.

She hadn't meant for any of it to happen. She hadn't even known what was going on until the night she'd finally discovered why Eberhard had been sending her on all those solitary vacations. *So lovely and stupidly gullible.* Wasn't that how she'd heard him describe her that night she'd returned unexpectedly from London, hoping to surprise him?

And surprise him she had.

Slipping in the back door of the garage and into his luxurious home, Adrienne overheard a conversation not meant for her ears.

A conversation he would have killed her for hearing.

She hadn't called out his name as she'd placed her hand on the door to his den. Gerard's voice carried clearly through the door.

"Did Rupert meet her in London?"

Adrienne froze. They were talking about her. How had they known that Rupert was in London? She'd just met him there yesterday. She hadn't even called Eberhard and discussed anything with him yet. She'd come back on the red-eye and it had taken all day and half the night to get home. She pressed her ear to the door, listening curiously.

Eberhard laughed. "Just as we'd planned. He told her he was in town to buy a gift for his wife. You know Adrienne, she'd believe anything. She didn't notice a thing when he swapped her luggage. She's so lovely and gullible. You were right about her from the first, Gerard. She's the perfect pigeon. And she'll never catch on to what we're doing until it's too late to matter."

Adrienne jerked violently, her hand frozen on the door.

"And when she finally gets caught, Eb? What will you do then?"

Eberhard's laughter chilled her blood. "Ah, that's the beauty of it. They'll dig up the records from the orphanage. I took the liberty of having them doctored a bit. They now reflect a juvenile delinquent with a natural inclination toward criminal behavior. She'll take the fall alone. There's not a cop in my fair city who'd try to pin anything on Mr. Eberhard Darrow Garrett—generous political patron. I never leave the Kingdom of N'Awlins. She's the one always in and out of the country."

Adrienne's eyes were wide with horror. *What was he saying?*

Gerard laughed. "We got a huge shipment out in her Mercedes last month, Eb. The Acapulco run was nothing but brilliant."

Shipment? Adrienne wondered frantically. Shipment of what? She backed soundlessly away from the door.

Stupid. Gullible. Innocent. What was so bad about being innocent? she wondered as she slunk through the darkened house, swallowing her sobs. At least there was honor in innocence. At least she never hurt anyone, never used anyone. So maybe she was a tad . . . gullible. Maybe she even lacked a bit of common sense. But she more than made up for it in other departments. She had a good heart. That should count for something.

Her throat tightened with suppressed tears. Stop it, she chided herself. Focus. Find the queen. Get back home. They don't make men like the Hawk in the twentieth century, and after the Hawk no man would ever be a temptation again.

The gatehouse loomed before her. Why hadn't they stopped her? She knew they were still there. Maybe he wanted them to let her go. Maybe she'd been so naive and unschooled that he really wasn't interested at all. After all, a man like that certainly wouldn't have a hard time finding a willing woman.

What would the king's whore care? There would always be another woman.

She kicked angrily at a pebble and watched it skitter into the wall of the gatehouse. Would they pull up the portcullis and draw back the sally port for her? Roll out the red carpet to celebrate her leave-taking?

And as she stepped into the archway, Grimm melted out of the shadows.

She stopped, relieved.

Try that again, she told herself. *Write that scene one more time, Adrienne de Simone. It reads, "she stopped, furious at being denied escape."*

No, definitely relieved.

She sighed, her shoulders drooping. "Grimm. Let me pass. It's my life. Move."

He shook his head. "Sorry, milady."

"Grimm, I must go back to the Comyn keep."

"Why?"

She studied him a moment in the breaking light. He looked truly confused, and his eyes kept scanning the northern bailey, as if he was expecting someone. "Because I'm homesick," she lied. Well, perhaps not exactly a lie—she *did* miss Moonie terribly.

"Ah!" Understanding dawned in his handsome features. He stood before her, his legs apart, muscular arms folded across his chest. "Are you looking for something?"

"What?" He couldn't know! Could he? "Grimm, did Lady Comyn—I mean my mother—say anything about . . . well . . . anything of mine that I might have left there . . . at home?"

"Like what?" Grimm asked, the veritable picture of innocence.

"Yes, like what?" echoed a voice behind her. Something in his voice had decidedly changed and for the worse. The Hawk's velvet purr had taken on the coldness of smooth, polished steel.

Was she responsible for that change?

"Take her to the Peacock Room. Lock the door and bring me the key, Grimm."

"No!" she cried, spinning around to face him. "I must go! I want to go to the Comyn keep!"

"What seek you, wife?" he asked icily.

Mute, she stared at him defiantly.

Hawk muttered a dark curse. Could it be true? Could she truly be from the future and looking for the way back home? The thought that she might leave him for Adam had made him near crazed.

But, he brooded darkly, if it was the black queen she was seeking, then she was most definitely doing it for a reason. Odds were she was from somewhere else if not some *when* else, and she thought the black queen could take her away from him.

One way to find out, he decided.

"Is it this you're after, lass?" he asked as he withdrew the chess piece from his sporran and raised it before her widening eyes.

CHAPTER 18

"COME, LASS." THE COMMAND WAS TONELESS AND UNMIS-takably dangerous. And even now, the mere word made her shiver with desire. The flush of heat stole her breath. "Hawk—"

"Don't." The word was a warning. "Now. Take my hand."

What was he going to do? she wondered frantically. Behind her, she felt Grimm step closer, edging her toward the Hawk.

"Wait!" She held out a hand to ward him off.

"Move, milady," Grimm said softly.

"Don't lock me in a room!"

"How could I not?" Hawk sneered. "Knowing that you would go back to a place where it seems you knew little joy—yet you would rather be there than here with me!"

"You don't believe I'm from the future!" she gasped.

"I'm beginning to," he muttered. "How do you think I knew about this?" The black queen glittered in his hand.

She shrugged. "How?"

"You, my sweet wife, talked about it when you were poisoned. Worried and fretted and tried to find it—"

"But I only just remembered."

"Your sleeping mind remembered sooner."

"But how did *you* get it?"

It was Grimm who told her. "The Lady Comyn saw it fall from your hand the night she claims you arrived."

"But how—"

"Lady Comyn entrusted it to me after the wedding. I gave it to the Hawk."

"She admitted that you're not her blood daughter. I can see no reason why she would lie on that score." *Unless Comyn keep is suffering some strange contagious madness,* he thought grimly. "Will it truly take you back to wherever you came from?" the Hawk asked carefully.

"I think so. As far as I can tell, it's what brought me here," she said, her gaze cast upon the cobbled walkway.

"And your plan was to get it and go home, lass? You planned to slip from Dalkeith, by yourself?"

"No! With your mother, Hawk!" she snapped absurdly. "Of course by myself!"

"So you were going to go to Comyn keep to get this chess piece and try to go back to wherever you came from? That was your plan this evening?" She missed the warning in his careful tone.

"Yes, Hawk. I admit it. All right? I was going to try. I'm not certain it will work, but it's the last thing I had in my hand before I ended up here, and legend says the chess set is cursed. It's the only thing I can think of that might have done it. If it brought me here, it might just take me back."

The Hawk smiled coolly. He turned the queen in his hand, studying it carefully. "Viking," he mused. "Beautiful piece. Well worked and well preserved."

"Do you believe me now, Hawk?" She needed to know. "That I really am from the future?"

"Suffice it to say—I don't believe in taking any chances." He still didn't quite believe, but infinitely better safe than sorry.

He turned sharply on his heel and stalked off toward the gardens. "Bring her, Grimm," he called over his shoulder, almost as an afterthought.

But Grimm didn't have to take her anywhere. A thousand warning bells clanged in her head, and she raced off behind him to catch up. His careful tone, his steely demeanor, his questions. He'd been neatly tying things down to the absolute letter. The Hawk was not a man lacking intellect and purpose. She only hoped she misunderstood his purpose now.

"Hawk!" she cried.

Hawk's shoulders tightened. He was beyond anger at this moment, he had slipped into the realm of icy resolve. He knew what he had to do as he broke into a run through the gardens, across the bailey, in the blushing Scottish morn. Until it was done, he couldn't afford to let her touch him, to put her sweet hands on his shoulders and beg. *I'll take no chances where my wife is concerned.*

"Wait!" Adrienne broke into a run, fear gripping her heart as she realized he was making a beeline for the northern edge of the bailey, where the forge was burning brightly.

"No, Hawk!" she screamed as he melted into the gardens. Her feet flew as she plunged through the lush greenery,

racing over the beds of anemones and purple iris. She leapt
the low stone walls and pushed thorny rose branches from
her face, tearing the soft palms of her hands until she
erupted from the gardens only to see him a dozen lengths
ahead of her.

Gasping for breath, she called on every ounce of fleet-
footed strength she had. If she made it at all, it would be
close—too close.

From a window high above, Lydia watched the scene
unfold.

Pushing against the pain of her unwilling muscles, Adrienne desperately tried to catch up to Hawk, but it was too
late—he already stood next to Adam near the brightly
glowing embers.

Gasping, she lunged forward just as Grimm's hand closed
upon her cape. He yanked hard on the fabric, pulling her
backward. The cape ripped and she fell, crying out as she
tumbled to the ground. "Hawk, don't!"

"Destroy this," Hawk commanded Adam.

"No!" Adrienne screamed.

Adam cast a momentary eye upon the felled beauty. "It
would seem the lady feels otherwise."

"I didn't ask you to think, Adam Black, and I don't give a
bloody damn what the lady thinks."

Adam smiled impishly. "I take it you have failed to jess
the falcon, Lord Hawk?"

"Burn it, smithy. Lest I satisfy myself by incinerating
you, rather than the queen."

"Adam! No!" Adrienne pleaded.

Adam seemed to ponder the situation a moment, then
with an oddly triumphant look, he shrugged and tossed the
piece into the forge.

To Adrienne, lying flat on the ground, everything seemed to happen in slow motion.

She watched in horror as the black queen soared through the air and sank into the glowing coals. Adrienne swallowed a sob as the flames licked greedily at the chess piece. Her only way out had been destroyed.

Hawk sighed his relief. Adrienne collapsed against the earth, staring blankly at the soil. The black queen was gone, the dense African wood no match for the blaze hot enough to forge steel.

No Moonie. No way home.

She was here in 1513—with him—forever.

Adam made a sound a shade too dark to be laughter as he leaned closer to the Hawk. Close enough that only the Hawk heard his low, mocking words. "She will warm my bed in no time at all now, fool Hawk."

Hawk flinched. The smithy was right. His wife would hate him for what he'd done.

"What the hell are you doing at the forge in the middle of the night anyway?" Hawk snapped.

Adam grinned impishly. "I am ever a merry wanderer of the night. Besides, one never knows what prime opportunity might present itself for the plucking."

Hawk snarled at the smithy.

Behind him, he heard Adrienne stagger to her unsteady feet. Her breathing was labored from her run, perhaps from shock as well. Bleakly, the Hawk studied the forge in rigid silence. Adrienne's voice trembled with fury.

"Know one thing, Lord Douglas, and it's all you'll ever need to know. Remember it, should you someday think I may have changed my mind. I won't. I *despise* you. You took from me what you had no right to take. And there's nothing you can *ever* do to earn my forgiveness. I *hate* you!"

"Despise me as you must," he said quietly, still staring at the forge. "But you can never leave me now. That's all that matters."

LUGHNASSADH

(Midsummer)

Double, double toil and trouble;
Fire burn and cauldron bubble . . .
SHAKESPEARE, *Macbeth*

CHAPTER 19

Twilight crept up from the ocean and over the cliffs with purple impatience that stained the walls of Dalkeith a dusky crimson. In his study, Hawk watched the night seep through the open doors on the west end.

She stood on the cliff's edge, unmoving, her velvet cape tossing restlessly in the wind. What was she thinking as she gazed blindly out to sea?

He knew what *he'd* been thinking—that even the wind sought to unclothe her. He tortured himself with the memory of the sultry rose peaks he knew crowned her breasts beneath the silk of her gown. Her body had been shaped for this time, to wear clinging silks and rich velvets. To be a fine laird's lady. To mate a proud warrior.

What the hell was he going to do? Things couldn't go on like this.

He'd been trying to provoke her, hoping she'd make him angry so he could lose his head and punish her with his body. But time and again when he'd pushed she'd given him only cool civility, and a man couldn't do a bloody thing with that kind of response. He whirled from the door and squeezed his eyes shut to erase all haunting memory of the vision of his wife.

Weeks had passed since that day by the forge—weeks lush with fragile days and delicate dawns, ruby nights and midsummer storms. And in those passing days, those jewels of Scotia's summer, were a thousand sights he wanted to share with her.

Damn it! He pounded his fist upon his desk, sending papers fluttering and statues scurrying. She was his wife. She had no way back to wherever she'd come from! When was she going to accept that and make the most of it? He would give her anything she wanted. Anything but to leave him. Never that.

His existence had all the makings of a gilded, living hell and he could find no exit.

As swiftly as it had assailed him, his rage evaporated.

Adrienne, his lips formed the word silently. *How did we come to this impasse? How did I make such a mess of it?*

✳   ✳   ✳

"Walk with me, lass," he said softly, and she whirled upon the cliff's edge, a breathtaking flutter of silver and cobalt blue. His colors, the Douglas colors. Unwittingly, it seemed, she wore them often. Did she even know that she donned in vivid splashes the very threads of the Douglas tartan, and that no name could have branded her more certainly his lady?

He waved a dismissive hand at his guards. He needed to steal precious moments with her alone, before he left. After hours of struggling, he had reached many decisions. First and foremost being that he was long overdue for a visit to Uster, one of his many manors and the most troublesome. He simply couldn't keep neglecting his estates in his lovesick idiocy. The laird had to put in the occasional appearance and take an interest in resolving his villagers' concerns.

Besides, he was making no progress here. If she chose Adam in his absence, then he could just die inside and get on with the pretense of living. It was how he'd survived the first thirty-odd years. What kind of fool had he become to expect the rest to be any different?

"Laird Douglas," she clipped.

In silence they walked the cliff's edge together, toward the forest.

"I will be leaving for a time," he said finally as they entered the forest.

Adrienne stiffened. Was he serious? "Wh-where are you going?" And why did it disturb her so much?

He took a sharp, indrawn breath. "Uster."

"What is Uster anyway?"

"One of my manors. Seventeen manors belong to Dalkeith. Uster holds the villages of Duluth and Tanamorissey, and they are an intemperate lot. 'Twas a problem even when the king's men held Dalkeith."

When the king's men held Dalkeith.

When her husband had been the king's whore.

In the last weeks the heat of Adrienne's anger had cooled, leaving a poignant regret. Hawk had mostly avoided her, except for the occasional times he'd seemed to be trying to pick a fight with her for some reason. She'd half expected him to lock her in his room, but after that terrible night he had retreated carefully to his study by the sea.

There he'd stayed every night—so quiet, so beautiful, and
so alone.

"Hawk?" she began tentatively.

"Yes?"

"What exactly did the king's whore do?"

Hawk stiffened. Could this be the chance he'd been waiting for? Perhaps he could dare to hope after all. His laughter
was full of bitter self-mockery. "Are you quite certain you
wish to know, lovely Adrienne?"

✳   ✳   ✳

Lurking behind a towering oak, Esmerelda studied Adrienne's silvery-blond mane, silvery eyes, sparkling face.
What did the Hawk see in that skinny, pale girl he couldn't
find in Esmerelda's sultry embrace?

For the first time in weeks the guards were gone and the
bitch walked unprotected enough that Esmerelda could
strike and flee into the shelter of the dark forest. Her
beloved Hawk might suffer a time of mourning, but he
would find solace and sweet passion in Esmerelda's arms
once the soil stilled upon his wife's grave.

She raised the arrow with a hand that trembled. Frown-
ing, she dug the edge of the notched head into her fleshy
palm until blood welled in her tawny-gold skin. She grimaced against the pain, but it steadied her nerves. This time
she would *not* fail. Esmerelda had chosen her weapon carefully. Poison had proved too chancy—her drawn and corded
bow would send the arrow flying true, with force enough to
lodge in the flesh and bone of Adrienne's breast.

Esmerelda dropped to her knee and coiled the leather
cord tighter. She notched the bow and took sight as Adrienne stepped into a clearing. She nearly faltered when she

saw the look on Hawk's face as he gazed at his wife. He loved Adrienne as Esmerelda would have loved *him*; a wild, claiming, know-no-bounds kind of passion. With this realization, any compassion Esmerelda may have felt for Adrienne evaporated. She steadied the bow and took aim at Adrienne's breast. With a soft *whoosh*, the arrow flew free.

Esmerelda swallowed a frantic scream. At the last minute the Hawk turned, almost as if he saw her lurking in the shadows or sensed the arrow's flight. He moved. No!

✳   ✳   ✳

"Ummmph!" Adrienne gasped as Hawk flung one powerful arm across her face and thrust her against a tree.

Adrienne struggled against his back, but he was an immovable mountain. Was this how he intended to win her back? After weeks of careful restraint, was he taking her into the forest to rape her?

"Oooof!" His breath hissed out softly, and she pushed harder at his back. "What are you doing, Hawk?" she demanded, but still he said nothing.

Hawk shuddered, battling the pain as his eyes scanned the trees. He felt his strength ebbing, but he couldn't give in to the weakness yet. Not until he found and stopped whoever was trying to kill his wife. But the bushes were still. The assailant, for whatever reason, had fled. Hawk felt relief rush through him as blood gushed from his wound.

When he swayed and crumpled at Adrienne's feet, she screamed and screamed.

✳   ✳   ✳

In the shadows, Esmerelda pressed a fist to her mouth. She could feel Hawk's eyes searching the very spot in which she cowered, but the shadows were too dense for even his eyes to penetrate.

He turned, and in profile she could see the arrow, still vibrating from the force of flight, just above his heart. She closed her eyes and swallowed tightly. She'd killed him! The arrow was wickedly notched and would be impossible to remove without ripping open his chest. She had deliberately designed it to do even more damage in the removing than in the entering. Even if it didn't kill the victim going in, it would certainly kill him coming out.

Esmerelda melted to the forest floor and crawled through the underbrush until she was certain she was safe. Then she surged to her feet and ran blindly, her crossbow forgotten on the damp forest floor. Branches slapped her face. A scream gathered and clotted in her throat. Esmerelda swallowed a bitter sob as she leapt a fallen log.

A hand shot out lightning-quick, halting her abruptly. Adam pulled her to him with a biting grip on her neck.

"Where have you been, lovely whore?" His eyes were preternaturally bright.

She panted into his face.

Adam glowered and shook her cruelly. "I said, where have you been?"

When she still didn't answer, Adam slid his hand up her neck to her throat and squeezed. "Your life means nothing to me, Gypsy." His eyes were as icy as his voice.

Haltingly, Esmerelda told him everything, begging Adam to save the man she loved, to use his unnatural powers and restore his life.

So she knew his identity. He wasn't surprised. The Rom were well versed in the ancient ways. "If you know who I am, Gypsy whore, you know I don't give a damn about your wishes—or anyone else's, for that matter. And I certainly don't care about your pretty Hawk. In fact, the Hawk is the son of a bitch I came here to destroy."

Esmerelda paled.

"Come," he commanded. And she knew he didn't mean it the way he used to. Not anymore.

CHAPTER 20

"WHAT DO YOU MEAN HE DOESN'T WANT TO SEE ME? I WANT to see him, so let me in," Adrienne argued. "Unless, of course, he's given you orders that he specifically doesn't want *me* to come in the room," she added coolly. Hawk would never do that.

Grimm didn't budge.

"He wouldn't! You can't be serious. H-he . . ." She trailed off uncertainly. The Hawk wouldn't refuse. Well, he hadn't yet, but . . .

Obdurate Grimm, his eyes grave, blocked the door.

Adrienne peered at him intently. "Are you telling me that I have been forbidden to enter my husband's room?"

"I have my orders, milady."

"I'm his *wife*!"

"Well, maybe if you'd bloody acted like his wife before now he wouldn't be in there!" Grimm's eyes flashed angrily in his chiseled face.

"Oh!" Adrienne stepped back, startled by his fury.

"I did my friend a grievous wrong. I made a horrible wish that I would take back now with all my heart, if I only could. But I can't."

"*You're* the one who wished it!" Adrienne exclaimed.

Grimm continued, unwavering. "And had I known how terrible was the wish I made, how far-reaching and painful the consequences would be, I would have taken my own life first. I am no captain of the guard." He spat his disgust upon the cobbled stone. "I am no honorable friend. I am the lowest droppings from the foulest beast. I wished *you* upon my best friend, may the gods forgive me! And now he lies wounded by an arrow meant for you!"

Adrienne's eyes widened in her pale face. "I'm not so bad," she whispered.

"You, milady, are the iron maiden without a heart. You have brought him nothing but pain since you came here. In all my years with the Hawk, I have never seen such suffering in his eyes and I won't tolerate it even one more day. He would climb into the very heavens and pluck down the stars, one by one, to bestow upon your shining brow, and I tell him you are *not* worth it. You scoff at his romantic feelings, you shun his freely offered love, you scorn the man himself. Doona tell me you're not so bad, Adrienne de Simone. *You* are the worst thing that's ever happened to that man."

Adrienne bit her lip. Grimm had such a slanted view of things! What about all the unfair things the Hawk had done to her? She was the innocent one!

"He burned my queen! He stole my freedom, and he trapped me here."

"Because he cares for you and refuses to lose you! That's such a terrible thing? He used his own body to save your life. He placed himself like the truest shield before you and took the arrow meant for you. Well, I say better he had let it find your breast. 'Twould cease his torment and he wouldna be bleeding inside or out!"

"I didn't ask him to save me!" she protested.

"Just the point. You didn't *have* to ask him. He gave it freely. As he would give you everything. But you condemn him, though you know *nothing* of the mighty Hawk! Tell me, had you seen the arrow flying for him would you have sacrificed your life for his? I see from your eyes you would not. I'm sorry I wished for you and upon every star, every night for the rest of my worthless life, I'll be wishing to undo the wrong I've done. Now get out of my sight. The Hawk won't see you now. Perhaps not ever. And 'tis good for him not to. Perhaps in time away from you he'll heal in more ways than one."

Adrienne raised her head proudly and met his blazing eyes. She refused to show the pain that closed around her heart. "Tell him I thank him for protecting me. Tell him I'll be back tomorrow and the next day and the next, until he sees me and allows me to thank him myself."

"I'll tell him no such thing," Grimm said flatly. "You're no good for him and I won't be stringing him along in your game."

"Then at least tell him I'm sorry," she said softly. And she meant it.

"You doona have enough human compassion to feel sorrow, lass. Heart of ice in a body of flame. You're the worst kind. You bring a man nothing but a brief sip of sweetness, then a keg full of bitter dregs."

Adrienne said nothing before she fled down the dim corridor.

✳   ✳   ✳

"Where is she? Is she all right? Who's guarding her?" Hawk tossed restlessly in bed, kicking the coverlet off.

"She's fine, Hawk. Two guards arc outside the Peacock Room. She's sleeping." Grimm fidgeted with the bottle of whisky the healer had left on the table, then poured a generous dollop into his glass. He moved abruptly to stand beside the hearth.

Hawk watched Grimm curiously. His loyal friend seemed unusually tense—probably blaming himself for not being there to prevent the attack, Hawk decided. He studied his bandaged hand carefully. "She didn't ask about me, Grimm?"

The silence grew until the Hawk reluctantly dragged his gaze from his hand to Grimm's rigid profile. Whcn Grimm finally glanced up from the flames, the Hawk flinched at the sadness he read in every line of his best friend's face. "She didn't even ask if I was going to be all right? Where the arrow hit? Anything?" Hawk tried to keep his voice level but it broke harshly.

"I'm sorry." Grimm drained his glass and poked at the red-hot embers in the fireplace with the toe of his boot.

"Bloody hell, the lass is made of ice!"

"Rest, Hawk," Grimm spoke into the fire. "You've lost a lot of blood. You came too close to dying tonight. If you hadn't raised your hand in defense, the arrow would have taken out your heart rather than just pinning your hand to your chest."

Hawk shrugged. "A wee scratch on my chest—"

"Hell, a hole the size of a plum through the palm of your hand! The old healer had to pull the arrow *through* your hand to get it out. And you heard him yourself. Had it gotten lodged in your chest, which it should have but for uncanny luck, there would have been naught he could do to save you, cruelly notched as it was. You'll bear scars and pain in that hand for life."

Hawk sighed morosely. More scars and more pain. So what? She hadn't even bothered to see if he was alive. She could have at least pretended to be concerned. Visited briefly to maintain the pretense of civility. But no. She probably hoped he was dying, for with him out of the way she would be a very wealthy woman. Was she even now lying in the Peacock Room, counting her gold and her blessings?

"Not even one question, Grimm?" Hawk studied the silky hairs around the bandage that covered almost his entire hand.

"Not even one."

Hawk didn't ask again.

"Grimm, pack my satchel. Send half the guard and enough staff to ready the manor house in Uster. I leave at dawn. And quit poking at that blasted fire—it's too damned hot in here already."

Grimm dropped the poker to the stone hearth with a clatter. He turned stiffly from the fire and searched Hawk's face. "Are you going alone?"

"I just told you to ready half the guard."

"I meant, what about your wife?"

Hawk's gaze dropped back to his hand. He studied it for a moment, then glanced up at Grimm and said carefully, "I'm going alone. If she couldn't even be bothered to see if I lived or died, perhaps it's time I quit trying. At the very least, some distance may help me gain perspective."

Grimm nodded stiffly. "You're sure you can travel with that wound?"

"You know I heal quickly. I'll stop at the Rom camp and get some of the camomile and comfrey poultice they use—"

"But to ride?"

"I'll be fine, Grimm. Stop worrying. You're not responsible." Hawk didn't miss the bitter smile on Grimm's face. It comforted him somewhat to know that his friend was so loyal when his own wife couldn't be bothered to care if he was dead or alive. "You're a true friend, Grimm," Hawk said softly. He wasn't surprised when Grimm hurried from the room. In all the years he'd known him, words of praise had always made the man uncomfortable.

*   *   *

In the Peacock Room's massive bed, Adrienne tossed restlessly, maddeningly awake. At this moment she was quite certain she would never sleep again. Her mind would never find respite from the bitter, icy clarity that raged through her brain, recoloring her every action since she'd arrived at Dalkeith a vastly different hue.

*   *   *

Hawk and Grimm rode out as dawn rose over the lush fields of Dalkeith. Satisfaction surged through Hawk as he surveyed his home. With his years of service to the king finally at an end, he could at last see to the needs of his people and be the laird he was born to be. Now he wanted just one more thing—for Adrienne to truly be a wife to him in every sense of the word, to help govern Dalkeith by his side. More than anything he wanted to see their sons and daughters walk this land.

Hawk cursed himself for a hopeless romantic fool.

"The harvest will be rich this Samhain," Grimm remarked.

"Aye, that it will, Grimm. Adam." Hawk nodded curtly to the smithy, who was approaching, the field of gold parting for his dark form.

"You're leaving the game? You admit defeat, dread Hawk?" Adam gazed mockingly up.

"Don't goad the devil, smithy," Grimm warned tersely.

Adam laughed. "Bedevil the devil and devil be damned. I fear no devil and bow to no man. Besides, this concerns you not, or little at least—certainly not so much as you appear to think. You vastly overrate yourself, gruff Grimm." Adam held the Hawk's gaze, smiling. "Fear not, I will care for her in your absence."

"I won't let him near her, Hawk," Grimm hastened to assure him.

"Yes you will, Grimm," Hawk said carefully. "If she *asks* for him you will let him near her. Under no other circumstances."

Adam nodded smugly. "And ask she will. Again and again in that husky, sweet morning voice she has. And Grimm, you might tell her for me that I have coffee from the Rom for her."

"You will not tell her that!" Hawk snapped.

"Are you trying to limit my contact?"

"I did not agree to provide you with a messenger! Yet— what will be will surely be. My guard stands for her, but it's you I will look to if she comes to harm."

"You give her into my keeping?"

"Nay, but I will hold you responsible if harm should befall her."

"I would never let harm come to any woman of mine—and she is mine now, fool Hawk."

"Only in as much as she wants to be so," the Hawk said softly. *And if she does, I will kill both of you with my bare hands and rest easier at night, dead inside.*

"You are either impossibly cocky or incredibly stupid, dread Hawk," the smithy said with scorn. "You will return to find the flawless Adrienne in my arms. Already, she spends most afternoons with me in your gardens—soon she will spend them in my bed," Adam taunted.

The Hawk's jaw clenched, his body tensed for violence.

"She didn't ask for you, Hawk," Grimm reminded tonelessly, shuffling from foot to foot.

"She didn't ask for him, captain of the guard?" Adam asked brightly. "Captain of honor, captain of truth?"

Grimm flinched as Adam's dark gaze searched his. "Aye," he said tightly.

"What a tangled web we weave. . . ." Adam drawled slowly, the hint of a smile on his burnished face.

"What passes now between the two of you, Grimm?" Hawk asked.

"The smithy's a strange man," Grimm muttered.

"I would wish you Godspeed, but I believe God suffers little, if any, commerce with men such as us. So I wish you only a warrior's farewell. And never fear, I shall keep safe the lovely Adrienne," the smithy promised as he patted Hawk's stallion on the rump.

Shadows flickered behind the Hawk's eyes as he took his leave. "Watch her, Grimm. If there are any more attempts on her life, send word to me at Uster," he called over his shoulder as he rode away. His guards could keep her alive, in that he felt secure. But now there would be nothing to keep her from Adam.

As Grimm watched his best friend leave, Adam studied the stoic warrior. "She didn't ask for him?" he mocked softly.

"Who the hell are you, really?" Grimm snarled.

CHAPTER 21

"TRY A BIT MORE STEAMING WATER," LYDIA DECIDED, AND Tavis obliged.

They both peered into the pan. Lydia sighed. "Well, drat and blast it all!"

"Milady! Such language for a woman of your position, I'll say." Tavis rebuked.

"It certainly doesn't act like tea, does it, Tavis?"

"Nay, not a bit, I'll say, but still no reason for you to be unladylike about it."

Lydia snorted. "Only you, dear Tavis, dare criticize my manners."

" 'Tis because you're usually the spit of perfection, so it fashes me more than a wee bit when you sally."

"Well, stir it, Tavis! Don't just let it sit there."

Tavis flashed her a disgruntled look as he began to stir the mixture rapidly. "These talented hands were made for curing the richest hides in all of Scotia, not stirring a lady's drink, I'll say," he grumbled.

Lydia smiled at his words. How he went on about his talented hands! One would think they were made of purest gold instead of flesh, bone, and a few calluses. She glanced at him a pensive moment while he stirred the brew. Ever faithful Tavis by her side. Her mornings and afternoons wouldn't be quite so rich without the man. Her evenings, well, she'd spent her evenings alone for so many years that she scarcely noticed it anymore—or so she liked to believe.

"Why don't you marry?" she had asked Tavis twenty long years ago, when he'd still been a young man. But he had only smiled up at her as he'd knelt by the vats where he'd been soaking a deerskin to buttery softness.

"I have all I need here, Lydia." He spread his arms wide, as if he could sweep all of Dalkeith into his embrace. "Why would you be shooing me on?"

"But don't you want children, Tavis MacTarvitt?" she probed. "Sons to take over your tannery? Daughters to cherish?"

He shrugged. "The Hawk is like a son to me. I couldn't ask for a finer braw lad, I'll say. And now we've the two wee ones running about, and well . . . you're without a husband again, Lady Lydia . . ." He trailed off slowly, his strong hands rubbing and squeezing the hide in the salt mixture.

"And just what does my being without a husband have to do with *you*?"

Tavis cocked his head and gave her the patient, tender smile that sometimes swam up to linger in her mind just before she drifted off to sleep at night.

"Just that I'll always be here for you, Lydia. You can always count on Tavis of the tannery, and I'll say that a thousand times more." His eyes were level and deep with something she was unable to face. She had already lost two husbands to two wars and the sweet saints knew there was always another war coming.

But Tavis MacTarvitt, he always came back. Scarred and bloody, he always came back.

Back to stand in the kitchens with her while she dried her herbs and spices. Back to lend a helping hand now and again as she dug in her rich black soil and pruned her roses.

There were times when they both knelt in the dirt, their heads close together, that she'd feel a fluttery sensation in her belly. And times when she sat by the hearth in the kitchen and asked his help brushing out her long dark hair. He'd take the pins out first, then unsmooth her plaits one by one.

"Nothing's happening Lydia." Tavis's voice shattered her pensive reverie and forced her mind back to the present.

She shook herself sharply, dragging her thoughts back to the task at hand. Coffee. She wanted coffee for her daughter-in-law.

"Maybe it's like the black beans or dried peas and has to soak overnight," she worried as she rubbed the back of her neck. Nothing was going right this morning.

Lydia had woken early, thinking about the lovely lass who had so bedazzled her son. Thinking about how the situation must seem from *her* point of view. Calamity after calamity had struck since her arrival.

Which is why she'd gone to the buttery to retrieve quite a store of the shining black beans her daughter-in-law so coveted. The least she could do was find Adrienne a cup of coffee this morning before she told her that the Hawk had left for Uster at dawn. Or worse, the news Tavis had discovered a scant hour ago: that Esmerelda had been trying to kill Adrienne but was now dead herself.

So it had come to this . . . peering into a pan full of glistening black beans that were doing not much of anything in the steaming water.

"Maybe we should smash the beans, Lydia," Tavis said, leaning closer. So close that his lips were scant inches from hers when he said, "What think you?"

Lydia beamed. "Tavis, I think you just might have it. Get that mortar and pestle and let's get at it. This morning I'd really like to be able to start her day off with coffee." *She's going to need it.*

*   *   *

"It's getting out of hand, fool. A mortal lies dead," King Finnbheara snapped.

"Of her own race's hand. Not mine," Adam clarified.

"But if *you* hadn't been here, it would not have come to be. You are perilously close to destroying everything. If the Compact is ever broken, it will be by my Queen's choosing, not through your act of idiocy."

"You had a hand in this plan too, my liege." Adam reminded. "Furthermore, I have harmed no mortal. I merely pointed out to the Rom that I was displeased. It was they who took action."

"You split hairs quite neatly, but you're too close to rupturing the peace we've kept for two millennia. This was not part of the game. The woman must go back to her time." King Finnbheara waved a dismissive hand.

*   *   *

Adrienne was walking in the garden, thinking about the advantages of the sixteenth century and the serene bliss of unspoiled nature, when it happened. She suffered a horrid falling sensation, as if a great vortex had opened and a relentless whirlpool tugged her down. When she realized that she recognized the feeling, Adrienne opened her mouth to scream, but no sound came out. She'd felt this way just before she'd found herself on the Comyn's lap; as if her body were being stretched thin and yanked at an impossible speed through a yawning blackness.

Agonizing pressure built in her head, she clutched it with both hands and prayed fervently, *Oh, dear God, not again, please not again!*

The stretching sensation intensified, the throb in her temples swelled to a crescendo of pain, and just when she was convinced she would be ripped in two, it stopped.

For a moment she couldn't focus her eyes; dim shapes of furniture wavered and rippled in shades of gray. Then the world swam into focus and she gasped.

Adrienne stared in shock at the fluttering curtains of her own bedroom.

She shook her head to clear it and groaned at the waves of pain such a small movement caused.

"Bedroom?" she mumbled dumbly. Adrienne looked around in complete confusion. There was Moonshadow perched delicately upon the overstuffed bed in her customary way, little paws folded demurely over the wood footrail, staring back at her with an equally shocked expression on her feline face. Her lime golden eyes were rounded in surprise.

"Princess!"

Adrienne reached.

*　　*　　*

Adam quickly made a retrieving gesture with his hand and glared at his king. "She stays."

King Finnbheara snapped his fingers just as quickly. "And I said she goes!"

✳   ✳   ✳

Adrienne blinked and shook her head, hard. Was she back in Dalkeith's gardens? No, she was in her bedroom again.

This time, determined to get her hands on Moonie, Adrienne lunged for her, startling the already confused cat. Moonie's back arched like a horseshoe, her tiny whiskers bristled with indignation, and she leapt off the bed and fled the room on tiny winged paws.

Adrienne followed, hard on her heels. If by some quirk of fate she was to be given a second chance, she wanted one thing. To bring Moonshadow back to the sixteenth century with her.

✳   ✳   ✳

Adam snapped his fingers as well. "Do not think to change your mind midcourse. You agreed to this, my King. It wasn't just *my* idea."

✳   ✳   ✳

Adrienne groaned. She was in the gardens again.

It happened three more times in quick succession and each time she tried desperately to capture Moonie. A part of her mind protested that this simply couldn't be happening, but another part acknowledged that if it was, she was damn well going to get her precious cat.

On the last toss, she almost had the bewildered little kitten cornered in the kitchen, when Marie, her erstwhile housekeeper, selected that precise moment to enter the room.

"Eees that you, Mees de Simone?" Marie gasped, clutching the doorjamb.

Startled, Adrienne turned toward her voice.

The women gaped at each other. A thousand questions and concerns tumbled through Adrienne's mind; how much time had passed? Was her housekeeper Marie living in the house now? Had she taken Moonie for her shots? But she didn't ask because she didn't know how much longer she had.

Sensing a reprieve, Moonshadow bolted for the door. Adrienne lunged after her, and abruptly found herself once again in the garden, shaking from head to toe.

Adrienne moaned aloud.

She'd almost had her! *Just one more time,* she whispered. *Send me back one more time.*

Nothing.

Adrienne sank to a stone bench to spare her shaky legs and took several deep breaths.

Of all the nasty things to have to endure first thing in the morning. This was worse than a bad hair day. This was insult to injury on a no-coffee day.

She sat motionless and waited again, hopefully.

Nothing. Still in the gardens.

She shivered. It had been terrible, being tossed about like that, but at least now she knew Moonie was okay and that Marie obviously hadn't waited *too* long before moving to the big house from her room over the garage. And although Adrienne's head still ached from being tossed back and forth, there was comfort in her knowledge that her Moonshadow was not a little skeleton cat traipsing through a lonely house.

*   *   *

"I am your King. You will obey me, fool."

"I found the woman, therefore one might say I started this game, my liege. Allow me to finish it."

King Finnbheara hesitated, and Adam pounced on his indecision.

"My King, she rejects over and over again the man who pleased our Queen. She humiliates him."

The King pondered this a moment. *He claims a woman's soul,* his Queen had said dreamily. He had never seen such a look on Aoibheal's face in all their centuries together, unless he himself had put it there.

Fury simmered in the King's veins. He didn't want to withdraw from this game any more than Adam did—he'd watched and savored every moment of the Hawk's misery.

Finnbheara studied the fool intently. "Do you swear to honor the Compact?"

"Of course, my liege," Adam lied easily.

A mortal pleased my Queen, the King brooded. "She stays," he said decisively, and vanished.

CHAPTER 22

"WELCOME, MILORD." RUSHKA'S GREETING SOUNDED PLEAS-
ant enough, but Hawk felt a strange lack of warmth in it.
Smudges of black marked the olive skin beneath the old
man's tired eyes and they were pink-rimmed, either from
sitting too close to a smoky fire or from weeping. And
Hawk knew Rushka didn't weep.

Hawk stood in silence while the man ran a callused hand
through his black hair. It was liberally streaked with gray
and white, his craggy face handsome, yet equally marked
by time. Absentmindedly, the man began to plait his long
hair, staring into the dying embers as full morning broke
across the valley.

Brahir Mount towered above this vale, its outline smoky
blue and purple against the pale sky. Hawk dropped to a
seat atop one of the large stones near the circle-fire and
sat in silence, a trait that had endeared him to this tribe of
Gypsies.

A woman appeared and deposited two steaming cups before leaving the two men to sit in companionable silence.

The old Gypsy sipped at his brew thoughtfully, and only when it was gone did he meet the Hawk's gaze again.

"You don't like our coffee?" he asked, noticing the Hawk had left his drink untouched.

Hawk blinked. "Coffee?" He peered into his cup. The liquid was rich, black and steaming. It smelled bitter but inviting. He took a sip. "It's good," he declared thoughtfully. With a hint of cinnamon, topped with clotted cream, the drink would be delicious. No wonder she liked it.

"A lass, is it?" The old man smiled faintly.

"You always did see right through me, Rushka, my friend."

"I hear you've taken a wife."

The Hawk looked piercingly at his old friend. "Why didn't you come, Rushka? When she was ill, I sent for you."

"We were told 'twas Callabron. We have no cure for such a poison," the old man said. Rushka shifted his attention away from the Hawk's steady gaze.

"I would have thought you'd have come, if only to tell me that, Rushka."

The old man waved a hand dismissively. "Would have been a wasted trip. Besides, I was sure you had more pressing things to contend with. All aside, she was healed, and all's well that ends well, eh?"

The Hawk blinked. He'd never seen his friend behave so oddly. Usually Rushka was courteous and cheerful. But today there was a heaviness in the air so tangible that even breathing seemed a labor.

And Rushka wasn't talking. That in itself was an oddity.

Hawk sipped the coffee, his eyes lingering on a procession of people at the far end of the vale. If he wanted answers, he'd simply have to ask around his questions. "Why did you move out here, Rushka? You've camped in my north field by the rowans for years."

Rushka's gaze followed the Hawk's and a bitterness shadowed his brown eyes. "Did you come for Zeldie?" Rushka asked abruptly.

I can't handfast Zeldie, Hawk had told this man a decade ago when he'd been bound in service to his king. The Rom had desired a match and offered their most beautiful young woman. He'd explained that it simply wasn't possible for him to take a wife, and while Rushka had understood, Esmerelda hadn't. Zeldie, as they called her, had been so infuriated by his refusal that she'd quickly lain with man after man, shocking even her own liberal people. The Gypsies did not prize virginity—life was too short for abstinence of any sort, which was one of the reasons the people had seemed so intriguing to him as a young lad. He'd been ten when he'd secretly watched a dusky Gypsy girl with budding breasts and rosy nipples make love with a man. Two summers later she had come to him saying it was his turn. Ah, the things he'd learned from these people.

"Esmerelda and I have parted ways."

The old man nodded. "She said as much." Rushka spat into the dust at his feet. "Then she took up with *him.*"

"Who?" Hawk asked, knowing what the answer would be.

"We do not speak the name. He is employed on your land with the working of metals."

"Who is he?" Hawk pressed.

"You know the man I mean."

"Yes, but who is he, really?"

Rushka rubbed his forehead with a weary hand.

Yes, Hawk realized with amazement, Rushka had definitely been weeping.

"There are situations in which even the Rom will not do commerce, no matter how much gold is promised for services. Esmerelda was not always so wise. My people apologize, milord," Rushka said softly.

Had the entire world gone mad? Hawk wondered as he drained the last of his coffee. Rushka was making no sense at all. Suddenly, his old friend rose and whirled about to watch the the stream of gypsies trailing down to the valley.

"What's going on, Rushka?" Hawk asked, eying the odd procession. It looked like some kind of Rom ritual, but if it was, it was one Hawk had never seen.

"Esmerelda is dead. She goes to the sea."

Hawk surged to his feet. "The sea! That's the death for a *bruhdskar.* For one who has betrayed her own!"

"And so she did."

"But she was your daughter, Rushka. How?"

The old man's shoulders rocked forward, and Hawk could see his pain in every line of his body. "She tried three times to kill your lady," he said finally.

Hawk was stunned. "Esmerelda?"

"Thrice. By dart and by crossbow. The bandage you wear on your hand is our doing. If you ban us from your lands, we will never again darken your fields. We have betrayed your hospitality and made a mockery of your good will."

Esmerelda. It fit. Yet he could not hold the levelheaded, compassionate, and wise Rushka responsible for her actions. Nay, not him nor any of the Rom. "I would never seek to bar you from my lands; you may always come freely to Dalkeith-Upon-the-Sea. Her shame is not yours, Rushka."

"Ah, but it is. She thought with your new bride gone you would be free to wed her. She was a strange one, though she was my daughter. There were times when even I wondered at the dark thing in her heart. But he brought her to us last night, and by the moon she confessed. We had no choice but to act with the honor we owed to all . . . parties . . . involved."

And now the procession to the sea, with every man, woman, and child carrying white rowan crosses, carved and bound and brilliantly emblazoned with blue runes. "What manner of crosses are those, Rushka?" Hawk asked. In all his time with these people he'd never seen the like before.

Rushka stiffened. "One of our rituals in this kind of death."

"Rushka—"

"I care for you like my own, Hawk," Rushka said sharply.

Hawk was stunned into silence. Rushka rarely spoke of his feelings.

"For years you have opened your home to my people. You have given with generosity, treated us with dignity and withheld censure, even though our ways are different from yours. You have celebrated with us and allowed us to be who we are." Rushka paused and smiled faintly. "You are a rare man, Hawk. For these reasons I must say this much, and the risk to my race be damned. Beware. The veil is thin and the time and place are too near here. Beware, for it would seem you are at the very core of it somehow. Take great care with those you love and no matter what you do, do not leave them alone for long. There is safety in numbers when this is upon us—"

"When what is upon us, Rushka? Be specific! How can I fight something I don't understand?"

"I can say no more, my friend. Just this: Until the feast of the Blessed Dead, keep close and closer those you love. And far and farther those for whom you can't account.

Nay." Rushka raised a hand to stop the Hawk even as he opened his mouth to demand more complete answers. "If you care for my people, you will not visit us again until we celebrate the sacred Samhain. Oh," Rushka added as an afterthought, "the old woman said to tell you the black queen is not what she seems. Does this mean something to you?"

The only black queen that came to mind was now scattered ashes in the forge. Hawk shook his head. The old woman was their seer, and with her far-reaching vision she had inspired awe in Hawk as a young lad. "Nay. Did she say more?"

"Only that you'd be needing this." Rushka offered a packet bound with leather cord. "The camomile poultice you came for." He turned back to the procession. "I must go. I am to head the walk to the sea. Beware, and guard thee well, friend. I hope to see you and all your loved ones at the Samhain."

Hawk watched in silence as Rushka joined the funeral walk for his daughter.

When one of the Rom betrayed the rules by which they lived, he or she was disciplined by their own. It was a tight-knit community. Wild they could be, and liberal-minded about many things. But there were rules by which they lived, and those rules were never to be mocked.

Esmerelda had disregarded one of great importance—those who gave shelter to the Rom were not to be harmed in any manner. By trying to kill the Hawk's wife, she had attempted to harm the Laird of Dalkeith himself. But there was something else, the Hawk could sense it. Something Rushka wasn't telling him. Something else Esmerelda had done that had brought strife upon her people.

As Hawk watched the procession wind toward the sea,

he whispered a Rom benediction for the daughter of his friend.

Easing himself back down by the fire, Hawk unwrapped the bandage and cleansed his wounded hand with Scotch and water. Carefully, he untied the leather pouch and wondered curiously at the assortment of stoppered flasks that fell out. He picked up the poultice and laid it to the side, sorting through the rest.

Just what had the seer seen? he wondered grimly. For she'd given him two other potions, one of which he'd sworn to never use again.

Hawk snorted. One was an aphrodisiac he'd tried in his younger days. That one didn't worry him too much. The one he despised was the potion that had been created to keep a man in a prolonged but detached state of sexual arousal.

He turned the flask with the vile green liquid in it this way and that, watching the sun reflect off the faceted prisms of the stoppered bottle. Shadows rose up and taunted him openly for a time, until his obdurate will banished them back to hell. Quickly he spread the poultice, which eased the pain and would speed recovery. In a fortnight his hand would be well knit.

Adam. Although he hadn't outright said it, Rushka had insinuated that it was Adam who had brought Esmerelda to them last night. Which meant Adam knew Esmerelda had been trying to kill Adrienne.

What else did Adam know?

And just what had made his friend Rushka, who had never once shown terror in all the thirty-odd years Hawk had known him, betray visible fear now?

Too many questions and not enough answers. Every one pointed an accusing finger toward the smithy, who even now was probably trying to seduce Hawk's wife.

*My wife who doesn't want me. My wife who wants Adam.
My wife who didn't care enough to even ask about me when
I was wounded.*

Esmerelda was dead, but Rushka had made it clear that
the real threat was still there, and close enough to Dalkeith
to drive the Rom away. Apparently, Adam was involved.
And he'd left his wife in the thick of it. *Keep close and
closer . . .*

The Hawk's mind whirred, sorting the scarce facts and
hunting for the most feasible solution to his myriad problems. Suddenly the answer seemed impossibly clear. He
snorted, unable to believe he hadn't thought of it before.
But the lass had a way of getting so far under his skin that
his mind didn't work in its usual logical fashion with her in
the vicinity. No longer! It was time to take control, rather
than allowing circumstances to continue to run amok.

His pact with Adam entailed that he could not forbid
Adrienne to see the smithy. But he could make it damned dif-
ficult for her to do so. He would take her to Uster with him.
Far away from the mysterious, compelling Adam Black.

So what if she hadn't asked about him? She'd made it
clear from day one that she didn't want to be wed to him.
She had vowed to hate him forever, yet he would swear her
body responded to his. He'd have her all to himself in Uster
and be able to test that theory.

Just when had he become passive? *When you felt guilty
for burning her queen,* his conscience reminded. *Trapping
her here, in spite of her wishes, if she is indeed from the future.* But guilt was for losers and fools. Not for Sidheach
Douglas. There was no guilt involved when she was at
stake. "I love her," he told the wind. "And so I've become
the greatest kind of fool."

A *nice* one.

Time to remedy that. Guilt and passivity dropped away from him in that clarifying instant. The Hawk who turned his steed around and headed for Dalkeith-Upon-the-Sea to claim his wife was the true namesake of the Sidheach of yore, the Viking conqueror who had run ramshod over any who dared oppose him. *I commit, I attain, I prevail.*

He leapt to his mount and spurred his charger into a full run. *Seel and jess, my sweet falcon,* he promised with a dark smile.

*   *   *

Beneath a bough of rowans, Adam stiffened. Not fair! Not fair! Get thee hence! But fair or not, he'd seen true. The Hawk had turned around and was coming back to take Adrienne away with him. That was simply unacceptable. He obviously had to do something drastic.

*   *   *

"How could this be?" Lydia paced the kitchen, a flurry of claret-colored damask and concern.

"I don't have any idea, Lydia. One minute I was in the gardens and the next thing I knew I was in my bedroom back in my own time."

"Your own time," Lydia echoed softly.

Adrienne met her gaze levelly. "Almost five hundred years from now."

Lydia cocked her head and fell still, as if having a brisk internal debate with herself. The silence stretched into a protracted length of time while she pondered the limits of her beliefs. Lydia had always thought that women were more open-minded and adaptable than men when it came to inexplicable happenings. Perhaps it was because women experienced firsthand the incomprehensible and astonishing miracle of childbirth. To a woman who could create life inside her own body, why, time travel seemed like a minor miracle in comparison. But men . . . men were always trying to find a rational explanation for things.

When the Hawk had told her what strange news Grimm had discovered at Comyn keep, Lydia had studied Adrienne closely, watching for any signs of instability or peculiar behavior. Through her close observation, she had only become more convinced that Adrienne was just as sane as a person could be. She had concluded that while something had hurt Adrienne deeply in her past, whatever had hurt her had far from weakened her mind—Adrienne had been strengthened by it, like tempered steel. Oh, Lydia knew there was a very lonely young woman behind some of Adrienne's caustic humor and sometimes cool façade, but Lydia had found that stern walls most often guarded a treasure, and a treasure her daughter-in-law was indeed. Lydia cared for her enormously and had every intention of having grandchildren from her son and this lovely young woman.

The idea that the entire Comyn clan was suffering some strange madness didn't make sense. Lydia knew Althea Comyn well from time spent at court together, years past. She was a practical, worldly-wise woman, and although over the years Althea had grown more reclusive, she still remained pragmatic and levelheaded.

Lydia had long suspected the Laird Comyn of acts of twisted violence. Could she believe he had killed his own daughter in an act of senseless violence? Easily. He'd had his youngest son slaughtered like a lamb to the sacrifice for crossing clan lines and taking up with one of the Bruce's grandnieces.

Through all of the Red Comyn's acts of twisted and petty vengeances, Althea Comyn had managed the aftermath to the continued benefit of her clan. She was an extraordinary woman, holding her children and grandchildren together with sheer will and determination.

And so to Lydia, the thought of the pragmatic Lady Comyn suffering a fit of fantasy was more difficult to believe than the possibility of time travel. Simply put, Althea Comyn was too much a cold realist to indulge in any nonsense.

Having reached her conclusions, Lydia smiled gently at Adrienne, who had been waiting in tense silence. "Hawk told me what Lady Comyn said, Adrienne. That you're not her daughter. That you appeared out of thin air. Indeed, I have heard your brogue ebb and flow like a stormy, unpredictable tide."

Adrienne was momentarily chagrined. "You have?"

Lydia snorted. "When you were ill your burr disappeared entirely, my dear."

Adrienne blinked. "Why didn't anybody ever ask me about it?"

"In case you haven't noticed, things haven't been exactly calm since you've come to Dalkeith. Not a day has passed that hasn't brought new surprises Murder attempts, unwelcome visitors, not to mention the Hawk behaving like a besotted lad. Besides, I hoped that one day you would confide in me of your own choosing. Now, the guards tell me they watched you disappear and reappear several times before their very eyes." Lydia rubbed her palms against the skirt of her dress, a far-off expression in her eyes. "From the future," she murmured softly. "My son believed it was some trauma that made you believe such madness and yet . . ."

"And yet what?" Adrienne urged.

Lydia met Adrienne's clear steady eyes. They stared at each other a long, searching moment.

Finally Lydia said, "Nay. Not a hint of madness in that gaze."

"I'm from another time, Lydia. I'm not mad."

"I believe you, Adrienne," Lydia said simply.

"You do?" Adrienne practically yelped. "Why?"

"Does it really matter? Suffice it to say, I am convinced. And when things finally return to normal around here, if they ever do, I want you to tell me all about it. Your time. I have many questions, but they will wait. For now, there are things we must be clear on." Lydia's brow furrowed in thought. "How did you get here, Adrienne?"

"I don't know." Adrienne shrugged helplessly. "Truly, I have no idea."

"The Hawk thought it was the black queen. The Lady Comyn said it was bewitched."

"I thought it was too."

"So it never was the black queen . . . hmmm. Adrienne, we must be absolutely clear on this. Exactly what were you doing at the moment when it happened?"

"The first time, when I wound up at the Comyn keep? Or this time?"

"This time," Lydia said. "Although we should investigate the first time as well, and look for similarities."

"Well . . . I was walking in the gardens and I was thinking about the twentieth century. I was thinking about how much—"

"You wanted to leave," Lydia finished for her, with a trace of bitterness.

Adrienne was equally surprised and touched. "No. Actually I was thinking about how nice it is here. In the 1990s, my God, Lydia, people were just out of control! Children killing parents. Parents killing children. Children killing children. They've all got cell phones stuck to their ears and yet I've never seen such distance between people trying so hard to be close. And just the day before I left you should have seen the headlines in the papers. A boy strangled a little girl when she wouldn't get off the phone and let him use it. Oh, I was thinking bitter thoughts of that time and comparing it to home and home was definitely winning."

"Say that again?" Lydia uttered softly.

"What?" Adrienne asked blankly. "Oh, headlines, papers, they're—" she started to explain, but Lydia cut her off.

"Home." Lydia's face lit with a beautiful smile. "You called this home."

Adrienne blinked. "I did?"

The two women looked at each other a long moment.

"Well, by the Sanhain, Lydia, give her the coffee, I'll say." Tavis's gruff voice came from the door. "Popping in and out like that, surely she's got a thirst on."

"Coffee?" Adrienne perked.

"Ah." Lydia smiled, pleased with herself and doubly delighted with her daughter-in-law who had called Dalkeith-Upon-the-Sea home without even realizing it. She quickly filled a porcelain mug with the steaming brew and placed it proudly on the table in front of her.

Adrienne's nose twitched as her taste buds kicked up a sprightly jig and she reached greedily for the mug. She closed her eyes, breathed deeply, and drank.

And choked.

Tavis pounded her on the back and looked accusingly at Lydia. "I told you!" he said.

When Adrienne could breathe again, she wiped the tears from her eyes and peered suspiciously in her cup. "Oh, Lydia! You don't leave the coffee grounds—no, not grounds quite . . . more like a paste, I think. What did you do? Mush the beans and mix them with water? Ugh!"

"Didn't I tell you to run it through a sieve?" Tavis reminded. "Would you want to drink it like that?"

"Well, with all the hubbub I forgot!" Lydia snatched the mug. "Since you're so certain you know how to do it, you do it!" She thrust the mug at Tavis, sloshing thick brown stuff on the floor.

"Fine. See if I don't, I'll say!" With a supercilious look he made off for the buttery.

Lydia sighed. "Adrienne, I know it hasn't been a very good morning so far. I so wanted to have coffee for you, but in lieu of coffee, how about a cup of tea and a chat?"

"Uh-oh," Adrienne said. "I know that look, Lydia. What's wrong? Besides my being tossed through time portals?"

"Tea?" Lydia evaded.

"Talk," Adrienne said warily.

How best to start this? Lydia was determined to hide nothing from her. Lies and half-truths had a nasty way of reproducing and breeding distrust. If Adrienne could see the Hawk clearly, the truth would hopefully not do damage; but lies, somewhere down the line, assuredly would. "Esmerelda is dead."

"I'm so sorry," Adrienne offered instantly. "But who's Esmerelda?"

"The Hawk's . . . er . . . well, ex-mistress probably explains it the best—"

"You mean in addition to Olivia? And where was he keeping *her*, by the way? In the dungeon? The tower? The room next to mine?"

Lydia winced. "It's not like that, Adrienne. He'd ended it with her months before you came. She lived with the Rom who camp on our fields in the warm seasons. According to what her people told Tavis this morning, she's the one who had been trying to kill you. The good news is, you're safe now."

"Haven't I been saying it all along? I told you it was probably one of *that man's* ex-girlfriends, didn't I? Oh!" She leapt to her feet.

"Adrienne."

"What now?"

Oh, bother, Lydia brooded. *Well buck up,* she told herself, knowing from the look on Adrienne's face that she was just spoiling for a good fight with the Hawk, and that she would be mad as a spitting banshee when she realized she couldn't get one. "Hawk left for Uster at dawn."

"For how long?" Adrienne gritted.

"He didn't say. Adrienne! Wait! We need to sort out what brought you here!" But Adrienne was no longer listening.

Lydia sighed as Adrienne stormed from the kitchen mumbling nonstop under her breath, "Arrogant pigheaded pain-in-the-ass Neanderthal . . ."

CHAPTER 23

JUST WHAT *IS YOUR PROBLEM, ADRIENNE DE SIMONE*? SHE asked herself furiously.

She shrugged and sighed before forlornly advising a nearby rosebush, "I seem to have a bit of a thing for the man."

The rosebush nodded sagely in the soft summer breeze and Adrienne willingly poured the whole of it upon her rapt audience.

"I know he's been with a lot of women. But he's not like Eberhard. Of course, probably there's nobody like Eberhard except maybe a five-headed monster from the jaws of hell."

When the rosebush didn't accuse her of being melodramatic or waxing poetical, she summoned up a truly pitiful sigh and continued. "I can't understand a blasted thing about the man. First he wants me—I mean, come on, he burned my queen to keep me here, which didn't really work apparently, but the intention was there. He saves my life repeatedly even though it was kind of indirectly his fault it was in danger to begin with, and then he refuses to see me. And if that's not enough, he just up and leaves without so much as a fare-thee-well!"

Adrienne plucked irritably at the rosebush.

"I don't think he quite understands the full necessity of clear and timely communication. Timely meaning *now*. Where exactly *is* Uster, anyway?" She fully considered trying to find a horse and go there herself. How dare he just up and abandon her? Not that she minded entirely being where she was—Dalkeith-Upon-the-Sea was certainly lovely, but what if she got zipped back to her own time for good and never saw him again?

Damned if that didn't put things in an entirely different perspective. A few soldiers of the war raging within her breast got up and traitorously switched camp on the heels of that thought.

How had she failed to realize that she could disappear and never see the man she was married to again? That she had no control over it whatsoever? Twenty more soldiers marched over to the Hawk's side of the fracas raging inside her. Holy cow.

Don't you wonder, Adrienne, what it would feel like to lie down next to him in the sizzling heat of magnificent passion?

Okay. She had one soldier left on her side and his name was Mr. Suspicious N. Fearful.

Traitors! She frowned at the Hawk's new camp. Just thinking about him made her feel hot. She trailed her fingers in the fountain's sparkling, chemical-free water.

She couldn't imagine never seeing this beautiful fountain again, never smelling the lavender virgin air of 1513. No Lydia, no Tavis. No castle by the sea. No Laird Hawk, man of steel and blazing passion. Just Seattle and bitter memories and fear keeping her inside her house. The 1990s, bargain packaged with smog and ozone holes.

She doubted Hawk would ever try to send her on vacations alone. He seemed to be the kind of man who would treasure his wife and keep her close to his side if the woman allowed it. Close to that beautifully muscled side, and under that kilt . . .

"Dream a wicked dream," she sighed softly. Adrienne squeezed her eyes tightly shut and dropped her head in her hands. A long eternity of questions tumbled through her head, and slowly but surely Adrienne helped the last little soldier to his feet, dusted him off, and let him lean on her as she walked him over to the other side of the war. She had made her decision. She would try.

She raised her head from her hands slowly to meet Adam's piercing gaze. How long had he been standing there watching her with worship in his eyes. Dark eyes, black as hate. *Now where had that come from?*

"You hate the Hawk, don't you, Adam?" she asked in a flash of crystal-clear intuition.

He smiled appreciatively. "You women are like that. Cut to the quick of it with a canny eye. But hate attaches a great deal of importance to its predicate," he mocked as he dropped himself beside her on the ledge.

"Don't play word games with me, Adam. Answer my question."

"This would please you? Honesty from a man?"

"Yes."

He shrugged a beautiful, sun-kissed shoulder. "I hate the Hawk."

"Why?" Adrienne asked indignantly.

"He's a fool. He fails to cede appropriate due to your beauty, Beauty."

"To my *what*?" The *least* important thing about her.

The smithy flashed a blinding smile. "He seeks but to spread them, to slip between your thighs, but those love-slick dewy petals *I* would immortalize."

Adrienne stiffened. "That's very poetic, but there's no need to be rude, Adam. And you don't even know me."

"I can think of nothing I'd rather do with my time than spend it knowing you. In the biblical sense, since you find my other references too graphic. Is that pretty enough for you?"

"Who are you?"

"I can be anyone you want me to be."

"But who are *you*?" she repeated stubbornly.

"I am the man you've needed all your life. I can give you whatever you wish before you even realize you're wishing for it. I can fill your every longing, heal your every wound, right your every wrong. You have enemies? Not with me at your side. You have hunger? I will find the most succulent, ripe morsel and feed you with my bare hands. You have pain? I will ease it. Bad dreams? I will chase them asunder. Regrets? I will go back and undo them. Command me, Beauty, and I am yours."

Adrienne shot him a withering look. "The only regrets I have are all centered around beautiful men. So I suggest you get yourself out of my—"

"You find me beautiful?"

Something about this man's eyes was just not quite right. "Aesthetically speaking," she clarified.

"As beautiful as the Hawk?"

Adrienne paused. She could be cutting at times, but when push came to shove it was her nature to go out of her way not to hurt people's feelings. Adrienne preferred to maintain her silence when her opinion was not the answer sought, and in this case, her silence was answer enough.

Adam's jaw tightened.

"As beautiful as the Hawk?"

"Men are different. You can't compare apples to oranges."

"I'm not asking you to. I'm asking you to compare a man to a man. The Hawk and myself," he growled.

"Adam, I am not getting into this with you. You're trying to force me to say something—"

"I am only requesting a fair answer."

"Why is this so important to you? Why do you even care?"

His mood changed, quicksilver. "Give me a chance, Beauty. You said aesthetically I please. You can't truly compare men until you've tasted the pleasure they can give you. Lie with me Beauty. Let me—"

"Stop it!"

"When you watched me forge the metal it made you burn." Adam's intense black eyes bored into hers, penetrating and deep. He claimed her hand and turned it palm up to his lips.

"Yes, but that was before I saw—" She broke off quickly.

"The Hawk," Adam spit out bitterly. "Hawk the magnificent. Hawk the living legend. Hawk the seductive bastard. Hawk—the king's whore. Remember?"

She gazed sadly at him. "Stop it, Adam," she finally said.

"Have you bedded him?"

"That's none of your business! And let go of my hand!" She tried to tug her hand out of his grasp, but his grip tightened and as his fingers caressed her wrist she felt confusion assail her senses.

"Answer me, Beauty. Have you lain with the Hawk?"

She swallowed tightly. *I won't answer him,* she vowed stubbornly even as her lips murmured, "No."

"Then the game still plays, Beauty and I have yet to win. Forget the Hawk. Think of Adam," he crooned as he claimed her lips in a brutal kiss.

Adrienne seemed to sink deeper and deeper into a murky sea that made her want to curl up and pull into herself.

"Adam. Say it, Beauty. Cry for me."

Where was the Hawk when she needed him? "H-h-hawk," she whispered against Adam's punishing mouth.

Enraged, Adam forced her head back until she met his furious gaze. As Adrienne watched, Adam's dark features seemed to shimmer strangely, changing . . . but that wasn't possible, she assured herself. Adam's dark eyes suddenly seemed to have the Hawk's flecks of gold, Adam's lower lip suddenly curved in Hawk's sensual invitation.

"Is this what I must do to have you, Beauty?" Adam asked bitterly.

Adrienne stared in horrified fascination. Adam's face was melting and redefining, and he looked more like her husband with every passing instant.

"Must I resort to such artifice? Is it the only way you'll have me?"

Adrienne extended a shaking hand to touch his oddly morphing face. "A-adam, s-stop it!"

"Does this make you burn, Beauty? If I wear his face, his hands? For I will, if it does!"

You're dreaming, she told herself. *You've fallen asleep, and you're having a really, really bad nightmare, but it will pass.*

Adam's hands were on her breasts and fingers of icy fire shivered a column of exquisite sensation through her spine . . . but it was not pleasure.

✳   ✳   ✳

A dozen paces away the Hawk froze, mid-step, after barreling up the long bridge to the gardens. Line by line, muscle by muscle, his face became a mask of fury and pain.

How long had he been gone? A dozen hours? Half a day?

The wound he'd taken while saving her life burned angrily in his hand as his desire for her throbbed angrily beneath his kilt.

He forced himself to watch a long moment, to seal permanently upon his mind just what kind of fool he was to want this lass. To love her even as she betrayed him.

The smithy's hard, bronzed body stretched the length of his wife's sultry curves as they lounged on the fountain's edge. His hands were twined in her silvery-blond mane and his mouth was locked on his wife's yielding lips.

Hawk watched as she whimpered, hands frantic against the smithy in her need . . . as she pulled at his hair, frantically clawed at his shoulders.

Grass and flowers ripped from the fragrant earth beneath his boot as Hawk turned away.

✳   ✳   ✳

Adrienne struggled for her sanity. "Go . . . back t-to whatever hell . . . from whence y-you c-c-came . . ." The words took every ounce of energy she still possessed and left her gasping limply for air.

The groping hands abruptly released her.

She fell off the ledge and landed in the fountain with a splash.

The cool water swept away the thick confusion instantly. She cringed in terror, waiting for the smithy's hand to reach in for her, but nothing happened.

"A-Adam?"

A breath of puckish wind teased her chilled nipples through the thin material of her gown. "Oh!" she covered them hastily with her palms.

"A-Adam?" She called, a little stronger. No answer.

"Who are you, really?" she yelled furiously into the empty morning.

CHAPTER 24

IN HER DEPRESSION, ADRIENNE CONSIDERED NOT EATING. SHE wondered if they had cigarettes in 1513, reconsidered, and decided to eat instead.

Until she found the Scotch.

About time, she mused as she sat in his study and propped her feet on his desk. She poured a healthy dollop of the whisky into a cut-crystal tumbler and took a burning swallow. "Och," she said to the desk thoughtfully, "but they do brew a fine blend, doona they?"

She spent the rest of the afternoon and evening in his sacred haven, hiding from the strange smithy's advances, Lydia's abiding concern, and her own heartache. She read his books as she watched the misty rain that started while she drained the tumbler of Scotch. He had fine taste in books, she thought. She could fall in love with a man who liked to read.

Later, when she rummaged through his desk, she told

herself she had every right because she *was* his wife, after all. Letters to friends, from friends, to his mother while he'd been away sat neatly ribboned in a box.

Adrienne picked through the drawers, finding miniatures of the Hawk's sister and brother. She discovered boyhood treasures that warmed her heart: a leather ball with often-repaired stitching, cunningly carved statues of animals, rocks and trinkets.

By her second glass of Scotch she was liking him entirely too much. *Enough Scotch, Adrienne, and it's long past time to eat something.*

On unsteady legs she'd made her way to the Greathall.

✳   ✳   ✳

"Wife." The voice held no warmth.

Adrienne flinched and gasped. She spun around and found herself face-to-face with the Hawk. But he'd gone to Uster, hadn't he? Apparently not. Her heart soared. She was ready to try, but something in his gaze unnerved her and she hadn't the foggiest notion why. She narrowed her eyes and peered at him intently. "You look downright cantankerous," she said. She emitted a squeak of fear when he lunged for her. "Wh-what are you doing, Hawk?"

His hands closed about her wrists with steely possession as he used his powerful body to force her back against the cool stone of the corridor.

"Hawk, what—"

"Silence, lass."

Wide-eyed, she stared into his face, searching for some clue that would explain the icy hostility in his eyes.

He forced his muscular leg between her thighs, cruelly pushing them apart. "You've been drinking, lass."

His breath was warm on her face, she could smell the

potent stench of alcohol. "So? So have you! And I thought you were in Uster!"

His beautiful lips contorted in a bitter smile. "Aye, I'm quite aware that you thought I was in Uster, wife." His brogue rasped thickly, betraying the extent of his rage.

"Well, I don't see why you're so angry with me! *You're* the one who's had nine million mistresses, and *you're* the one who left without saying goodbye, and *you're* the one who wouldn't—"

"What's good for the gander is not necessarily good for the goose," he snarled. He twined his hand in her hair and yanked her back sharply, baring the pale arch of her throat. "Neither in spirit consumption nor in lovers, wife."

"What?" He wasn't making any sense, talking about farm animals when she was trying to have a reasonably sober conversation with him. She gasped when he bit her gently at the base of her neck where her pulse pounded erratically. If she couldn't handle this man sober, she certainly couldn't handle him tipsy.

With excruciating leisure, he traced his tongue down her neck and across the upper curves of her breasts. Her mouth went dry and an entire flock of twittering birds took wing in her belly.

"You wanton," he breathed against her flawless skin.

Adrienne moaned softly, partly in pain from his words and partly in pleasure from his touch.

"Faithless, cruel beauty, what did I do to deserve this?"

"What did *I* do—"

"No!" he thundered. "No words. I will suffer no honeyed lies from that sweet snake's lair you call a mouth. Aye, lass, you have the most cruel of poisons. Better I had let the dart take you, or the arrow. I was a fool to suffer one moment of pain on your account."

I'm dreaming again? she wondered. But she knew she wasn't because never in a dream had she been so aware of every inch of her own body, her traitorous body that begged to get closer to this angry man who dripped sex appeal, even in his fury.

"Tell me what he has to give you that I don't have! Tell me what you hunger for in that man. And after I've shown you every inch of what I have to give you, then you can tell me if you still think he has more than I."

"The smithy?" she asked incredulously.

He ignored her question completely. "I should have done this long ago. You are *my* wife. You will share *my* bed. You will bear *my* children. And most assuredly, by the time I'm done with you, you will never say that word again. I told you the Hawk's rules once. Now I'm reminding you for the last time. *Smithy* and *Adam* are two words that you will never say to me. If you do, I will punish you so innovatively and cruelly that you'll wish you'd never been born."

The words were spoken with such white-hot yet carefully controlled anger that Adrienne didn't even begin to question what punishment he might have in mind. She knew instinctively that she never wanted to find out. As she parted her lips to speak, Hawk rubbed his body against hers, intimately pressing his hard cock between her thighs. The words she'd planned to say were exhaled instead as a soft *whoosh* of air that tapered into a husky moan. Adrienne wanted to melt against him, to arch herself into his body with complete abandon. She couldn't even stand next to this man without wanting him.

His smile was mocking and cruel. "Does he feel like this, lass? Does he have this much to pleasure you with?"

No man has that, she thought feverishly, as her hips

moved hungrily against him. Hawk growled softly, closing his mouth over hers in a ruthless, punishing kiss.

Adrienne felt his hand, raising her skirt and realized that in his current rage the Hawk was going to take her, right here in the dim and chill hallway. Tipsy or not, this was not how Adrienne planned to part with her hard-kept virginity. She wanted him, but not like this. Never like this. "Stop! Hawk, whatever you think I've done—I haven't!" she cried.

He silenced her with his mouth, his kiss hot, hungry, and cruel. She understood he was punishing her with his body, not making love to her, but she couldn't resist his tongue and couldn't prevent herself from breathlessly kissing him back.

Hawk dropped his head and grazed her neck with his teeth, then teased her hardened nipples through her gown. Adrienne was so lost in pleasure that she didn't realize what he was doing until it was too late.

She felt the rasp of a rope against her wrists as he yanked her arms down and spun her around, securing her hands at the base of her back.

"You son of a bitch!" she hissed.

"Son of a bitch," he repeated thoughtfully. "Now you don't like my mother?"

"I don't like *you* when you're like this! Hawk! Why are you doing this? What have I done?"

"Silence, lass," he commanded softly, and she learned then that when his voice was soft and supple as oiled leather was when she was in the most extreme danger. It was the first of many lessons he would teach her. When the silken hood slid down over her face she screamed her fury and lashed out against him with her feet. Struggling, kicking, raging in his arms, she cursed raggedly.

"Wife," he said right against her ear through the silk hood, "you belong to me. Soon you will not remember that there was ever a time when you didn't."

✳   ✳   ✳

Adam stood amidst the shadow of the rowans and watched as the Hawk stalked through the night, the hooded woman fighting his grasp. So he thought he could escape Adam Black, did he? Hawk thought he could take her away? Clever. Adam hadn't negotiated that point. Hawk had obviously decided to play cutting-edge close to the letter of their law.

The man was becoming downright infuriating.

No, this was not what Adam had expected at all when he'd staged his scene in the gardens.

So, the man was more brute than he had thought. He had vastly underestimated his opponent. He'd thought the Hawk was too decent and too *nice* to know when a man had to be as hard and unforgiving as steel with a woman. He'd counted on the noble Hawk being so wounded by seeing her with the smithy that he'd curse her and swear her off, maybe divorce her—any of which, according to his plan, would send her scurrying to his blazing forge at the rowans. He'd thought, quite mistakenly it seemed, that the Hawk had at least one or two weaknesses of character.

"Silence, wife!" The Hawk's baritone resonated in the darkness. Adam shuddered. No mortal should have such a voice.

Well, this just wouldn't do. He'd have to seriously intervene, because if such a man carried off a woman and kept her for a time, the woman would surely belong to him when he was through.

And Adam never lost at anything. Certainly not this.

He stepped forward from the shadows, prepared to confront the Hawk, when he heard a harsh whisper behind him.

"Fool!"

"What now?" Adam snarled, turning to face King
Finnbheara.

"The Queen demands your presence."

"Now?"

"Right now. She's on to us. I think it's that snoopy little
Aine again. You'll have to leave this game at least long
enough to allay the Queen's suspicions. Come."

"I can't come *now.*"

"You have no choice. She will come for you herself if
you don't. And then we'll have no chance left at all."

Adam stood still a long moment, allowing his rage to
burn through him and leave cinders of resolve in its wake.
He had to be very careful where his Queen was concerned.
It would do him no good to bar her whim or will in any
manner.

He allowed himself one long look over his shoulder at
the retreating figure on horseback. "Very well, my liege.
Through this rotten hell, bar my will, pledged to none but
the *fairest* queen, lead on."

CHAPTER 25

SHE STOPPED SCREAMING ONLY WHEN HER VOICE GAVE OUT. *Stupid*, she told herself. *What did that accomplish? Not a thing. You're trussed up like a chicken about to be plucked and now you can't even peep a protest.*

"Just take the hood off, Hawk," she begged in a gravelly whisper. "Please?"

"Rule number nine. My name from this moment forward is Sidheach. *Sidheach,* not Hawk. When you use it, you will be rewarded. When you don't, I will permit no quarter."

"Why do you want me to use that name?"

"So I know you understand who I really am. Not the legendary Hawk. The man. Sidheach James Lyon Douglas. Your husband."

"Who first called you Hawk?" she asked hoarsely.

He stifled a swift oath and she felt his fingers at her throat. "Who first called me Hawk doesn't make the difference. Everyone did. But 'twas all the king ever called me," he gritted. He didn't add that in all his life he had never given a lass leave to call him Sidheach. Not one.

He untied the hood and lifted it from her face, then poured cool water into her mouth, relieving some of the burning that made her voice so rough. "Try not to scream anymore tonight, lass. Your throat will bleed."

"King James used only that name?" she asked swiftly.

Another sigh. "Yes."

"Why?"

She could feel his body tense behind her. "Because he said I was his own captive hawk, and it was true. He controlled me for fifteen years as surely as a falconer controls his bird."

"My God, what did he *do* to you?" she whispered, horrified at the icy depths in his voice when he spoke of his service. The Hawk controlled by another? Incomprehensible. But if the threat of destruction of Dalkeith, his mother, and his siblings had been held over his head? The threat of killing the hundreds of his clanspeople? What would the noble Hawk have done to prevent that?

The answer came easily. Her strong, wise, ethical husband would have done whatever he had to do. Any other man the Hawk would have simply killed. But one couldn't kill the King of Scotland. Not without having his clan's existence completely eradicated by the king's army. Same result, no choice. A sentence of fifteen years, all because of a scorned and spoiled king.

"Can't you just accept me as I am now, lass? It's over. I'm free." His voice was so low and resonant with anguish that she froze. His words threw her off balance; it was something she might have said herself if confronted with her past by someone she cared for. Her husband understood pain, and perhaps shame and, oh so surely, regret. What right had she to judge and condemn a person for a dark past? If she were honest with herself, she would even point out that her past had been the result of her own naive mistakes, where his painful ordeal had been one he'd been forced to endure to keep safe his clan and his family.

She wanted to touch and heal the man who sat so stiffly away from her now, yet she was not quite sure how to begin. This much was clear—he hadn't been the king's whore, whatever that was, because he'd wanted to; that fact went a long way toward easing her mind. More than anything, she wanted to understand this fierce, proud man. To brush away the shadows in his beautiful dark eyes. She jerked swiftly when she felt silk graze her jaw.

"No! Don't put the hood back on me. Please."

Hawk ignored her protests, and she sighed as he retied the cords.

"Will you just tell me why?"

"Why what?"

"Why are you 'seeing' me now?" What had she done to provoke his anger?

"I stepped back, lass. I gave you what no other man would have given you. I allowed you the time to choose me of your own will. But it seems your will is wildly foolish and needs persuading. Choose me, you will. And when you do, there will be no other man's name on your lips, no other man's shaft between your thighs, no other man's face in your mind's eye."

"But—" She wanted to know why her time had so suddenly run out. What had made him snap?

"No buts. No more words, lass, unless you would have me bind your mouth as well. From this time forward you see without the benefit of those beautiful, lying eyes. Perhaps

I'm not a complete fool. Perhaps you might see true with your inner vision. Then again, perhaps not. But your first lesson is that what I look like has nothing to do with who I am. Who I might have had to be in the past has nothing to do with who I am. When you finally see me clearly, then and only then will you see with your eyes again."

*   *   *

They arrived in Uster shortly after dawn. Pushing his horse hard through the night, Hawk turned a two-day journey into less than one.

He guided her into the laird's residence, past the gawking staff, up the stairs and to the bedroom. Without a word, he cut the bonds on her wrists with a dagger, pushed her to the bed, locking the door behind him as he left.

*   *   *

The instant Adrienne's hands were free she ripped off the silken hood. She'd been prepared to shred it into tiny silken tatters but realized he'd probably just use something else if she destroyed it. Besides, she mused, she had no intention of fighting him. She had enough of a battle on her hands trying to face her own emotions; let him do what he felt he needed to do. It granted her more time to grow familiar with the new feelings inside her. Dear heaven, but he was angry with her. Just what he was angry about she wasn't certain, but her resolve was still true. In the face of his fury, her soldiers had not changed their minds. They all stood proudly on the Hawk's side, and she was with them to a man.

He planned to seduce her callously? To open her inner vision to him?

He didn't need to know that it had already been opened, and that she shamelessly anticipated every moment of the seducing.

$$* \quad * \quad *$$

The Hawk walked slowly through the streets of Uster. It was nearly deserted at this late hour, only those of courage, abject stupidity, or evil intent walked the streets late at night when a heavy fog was roiling in. He wondered into which category he fell.

Much had been begun this day, yet even more remained unfinished. He'd spent most of his morning going over the miller's books and talking with angry villagers who accused the man of substituting their grain. There was only one miller, so positioned by the king's men before Hawk had been released from his pledge of service. Being the only one, he had been able to exert absolute control over the villager's grain and had, in collusion with the local bailiff, indeed been cheating on weights, substituting moldy meal for better grains, and turning a tidy profit three towns northerly.

Hawk sighed. That had been only the first of a dozen problems demanding his attention. He would have to hold the courts for a fortnight to catch up on all that had gone wrong under his benign neglect while he had been off in service to James.

But he had time to remedy the villagers' many ills, and remedy them he would. His people had been well pleased to have him back and once again taking an interest in their needs. As of this day, three men in Uster now held miller's tools and miller's rights. The Hawk smiled. Competition would be good for his people.

Tansy and mint swirled out the door of an open establishment as he passed by. A woman beckoned from the doorway, clad only in a filmy bit of stained and tattered silk. The Hawk cocked an amused brow and smiled, but declined as he continued down the street. His eyes turned dark and bitter. He had more than he could handle waiting for him at home.

* * *

Adrienne sat up with a start when she heard the Hawk throw open the door to her chamber. She had been imagining the sweet seduction he had in store for her and had to use all her composure to hide her excitement at his return.

"Oh, you're back," she drawled, hoping she had succeeded in masking her delight.

He crossed the room in two awesome strides, took her in his arms, and frowned darkly down at her. He lowered his head inexorably toward her lips, and she turned her face away. Undeterred, he grazed her neck with his teeth until he reached the base where her traitorous pulse beat raggedly. Her breath caught in her throat as he nipped her and ran his tongue up the column of her neck. If his very nearness made her shiver, his kisses would be her complete undoing. His rough shadow beard chafed her skin when he tugged her head back and gently nipped the lobe of her ear. Adrienne sighed her pleasure, then added a little squeal of protest just to be convincing.

"You will forget the smithy, lass," he promised. A swift yank of her hair forced her to meet his gaze.

"I had no intention of remembering him anyway. He's nothing more than a pushy, overbearing, liberty-taking scoundrel."

"Nice try, wife," Hawk said dryly.

"What do you mean, nice try? Why are you so obsessed with the smithy?"

"*Me?* You're the one who's obsessed with the smithy!" He raised the hood toward her head.

"You are so thickheaded you don't even see the truth when it's right in front of you."

"Oh, but that's just the point, lass. I saw the truth clearly with my own eyes that day in the garden. Aye, too clearly, and the memory of it seethes in my mind, mocking me. I had just been wounded saving your fickle life, but you had no care for that. Nay, you had other sweet plans in the making. And my absence only made it easier for you. Gone from your side for all of a few hours and so quickly you lay beneath him on the fountain. *My* fountain. *My* wife."

So that was it, she mused. He'd returned and seen the smithy when he'd been doing those foggy frightening things to her, when she'd been fighting him. He'd been standing there watching the smithy practically rape her and, in his mind, believed she was willing. He hadn't even thought to help her.

"Perhaps I'm not the only one who can't see so clearly," she said scathingly. "Perhaps there are two in this room who could benefit from a little inner vision."

"What say you, lass?" Hawk said softly.

She would not dignify his stupidity with a response. A man had practically raped her, and in his jealousy her husband had simply watched. The more she protested her innocence, the guiltier she would look. And the more she thought about it, the angrier it made her. "I merely suggest you find that inner eye yourself, husband," she said, just as softly.

Her quiet dignity gave him pause. No mewling or lying or groveling. No justifications. Could it be he had misunderstood what he had seen on the fountain? Perhaps. But he would erase her memories of the smithy, that he vowed.

He smiled darkly and seeled her with the silken hood again. Yes, by the time he was finished she would forget Adam Black even existed.

That he knew he could do. He'd been trained for it. First by the Gypsies and then by the Duchess of Courtland. "Sex is not merely a momentary pleasure," she'd instructed him. "It is an art to be practiced with studied hand and discriminating taste. I am going to school you in this, the finest of forays into human scandal. You will be the best lover the land has ever known by the time I am done. Easily, for there is no question that you are the most beautiful."

And the lessons had begun. She'd been right—there had indeed been much he hadn't known. And she showed him, this spot here, that curve there, this way of moving, a thousand positions, the subtle ways to use his body to bring many different kinds of pleasure, and finally, all the mind games that went with it.

He learned well, committing this art to memory. And in time, his eager boyish hunger was lost adrift a meaningless sea of conquests and mistresses.

Oh, he was the best, no question about it. He left the lasses begging for his attention. The legend of the Hawk grew. Then one day, a woman whom Hawk had spurned repeatedly—Olivia Dumont—petitioned King James for his favors as if he were a piece of property to be granted.

And like royal property, James had granted him, wielding the same threat of harm to Dalkeith should he disobey.

How James had loved that—especially when he realized how much the Hawk had been humiliated by it. And so the king had said, *you will be whoever We want you to be, even if it's a thing so trivial as Our whore, to please Our favored ladies*. Other men were sent to battle. The Hawk was sent to bed with Olivia. Doubly humiliating.

Many men had envied the Hawk—the lover of so many beautiful women. Still more men had hated the Hawk for his prowess and virility, and for the legends the ladies wove about him.

Eventually, James had grown tired of hearing the legends. Sick of his ladies clamoring about the beautiful man, James had sent the Hawk abroad on absurd and risky missions. To steal a crown jewel from Persia. To beguile a priceless objet d'art from an old heiress in Rome. Whatever odd treasure the greedy James had heard of, the Hawk was sent to acquire by fair means or foul. The king's whore had been simply that: a man who did the king's "dirty work," whatsoever his fickle liege wished at the time.

Now his eyes returned to the lass standing in silence before him.

She was so different from any he'd ever known. From the first day he'd seen her, he'd recognized that she was truly without artifice or coy subterfuge. Although she might have hidden depths, they were neither malicious nor self-serving but had been born of suffering and loneliness, not of deceit. He'd recognized that she had a pure heart, as pure and real and full of possibility as his Gypsy fields had been, and that it had already been given to a man who was undeserving! To the epitome of deceit and strange artifice. To Adam Black.

By hook or crook or whatever fashion was necessary, he would woo and win her. He would make her see the error of her ways—that she'd given her heart to the wrong man.

She was seeled both from him and to him, until she learned to see again with that pure heart which had recoiled into hiding. He would wake it, shake it up, and force it to come out and face the world again. And when she'd learned to see him for what he really was, then she could see him with her eyes again.

Adrienne stood stock-still and uncertain. It was strange, knowing he was in the room but not knowing where or what he was doing. He could be standing in front of her even now, his body nude and glistening in the oil lights. She imagined him lit by the soft glow of candles. She loved the fires and torchères of this century. What kind of romance could live and breathe beneath fluorescent lights of her own time?

She regretted the hood as it deprived her of seeing him, but decided that was for the best. If she could see him, that meant he could see her eyes, and they would surely betray her fascination, if not her willingness.

She felt the whisper of a breeze. Was he to her left? No, her right.

"The first time is for erasing all your memories of another man."

He was circling round her. Her heart thundered. With any other man, being unable to see would have felt threatening, but not with the Hawk. For despite his fury, he had proven himself to be honorable to the core. She knew that although he'd seeled her, he had done so in an attempt to win her love and trust—not to dominate or subdue her. There was nothing threatening in the fact that he'd closed her eyes to him; he'd opened her heart with his silken hood. Her lack of vision heightened all her other senses to an exquisite state.

When his hand caressed the column of her neck, she swallowed a sigh of pleasure.

Hawk continued circling her; to her side, then to her back, and, in what seemed like an eternity later, around to her front. Her ears strained for clues, her body vibrated with tension, wondering, waiting.

"The second time will be for teaching. Teaching you how it feels to be loved by a man such as me. 'Tis a thing you'll never forget."

His breath fanned the nape of her neck, his fingers picked up a fall of her hair. She could hear only ragged breathing—his or hers, she wasn't certain. She stiffened at the brush of his hand against the curve of her hip, feeling a wild jolt of electricity charge through her body.

"The third time will be for the jessing and leashing. I promise you that time will be the end of your resistance."

He trailed his fingers down her neck, across her breasts from nipple to nipple, then down over her taut stomach. His light caress feathered between her legs and was gone, leaving behind an aching hunger.

"But the fourth time, ah, the fourth time when I hear your sweet cries, that one's for me, lass. For the waiting and the hunger and the agony of wanting you. Just for me."

His hands were on her shoulders, sliding the silk of the gown over her skin. Undoing tiny pearl buttons at the nape of her neck one by one with something that felt like . . . teeth? Oh! His tongue flickered against the sensitive skin at the nape of her neck then moved lower still.

Oh dear heavens but this sensuous stroke of his tongue could be her complete undoing. The rough velvet of his tongue traced its way all the way down her spine, then lower still. She trembled.

Her knees weak, she swayed in silence. Can't make a sound, she reminded herself. Not a good sound, anyway. Only protests.

Just when she was certain she couldn't maintain her silence a second longer, he stepped back, and she felt a slow breeze in his wake. She turned, attempting to track him in the silence.

The back of her gown was open, her skin damp from his kisses. She waited in mute anticipation. *Where was he?*

There, she thought as she suddenly felt him grasp the fabric of her dress. He tugged her gown and it fell to the floor in a rustle of silk. The chemise fell next, and then there was nothing but stockings, lace stays, and slippers.

Hawk was grateful she was seeled, that she couldn't see the tremor in his hands as he slid to his knees and removed one stocking slowly, rolling it down inch by inch as he knelt before her. He trailed reverent kisses down her long, silky leg. From her supple thigh to the back of her knee to her trim ankle, he lavished her legs, first one, then the other, with hot kisses, making certain he didn't miss one delectable inch of the creamy flesh he'd been dying to taste.

She made not a whimper, but he understood her game. Hating him as she did, she would surely not utter one sound of pleasure unless he could rip it from her throat. And to do that he must keep a clear head. He must not lose control and start thinking about those shimmering curls at the sweet juncture of her thighs, only inches from his mouth, or the silken nub that nestled within, the very center of her passion. From his position at her feet he reveled in every plane and curve of her perfect body. His eyes skimmed over her firm thighs, up her taut, slightly rounded belly, over her creamy breasts to the alabaster column of her neck where it met the black silk hood.

Adrienne knew that if something didn't happen fast, her legs were going to simply buckle beneath her and she would fall on his face. *Not a bad idea,* her mind offered. She was shocked. Aghast. But maybe . . .

She swayed forward slightly.

Hawk groaned as her shimmering curls brushed his unshaven cheek. Kneeling at her feet, he squeezed his eyes
shut to banish the vision, the need, unaware that his tongue
wet his lip and his mouth demanded . . .

Shaking, he growled and surged to his feet, and then his
hands were on her body and he knew he was in serious trouble. *Where the hell had the Hawk gone?* he wondered as
he tumbled her roughly back to the bed. Where was the
Lothario? That legendary master of control who was going
to tease her beyond endurance and shatter her defenses?
Just where the hell had his will gone? *What will?* he wondered, for he was lost in a green field of innocence more
sweet and lush than any he'd ever known.

Adrienne moaned when his body covered hers, pressing
her down into the soft bed. He was every inch a hot, demanding man. *Oh, heavenly,* the woman within her purred.
Take me, she wanted to cry. But not that easily, she wouldn't
give in too quickly.

In a swift motion the Hawk ripped the hood off her head
and kissed her, burying his hands in her hair. He kissed her
so deeply that she lost her breath and the last remnants of
her fear.

She'd kissed a few men before. More than a few. Timid
kisses, passionate kisses. Eberhard kisses that had left her
cold. A man didn't kiss like *this* unless he was very deeply
in love.

He loved her. The awareness trembled in her, just under
the top layer of her skin, then seeped deeper, penetrating
fully. How magnificent, to know he loved her so much. No
question about it. He was cradling her face with his strong
hands as if she were the most precious thing in the universe. She opened her eyes and met his troubled gaze, trying to say with her silvery silence all that she really felt,

because she couldn't say the words. She didn't know how. No practice.

When he shifted her beneath him and his hard arousal rode between her legs she did it, made all that sound she'd sworn she wasn't going to. Practically roared. So this was it. This was what made people crazy with passion and longing and hunger. This was what Shakespeare had known at some time in his life to write *Romeo and Juliet*, to pen such sweet verses of love. This is what the Hawk had meant by Valhalla.

She arched up against him, the muscles deep within her on fire, burning for something, aching and empty.

"Ari," he breathed as he dropped his head to suckle one nipple into his mouth. He kissed and tugged and tortured it. He released the tightened crest and blew cool air on the heated tip. Nipped it lightly, then rubbed his rough, shadow beard gently across it. A flash of fire erupted in her, radiating outward from her breasts and flooding her entire body with waves of desire.

He scattered kisses lower, trailing across her stomach, the curve of her hips, her thighs. When he paused directly above her honeyed heat, his mere breath fanning her sensitive skin was sheer torture.

A heartbeat turned into a dozen, and she waited, frozen, for his next caress.

When it came, she whimpered softly. He dropped kisses on the satiny insides of her legs, then tasted the very center of her hunger. When his tongue flickered out, stroking her tiny, taut nub repeatedly, she cried out and her body quivered against him. She felt herself reaching, soaring for something just beyond her reach and then . . . oh!

How was it that she'd never experienced anything like this before? The Hawk flung her to the starlit heavens and spun her out between the planets, slid her down the Milky Way and through a star going supernova. Rocked her universe from end to end of its solar system. And when he finally, gently let her come back down, she shuddered beneath him with agony and ecstasy, knowing she would never be the same. Something had woken up inside her and blinked pale eyes, unaccustomed to the blinding brightness and stunning intensity of this new world.

She lay, panting and a little bit frightened, but ready. Ready to truly and completely give herself to her husband and make their marriage soar as she knew it could. Ready to try to begin to tell him the things she felt for him. How much she really admired his sensitivity and compassion. How much she adored his strength and fearlessness. How much she even cherished his brash and passionate rages. How glad she was to be his wife. "Hawk—"

"Ari, Ari . . . I . . . no. I don't . . ." His face was fierce and wild, and she reached for him. But she missed.

Because the Hawk stiffened with a roar of agony and leapt from the bed. Leapt from her, and practically ran from the room without looking back.

The room fell silent except for the click of a lock.

Adrienne stared in total confusion at the door.

This was like being bedded in roses and waking up in the mud.

How could he just up and leave her after *that*?

CHAPTER 26

SIDHEACH JAMES LYON DOUGLAS DOES NOT SHAKE, HE RE-
minded himself. Does not lose control. Does not almost
start mooning about like some lovesick boy just because he
gives a lass the orgasm of her life. He hadn't missed that.

But it wasn't the orgasm. Not even the way she'd shuddered against him, or how beautiful she'd looked as she'd
panted, love-slicked, beneath his tongue.

It was that he'd been about to do something he'd never
done in all his life—lose his seed outside of a lass. That and
more, it was that he loved her and she still hadn't said his
name. Not even in the apex of her passion had she cried
his name. Nothing. For all he knew, she could have been
thinking of Adam. It was part of why he'd had to pull the
damned hood off her. The hood had seemed a good idea at
the start, but it just had to go.

The next time he loved her, he'd have her eyes open and
seeing him from start to finish, and finish it he would. His

throbbing shaft would not be able to handle that torture again.

But he didn't want to give her his seed until he knew she belonged to him. Didn't want the possibility of not knowing whose child she might bear.

And then he recalled the flask that the old Rom had given him. He considered it thoughtfully, wondering if now was the time to use the potion it contained.

He may as well, he mused, although he hated the side effects. The way it would leave him cold and remote in the middle of the greatest passion he'd ever known.

✳   ✳   ✳

The next time he came to her was in silence, from beginning to end.

A scarce quarter of an hour before, he'd grimaced as he'd pulled out the stopper with his teeth. He had sworn never to take the potion again, but this time it was necessary. He had to make her want him, to bind her to him with desire so he could start working on making her love him. And he needed a clear head to do it.

Last night he'd almost made a fool of himself. He'd certainly lost control. Come close to spilling on her with both body and heart; foolish words of love and seed and hope for babies and a lifetime together.

So he tossed his head back and swallowed the bottle's bitter contents, and waited.

When he could feel its eerie fingers unfurling through his body, only then did he go to her.

He stripped her bare and guided her to the floor. She made no move to stop him; she remained mute, with an unfathomable expression in her eyes. It was mute fascination, but he didn't know that. Her eyes lovingly wandered over every inch of his body when he looked anywhere besides her face. She marveled at the sensation of cool floor to her back and hot man to her front, but he seemed somehow different this time as with his hands and his mouth he brought her to that shining place in the sky not once but a half-dozen times. Perfectly skilled, almost frighteningly controlled, while she lay aching beneath him.

She didn't like it one bit.

When he turned away from her, she felt somehow cheated. As if he hadn't really been there with her at all. So what if he pleasured her well? She wanted the same sun glowing in his eyes, the same uncontrollable, wild passion that burned white-hot between them.

"Hawk!" she called to his back.

He stiffened and paused a long moment. Muscles bunched in his shoulders and back. He seemed so untouchable.

"Oh. Never mind . . ." she said softly, her eyes luminous and brimming with hurt.

*   *   *

Hours later the Hawk rinsed his mouth for the fifth time and spat into a basin. Well, that had been a disaster of epic proportions. It had hurt him more than it had helped him. The potion had kept up his enormous erection and not allowed him to spill anything.

Was there such a thing as a fire that froze?

He would never take that potion again. Not with his wife.

When he'd finally gotten the foul taste of it out of his mouth, he dressed and headed for the village gathering hall to hear more cases. More decisions and more people with needs he must see to. And all the while he knew he'd be wondering if he, who ruled numerous manors, villages, keeps, and men, was ever going to be able simply to make his own wife say his name.

Sidheach.

That's all he wanted.

*   *   *

Adrienne paced the room restlessly. What had happened this afternoon? She felt dirty, as if she'd been touched too intimately by a stranger, not been made love to by her husband. Not like the night before when she'd seen that look in his eyes, that warmth and tenderness along with the epic desire. He'd been detached somehow this afternoon. When he'd returned to their room to dress before he'd left again, he'd still been eerily distant. Had he done something, taken some drug to make him . . .?

Those flasks she'd seen. Lying in a leather pouch on the bed table last night.

Her jaw jutted as she stomped to the bed table. Not there.

Where had he put them? Her eyes flew to the clothes he'd dropped in the chair when he'd changed this afternoon. Rummaging through the pile, she found what she sought and dumped the little leather pouch. One empty, a full one left. Ha! That and the healing poultice he'd been using when he changed the bandage on his hand.

An empty flask. Hmmph! Well two could play that game, and he'd rue the day he left the other one just lying about. Wait until he saw just how cold she could be!

*   *   *

When the Hawk returned to the manor that night, he was unequivocally convinced he must have gone to the wrong house. His wife was waiting for him in the locked bedroom, completely nude, with a wild look in her eyes that made him quite certain he was dreaming, or lost or mad.

"Hawk," she purred as she glided to him.

"Adrienne?" he asked warily.

His wife was so damned beautiful. And for an instant he didn't care why she was acting this way. He was sick of the waiting and tired of the wanting. So he swung her up into his arms and kissed her, his hot mouth moving over hers hungrily.

Then he saw the flask lying on the floor by the bed, looking as if it had been dropped shortly after consumption.

Hawk blew out a breath of frustration and allowed himself one more longing look at his wife's flushed cheeks, her magnificent breasts, and curves that went on forever. One glance at her darkly dilated eyes and her pouty mouth, plum-ripe and begging to be kissed.

"Lass, did you take that potion?" he said wearily.

"Uh-hmm," she drawled as she reached for his lips hungrily.

He dumped her on the bed with a thump. The aphrodisiac. He figured it should last about twelve hours before he could be certain she was back to her normal shrewish self.

It would serve her right for him to just take her right now, honor be damned, he thought darkly.

Unfortunately there were no circumstances under which honor could be damned. Not even when his throbbing shaft was making him wonder how the hell honor had anything to do with tupping his own wife.

Oh, she would surely want to kill him the next time she saw him.

He locked the door and stationed four guards outside it,

telling them he'd kill any one of them who went in that room for any reason during the next twelve hours.

Then the legendary Hawk sat down on the stairs to wait it out.

✳   ✳   ✳

The next time he came to her, she was indeed furious. "What was in that flask?" she raged.

Hawk couldn't help but smile. He tried to duck his head before she saw it, but failed.

"Oh! You think it's funny, do you? I'll have you know that you left me in here for a whole night thinking . . . oh my God! You have no idea how much I needed—"

"Not me, lass." His eyes were dark. "It was not me you needed. You took a bit of an aphrodisiac the Rom brew. I had no intention of giving it to you or using it myself. I didn't even ask them for it. And you snooped—"

"You took a potion to make yourself cold to me!" she shouted. "You hurt me!"

Hawk stared. "Hurt you? Never! I would not hurt you, lass."

"Well, you did!" Her eyes were wide and luminous and her lip trembled.

He was at her side in an instant. "How did I hurt you? Only tell me, and I will make it up to you."

"You were cold. You touched me and it was like you were a stranger."

Hawk's heart sang. Desire coursed through him in hot waves. She liked his touch.

"You like my touch?" he breathed before stealing a kiss from her pouty lips.

"Not when you do it like you did yesterday!" There was a furrow of consternation between her lovely brows and he kissed it away. "Besides, being that you wanted to bed me, why didn't you just take advantage of it when I was so willing?" she sighed as he traced soft kisses across her eyelids and her lashes fluttered closed. His lips were warm and infinitely tender as he kissed the tip of her nose, then not quite so tender when he claimed her mouth with his.

"When I love you, 'twill not be because some drug has intoxicated you, but because you are intoxicated with me, as surely as I am bewitched by you."

"Oh," she breathed as he unbound her hair and let it tumble free down her shoulders.

"Why did you bind it?" He combed his fingers through her heavy mane.

"That potion was terrible. Even my own hair rubbing against my skin was too much to bear."

" 'Tis too much for me to bear, this mane of yours," Hawk said, playing it gently through his fingers. His eyes turned hooded, darkly heavy with sensual promise. "You have no idea how often I imagined the feel of this silvery-gold fire spread across my shaft, lass."

Desire enveloped Adrienne as she pondered the image his words conjured.

He backed her slowly toward the bed, encouraged by the haze of desire in her wide eyes.

"The thought interests you, lass?" he purred smugly.

She swallowed hard.

"You have only to tell me, whisper to me what pleases you. I will give you it all."

She gathered her courage. "Then kiss me, husband. Kiss me here . . . and here . . . oooh!" He obeyed so quickly. His lips were hot, silky and demanding. "And here . . ." She lost her voice completely when he slid her gown from her body and tumbled her to the bed beneath him.

"I want to pull the drapes around this bed and keep you in here for a year," he mumbled against the smooth skin of her breast.

" 'S'all right, with me," she mumbled in response.

"Aren't you supposed to be fighting me, lass?" Hawk drew back and studied her intently.

"Um . . ."

"Yes, do go on," he encouraged. He knew his eyes must be dancing with joy. He knew he must have an absolutely absurd expression on his face right now. Was it possible? The taming had begun and was working?

"Just touch me." She wrinkled her brow. "Don't ask me so many questions about it!"

He rumbled with soft laughter and promise of infinite passion. "Oh, I'll touch you, lass."

*   *   *

"Too deep. You're in too far."

"I don't know what you mean."

"I've given it thought, fool. We must end this. Queen Aoibheal is on to us. Even your time by her side has not allayed her suspicions. I, for one, do not wish to suffer the consequences of her wrath. The woman is simply going to have to return to her time."

King Finnbheara waved his hand.

*   *   *

And the Hawk collapsed onto the bed. Stunned, he looked around the empty room.

Adrienne fell to the floor of her modern kitchen with a thud.

*   *   *

"Did you see what I saw?" King Finnbheara gasped.

Adam was stunned. "She was nude. He was panting. She was—oh shit!"

The King nodded emphatically as they both gestured. *"She stays."*

It was one of the golden rules. Some things could never be interrupted.

*   *   *

"You really are from the future, aren't you?" Hawk whispered hoarsely, when Adrienne reappeared scant moments later, a few feet away from him on the bed. While Adrienne had been drinking in his study, Lydia had told him of the disappearance in the garden. The Hawk had tried to convince himself that Lydia was mistaken, but his guards had confirmed that they'd watched his wife disappear and reappear several times in quick succession.

So, she could still return to her own time, even without the chess piece. *The black queen is not what she seems.* The seer had spoken true.

Adrienne nodded, still dazed by her abrupt transfer through time. "And I can't control it! I don't know when it's going to happen again!" Her fingers flexed convulsively on the woolen coverlet as if a tight grip might prevent her from being taken again.

"By the saints," he breathed slowly. "The future. Another time. A time which hasn't happened yet."

They stared at each other, dumbstruck, for a prolonged moment. His raven eyes were deep with shadows, the beautiful golden flecks extinguished completely.

Suddenly Adrienne realized all too clearly that she *never* wanted to go back to the twentieth century. She didn't want to be without him for the rest of her life! Desperation curled cold fingers around her heart.

It was already too late. How she loved him! The abruptness with which she had been reminded that she had no control over how much longer she could stay; the knowledge that she might be shuttled back, never to return; the fact that she had no idea how, or if, she could come again by herself terrified her.

To be consigned, no, *condemned,* back to that cold and empty twentieth-century world, knowing that the man she would love for eternity had died almost five hundred years before she'd even been born, oh dear God, *anything* but that.

Awestruck by her realizations, she gazed at him, her lips parted, openly vulnerable.

Hawk sensed the change in her; some kind of wordless admission had just occurred in that part of Adrienne he'd been trying to reach for so long. She was gazing at him with the same unfettered expression he'd seen that night on the cliffs of Dalkeith when she'd wished on a star.

It was all Hawk needed to see. He was on her in an instant. His awareness that she could be ripped from him at any moment made time infinitely precious. The present was all they had, and there were no guarantees for tomorrow.

He claimed her body, raining down upon her a storm of unleashed passion. He kissed and tasted, desperate with fear that any instant her lips might be torn from his. Adrienne kissed him back with complete abandon. Heat flared between them as it should have, as it would have from the very beginning had she permitted herself to dare to believe such passion, such love was possible.

Falling back on the bed, she melted beneath him. She wrapped her arms around his neck and pulled his hungry head closer.

"Love me . . . oh, love me," she whispered.

"Always," he promised into her wide-open eyes. He cupped her breasts and lavished them with kisses, savoring how wildly she responded to him. This time was different. She was really seeing *him*, Sidheach, not some other man she'd had before, and hope exploded in his heart. Was she coming to crave him as he did her? Could it be his wife was developing a hunger for him that matched his own appetite?

"Oh, please . . ." Her head arched back against the pillows. "Please . . ." she breathed.

"Do you want me, Adrienne?"

"Yes. With every ounce of my body . . ." *and soul* she was going to add, but he claimed her mouth with deep, hot kisses.

She wanted him, eyes open and seeing him. He could tell, this time it was real.

When her hand closed around his engorged phallus, a groan ripped from his throat.

"I saw you, you know," she whispered, her eyes dilated and dark with passion. "In the Green Lady's room. You were lying flat on your back."

He stared at her in mute fascination, the muscles in his neck working furiously as he struggled to say something intelligible, anything, but only a husky purr came out as her hand tightened on him. So, she had watched him too? As he had spied on her every chance he got?

"You were lying there in your sleep like some Viking god, and that's the first time I saw this." She squeezed her hand gently for emphasis. He growled. Emboldened by his response, Adrienne pushed him back and scattered kisses across his sculpted chest. She ran her hungry tongue down over his abdomen, tasting each defined ripple in turn. She explored his powerful thighs and throbbing manhood, pausing to drop a tantalizing kiss on the velvety pink tip of the shaft a stallion would have envied.

"Did you find it passing . . . fair?" he croaked, "what you saw then, and see now?"

"Ummm . . ." She pretended to ponder his question, then licked a long, velvety stroke up his shaft from base to tip. "It'll do in a pinch."

He tossed his dark head back with a smile and roared. "A pinch . . . a pinch? I'll show you . . ." His words trailed off as he pulled her roughly into his embrace. His mouth claimed hers and he rolled her onto her back.

Too late to pull back or worry about seed or children, far beyond rational thought of any kind, and adrift in a musky madness named Adrienne, the siren witch who owned him, he slid between her legs and positioned himself above her.

Just before he ceded to her beckoning heat, he said, "I have always loved you, lass." Quietly and regally.

Tears shimmered in her eyes and rolled down her cheeks. He touched a glistening drop with his finger and marveled for a moment at how good it felt to have her accept him at last. Then, past waiting, he plunged into her. More tears misted her eyes at the sudden pain. Above her, barely in her, the Hawk clenched his jaw and froze. He stared down at her a speechless moment, stunned and awed.

"Please," she urged. "Don't stop now. Please, I want this."

"Adrienne," he breathed, his face dark. "Virgin," he muttered dumbly. Ebony eyes held her gaze a breathless moment as his body lay rigid atop hers.

Then she felt an involuntary jerk rage through him and he pushed past the barrier, ripping into her with barbaric intensity. "Mine," he swore roughly, his black eyes flashing. "Only mine. First . . . best . . . and last." His beautiful head

arched back, and she buried her hands deep in his hair.
Again she felt that involuntary shudder that rocked him
from head to toe.

There was momentary pain, but waves of heat quickly
replaced it and the stars called her name, beckoning her to
come fly. This time it was even more intense, calling from
deep inside her where his hot shaft filled her all the way. An
instinctive voice told her how to move, how to gain her
pleasure and assure his in the same breath.

"Don't . . . move," he gritted against her ear, struggling
to not spill the moment her sleek tightness encased him. He
was beyond aroused, driven nearly insane by passion coupled with the knowledge that the smithy had never been
where he was now. Not even the legendary Ever-hard, whoever he was. He was her first man, her first and only lover.

"I can't help it . . . feels too . . . oh! . . . Delicious!" Her
hands caressed his back, then her nails lightly scored the
bronzed skin of his shoulders as he rocked her slowly beneath him.

"Stop moving, lass!"

"I thought I was supposed to move . . . too," she mumbled, very nearly incoherently. "Please . . ."

"Be still. I would teach you slow first. Then the next time
will be for the wild, rough love."

"Wild, rough love *now*," she demanded quite clearly, and
it broke the tether that had been holding him so tautly in
check. He raised her legs and drove into her, pushing the
worry of her virgin sensitivity from what little of his mind
remained. He came into her the way he'd wanted to from the
very first moment he'd seen her—rough and claiming. Hard
and demanding, with possession. Hungry and almost brutal, branding her his.

Adrienne spiraled beneath him, the tips of her fingers

trailing against the stars as she fragmented into a thousand shimmering pinpoints. She felt him stiffen, then pulse heavily inside her. They exploded together in perfect rhythm, perfect harmony.

Hawk lay breathing harshly atop her for a long time while she contentedly petted her husband. His silky hair had come free from its thong. She traced the soft skin of his solid, muscled back. *Beautiful man,* she mused, and the thought no longer carried any taint of fear. She stroked his hair in silence, marveling at her life and how rich it was with him in it.

It was in silence that at last he raised himself from her and went to stand by the window, staring out into the night of Uster.

"Och, lass, what have I done?" he whispered to the glass pane.

Silence from behind him. Adrienne's eyes moved lovingly over every inch of her man.

"I judged thee inconstant and shrewish. I judged thee, sweet falcon, to be the worst of faithless vipers. My dark imaginings feathering in my heart with spiky wing. And I could not have been more wrong."

Still silence. He didn't know that behind him his wife had a tender smile curving her lips.

"Lass from future's distant short, you were dumped into a man's lap, wed to me sight unseen and have lived through hells of your own before ever coming to me. I have only given you one more hell to add to it. Full of my—och, wife, what have I done? Oh God, what have I done to you?"

"You loved me."

It wasn't a question, but he answered it readily. "I do. More than life. My heart. I didn't just pick a sweet turn of phrase to name you, but spoke from my soul when I named you thus. Without my heart I couldn't live. And I couldn't breathe without you."

"Are you a man who has more than one heart?"

"Nay. Only this one. But it's bitter and dark now from the pain I've brought you."

He stared out the window into the bottomless night. Virgin blood on his shaft. Virgin tears on his hands. Virgin wife who'd never lain with Adam, and in all her years, with no man. A trembling gift she'd had to give and he'd forced it from her with his own dark passion.

"Sidheach." The word was a steamy caress from her lips.

It must have been a figment of his imagination. Hawk thought he would suffer his life long the torture of waiting in vain for a word he knew he would never hear tumble forth from her lips. "I have so abused you, my heart. I will atone, I swear to you, I will find a way—"

"Sidheach." He felt her hands on his sides, her arms slipping around him from behind. She couldn't keep the truth from him any longer. She had to tell him, had to have whatever time the fickle gods would allow them to enjoy. She rested her cheek lovingly against his back, and felt a shudder steal through his powerful frame.

"Do I dream a twisted dream?" he whispered hoarsely.

"I love you, Sidheach."

He whirled about to face her, his eyes dark and shuttered. "Look at me and say that!" he thundered.

Adrienne cupped his darkly beautiful face in her hands. "I love you, Sidheach, flesh-and-blood husband. 'Tis the only reason I was ever able to hate you so well."

A shout of joy burst from his lips, but his eyes were still disbelieving.

"I've loved you since that night by the sea. And hated you harder for every minute of it."

"But the king's whore—"

"Say no more. I'm a selfish woman. Adrienne's husband is who you are now. No one else. But I thank the good king for so perfecting your skills," she teased saucily. Some things were better left to heal, unpicked at. And it didn't threaten her anymore, because she understood that it was the noble, chivalrous part in him that had forced him to do whatever he'd had to do to protect those he loved. Although neither he nor Lydia had told her much, she'd been able to figure out a few things for herself.

He laughed at her audacity, then sobered quickly.

"I must wed you again. I want the vows. Between *us*, not some proxy." Was it magic that had tossed her through time? When she'd disappeared right out of his arms, he'd finally accepted it, that his wife had come to him from time's distant shores, and what could that be except magic? A magic he could not control.

But what if they could make some wee magic of their own? There were legends that wedding vows taken within the circle of the Samhain fires, on that powerful eve before the feast of the Blessed Dead, were binding beyond human understanding. What if they made their wedding vows, pledged before the mystical Rom, on such a sacred night? Could he bind his wife to him across any boundaries of time? He would try anything.

"Aye," she breathed with delight, "make it so."

"I'm only sorry I missed it to begin with. And had I known that it was you waiting for me at the Comyn keep I would have come myself, my heart. On the very first day of the troth."

But his eyes were still troubled and she raised a hand to brush the shadows away. He caught it and placed a kiss tenderly in her palm, then closed her fingers over it.

"Do you trust me, lass?" he asked softly.

Trust. Such a fragile, tenuous, exquisitely precious thing.

The Hawk watched her, the emotions flashing across her expressive face, wonderfully open to him now. He knew she was thinking of those black times of which she'd never spoken. One day she would confide in him all her most private thoughts and fears, and she would come to understand that no matter what had happened in her past, it could never change his feelings for her.

Adrienne gazed lovingly at the man who'd taught her how to trust again. The man she'd lost her heart to hopelessly and helplessly. This man who liberally dripped honor, valor, compassion, and chivalry. Neither her past nor his had any relevance to love such as theirs. "Trust you, Sidheach? With all my heart and further then."

His smile was blinding. "Adrienne . . ."

"My lord?" her voice was soft and warm and carefree as a girl's.

When he took her in his arms, she shivered with desire. "My lord!"

*   *   *

Adrienne didn't see that above her head his eyes grew dark. How was he going to protect her? How could he assure her safety? How quickly could he get to Adam and find what was going on? Because no matter what winding corridors his mind wandered trying to unravel the strange happenings that involved his wife, they all seemed to come circling back to a grinding halt directly in front of that damned smithy. And it *wasn't* mere jealousy, although the Hawk would readily admit to an abiding dislike for the man.

It wasn't the black queen that had brought Adrienne to him, or so cruelly ripped her from him. That was a fact.

So what was it?

Someone or something else had that power. The power to destroy the laird of Dalkeith with one blow—by taking his cherished wife away from him. What game, what terrible, twisted amusement was being played out upon Dalkeith's shore? What power had taken an interest and why?

I came here to hate you, Hawk. But I did not come here to hate the woman you claim as wife. Adam's words echoed in his mind, and he began to see just the vague outline of a carefully plotted revenge. But that would mean Adam Black had powers the Hawk had never quite believed existed. Bits and pieces of Rom stories he'd heard as a lad resurfaced in his whirring mind, raising questions and doubts. Stories about Druids and Picts and, aye, even the nefarious and mischievous Fairy. Lydia had always said that any legend was based in some part on fact, the mythical elements being merely the inexplicable but not necessarily untrue.

Oh, his love was testing the limits of his belief in the natural world and blowing them wide open.

But if he conceded belief in such magic as time travel, what magic could he discard as too outrageous? None. He could discard no possibility, however unearthly, without thorough consideration.

Adam Black had been able to cure the previously incurable poison of Callabron. Adam Black always seemed to know too damned much. Adam Black admitted flatly that he had come to Dalkeith for revenge.

The Rom had moved far from the smithy's forge. The Rom who *believed* the myths and legends.

And the Hawk, indebted to Adam for his wife's life, had

forced himself to overlook all the oddities, attributing them to his intense dislike of the smithy, convincing himself that he was seeing dragons in the puffy shapes of harmless clouds.

He would never let her go, but someone or something else could take her from him at a moment's whim.

He would seek it, destroy it, and free her—on his life he vowed it.

For there was no life for him without her.

CHAPTER 27

ALTHOUGH THE HAWK INSISTED ON LEAVING EARLY THE NEXT morning, he also made sure they took their sweet time on the way back to Dalkeith. He sent half the guards to ride ahead and commanded the other half to stay well behind him and his lady, to allow them privacy. He would return to Uster and oversee the rest of the manorial courts in the future, after this battle was done.

Adrienne was thrilled by his urgency to return to Dalkeith to seal their vows. She was equally thrilled by the three-day journey, with long dalliances in chilly pools of bubbling spring water. Longer interludes of passion on springy moss beneath the canopy of brightly fluttering leaves. Moments in which he teased, coaxed, and taught her until the blushing virgin grew confident in her newly discovered womanhood, thrilled to feel a woman's power over her man. She soon became expert in the subtle ways of touching or speaking, of wetting a lip and beckoning with her eyes. She knew the stolen caresses and the instant responses that turned her sweet, beautiful man into a throbbing, hardened savage.

She was mildly stunned to discover that autumn had painted the hills with the inspiration of a master; leaves in brilliant shades of pumpkin, bloodwine, and buttery amber rustled crisply beneath the horse's hooves as they rode beneath boughs of harvest gold. Squirrels chirped and skittered through the trees with gravity-defying leaps. Scotland in all her majestic glory, airbrushed by love, colored the simple gifts of nature into a tapestry of miracles. Adrienne had never realized the world was such a wonderful place.

She would remember the leisurely return journey to Dalkeith as her honeymoon; a time of phenomenal passion and tender romancing. A time of blissful healing and loving. Quite simply, the happiest days of her life.

*   *   *

Late on the second day, as they lay on a Douglas tartan of blues and grays, an unaddressed hurt surfaced to poke at Adrienne and she couldn't stay her tongue. Gripping the Hawk's face between her hands, she kissed him hard, hot, and tempting, then pulled back and said, "If you ever forbid me from you again, my husband, I will tear down the walls of Dalkeith, stone by stone, to get to you."

The Hawk shook his head, his thoughts completely muddled by the tantalizing kiss and further bewildered by her words. He claimed her lips in a long, equally fierce kiss, and when she lay panting softly beneath him, he said, "If you ever fail to see how I am faring after being wounded, I will add a stone tower onto Dalkeith and lock you in there, my captive love-slave, never to refuse me anything again."

It was her turn to study him with a bewildered expression, her lips full and rosy from the heat of his kiss. "If you mean after you were injured by the arrow, I *tried* to see you. Grimm wouldn't let me."

Hawk's gaze battled with hers. "Grimm said you never came. He said you were sleeping soundly in the Peacock Room with naught a worry in your mind, save how soon I would die and leave you free."

Adrienne gasped. "Never! I was right outside your door. Arguing and fighting with him. Still, he swore you refused me entrance!"

"I have never refused you entrance. Nay, I opened my very soul and bade you enter. Now you're telling me that you came to see me that night, and Grimm told you I had given orders that you were to be refused?"

Adrienne nodded, wide-eyed.

Dark fury flitted across the Hawk's face as he recalled the agony he'd endured, believing she'd not cared enough to see if he still lived and breathed. Suddenly he understood his friend's stiff behavior that night. The way Grimm's gaze had not seemed quite steady. The nervous way he'd built up the already blazing fire and had poked aimlessly at the crackling logs. "Grimm, what mischief do you play?" he murmured. Could Grimm wish Adrienne ill? Or had Grimm only been trying to protect him, his friend and brother-in-arms, from further harm?

Regardless, his actions were unacceptable. No matter how long-standing their friendship, lies were never tolerable. And Grimm's lies had driven a wedge between him and his wife, a wedge that had sent the Hawk rushing off to Uster. What if he hadn't returned for Adrienne? How far might Grimm's lies have taken them apart from each other? What might Adam have done to his wife if he hadn't returned for her?

The Hawk's mouth tightened. Adrienne laid her palm

against his cheek and said softly, "Hawk, I don't think he meant any harm. He seemed to be trying to protect you. He said I had brought you nothing but pain, and that it was all his fault."

"*His* fault?"

"For wishing on a star."

The Hawk snorted. "Wishes on stars don't come true, lass. Any addlebrained bairn knows that."

Adrienne cocked a mischievous brow at him. "But he did say he wished for the perfect woman." She preened. "And I do fit the bill," she teased.

"Aye, that you do," the Hawk growled. With a wicked smile, he cupped one of her perfect breasts in his hand and pushed her back upon the tartan as their passion began once again. His last coherent thought before he lost himself in the beauty and wonder that was his wife, was that Grimm owed him some answers and his wife an apology. And, if he had to admit it, that for all he knew maybe wishes on falling stars did come true. Stranger things had happened of late.

✳   ✳   ✳

On the last day, Hawk rode as if hell-bent. *Stole three days,* he mused darkly, holding his wife to his chest in his possessive embrace, his cheek brushing her silky hair.

In the woods he had felt safe, that whatever enemy threatened her didn't know where she was at that moment. So he'd prolonged it and spun it out to make it last, keeping his worries away from his wife, wanting nothing to spoil her pleasure.

Besides, he kept collapsing into near slumber every time his demanding young wife had her way with him. Damnedest odd thing. He'd never fallen so replete and satisfied to the ground. Oh, but that lass had some *serious* magic.

But now his mind turned darkly to the matter that lay ahead. Until the feast of the Blessed Dead, Rushka had warned. The Samhain was tomorrow, the day after the Samhain was the feast of the Blessed Dead—or All Saints, as some called it.

The Samhain was a perilous time for any to be alone. It was rumored that the Fairy walked the earth in full glamour on such a night. It was rumored that wickedness abounded on the Samhain, which was why the clans laid the double bonfire of birch, rowan, oak, and pine, and carved deep trenches around it. There they gathered to a one, every man, woman, and child, and feasted together in the protective rim of light. Within that ring, he would pledge his life to his wife and try to make some magic of their own.

He could just feel it in his bones that something was about to go very wrong.

SAMHAIN

(Harvest)

For nothing this wide universe I call,
Save thou, my rose; in it thou art my all.
SHAKESPEARE, SONNETS CIX

CHAPTER 28

ADAM HISSED AS HE LEFT THE FAIRY ISLE OF MORAR. TIME, usually of no significance to him, had flashed past him, day by precious day. When he played a mortal game, time became a nagging concern. For too long he'd neglected his doings at Dalkeith, but it had taken some time to convince his Queen that he was up to no mischief.

Now the far-seeing Adam turned his mind toward Dalkeith to study the changes in his game. He stiffened and hissed again. How dare they?

When his Queen had said the damning words sealing the Hawk's fate, Adam had searched far and wide for the perfect tool of revenge. He had wandered through the centuries, listening, watching, and finally choosing the perfect woman with careful precision. Adam was not one to muck in the lives of mortals often, but when he did, legends arose. And Adam liked that.

Some called him Puck. A Bard would name him Ariel.

Still others knew him as Robin Goodfellow. The Scots called him the *sin siriche du*—the black elf. Occasionally, Adam donned the visage of a charging and headless horseman, or a grim-faced specter carrying a scythe, just to live long in the memories of mortals. But whatever the glamour chose, he *always* won what he set out to win. And he'd been so certain of success this time! The woman had not only grown up in magical New Orleans, she'd sworn off men so vehemently that he'd heard her through the centuries. Adam had watched her for weeks before he'd made his careful choice; he'd studied her, learned everything there was to know about the fascinating Adrienne de Simone. Things even her beloved husband didn't know about her. He had been convinced that she was the one woman guaranteed to hate the legendary Hawk.

Now, as Adam moved toward Dalkeith-Upon-the-Sea, his far-reaching vision revealed a blissful Adrienne, wedding plans lazing dreamily in her mind.

But the Hawk, ah. . . . the Hawk wasn't so comfortable right now. He sensed something was wrong. He would be prepared.

Adam had brought Adrienne here to reject the Hawk, and of course, to claim the beauty for himself. Rarely was such a stirring mortal creature born as that woman. Even the King had commented on her perfection. What sweet revenge, to wed the Hawk to a woman who would never love him, while Adam made her his own. To cuckold the man who'd humiliated the Fairy King. But it seemed that he'd been as wrong about Adrienne as he'd been about the Hawk. Underestimated them both, he had.

She loved the Hawk as intensely as the Hawk loved her.

Adam drew up short, and grinned craftily as inspiration

struck. What a tiny revenge that would have been to merely cuckold the Hawk.

A new and truly devastating possibility now occurred to him.

*   *   *

Lydia and Tavis were sitting on the cobbled terrace of Dalkeith when the Hawk and Adrienne arrived late that night.

Deep in the shadows, talking softly and sipping sweet port, they watched the younger couple ride in, dismount, and link hands as they moved toward the terrace. Lydia's eyes shimmered with happiness as she watched.

Adrienne said something that made the Hawk laugh. When he pulled her to a lazy halt and kissed her, she tugged the thong free from his hair and flung it into the night. What started as a tender kiss deepened hungrily. Long moments rippled by as the kiss unfurled. Lingering and savage and hot, the laird of Dalkeith-Upon-the-Sea and his lady kissed. Beneath an almost full moon, on the lawn directly in front of the terrace, they kissed.

And kissed.

Lydia's smile faded, and she shuffled in her chair uncomfortably. She forced herself to draw a deep, difficult breath and willed her heart to stop that ridiculous thundering. She'd thought her body might have finally forgotten such passion. Little chance of that.

"That's quite a kiss, I'll say." Tavis's rich brogue rolled over her.

"Qu-quite . . . a kiss." Lydia swallowed. How long had it been since a man had kissed her that way?

Tavis moved imperceptibly closer and Lydia glanced sharply at him.

Then her gaze turned speculative.

Tavis MacTarvitt was one fine figure of a man, she noted. How did it come to pass that she had failed to see that before now? And why that secretive smile on his face? she wondered. "What are you smiling about?" she snapped.

" 'Tis a fine night on Dalkeith, I'll say," he offered benignly. "They've come home. And it looks to me like we'll be having wee bairns around here soon, and I'll say that again."

"Hmmph." Lydia snorted. "Have you figured out how to make coffee yet, old man? I'd love to have a good cup for her in the morning."

"Milady." His gentle gaze chided her. "I'm a man of talented hands, remember? Of course I can make coffee."

Talented hands. The words lingered in her mind a moment longer than she would have liked, and she stole a surreptitious peek at those hands. Good hands, they were, indeed. Broad and strong, with long, clever fingers. Able. They tanned soft hides and tenderly pruned young roses. They brushed her hair gently, and made tea. What other pleasures might those hands be capable of lavishing upon a woman? she wondered. *Och, Lydia, you've been wasting many fine years, haven't you, lass?* the true voice of her heart, silent all these years, finally found its tongue.

Lydia subtly shifted closer to Tavis so that their arms rested lightly side by side. It was a soft touch, but it was meant to tell him many things. And it did.

Deeper in the night, when Tavis MacTarvitt laid one aging yet still strong and capable hand atop hers, Lydia of Dalkeith pretended not to notice.

But she curled her fingers tightly around his, just the same.

*   *   *

It was early in the morning, the time when the cool moon briefly rides in tandem with the sun, that Adrienne felt the Hawk slip from the hand-hewn bed in the Peacock Room. She shivered in the fleeting coolness before the covers draped snugly to her body again. The spicy scent of him clung to the blankets and she buried her nose in it.

When they'd ridden in last night, the Hawk had swept her into his arms and vaulted the stairs three at a time, carrying his blushing wife past gaping servants. He'd called for a steaming bath to be delivered to the laird's bedroom and they had bathed in scented, sensuous oil that clung to their bodies. He'd made fierce and possessive love to her on a mound of tangled throws before the fire, and oiled by the fragrant blend, their bodies had slipped and slid with exquisite friction.

Adrienne had been claimed and branded by the man's hand. Conquered and ravished and utterly devoured. She had willingly dismissed all conscious thought, become an animal to mate her wild black charger. When he carried her to the bed, she'd run her hands over his body, over his face in the sweet afterglow, memorizing every plane and angle and secreting that memory away in her hands.

But somehow between the magnificent lovemaking and the sleeping, a silence had fallen between the lovers. It lay there, a stranger's gauntlet downflung in their bed. She had felt it grow into a fist of silence as she'd gotten lost in fears over which she had no control.

Desperately, she'd threaded her fingers through the Hawk's. Perhaps if she held on to him tightly enough, if she was tossed back to the future, she might take him with her.

She had spent many stiff hours pretending to sleep. Afraid to sleep.

And just now, as he slipped from the bed, she felt the fear returning.

But she *couldn't* hold his hand every minute of every day!

She rolled silently onto her side, peeped out from the pile of covers, and marveled.

He stood at the arched window, his head cocked as if listening to the breaking morn and hearing secrets in the cries of the wakening gulls. His hands were splayed on the stone ledge of the opening, the last rays of moonbeam caressing his body with molten silver. His eyes were dark pools of shadow as he gazed into the dawn. His stern profile might have been chiseled of the same stone used to build Dalkeith-Upon-the-Sea.

She closed her eyes when he reached for his kilt.

The silence unfisted and wrapped its fingers around her heart as he left the Peacock Room.

*   *   *

Hawk stood in the doorway on the second floor, his eyes dark with rage.

Rage at his own helplessness.

Bringing her back to Dalkeith had been a mistake. A big mistake. He knew it. The very air inside Dalkeith seemed charged, as if someone had sloshed lamp oil all over the castle and now lay in wait, ready to drop a lit candle and step back to watch their lives be devoured by the ensuing inferno. No question remained in his mind—Dalkeith was not safe for her.

But she'd disappeared in Uster too.

Then they'd just have to go farther away. China, perhaps. Or Africa. At least get the hell out of Scotland.

Damn it all! Dalkeith was *his* place. *Their* place.

Dalkeith-Upon-the-Sea had been his entire life. He'd endured so much to have this time. To come home. To watch their sons play at the cliff's edge. To watch their daughters race through the gardens, little feet pattering across mosses and cobbled walkways. On a warm day, to bathe their children in a clear blue loch. On a balmy summer night, to seduce his wife in the fountain beneath shimmering stars.

He deserved to spend the remainder of his years walking with Adrienne over these hills and vales, watching the sea and the seasons' eternal march across the land, building a home rich with love and memories and adventures. Every bit of it—damn it—he was a selfish man! He wanted the whole dream. *Should have stayed away, Hawk, and you know it. What made you think you could fight something you can't even name?* He closed his eyes tightly and swayed in the dark. Give up Dalkeith for her? His head fell forward, bowed beneath the weight of crushing decisions. A sigh to extinguish bonfires shuddered through his body. *Aye.* He would wed her at the Samhain. Then he would take her as far away from here as they had to go. He'd already started to say his goodbyes in a strained silence. Goodbyes took some time, and there was much he needed to bid farewell at Dalkeith-Upon-the-Sea.

To risk staying where whatever forces commanded his wife? Patently impossible. "We can't stay," he told the silent, waiting room—the one room he needed to bid farewell most strongly. His nursery. "Running is the only intelligent thing to do in this case. 'Tis the only sure way to keep her safe."

He rubbed his eyes and leaned an arm against the door-jamb, struggling to tame the emotions coursing through him. He was captivated, bound beyond belief to the lass sleeping innocently in his bed. This night shared with her had been all he'd ever dreamed he might one day know. The incredible intimacy of making love to a woman whose very thoughts he could read. It wasn't just making love—tonight when their bodies had melded together in passion, he felt such complete kindred that it knocked him off balance. If nothing else, it shifted and tumbled his priorities into perfect position. *She comes first.*

Hawk's jaw tensed, and he cursed softly. His eyes wandered lovingly over the cradles, the carved toys, the soft woolens, and the high windows opening to a velvet dawn. He could give her a babe—hell, she might carry his already. And someone or something could rip her and the babe right out of his arms and his life. It would destroy him.

Dalkeith would prosper without him; Adrian would make a fine laird. Lydia would summon him home from France. Ilysse would keep his mother company and Adrian would wed and bring babies to this nursery.

He would suffer no regrets. He could have babies with Adrienne in a crofter's hut and be just as happy.

The Hawk stood a few moments more, until the flicker of a smile curved his lip.

He closed the door on his old dream with a gentle smile and a kind of reverence only a man in love fully understands. A room had never been his dream at all.

She was his dream.

*   *   *

"Hawk!" Lydia's lower lip trembled an unspoken protest. She averted her gaze to study an intricate twining of roses.

"It must be done, Mother. 'Tis the only way I can be certain she's safe."

Lydia busied her hands with the careful pinching away of dried leaves, pruning her roses as she'd pruned them for thirty years. "But to leave! Tonight!"

"We can't risk staying, Mother. There's no other choice I can make."

"But Adrian isn't even here," she protested. "You can't relinquish the title if no one's here to claim it!"

"Mother." Hawk didn't bother to point out to her how absurd that protest was. From the sheepish look on her face it was obvious she knew she was grasping at any excuse she could find.

"You're talking about taking my grandbabies away!" Lydia squinted hard against tears.

Hawk regarded her with a mixture of deep love and amused patience. "They're grandbabies you don't even have yet. And ones we won't get a chance to make if I lose her to whatever it is that controls her."

"You could take her far from these shores and *still* lose her, Hawk. Until we discover what controls her, she won't ever really be safe," Lydia argued stubbornly. "She and I had planned to investigate the details of each time she traveled, to discover similarities. Have you done that?"

Hawk shook his head, his gaze shuttered. "Not yet. Truth be told, I've been loath to bring it up. She doesn't. I keep my silence. Once we've wed and left, there will be time to speak of it."

"Hawk, perhaps the Rom—"

Hawk shook his head impatiently. He'd already tried that tactic this morning. It had been his last ditch chance. He'd found Rushka up on the southwest ridge with his people, digging the trenches and gathering the seven woods for the fires. But Rushka had flatly refused to discuss his wife in any capacity. Nor had the Hawk been able to lure him into a conversation about the smithy. Damned irritating that he couldn't even force answers from those who depended upon him for his hospitality. But the Rom—well, the Rom truly depended upon no man's hospitality. When things became difficult, they moved on to a better place. Absolute freedom, that.

Nor had the Hawk, for that matter, been able to find the damned smithy.

"Mother, where's Adam?"

"The smithy?" Lydia asked blankly.

"Aye. The forge was cold. His wagon's gone."

"Fair to tell, I haven't seen him since . . . let's see . . . probably since the two of you left for Uster. Why, Hawk? Do you think he has something to do with Adrienne?"

Hawk nodded slowly.

Lydia attacked from another angle. "Well, see! If you take Adrienne away and Adam does have something to do with it, he can just follow you. Better to stay here and fight."

She gasped when the Hawk turned his dark gaze toward her. "Mother, I will not risk losing her. I'm sorry that doesn't please you, but without her . . . ah, without her . . ." He lapsed into a brooding stillness.

"Without her what?" Lydia asked faintly.

The Hawk just shook his head and walked away.

*   *   *

Adrienne walked slowly through the bailey looking for the Hawk. She hadn't seen him since he'd left their bed early that morning. Although she knew she'd be standing beside him soon pledging her vows, she couldn't shake the feeling that something was about to go wrong.

She approached the mossy stones of the broch. Looking at it reminded her of the day Hawk had given her the first lesson in how a falcon was tamed.

How *deliciously* a falcon was tamed.

She opened the door and peered inside, a faint smile curving her lip. How frightened and fascinated she'd been by the Hawk that day. How tempted and hopeful, yet unable to trust.

Was that the flutter of wings she heard? She squinted into the gloom, then stepped in.

A part of her wasn't surprised at all when the door closed swiftly behind her.

As she was plunged into darkness she had an abrupt flash of understanding. This was the danger she had so feared—whatever or whoever was behind her.

Adrienne felt as if she'd been balancing on the edge of a razor since last night, waiting for something bad to happen. Now she understood perfectly what had kept her awake all night—it had been her instincts again, warning her of impending doom, clamoring that it was just a matter of time before her world fell apart.

And whoever was behind her was certainly the harbinger of her destruction.

"Beauty."

Adam's voice. Adrienne's body went rigid. Her jaw tensed and her hands fisted when he grabbed her in the darkness and pressed his hips hard against the curve of her rump. She lurched forward but he tightened his arms around her and dragged her back against his body.

When his lips grazed her neck she tried to scream, but not a sound came out.

"You knew I'd come," he breathed against her ear, "didn't you, lovely one?"

Adrienne wanted to protest, to scream denial, but some part of her *had* known—on a visceral, deeply subconscious level. In that instant, all her strange encounters with Adam Black were suddenly washed crystal-clear in her mind. "You made me forget," she hissed, as memories flooded her. "The strange things you did—when you took the Hawk's face at the fountain—you made me forget somehow," she accused.

Adam laughed. "I made you forget when I took you to Morar too, even earlier than that. Do you remember lying in the sand with me now, sweet Beauty? I'm giving them back to you, those stolen times. Remember me touching you? Remember when I took you to my world to cure you? I touched you then, too."

Adrienne shuddered as the memories unfogged in her mind.

"I take from you what you don't need to recall, Beauty. I could take from you memories you'd love to lose. Shall I, Beauty? Shall I free you from Eberhard forever?" Adam pressed his lips to her neck in a lingering kiss. "No, I have it, I shall erase every memory you have of the Hawk—make you hate him, make him a stranger to you. Would you like that?"

"Who are you?" Adrienne choked as tears filled her eyes.

Adam turned her slowly in his arms until she faced him. His face was icy and definitely not human in the grayish half-light. "The man who's going to destroy your husband and everything at Dalkeith if you don't do exactly as I say, lovely Adrienne. I suggest you listen to me very, very carefully if you love him."

✳   ✳   ✳

Hawk couldn't find Adam. He couldn't find Grimm. And now he couldn't find his own wife. What the hell kind of wedding day was this?

The Hawk paced through the lower bailey calling her name, his hands clenched into fists. On the ridge, people had already started to gather. Clanspeople were arriving in droves from miles around. Come twilight there would be nearly seven hundred plaids gathered on Dalkeith's shore; the Douglas was a large clan with many crofters tilling the land. Earlier in the morning the Hawk had sent his guard into the hills and vales announcing the laird's wedding this eve, thus ensuring the attendance of every last person, young and old.

But there wouldn't be any wedding if he couldn't find his wife.

"Adrienne!" he called. Where the hell had she gone? Not in the castle, not in the gardens . . . not at Dalkeith?

Nay!

"Adrienne!" he roared, his pace quickening to a run. Calling her name, he sped past the falcon broch.

"Hawk, I'm here!" He heard her cry echo behind him.

"Adrienne?" He skidded to a halt and turned.

"I'm right here. Sorry," she added as she closed the door to the broch and stepped outside.

"Don't *ever* leave me again without telling me where you're going. Didn't you hear me calling you?" he growled, fear roughening his voice.

"I said I'm sorry, Hawk. I must have been wool-gathering." She paused where she stood.

Hawk's heart twisted in his chest. He'd found her, but why hadn't that erased his fear? Something nagged—a thing intangible, yet as real and potentially treacherous as the jagged cliffs of Dalkeith. There was an almost palpable odor of wrongness hovering in the air around the broch.

"Lass, what's wrong?" he asked. Every inch of him tensed as she stepped out of the shadows that darkened the east side of the squat tower. Half her face was deeply shadowed by the sun's descent, the other half was visibly pale in the fading light. Hawk suffered a fleeting moment of impossible duality; as though half her face was smiling while the other was drawn tightly in a grimace of pain. The macabre illusion chased a spear of foreboding through his heart.

He extended his hands, and when she didn't move from that strange half domino of light and darkness, he strode brusquely forward and pulled her into his arms.

"What ails you, sweet wife?" he demanded, gazing down at her. But he hadn't pulled her forward far enough. That hated shadow still claimed a full third of her face, concealing her eyes from him. With a rough curse he back-stepped until she was free of darkness. That shadow, that damned shadow from the broch had made him feel as if half of her was becoming insubstantial and she might melt right through his hands and he would be helpless to prevent it. "Adrienne!"

"I'm fine, Hawk," she said softly, sliding her arms around his waist.

As the fading light bathed her face, he felt suddenly foolish, wondered how he could have thought, even for a moment, that there was a shadow eclipsing her lovely face. There was no shadow there. Naught but her wide silver eyes brimming with love as she gazed up at him.

A trembling moment passed, then her lip curved in a sweet smile. She brushed a stray fall of dark hair back from his face and kissed his jaw tenderly. "My beautiful, beautiful Hawk," she murmured.

"Talk to me, lass. Tell me what fashes you so," he said roughly.

She flashed him a smile so dazzling that it muddled his

thoughts. He felt his worries scattering like petals to the wind beneath the soft promises unspoken in that smile.

He brushed his lips to hers and felt that jolt of immediate response tingle through his body from head to toe. *What shadow?* Foolish fears, foolish fancy, he realized wryly. He was letting his imagination run wild at the slightest provocation. A silly shadow fell across her face and the great Hawk suffered visions of doom and desolation. Bah! No lass could smile like that if she was worried about something.

He took her lips in a brutal, punishing kiss. Punishing for the fear he'd felt. Punishing, because he needed her.

And she melted to him like liquid flames, molding and pressing herself against him with fierce urgency. "Hawk . . ." she whispered against his lips. "My husband, my love, take me . . . again, please."

Desire surged through his veins, conquering all traces of his panic. He needed no further encouragement. They had a few hours left to them before the man of God would bind them beneath the Samhain mantle. He pulled her toward the broch.

Adrienne stiffened instantly. "Nay, not in the broch."

So he took her to the stables. To a thick pile of sweet purple clover where they spent the remaining hours of the afternoon of their wedding like a beggar's precious last coins on a splendid feast.

CHAPTER 29

ADRIENNE'S WEDDING DRESS SURPASSED ALL OF HER CHILD-hood dreams. It was made of sapphire silk and elegant lace, with shimmery threads of silver embroidered at the neck, sleeves, and hem in patterns of twining roses. Lydia had produced it proudly from a sealed chest of cedar-lined oak; yet another of the Hawk's clever inventions. She'd aired it out, steamed it in a closed kitchen over vats of boiling water, then lightly scented it with lavender. The gown clung at the bosom and hips, and fell to the floor in swirls of rich fabric.

It had been stitched by the Rom, Lydia told her as she and a dozen maids fussed over Adrienne, for Lydia's wedding to the Hawk's father. Lydia's wedding had also been celebrated at Dalkeith-Upon-the-Sea at the Beltane festival, before the same kind of double fires laid at the Samhain.

But Lydia had gone ahead now, up to the ridge. The maids were gone too, shooed on by Adrienne a quarter-hour past. It had taken every ounce of Adrienne's courage to get through the past few hours.

Lydia had been so elated, practically dancing around the room, and Adrienne had felt so wooden inside—forcing herself to pretend. She was about to do something that was guaranteed to make Lydia and Hawk despise her, and she had no other choice.

How could she bear the looks on their faces when she did it? How would she endure the hate and betrayal she would see in their eyes?

Adrienne stood alone in Lydia's lovely bedroom, amidst slowly cooling round irons and discarded choices for underthings and half-empty cups of tea, left undrunk in nervous anticipation.

The time was nearing.

And her heart was freezing, breath by bitter breath. She shivered as a crisp breeze tumbled through the open window of Lydia's bedroom. She crossed the room intending to close it, but froze, one hand upon the cool stone ledge. She stared mesmerized into the night.

I will remember this, always.

She drank in Dalkeith, committing each precious detail to memory. The full moon held her spellbound as it bathed the ridge in silvery brilliance. It seemed closer to the earth and so much larger than usual. Maybe she could step into the sky to stand right next to it—perhaps give it a firm nudge and watch it roll across the horizon.

Adrienne marveled at the beauty of it all. *This place is magic.*

She had a perfect view of the feast from the window. The ridge was alive with hundreds of people spread about the fires on bright tartans, talking, feasting, and dancing. Wine, ale, and Scotch flowed freely as the people celebrated the harvest to come. A rich harvest, her husband had seen to that.

Children played children's games, running and squealing and circling back to loving parents. And the music . . . oh, the music drifted up to the open window, blending with the soft roar of the ocean. The powerful hypnotic beat of the drums, the pipes and wild chanting.

Between the two circles of fire, she could just make him out, the laird of Dalkeith-Upon-the-Sea was dancing with his people, his head tossed back, adding his deep butterscotch cry to the song. Her husband. At least she'd gotten to love him for a while—maybe not forever, but . . .

The beat of drums intensified, and she watched him circle the fire. So primitive and savage, yet so incredibly tender and loving.

I adore this place, she thought. *If I could have ever dreamt a place to go, back in the twentieth century, I would have dreamt this one.*

She let her forehead fall against the cool stone wall a long moment and squeezed back the tears. "I love him more than life itself," she whispered aloud.

And *that* had been the deciding point.

*   *   *

"Nay." The Hawk raised his hands in mock protestation. "You must leave me with strength to wed and bed my wife, this eve," he teased the laughing women who tried to lure him into yet another dance.

Despite the disappointed looks and saucy remarks about his virility, the Hawk made his way higher up the ridge. He'd seen Lydia wander that way with Tavis while he'd been dancing. He paused a moment and looked back at the castle, his eyes searching the windows intently. There it was. Lydia's room, his wife's silhouette visible against the brightly lit window. He watched her turn her back. She was on her way.

A chill slithered up the nape of his neck as he studied her back. He watched a long moment, and when she didn't move, he wondered what she was doing.

I should have insisted she keep the guard with her.

Will they button my gown for me? she'd teased, and a swirl of jealousy at the thought of any of his guards touching his wife's silken skin had sealed it.

He could watch every step of her progress from the ridge, and the castle wasn't entirely deserted. The ridge was a short walk, a few minutes or less. *She should be fine.* Yet he worried . . .

"Have you seen Grimm?" Lydia touched his arm lightly to get his attention.

Hawk tore his gaze from the window. "Nay. Have you?"

"Nay. And that worries me. He's your best friend, Hawk. I thought he'd be here. What might have kept him?"

Hawk shrugged and glanced quickly at the castle. Ah, finally. The candles were out and his wife was on her way. Lydia's room was full dark. Suddenly Grimm seemed inconsequential. Even his irritation at Grimm's lies slid off his shoulders with the thought of his beloved Adrienne.

Tonight I will bind her to me for all eternity, he pledged silently.

"Hawk?" Lydia waved her hand in front of his face and he dragged his gaze from the castle with an effort.

"Hmmm?"

"Oh my," Lydia sighed. "How you *do* remind me of your father when you look like that."

"Like what?" Hawk drawled, watching the front steps for the first glimpse of his wife.

"Like some savage Viking set to conquer and take captive."

"I'm the captive in this, Mother," Hawk snorted. "The lass has fair spelled me, I think."

Lydia's laughter tinkled merrily. "Good. 'Tis as it should be, then." She gave him a brisk kiss. "She'll be here any moment." Lydia straightened his linen that didn't need straightening, smoothed his perfect hair that didn't need smoothing, and in general clucked over him like a nervous hen.

"Mother," he growled.

"I just want you to look your best—" Lydia broke off. She spared a nervous laugh for herself. "Just look at me, a jittery mother, all in a tizzy at her son's wedding."

"She's already seen me at my worst and loves me in spite of it. And what are you doing fussing over me? I thought we weren't speaking. What plans are you devising now?" he demanded. He knew her too well to believe she'd just capitulated quietly to his plans to leave this evening.

"Hawk," Lydia protested, "you wound me!"

Hawk snorted. "I'll ask you again, what nefarious plot have you devised to try to keep us here? Did you drug the wine? Hire ruthless mercenaries to hold us captive in my own castle? Nay, I have it—you dispatched a messenger to the MacLeod telling them now might be a good time to lay siege to Dalkeith, right?" He wouldn't be surprised if she'd done any of those things. Lydia was formidable when she set her mind on something. Nothing was beyond her if it might mean keeping Adrienne by her side. *Like mother like son,* he acknowledged ruefully.

Lydia glanced studiously away. "I simply refuse to think of you leaving until the time comes that you try to. Until then, I intend to enjoy every last moment of my son's wedding. Besides, 'tis apparent Adrienne has no idea what you're planning. I'm not so certain she won't side with me," she snipped pertly.

"Here she comes." Tavis interrupted their squabbling and waved their attention to the stone stairs that cascaded into the upper bailey.

"Oh! Isn't she lovely?" Lydia breathed.

A collective sigh ruffled the night and blended with the fragrant breeze dappling the ridge.

"Could be a princess!"

"Nay, a queen!"

"Prettier than a fairy queen!" A wee lass with blond ringlets clapped her hands delightedly.

"The Lady of Dalkeith-Upon-the-Sea." A crofter doffed his cap and clasped it over his heart in a gesture of fealty.

Lydia's smile faded as she watched Adrienne head for the stables.

No one spoke until she reappeared a few moments later, leading a horse to a nearby wall. "But what? What is that . . . a horse? Ah, I suppose she's riding a horse up," Lydia murmured, perplexed.

"A horse? Why wouldn't she just walk? 'Tis fair short space to cross, I'll say," Tavis wondered.

Beneath the brilliant moon they could clearly see her stepping up on a low stone wall and mounting a horse— wedding dress and all.

Hawk's eyes narrowed thoughtfully. His body tensed and he stifled an oath when he saw Rushka, who had been standing silently beside them, trace a gesture upon the air. "What are you *doing*?" Hawk growled, closing his hand around the Rom's arm.

Rushka stopped and his brown eyes rested on the Hawk with deep affection and deeper sorrow. "We had hoped he wouldn't come, my friend. We took all the precautions . . . the rowan crosses. The runes. I did everything I could to prevent it."

"Who wouldn't come? What are you talking about? Prevent what?" Hawk gritted. Every inch of his body was suddenly alive. All day something had been gnawing at him, demanding that he take action, and now it exploded to a fever pitch in his blood. He'd like nothing more than to take action—but against what? What was happening? The thunder of approaching horses rumbled the earth behind him.

"He comes." Rushka tried to retrieve his arm from the Hawk's deadly grip, but dislodging a boulder from his chest might have been easier.

The clip-clop of horses' hooves canted up the ridge, drawing nearer.

"Talk to me," Hawk gritted, glaring down at Rushka. *"Now."*

"Hawk?" Lydia asked, worried.

"Hawk," Tavis warned.

"Hawk." His wife's husky voice cut through the night behind him.

The Hawk froze, his gaze locked on the elderly Rom who'd been like a father to him for so many years. A flicker in the man's eyes warned him not to turn. To just pretend nothing was happening. *Do not look at your wife,* Rushka's eyes were saying. He could see her, mirrored deep in the Rom's brown eyes. Not turn around? Impossible.

Hawk tugged his furious gaze from Rushka. He turned on one booted heel, slowly.

His wife. And next to her, upon the Hawk's own black charger, sat Adam. Hawk stood in silence, his hands fisted at his sides. The ridge was eerily still, not one child peeped, not one crofter breathed so much as a whisper or troubled murmur.

"Lorekeeper." Adam nodded a familiar acknowledgment to Rushka, and Hawk's gaze drifted between the strange smithy and his Rom friend. Rushka was white as new-fallen snow. His brown eyes were huge and deep, his lean body rigid. He did not return the greeting, but cast his eyes to the ground, signing those strange symbols furiously.

Adam laughed. "One would think you might have realized that it hasn't helped so far, old man. Give it up. Not even your. . . . sacrifice. . . . helped. Although it did mollify me slightly."

Lydia gasped. "What sacrifice?"

No one answered her.

"What sacrifice?" she repeated tersely. "Does he mean Esmerelda?" When no one responded, she shook Rushka by the arm. "Does he?" Her eyes flew back to Adam. "Who are you?" she demanded, her eyes narrowing like a mother bear's as she prepared to defend her cubs.

Rushka dragged her against him. "Be still, milady," he gritted. "Do not interfere in that which you don't understand."

"Don't tell me what I—" Lydia began heatedly, then shut her mouth beneath the Hawk's lethal gaze.

Hawk turned back to Adrienne and calmly raised his hands to help her dismount, as though nothing were amiss.

Adam laughed again, and it made Hawk's skin crawl. "She goes with me, Lord Buzzard."

"She stays with me. She is my wife. And it's Hawk. Lord *Hawk* to you."

"Nay. A vulture, a sad scavenger to pick over the unwanted remains, Lord Buzzard. She chooses was the deal made, do you recall? I saved your wife for a price. The price is now paid. You've lost."

"Nay." The Hawk shook his head slowly. "She chose already, and 'twas me she chose."

"It would appear she *un*chose you," Adam mocked.

"Get off my horse, smithy. Now."

"Hawk!" Rushka warned, low and worried.

"Hawk." It was Adrienne's voice that stilled him. Froze him in mid-step toward the smithy. Until now, the Hawk had been focusing his attention and anger on the smithy. And he knew why. It was the same reason he had delayed turning around when he heard the horses approaching. The reason why he'd looked at Rushka instead. He was afraid to look at his wife, of what he might see in her lovely eyes. Might she truly have unchosen him? Could he have been so completely wrong? He paused, hand on his sword hilt, and forced his eyes to hers. The insecurity that had seized him the very first day he'd found his wife at the smithy's forge reclaimed him with a vengeance.

Her face was smooth and void of emotion. "He speaks the truth. I have chosen him."

Hawk gaped at her, stunned. Not so much as a flicker of emotion in her silver eyes. "How is he making you lie, lass?" Hawk refused to believe her words, clinging to his faith in her. "What is he threatening you with, my heart?"

"Nothing," Adrienne said coldly. "and stop calling me that! I have never been your heart. I told you that from the beginning. I don't want you. It was Adam all along."

Hawk searched her face. Cool, composed, she sat the mare like a queen. Regal and untouchable. "And just what the hell was Uster, then?" he growled.

She shrugged, her hands palms up. "A vacation?" she replied flippantly.

Hawk tensed, his jaw gritting. "Then just what were the stables this afternoon—"

"A mistake," Adam cut him off flatly. "One she won't be repeating."

Hawk's gaze never wavered from Adrienne's. "Was it a mistake?" he asked softly.

Adrienne inclined her head. A pause the length of a heartbeat. "Yes."

The Hawk saw not so much as a flicker in her face. "What game play you, lass?" he breathed, danger emanating from every inch of his rigid stance, charging the air around them.

The night hung still and heavy. On the ridge not one person moved, riveted to the terrible scene unfolding.

"No game, Hawk. It's over between us. Sorry." Another nonchalant shrug.

"Adrienne, stop jesting—" he growled.

" 'Tis no jest," she interrupted him with sudden anger. "The only joke here is on you! You didn't really think I could stay here, did you? I mean, come on!" She waved a hand dismissively at the splendor of the wedding feast. "I'm from the twentieth century, you fool. I'm used to luxuries. It's the little things that spoil. Coffee. Steaming showers, limousines, and all the glitter and hubbub. This was a lovely diversion—quite a little getaway with some of the most *fascinating* men. . . ." She smiled at Adam, and it took every ounce of the Hawk's will not to leap at the smithy and choke the life from his arrogant body.

Instead, he stood like a marble effigy, hands curled at his side. "You were a virgin—"

"So? You taught me pleasure. But the smithy gave me more. It's that simple." Adrienne fiddled with the reins of her mount.

"Nay!" Hawk roared. " 'Tis some game! What have you threatened my wife with, smithy?"

But it was Adrienne who answered, in that same calm, utterly detached voice. That husky voice that made him think he'd gone mad, for the words tumbling forth must surely be lies. Yet she didn't look as if she was being forced. There was no sword to her throat. No shimmer of tears in her eyes. And her voice, ah . . . it was level and calm. "He has threatened me only with greater pleasure than you ever gave me. He has true magic at his command. Don't waste your time hunting for us. You won't find us. He has promised to take me to places I've never dreamed existed." Adrienne nudged her mount closer to the smithy's.

Adam flashed a blinding smile at the Hawk. "Looks like you lost after all, pretty bird."

"Nay!" Hawk roared, lunging for the smithy and drawing his sword in one fluid sweep. The charger bucked at the Hawk's bellow and sidestepped wildly.

Rushka grabbed the Hawk's arm and cleaved his blow down so hard that the sword lodged in the earth at his feet.

Adam raised his hand.

"Nay!" Adrienne quickly restrained the smithy's hand. "You will not hurt him! No bloodshed. You prom—it's messy," she appended. "I don't like blood. It makes me ill."

Adam cocked his head and lowered his hand. "Your wish is my command, Beauty."

"Is this truly what you wish, lass?" Hawk's eyes were black and soulless.

"Yes," she said softly. Carefully.

"He is not forcing you?" *Tell me, just say the word, wife, and I will kill him with my bare hands.*

She shook her head and met his gaze levelly.

"Say it," Hawk gritted. "He's not forcing you?"

"He uses . . . no coercion against . . . me."

"Do you . . . love . . . him?" He hated himself when his voice broke roughly over the words. His throat was so tight he could scarcely breathe.

"I love him the way I loved Eberhard," she sighed. She smiled vapidly at Adam, who suddenly narrowed his eyes at her last words.

"Enough, Beauty." Adam captured her hand in his. "The universe awaits us and your pleasure is my command."

Hawk's heart wrenched and twisted. The damned Everhard. Her first love, whether he'd ever made love to her or not. He turned away before he could make a bloody massacre of the ridge singlehandedly.

When he finally returned his gaze to her, it was too late—she was gone.

The mass of hundreds on the ridge at Dalkeith-Upon-the-Sea stood numbly as both horses and riders simply vanished into the night air. One moment they were there. The next—nothing.

But a soft voice floated on the breeze. *You were right about your falcons, Sidheach,* came the strange last words of the woman he'd loved and who had effectively destroyed the once proud laird of Dalkeith-Upon-the-Sea.

Lydia clutched at his sleeve limply.

Rushka cursed harshly in a language no one had ever heard before.

Hawk only stared blindly into the night.

CHAPTER 30

"WHERE ARE WE?" ADRIENNE ASKED ADAM WOODENLY.

He was leading her mount by the reins down a dark path through a strange forest. Twisted branches wove a gnarled canopy above her head. Occasionally a ray of faint light would pierce the dense gloom and the creaking branches would glimmer like bleached bones.

No crickets. No normal noises, only the screech of flying creatures. The bracken rustled, revealing brief glimpses of dwarfed gnomes with wild faces. She shivered violently and hugged her arms around herself.

"You are in my realm."

"Who are you *really*, Adam Black?" Her voice broke on the simple sentence, raw and full of anguish.

For an answer, she received a mocking smile. Nothing more.

"Tell me," she demanded dully. But the dark man at her side rode in silence.

"At least tell me *why*."

"Why what?" He cocked a curious brow at her.

"Why did you do this to me? What did I do? Why did you send me back in time and take me away again?" *And break my heart and leave me dying inside?*

Adam stopped their mounts, amusement lighting his dark visage. He reached out a hand to stroke her pale cheek and she shuddered beneath his hand. "Oh, Beauty, is that what you think? How very self-engrossed and utterly charming you are." His laughter rolled. But it was his next words that shafted through her soul like a knife. "It had nothing to do with you, my winsome beauty. Any beautiful woman would have sufficed. But I thought you hated beautiful men. I heard you, there in your library, swearing off men, all men. Yet, it would seem I was mistaken. Or you lied, which is more likely."

"What are you saying?" she breathed faintly. Any woman would have sufficed? Her heart was laid bare and cleaved through by this man's twisted game, and he dared say so baldly that it hadn't mattered one whit who she was? A pawn? Again? Her jaw locked temporarily. *I will not scream. I will not.* When she was certain she could speak without raging she said coolly, "You got what you wanted. Why won't you just tell me who you are?" She had to find out more about this man to avenge herself. To avenge her husband.

"True. I did get what I wanted. The Hawk looked utterly destroyed, wouldn't you say? Crushed." Adam flicked his hand lightly over hers. "You did very well tonight, Beauty. But tell me"—his eyes searched hers intently, and she stiffened when it seemed they might penetrate into her very soul—"what did you mean about his falcons?"

Adrienne's breath hitched. "He told me once that all his

falcons had flown him," she lied evenly. "You told me I had to be utterly convincing or you would kill him, so I chose that reminder to drive the point home. That's all."

"That had better be all." His face was cold and unforgiving. Just as it had been in the broch before the Hawk had come looking for her. Before what should have been the wedding of her dreams. Icily, he'd explained to her in exact and excruciating detail precisely how he would destroy the Hawk and everyone at Dalkeith if she failed his will. Then he'd shown her things he could do. Things her mind still couldn't quite comprehend. But she'd understood that he was perfectly capable of carrying out the mass destruction he'd threatened. Two choices he'd given her—either lie to the Hawk and break his heart, not to mention her own, or stand by while Adam used his unnatural powers to kill him. Then Lydia. Followed by every man, woman, and child at Dalkeith.

No, there had been no choice at all. The hellish decision had given her an intimate understanding of what a man called the king's whore might once have suffered.

When she'd left the broch shaking and pale, she'd seized one last moment of glory. She'd made love to the Hawk with all the passion in her soul. Saying goodbye, and dying inside. She'd known it would be horrible to lie to him, but she hadn't anticipated just how deeply it would cut her.

Adam had been unyielding on that point. He'd made it clear that she must fully convince the Hawk she desired Adam. After the incredible intimacy she and Hawk had shared, she'd known she would have to say hateful, horrid things to convince him.

She shivered violently as Adam's thumb brushed her lower lip. She slapped his hand away in spite of her fear. "Don't touch me."

"If I thought for a moment you had tried to tell him something more, I would go back and kill him even as we speak, Beauty."

"I gave you what you wanted, you bastard!" Adrienne cried. "All of Dalkeith is safe from you now."

"It doesn't matter." Adam shrugged indolently. "He's dead anyway." Adam tugged at her reins and resumed their slow passage beneath the rustling limbs.

"What?" Adrienne hissed.

Adam smiled puckishly. "I thought you might enjoy the scenic route back. This trail is a timeline and we just passed the year 1857. It's that misty bend back there between the . . . trees . . . for lack of a better word. He's been dead for over three hundred years.

A silent scream began to build inside her. "Who *are* you?"

"They used to call us gods," he said dispassionately. "*You* would do well to worship me."

"I'll see you in hell, first," she breathed.

"Not possible, Beauty. We don't die."

CHAPTER 31

ADRIENNE DREW HER ARM BACK AND WINGED THE BOOK like a Frisbee. It was supposed to fly across the room and crash with a resounding thump against the wall. Instead, it dropped limply, landing on the floor at the foot of her bed.

She glanced at the volume in disgust and noticed that it had fallen open to a page. She squinted to read it from her perch at the footrail.

> *Dreams about stopped-up commodes can symbolize many things:* the dreamer is emotionally repressed. Emotional and/or physical purging is recommended. A recurring dream of this nature signifies the dreamer has endured a traumatic experience from which he/she *must* find some kind of release or serious psychological damage may occur.

So much for a sign from heaven.

Adrienne swallowed a choked laugh that turned into a sob. *Who writes this stuff?*

She dangled her bare foot over the bed and poked the book shut with her toe. *1001 Little Dreams.* How bizarre. She hadn't even realized she had that book in her library. Even more bizarre that she'd been dreaming about toilets for ten nights in a row. Nothing else. Just backed-up, overflowing commodes.

Lovely.

But she didn't have to be hit over the head with a dream guide. She knew what was wrong with her. Fifteen days ago she had materialized in her sprawling Victorian house at 93 Coattail Lane, Seattle, U.S. of A.

And she hadn't spoken to a single soul since then. Every scrap of energy she had went toward maintaining her composure—her tight skin. Tight dry eyes. Tight little death going on inside. She understood perfectly well that if she let even one tiny tear sneak out of the dry corner of her eye, she couldn't be held responsible for the flooding that could cause mass evacuations throughout the state.

She scratched her tight scalp with a tight little hand as she tightly petted Moonie's silky back. She touched Moonie's pink nose in a tight, economical motion. *No stopped-up commodes in a cat's world,* Adrienne mused as Moonie curled her paws into her hair and began a thrumming little purr.

It was Moonie's hungry mews that roused her from the bed. Adrienne eased her aching body from the down coverlets and padded slowly to the kitchen.

God, but she felt five hundred years old herself, in pain from head to toe from a heartache she knew would never heal.

Adrienne woodenly opened a can of tuna. White alba-core. Only the best for Moonie. She slumped down on the floor and brushed irritably at the hand that shoved a book in front of her. "Go away, Marie, I need to be alone." Adrienne marveled at the pale swirls of lime in the jade tile of the kitchen floor, and wondered why she'd never noticed them before. She rubbed lightly at one of the swirls. Slate tile could be so interesting. Riveting, in fact.

"Eees book you dropped," Marie said in her thick accent.

Adrienne didn't move. The book brushed her cheek. Heavens, but the woman was insistent. The book's sharp corner poked the soft underside of her neck. Probably another stupid dream book. Well, she just wouldn't look at it.

"Quit shoving at me." Adrienne took the book blindly, her eyes squeezed shut. "Go away now," she mumbled. There. That wasn't too bad. She applauded herself for performing a simple function with precision. No tears. Not one thought of . . . the thing she wasn't thinking of. Adrienne took a deep breath and forced a grim, tight smile.

She was going to be fine. Small things now—big things soon.

"I think I make for you some tea," Marie said.

Adrienne's stomach heaved and rolled. "No."

"I think, then, I make dinner for *señorita*."

"I'm not hungry. Go away."

"Okay. I move things to garage," Marie grunted.

Move things? Leave the house? "No!" Adrienne controlled her voice with a tremendous effort. "I mean, that's not necessary, Marie. God knows this old house is big enough for both of us."

"Eees no good. I no good to you. I move now back to garage." Marie watched her carefully.

Adrienne sighed. Marie simply *had* to stay in the house.

She couldn't stand the huge, aching silence, the empty rooms. The hum of the refrigerator might drive her mad.

"Marie, I don't want you to move back out. I really want you to stay with . . ." Adrienne opened her eyes, her voice trailing off as she stared in horror at the book in her hands. *A Study of Medieval Falconry*.

Stay tight!

Would you soar for me, falcon? I'll take you higher than you've ever been. I'll teach you to bank heights you only dreamed existed.

He'd certainly made good on that promise. And now she was falling from those incredible heights without a parachute, or a Mary Poppins umbrella, or anything else to break her fall. Adrienne de Simone Douglas squeezed her arms around her stomach and started screaming.

The tiny Cuban woman dropped to her knees and very carefully pulled Adrienne into her arms. Then she rocked her, smoothed her hair, and did her best to comfort her.

For days and days Adrienne lay on her back replaying every precious memory on the blank screen of her ceiling. She'd pulled the drapes shut and turned all the lights out. She couldn't stand the world to be bright without him.

Marie floated in and out, bringing food and drink that remained untouched, and Moonie stayed at her side unceasingly.

Adrienne just drifted in and out of consciousness, as the mind does when grief runs too deep to handle. Eventually she came back to herself, but she went the long way around.

*   *   *

On the glistening silica sands of Morar, Adam Black sauntered with arrogant grace to his Queen's side.

"Where have you been wandering, minstrel-mine?"

Queen Aoibheal asked silkily. "What new tales and entertainments have you collected for me?"

"Oh, the finest of tales! An epic, grand adventure," Adam bragged, drawing the elegant courtiers near.

The Fae loved a good tale, the thicker the subterfuge, the more intense the passions, the more aroused the court. They'd long since tired of happy endings; immune to suffering themselves, they were enamored with mortal struggles and casualties. The Queen herself was most especially partial to a tragicomedy of errors, and this new tale did suit that genre well.

"Tell us, jester, sing and play for us!" the court of the Tuatha De Danaan cried.

Adam's smile gleamed brightly. He met his Queen's eye and held it long. "Once upon a time there was a mortal man. A man so fair even the Fae Queen herself had noticed him . . ."

The Queen's eyes glittered brightly as she listened, at first in amusement, after a time with obvious agitation, and finally with a sensation that vaguely resembled remorse.

CHAPTER 32

LYDIA SIGHED AS SHE PICKED THROUGH HER SEEDS. THE NEW Year had inched past them as if it traveled on the humped back of a snail. She didn't even want to recall the grim scene Christmas had been. Winter had descended upon Dalkeith in force—icicles twisted obscenely from the shutters, and the dratted door to the front steps had been frozen shut this morning, effectively sealing her in her own home.

Lydia could remember a time when she'd loved the winter. When she'd reveled in each season and the unique pleasures it brought. Christmas had once been her favorite holiday. But now . . . she missed Adrian and Ilysse. *Come home, children. I need you,* she prayed silently.

The sound of splintering wood suddenly rent the air, causing her to jerk her head up in an involuntary gesture that sent her precious seeds flying.

Damned inconsiderate of them to split firewood right outside the window.

Lydia pushed irritably at her hair and began to reorganize the scattered seeds. She dreamed of the flowers she would plant—if spring ever came again.

Another resounding crash shuddered through the Greathall. She stifled a very unladylike oath and laid her seeds aside. "Keep it down out there! A body's trying to do a bit of thinking!" she yelled.

Still the deafening crashes continued. "We aren't all that short of firewood, lads!" Lydia roared at the frozen door.

Her words were met with a terrible screeching noise.

"That's it. That's *it*!" She leapt up from her chair and seethed. That last one had seemed to come from . . . upstairs?

She cocked her head at an angle.

Someone had either decided it was too cold to split firewood outside or was quite busily turning the furniture into kindling instead.

The crash was followed by the shattering of glass. *"Holy shit!"* Lydia muttered, as her lovely daughter-in-law would have offered quite perkily. She spun on her heel, grabbed up her skirts, and raced the stairs like a lass of twenty. Hand on her heart she flew down the corridor, skidding past gawking maids and tense soldiers. How many people had stood about listening to this insane destruction while she'd been sitting downstairs?

Not the nursery, she prayed, *anything but that.*

Her son would never destroy that room of dreams. Granted, he'd been a bit out of sorts, but still . . . No. He definitely would not do something so terrible. Not her son.

By all that's holy, oh yes he would. And he was.

Her breath came in burning gasps as she stared, dumbfounded. Her son stood in the nursery surrounded by a twisted heap of horrid broken wooden limbs. He'd been literally ripping apart the lovingly crafted furnishings. He was clad in only a kilt, his upper body glistening with sweat. The veins in his arms were swollen and his hands were raw and bloody. His raven hair was loose but for the two war braids at either temple. *By the sweet saints, just paint his face blue and I wouldn't even know him for my son!* Lydia thought.

The Hawk stood silently, wild-eyed. There was a smudge of blood on his face where he'd wiped at sweat. Lydia watched, frozen in horror, as he tilted an oil bowl, drizzling its contents over the splinters of furniture, the toys and books, the magnificent dollhouse that had been squashed flat in his gargantuan rage.

When he dropped the candle, a soft scream wrenched her mouth wide.

The flames leapt up, greedily devouring the pile of Hawk's and Lydia's shattered dreams. Shaking with hurt and fury, Lydia pressed a hand to her mouth and swallowed a sob. She turned away before the animal that used to be her son could see her tears.

*   *   *

"We have to do something," Lydia murmured woodenly, staring blankly at the kitchen hearth.

Tavis stepped close behind her, his hands suspended in the air just above her waist. He dropped his head forward and inhaled deeply of her scent. "I'll speak with him, Lydia—"

"He won't listen," she choked as she spun around. "I've tried. Dear God, we've all tried. He's like some rabid dog, snarling and foaming and oh, Tavis! My nursery! My grandbabies!"

"*I* haven't tried yet," Tavis said calmly, dropping his hands to grip her waist.

Lydia cocked her head, marveling at the implicit

authority in his words. He'd managed to surprise her once
again, this gentle man who'd stood patiently by her side for
so long.

"You'll speak with him?" she echoed hopefully, her eyes
glimmering with unshed tears.

"Aye," he assured her.

Strength and ability laced his reply. How could it have
taken her so long to begin to see this man clearly?

Some of her astonishment must have been evident in her
gaze, because he gave her that patient smile and said tenderly, "I knew one day you'd finally open your eyes, Lydia. I
also knew it would be worth every minute of the wait," he
added quietly.

Lydia swallowed hard as a fission of heat and hope and
heady, tumultuous love spread through her in a wave. Love.
How long had she been in love with this man? she wondered dumbly.

Tavis brushed her lips with his, a light friction that promised so much more. "Doona worry. I care for him like my
own, Lydia. And, as if he were my own, 'tis time we had a
good thorough father-son kind of talk."

"But what if he refuses to listen?" she fretted.

Tavis smiled. "He'll listen. You can take Tavis Mac-
Tarvitt's word on that, I'll say."

✳   ✳   ✳

The Hawk brooded into the fire, watching ghosts dance
whitely in the spaces between the flames. They were
memory-born and hell-bound, as he surely was. But purga-
tory—if not heaven—was within his reach, tidily captured
in a bottle, and so he toasted the ghosts as he raced them to
oblivion.

He picked up another bottle of whisky and turned it in

his hand, studying its rich amber color with drunken appreciation. He raised the bottle to his lips, his hand fisted about
the neck, and bit out the stopper. Briefly he remembered
biting out the stopper of a Gypsy potion. Remembered covering his wife's body with his own and tasting, touching,
kissing . . . He'd been fool enough then to believe in love.

Bah! Adam! It had always been him. From the first day
he'd seen her. She'd been standing pressed against a tree
trunk watching the blasted smithy with hunger in her eyes.
He tossed back a swallow of whisky and considered going
back to court. Back to King James.

A crooked, bitter smile curved his lip. Even as he pic-
tured himself prowling the boudoirs of Edinburgh again,
another part of his mind recalled the roiling thick steam rising from a scented bath, the sheen of oil upon her skin as
she'd tossed her head back, baring the lovely column of her
throat to his teeth. Baring everything to him, or so he'd
thought.

Adrienne . . . Treacherous, traitorous, lying unfaithful
bitch.

"Lay me into the dead earth now and be done with it," he
muttered to the fire. He didn't even react when the door
to the study was flung open so hard that it hit the wall.
"Close the door, man. A bit of a draft chilling my bones,
there is," the Hawk slurred unsteadily without even bothering to see who had invaded the drunken squalor of his private hell. He again tilted the bottle to his mouth and took a
long swallow.

Tavis crossed the room in three purposeful strides and
smashed the bottle out of Hawk's hand with such force that
it shattered in a splash of glass and whisky on the smooth
stones of the hearth. He gazed at Tavis a befuddled moment, then reached, undeterred, for a second bottle.

Tavis stepped between the Hawk and the crated liquor.

"Get out of my way, old man," Hawk growled, tensing to rise. He had barely gained his feet when Tavis's fist connected solidly with his jaw, spilling him back into the chair.

Hawk wiped the back of his hand across his mouth and glared up at Tavis. "Why'd you go and do that for, Tavis MacTarvitt?" he grumbled, making no move to defend himself.

"I don't give a bloody hell what you do to yourself, *laird*," Tavis sneered. "Just get the hell out of this castle and don't do it in front of your mother."

"Who the hell d'you think you are?"

"I know who I am! I'm the man who watched you grow from wee lad to braw laird. I'm the man who burst with pride while he watched you make some hard choices." Tavis's voice dropped a harsh notch, "Aye, I'm just the man who has loved you since the day you drew your first hungry breath in this world. And now I'm the man who's going to thrash you within an inch of your worthless life if you don't get a grip on yourself."

Hawk gaped, then swiped irritably at Tavis. "Go 'way." He closed his eyes wearily.

"Oh, I'm not done yet, my boy," Tavis said through gritted teeth. "You are not fit to be laird of a dunghill. 'Tis obvious you have no intention of pulling yourself together, so until you do you can just get the bleeding hell out of Lydia's castle. Now! I'll send word to Adrian and bring him home. He'll make a fine laird—"

The Hawk's eyes flew open. "Over my dead body," he snarled.

"Fine. So be it," Tavis spit back. "You're no use to anyone as you are now anyway. You may as well fall on your own claymore for all the good you're doing your people!"

"I am laird here!" Hawk slurred, his eyes flashing furiously. "And you . . . you, old man, oh hell, you're fired." Although he had intended—when he'd still had his wife—to relinquish his place to Adrian, it was currently damned cold outside and he wasn't going anywhere just yet. Maybe in the spring, if he hadn't drowned himself in whisky yet.

Tavis yanked Hawk to his feet in a swift motion, surprising the drunken laird. "Pretty strong for an old man," Hawk muttered. Tavis pulled the stumbling Hawk to the doors of the study.

"Get off me!" the Hawk bellowed.

"I expected more from you, lad. A fool I must be, but I thought you were the kind of man who fought for what he wanted. But no, you just fell apart in the face of a wee bit of adversity—"

"Och, and my wife leavin' me for another man is only a wee bit of adversity? That's what you call it?" Hawk slurred thickly, his burr deepening with his anger.

"Regardless of how *you* perceive what happened, you still have a family here, and a clan who needs its laird. If you can't do the job, then step aside for someone who can!"

"Who the hell put you in charge of me?" Hawk roared.

Tavis's own burr thickened as his temper mounted. "Your mother, you bletherin' idiot! And even if she hadna asked me, I would have come after you myself! You may be killing yourself, lad, but I'll no' be having you torturing Lydia while you're doing it!"

"All I'm doing, old man, is having a wee bit of a drink," Hawk protested.

"You've been having a 'wee bit of a drink' for over a month now. I, for one, am tired of watching you guzzle yourself to death. If you canna put down the bottle, then just get the hell out. Go piss the night away in a snowdrift where the people who love you are no' forced to watch."

Tavis kicked open the doors and tossed the stumbling Hawk face-first into the snow.

"And doona be coming back in until you can be nice to your mother! When you're ready to be laird again, *and* you've given up the bottle, you can return. But not until then!" Tavis roared as the Hawk struggled to pull his head out of a drift.

When Hawk finally managed to struggle upright, he snorted disbelievingly when he saw the man he'd thought of as a mild-mannered tanner send the Hawk's own guards to stand wide-legged in front of the door, crossed arms clearly barring him entrance into his own castle.

"Just stay out!" Tavis bellowed with such volume that Hawk heard him through the castle's heavy wooden doors.

✻   ✻   ✻

Adrienne hadn't realized how thoroughly she hated winter.

The pale face of the clock above the mantel chimed once, twice, then lapsed into silence. Two o'clock in the morning; a time when being awake could make a person feel like the only living creature left in the world. And Adrienne did feel that way, until Marie silently entered the library. Adrienne glanced up and opened her mouth to say good night, but instead a deluge of words flooded out despite the dam she'd so painstakingly erected.

Marie tucked herself into an armchair and smoothed an afghan across her lap.

Adrienne poked at the fire and opened a bottle of sweet port while she told Marie a story she'd never told anyone. The story of the orphan girl who thought she'd fallen in love with a prince, only to discover that Eberhard Darrow Garrett had been a prince of organized crime and that he'd been sending her on vacations to get drugs across the border in her luggage, her car, sewn into her clothing. And how, since she had always been packed and unpacked by his attendants, she hadn't known. She'd simply enjoyed wearing his incredible ten-carat diamond engagement ring, riding in his limos, and thumbing her nose at the Franciscan nuns in the old orphanage on First Street. How she hadn't known that the FBI had been drawing its net around him ever tighter. She'd seen that a wealthy, undeniably attractive man was showering her with love, or so she'd thought at the time. She'd had no idea she was a last-ditch effort to get a series of shipments out of the country. She'd never suspected that she was less than nothing to him—a beautiful, innocent young woman no one would ever suspect. His perfect pigeon.

Until the day she'd overheard a terrible conversation she'd never been meant to hear.

She told Marie in a hushed voice how she'd turned state's evidence and bought her own freedom. And then how Eberhard, whom the FBI had managed to miss after all, had come after her in earnest.

Marie sipped her port and listened.

She told Marie how when she'd finally been trapped by him in an old abandoned warehouse, sick of running and hiding and being afraid, she'd done the only thing she could do when he'd raised his gun.

She'd killed him before he could kill her.

$$* \quad * \quad *$$

At that point Marie waved an impatient hand. "Eees not real story. Why you tell me this?" she asked, accusingly.

Adrienne blinked. She'd just told the woman what she'd been afraid to tell anyone. That she'd killed a man. She'd done it in self-defense, granted, but she'd killed a man. She told Marie things she'd never trusted to anyone before, and the woman waved it away. Pretty much accused her of wasting her time. "What do you mean, Marie? It was real," she said defensively. "It happened. I was there."

Marie rummaged through her small reticule of English to find the right words. "Yes yes, *señorita*. May be ees real, but ees not important. Ees over and forgotten. And ees not why you weep like world ees ending. Tell me real story. Who cares where you come from, or I? Today matters. Yesterday ees skin on a snake, to be shed many times."

Adrienne sat very still for a long moment as a chill worked its way down her spine and into her belly. The hall clock chimed the quarter hour and Adrienne gazed at Marie with new appreciation.

Drawing a deep breath, Adrienne told her of Dalkeith-Upon-the-Sea. Of Lydia. And of Sidheach. Marie's brown eyes lit with a sparkle, and Adrienne was treated to a rare sight she'd bet few people had ever seen. The tiny olive-skinned woman laughed and clapped her small hands to hear of her love and of her time with the Hawk. She latched on to details, oohing over the nursery, glaring at her for saying Adam's name too many times, ahhing over their time together in Uster, sighing over the wedding that should have been.

"Ah . . . finally . . . this ees *real* story." Marie nodded.

*   *   *

In 1514, the Hawk was trying desperately to sleep. He'd heard a man could freeze to death if he fell asleep in the snow. But either it was too damned cold in that drift or he wasn't quite drunk enough. He could remedy that. Shivering, he pulled his tartan closer against the bitter, howling wind. Stumbling to his feet, he teetered unevenly up the exterior stairs to the rooftop, knowing the guards often kept a few bottles up there to keep them warm while they stood watch.

No such luck. No bottles and no guards. How could he have forgotten? The guards were all *inside*, where it was warm. He was the only one *outside*. He kicked aimlessly at the snow on the roof, then stiffened when a shadow shifted, black against the gleaming snow. He squinted and peered through the wet swirling flakes. "What the hell are you doing up here, Grimm?"

Grimm reluctantly abandoned his persistent survey of the falling dusk. He was about to explain when he saw the Hawk's face and kept his silence instead.

"I said, what are you doing up here, Grimm? They tell me you practically live on my roof now."

Suddenly furious, Grimm retorted, "Well, they tell me you practically live in a bottle of whisky now!"

Hawk stiffened and rubbed his unshaven jaw. "Don't yell at me, you son of a bitch! You're the one who lied to me about my —" He couldn't say the word. Couldn't even think it. His wife, about whom Grimm had been right. His wife, who had left him for Adam.

"You are so unbelievably dense you can't even see the truth when it's right in front of you, can you?" Grimm snapped.

The Hawk swayed drunkenly, God, where had he heard those words before? Why did they make his heart lurch inside his chest? "What are you doing up here, Grimm?" he repeated stubbornly, clutching at the parapet to steady himself.

"Waiting for a blasted falling star so I can wish her back, you drunken fool."

"I don't want her back," Hawk snarled.

Grimm snorted. "I may have mucked it up once, but I'm not the only one who let his emotions interfere. If you would just get past your foolish pride and anger, you'd realize that the lass would never have left you willingly for that blasted smithy!"

Hawk flinched and rubbed his face. "What say you, man?"

Grimm shrugged and turned away, his dark eyes searching the sky intently. "When I thought she was breaking your heart, I tried to keep the two of you apart. 'Twas a damn fool thing for me to do, I know that now, but I did what I thought was best at the time. How the hell was I supposed to know you two were falling in love? I've had no such experience. It seemed like a bloody battle to me! But now, thinking back on it, I'm fair certain she loved you from the very beginning. Would that we all could see forward with such clarity. If you'd pull your head out of that bottle and your own stubborn ass long enough, you might develop keen vision as well."

"She-said-she-loved-the-smithy," Hawk spit each word out carefully.

"She said, if you'll recall, that she loved him like Everhard. Tell me Hawk, how did she love her Ever-hard?"

"I don't know," Hawk snarled.

"Try to imagine. You told me yourself that he broke her heart. That she talked of him while you held her—"

"Shut up, Grimm!" the Hawk roared as he stalked away.

*   *   *

Hawk wandered the snow-covered gardens with his hands pressed over his ears to stem the flood of voices. He removed his hands from his ears only long enough to take another swig from the bottle he'd pilfered from the stable boy. But oblivion never came and the voices didn't stop—they just grew louder and clearer.

I love you, Sidheach. Trust you, with all my heart and further then.

None of my falcons have ever flown my hand without returning, he had warned her at the beginning of that magic summer.

You were right about your falcons, Sidheach, she'd said when she left with Adam. He'd wondered many a night why she'd said those words; they'd made no sense to him at all. But now a hint of understanding penetrated his stupor.

Right about his falcons . . .

Had his own jealousy and insecurity about the smithy so muddled his vision?

None of my falcons have flown my hand . . .

Hawk lurched to his feet as a terrible thought occurred to him.

The day of their wedding she'd been gone from his side for more than two hours. He hadn't been able to find her. Then she'd walked hurriedly out of the broch. He'd wanted to take her back into the sweet coolness to make love to her and she'd carefully and determinedly steered him away. They'd gone to the stable instead.

What had she been doing in the broch on their wedding day?

He sped through the frosty garden and leapt the low stone wall, racing through the lower bailey. He threw open the door of the broch and stood, gasping great breaths into his lungs. It was too dark with night falling. He went back outside and drew open the shutters. Not much light, but maybe it would be enough.

Hawk stood in the center of the round tower, memories tumbling around him. Eventually his eyes adjusted to the gloom. *What were you trying to tell me, lass?*

His mind whirled while his eyes searched the floor, the ceiling, the walls . . .

There.

He crossed to the wall by the door and there it was in tiny letters. Printed on the dark wall with chalky white limestone.

None of your falcons have flown you willingly, my love. Always yours! A.D.S.D.

A tiny leak sprang in the dam that had held back his anguish, releasing a trickle of pain that went on and on. She'd tried to tell him. *He uses no coercion against me,* she'd said. But coercion the smithy had obviously used against someone or something that Adrienne cared about more than she'd cared for her own happiness.

How could he have not figured it out before? That his cherished wife would have sacrificed everything to keep Dalkeith safe, just as he would. That hers was a love so deep, so unselfish, she would have walked through hell and back again to protect what she loved.

Hawk groaned aloud as memories tumbled through his mind. Adrienne bathing with him in a cool spring on their return from Uster, and the simple reverence in her eyes as she surveyed the untamed landscape that was Scotia. Adrienne's eyes glowing every time she gazed up at Dalkeith's stone walls. Adrienne's tenderness and gentle heart hidden carefully behind her aloof façade.

The bastard smithy must have found her in the broch, or perhaps he'd been trailing her. Adam had obviously threatened to use his strange powers to destroy Dalkeith, and Adrienne had done whatever he'd asked to prevent that. Or was it he, the Hawk, Adam had threatened to destroy? That thought sent him into an even bleaker rage. So, his wife had given herself up to protect him and left him a loving message to let him know what she couldn't risk telling him. That she would always love him. Her strange words had been carefully selected to make him wonder why she'd said them. To make him go to the falcon broch and look around. She hadn't been able to risk being any more explicit for fear Adam would catch on.

She must have written the words only moments before he'd found her the day of the wedding. Knowing that she had to leave him to keep him safe, she had wanted one last thing—for him to hold fast to his belief in her.

But he hadn't. He'd raged like a wounded animal, quickly believing the worst.

He swallowed the bitter bile of shame. She'd never stopped loving him. She'd never left him willingly. Small comfort now.

How could he ever have doubted her for even a minute?

The bottle dropped from his hands with a thump. Sidheach James Lyon Douglas, most beautiful man and renowned lover of three continents, man the very Fae might have envied, sank to the ground and sat very still. So still that the tears almost froze on his cheeks before slipping to the ground.

*   *   *

Hours later, Hawk made the slow, sober journey back up to the rooftop and sat heavily beside Grimm. As if their earlier conversation had never been interrupted he said, "Everhard . . . She said he used her for a fool, and she cried."

Grimm looked at his best friend and almost shouted with relief. The wild black eyes were mostly sane again. The jagged, brittle pieces of his heart no longer dangled from his sleeve. There was just a glimmer of the old Hawk's determination and strength in his face, but a glimmer was a good start. "Hawk, my friend, there is not a man, woman, or child at Dalkeith who believes she left you willingly. Either I can stay up here and freeze my ladycrackers off trying to find a falling star, or you can do something about it yourself. I—and my freezing nether regions—would thank you most assuredly. As would all of Dalkeith. *Do* something, man."

Hawk closed his eyes and took a deep, shuddering breath. "Like what? You saw them vanish into thin air. I don't even know where to look."

Grimm pointed to the smoky crest of Brahir Mount in silence, and the Hawk nodded slowly.

"Aye. The Rom."

Grimm and the Hawk passed a moment staring silently into the swirling gray mists.

"Hawk?"

"Hmmm?"

"We'll get her back," Grimm promised.

CHAPTER 33

IT TOOK MORE THAN A MONTH OF FRUSTRATED SEARCHING TO find the Rom. They'd moved on to warmer climes for the winter. It was Grimm who finally tracked them down and brought Rushka back to Dalkeith. Unknown to the Hawk, recovering Adrienne had become Grimm's personal penance, and finding the Rom had been but a minor step along the way.

"Who *is* Adam Black, really?" Hawk asked.

Everyone gathered in the Great Hall had wondered that same question at some point during the strange smithy's stay, and they all leaned closer to hear the answer.

"You Highlanders call his people the *daoine sith*. Adam is the fairy fool. The jester at the Fairy Queen's court." Rushka sighed and ran worried hands through his silver hair.

"Fairies," Grimm echoed carefully.

"Oh, don't go getting spooked on me, Grimm Roderick,"

Rushka snapped. "*You* heard the banshee yourself the night your people were killed. You saw the *bean nighe,* the washerwoman, scrubbing the bloody gown of your mother before she died. Just makes me wonder what else you've witnessed of which you speak naught." Rushka broke off abruptly and shook his head. "But that's neither here nor there. The simple fact is that the Fairy inhabit these islands. They have since long before we came, and they probably will continue to do so long after we're gone."

"I've always believed," Lydia said softly.

Hawk shifted uneasily by the fire. He had been raised on legends of the Fairy, and the fairy fool—the *sin siriche du*—was the most dangerous of the lot. "Tell me how to beat him, Rushka. Tell me everything there is to know."

Keeping track of the past was an astonishing feat of memory, and not all of the Rom could maintain such exhaustive records in their heads. But Rushka was one of the finest lorekeepers, and he was revered for being able to recite the ancient tales word for word—his father's words, and those of his father's father before him—back fifty generations.

"It was told to me as follows." Rushka took a deep breath and began.

"There are two ways to be certain one is safe from the Fae. One is to exact the Queen's oath upon the pact of the Tuatha De Danaan. That is nearly impossible to obtain for she rarely bothers herself with the doings of mortals. The other is to secure the true name of the fairy with whom one is dealing. One must then pronounce the name correctly, in the being's own tongue, while looking directly into the fairy's eyes, and issue one command. This command must be explicit and complete, for it will be obeyed precisely and only to the letter. There is no limit on the length of the command but that it must be spoken unbroken, conjoined, never-ending. One may pause, but one may never finish a sentence until the entire command is complete. If the command is broken to resume conversation with anyone, the extent of obedience summarily ends." Rushka paused a moment studying the fire. "So you see, our histories say that if you look directly into his eyes while calling his true name, he is yours to command." Rushka paced uneasily before the fire in the Greathall.

"What is his true name?"

Rushka smiled faintly and sketched several symbols in the ash of the hearth. "We do not speak it aloud. But he is the black one, the bringer of oblivion. He has many other names, but 'tis only this one that concerns you."

Hawk was incredulous. If he had only spoken Adam's name in Gaelic, he would have had it. "That simple, Rushka? You mean to tell me he was so smug and sure of himself that he called himself Adam Black?" *Amadan Dubh.* Hawk echoed the name in the privacy of his mind. Literally translated it meant Adam Black.

"Aye. But there's still a catch, Hawk. You have to find him first. He can only be compelled if he is present and you utter his name while looking directly into his eyes. And they say his eyes can send a man swiftly into madness."

"Been there already," Hawk murmured absently. "Why didn't you tell me this when he was still here? Before he took Adrienne back?"

Rushka shook his head. "Would you have believed me if I had told you that Adam was of a mythical race? That we believed he had brought the lass here for some strange revenge? Lydia tells me you wouldn't even believe she was from the future until you finally saw her disappear yourself."

Hawk's eyes clouded and he rubbed his jaw impatiently. "There is that," he allowed finally, grudgingly. "But you could have warned—"

"I did, Hawk, remember? In as much as I could the day of Zeldie's burial."

The Hawk nodded soberly. True. And his mind had been so filled with thoughts of his wife that he had put his own desires before the warnings.

"Besides, even if I had thought you would have believed, I still probably wouldn't have told you. Compelling the Fairy is a last resort. 'Tis a dangerous thing. With the fool's true name you may compel him only once—and precisely to the letter of your law. The fool obeys only exactly what you say. Were you to say, "I command you to bring Adrienne back, he would have to bring her. But she might be dead because you didn't specify in what condition."

The Hawk threw his head back and let out a wail of frustration.

Rushka continued. "Or, if you were to say, 'Take me to her,' he would have to, but *you* might be dead. Or turned into a lizard if the thought appealed to him. 'Tis a very dangerous thing to try to compel the fairy fool."

The Hawk rubbed his clean-shaven face and brooded into the flames, listening intently as Rushka went on. He sorted through the flood of information, picking and choosing carefully. It could be done. Aye, it could. When Rushka finally fell still, they passed a time in silence unbroken but for the crackle of the hearth fire.

"If you choose to try it, we still have one small problem, my friend," Rushka warned.

"What's that?" the Hawk asked absently.

"He's gone. How will you find him? I've known men

who searched for the legendary Fairy their entire lives, yet never saw so much as a stray kelpie, Hawk."

Hawk considered that a moment, then smiled. "Egotistical, you say he is?"

"Aye."

"Vain, obviously."

"Aye," Rushka confirmed.

"Prone to fits of anger and mischief was how I believe you put it."

"Aye."

"And it would appear he came here, goaded by such a human thing as jealousy. Of me."

" 'Tis true."

"Good. Then I'm about to really shake up his nasty little world."

"What do you have in mind, Hawk?" Rushka asked, the faint trace of a smile carving his weathered face.

The Hawk grinned and rose to his feet. He had work to do.

*　　*　　*

Adrienne raced up the steps at 93 Coattail Lane with more energy than she'd had in months.

"Marie! Marie!" she cried as she plunged through the door, searching for the diminutive Cuban woman who'd become more than her housekeeper in the past month; she was now more like a mother and a dear friend.

Adrienne had flatly ordered Marie to move into the house with her, and cautiously the two of them had settled into the lovely rituals of friendship; the nightly teas, the morning chats, the shared laughter and tears.

"Marie!" She called again. Then, spying Moonie, she

scooped her up and twirled the bewildered kitten around the foyer.

"Adrienne?" She appeared in the doorway, her eyes bright with hope. Marie measured Adrienne a careful moment; her shining face, her sparkling eyes. "You saw him—zee doctor?"

Adrienne bobbed her head and hugged Moonie tightly. The cat gave a disgruntled snort and squirmed. Adrienne and Marie beamed dumbly at each other over the kitten's head.

"And zee doctor said . . ." Marie encouraged.

"You were right, Marie! That *is* why I felt so sick. I'm having Hawk's baby, Marie," Adrienne exclaimed, unable to keep the news inside a moment longer. "I have the Hawk's baby inside me!"

Marie clapped her hands and laughed delightedly. Adrienne would heal in time. Having the baby of the man she loved could graft hope into any woman's heart.

✷   ✷   ✷

The Hawk hired fifty harpers and jesters and taught them new songs. Songs about the puny fairy fool who had been chased away from Dalkeith-Upon-the-Sea by the legendary Hawk. And being such a legend in his own time, his tales were ceded great truth and staying power. The players were delighted with the epic grandeur of such a wild tale.

When they had rehearsed to perfection the ditties and refrains portraying the defeat of the fool, the Hawk sent them into the counties of Scotland and England. Grimm accompanied the group of players traveling to Edinburgh to help spread the tale himself, while Hawk spent late hours by the candle scribbling, crossing out and perfecting his command for when the fool came. Sometimes, in the wee hours of the morning, he would reach for his set of sharp awls and blades and begin carving toy soldiers and dolls, one by one.

*　　*　　*

On the Island of Morar, the Queen smothered a delicate laugh with a tiny hand as strains of the new play drifted across the sea. Adam snarled.

The fool had been gloating for months now over his defeat of the Hawk. Smugly he had said to the King, and to anyone else who would listen, "He may have been pretty, but he was no match for me. Just a stupid pretty face."

The King cocked a mischievous brow, unable to resist taunting the fool. "Stupid, is he? Defeated, was he? My, my, fool, 'twould seem we named you thusly in truth. The legend of the fairy fool has just been rewritten. For all eternity mortals shall remember your defeat, not his."

The fool loosened a giant howl of rage and disappeared. This time, Finnbheara went directly to his Queen's side.

"The fool goes to the Hawk," he told her. Adam was in a dreadful temper, and the fool had nearly destroyed their race once before. *The Compact must not be broken.*

The Queen rolled onto her side and measured her consort a long moment. Then she offered her lips for his kisses and Finnbheara knew he was once again in the good graces of his love.

"You did well to tell me, my dear."

*　　*　　*

Sometimes, very late at night, Adrienne would dream that she walked the green slopes of Dalkeith again. The fresh tang of salt air scented with roses would lick through her hair and caress her skin.

In her dreams the Hawk would be waiting for her by the

sea's edge; her kilt-clad, magnificent Scottish laird. He would smile and his eyes would crinkle, then turn dark with smoldering passion.

She would take his hand and lay it gently on her swelling abdomen, and his face would blaze with happiness and pride. Then he would take her gently, there on the cliff's edge, in tempo with the pounding of the ocean. He would make fierce and possessive love to her and she would hold on to him as tightly as she could.

But before dawn, he would melt right through her fingers.

And she would wake up, her cheeks wet with tears and her hands clutching nothing but a bit of quilt or pillow.

CHAPTER 34

1 APRIL 1514

HE WAS NEAR. THE HAWK COULD FEEL HIM AS HE SAT IN HIS study polishing a toy soldier to a smooth, scaled grain while he watched the dawn move over the sea. A tingling awareness started at the base of his spine and worked its way up, heightening all his senses.

The Hawk smiled darkly and laid the toy carefully aside. Something wicked this way comes. *Aye. And I am ready this time, you bastard!*

The Hawk crossed his study to his desk and rolled the thick sheaf of parchment, tucking it into the leather girth of his sporran. He was ready to use it, but only after he had the satisfaction of fighting the smithy on mortal terms.

He stepped into the morning feeling more alive than he'd felt in months. *Hold fast and believe in me, love,* he whispered across the centuries.

Because love and belief were serious magic in and of themselves.

*   *   *

"Come out, coward," he called, his breath frosting in the chill morning air. The snowfall had stopped a few weeks ago, only sparse patches remained, and soon spring would grace Dalkeith-Upon-the-Sea once more. *As will my wife,* he vowed fiercely. For days now he'd been tense, knowing something was about to happen. Feeling it in his heart, as the Rom sometimes suffered their premonitions. Then, this morning, he'd woken in the wee hours knowing the time was at hand. The battle would be waged this day, and it was a battle he would win.

"Come on! 'Tis easy to fight anonymously. It only tells me you're too much a coward to declare yourself and face me," he taunted the misty air.

He felt foolish for a moment, then pushed the feeling brusquely aside. Adam Black was near, he knew it clear to the marrow in his bones, goaded by the minstrel plays and a fool's weakness.

"Foe! Face me! Cowardly, puny, sniveling whelp. I bet you used to hide behind your mama's skirts as a wee lad, didn't you? Quiver and taunt from behind a lass as you do now?" Hawk scoffed into the silent morning. "You used a lass as your pawn. *Anyone* could have played such a weak game. I challenge you to a true contest, gutless worm."

The breeze kicked up, more puckish now, but still no one came. The air swirled thickly in a rush of fast-scuttling clouds with black underbellies. Hawk laughed aloud, feeling exhilaration and strength course through his veins.

"Mortal man knows the truth about you now, Adam—that you couldn't win my wife, that she scorned you for me." Naturally, he omitted the truth that Adam had temporally convinced him that Adrienne had gone willingly. But the Hawk had regained his senses, along with his belief and trust in his wife. "I know she rejected you, smithy! I know you forced her to leave me against her will. She chose me over you and the whole country knows it now."

"Cease, mortal," Adam's voice whispered on the breeze.

The Hawk laughed.

"You find this amusing? You think to incite my wrath and live to laugh about it? Are you truly such a madman? For you are *not* my match."

The Hawk was still smiling when he said softly, "I was more than your match when it came to Adrienne."

"Face your executioner, pretty bird." Adam stepped menacingly out of the dense Highland mist.

The two men regarded each other savagely.

Adam stepped closer.

So did the Hawk. "Fair battle, fickle fae. Unless you're too afraid."

"This is what you called me for? A fistfight?"

"Take a mortal form, Adam. Fight me to the death."

"We don't die." Adam sneered.

"Then fight me to the draw. Fight me fair."

They circled each other warily, muscled frames abristle with unleashed hostility. The violence that had simmered since the moment these two men had met escalated to a roiling boil. It was a relief to the Hawk to have it out, to have it done with. And oh, get his hands on that bastard smithy at last!

"Fair battle is all I've ever done."

"You lie, fool. You cheated at every turn."

"I've never cheated!"

"Well, don't cheat now," Hawk warned as they faced off. "Bare-handed. Man to man, you are my match in size. Are you in strength, agility, and cunning? I think not."

Adam shrugged indolently. "You will rue the day you were born, pretty bird. I've already beaten you and taken your wife, but this day, I will seal your fate. This day I will destroy Dalkeith, until nothing but granite crumbs blow over the cliff's edge to meet the hungry sea. Your bones will be among them, Hawk."

Hawk threw his dark head back and laughed.

*   *   *

Shrouded in the heavy mist, the court of the Tuatha De Danaan watched the fight.

"The Hawk is winning!"

Silvery sigh. "So much man."

"See him move! Fast as a panther, deadly as a python."

"Think not of him, he is safe from all of us now. So I have commanded," the Queen snapped on a frigid gust of air.

A long silence.

"Will the fool play fair?" queried Aine, the quiet, mousy fairy.

The Queen sighed. "Has he ever?"

*   *   *

Adrienne clutched Marie's hand and gasped aloud as she felt the soft kick in her womb. Somehow it felt as if the Hawk were near and needed her strength and love. As if something magical hovered, almost tangible enough to grasp with her slender fingers. She squeezed her eyes shut tightly and willed her heart across the chasms of time.

*   *   *

Adam snarled. "Enough of this mortal idiocy. It's time to end this once and for all." He was bleeding, his lip cut and nose shattered. Adam used his immortal strength to fling the Hawk to the ground at his feet. A sword appeared in Adam's hand, and he laid the blade against the mortal's throat. "Compact be damned," Adam muttered, balancing the razor-sharp edge flush to the Hawk's jugular. He cocked a brow and taunted the fallen mortal. "You know, for a moment there, I was worried you might have managed to learn something about my race, the kind of thing we don't like mortals to know. But it seems I was right about you all along, and my worry was for naught. You are truly thick-witted. You really thought you could best me in a fistfight?" Adam shook his head and tsk-tsked. "Hardly. It takes more than that to defeat my kind. Oh, and by the by, prepare to die, mortal."

But his threat elicited nary a quiver from the legend at his feet. Instead the Hawk arrogantly wrapped his hand around the blade and looked deep into Adam's eyes. The intensity of the mortal's gaze latched on to Adam's and held with a strength all its own.

Adam tensed, and a flicker of uncertainty flashed across his face.

Hawk smiled. "*Amadan Dubh,* I compel you thusly . . ."

Adam froze and his jaw dropped, belying a very human expression of astonishment. The sword melted from his hand as the words of the ancient ritual of binding mired him tightly. "You can't do this!" Adam spit out.

But the Hawk could, and did.

Adam growled low in his throat. It was not a human sound at all.

Twenty minutes later, Adam was gaping in disbelief. The Hawk had actually unrolled a parchment scroll from his sporran and was reading a very long, very specific list of demands.

". . . and you will never come near Dalkeith-Upon-the-Sea again . . ."

Adam shuddered. "Are you almost done, pretty bird?"

The Hawk continued without interruption, unrolling his scroll farther.

"Did you write a goddamn book? You can't do it like this," Adam said through gritted teeth. "You get one command. You can't read that whole thing."

Hawk almost laughed aloud. The trickery would begin now. Any loophole the fickle fairy could find he would try to use. But the Hawk hadn't left any loopholes. He kept reading.

"I said give it up, you infantile, mewling mass of mortality. It won't work."

". . . and you will never . . ." Hawk continued.

Adam snarled and raged, his icy face turning whiter. "I will curse your children, your children's children; I will curse Adrienne and all her children . . ." Adam dangled evilly.

Hawk stiffened and paused. His eyes flew to Adam's.

Adam stifled a snicker of glee, certain that the Hawk would slip and break his command.

Hawk's lips drew back in a fierce snarl, ". . . and you will never seek to lay a curse upon my family, my seed, myself, or the family, seed, or self of anyone I command you to forsake or any Douglas commands you to forsake . . . including Adrienne; with Douglas being expressly defined as any relative by direct blood tie, marriage, or adoption, seed being defined as progeny, children adopted or otherwise obtained, you will not harm any animal belonging to . . ."

Adam paced a stunted space of earth, fear now evident in his every step.

". . . obedience being defined as . . . and when you return

Adrienne to me, all will be in order at Dalkeith-Upon-the-Sea . . . the Hawk and all his people being protected from any harm, alive and in the best of health with no tricks played . . . and Adrienne will be bringing her cat safely back through time with her . . . and . . ."

Adam's face, once beautiful, was a livid mask of hate, "I will *not* lose! I will find a way to defeat you, Hawk."

". . . and you will forgo any thoughts or actions of revenge against the Douglas . . ."

Adam waved his hand and Adrienne appeared, looking utterly stunned, clutching a clawing cat in her arms.

The Hawk shuddered imperceptibly, knowing this was just one more trick by Adam to get him to break his command. Five months, five horrible, heartless months without a glimpse of his beloved's face, and now she stood before him. Breathtakingly, heart-wrenchingly lovely. Hawk's gaze rested hungrily on her face, her silvery mane, her lush body, her round belly . . .

Her round belly? His eyes flew to Adrienne's, wide with astonishment and awe, as a violent possessiveness rocked his frame.

His child! His daughter or son. Blood of his blood—his and Adrienne's.

Adrienne was pregnant.

Hawk was speechless.

Adam grinned wickedly—and the Hawk saw it.

He would *not* lose Adrienne. He had too much to read yet. With iron force of will, Hawk averted his eyes from his beloved wife.

It was the hardest thing he'd ever done in his entire life.

Adrienne's eyes devoured him.

She was afraid to interrupt, afraid to move. Somehow she'd been miraculously yanked right out of her library, and

Moonie, who had been across the room by the fire, was curled snugly in her arms. She could still see Marie's startled face fading before her eyes.

And there was the Hawk, beloved husband and life itself.

"How could you resist me, Beauty?" Adam was suddenly the smithy again, kilt-clad and glistening. "I am every bit as beautiful as the Hawk and can please you in ways you can't even dream. I could turn you inside out and make you weep with ecstasy. How could you forsake me?"

"I love my husband." She'd spent many months clinging to the hope of the Hawk's child growing inside her and studying everything about Celtic lore she could get her hands on in hopes of finding a way back. But the Hawk, it seemed, had found it for her.

"Love. What is this love thing you mortals prize so highly?" Adam sneered.

Enough, fool, came a silvery peal of the Fairy Queen's sigh.

Even Hawk slurred over his words, midsentence, at that voice.

And enough from you, too, beautiful man, legendary Hawk.

Sweeter than the chiming of bells, her voice was a sensuous stroke of heaven. But Hawk continued, without interruption, ". . . and as used in this command, the word *person* shall mean and include, where appropriate, an individual or other entity; the plural shall be substituted for the singular and the singular for plural when appropriate; and words of any gender shall include any other gender . . ."

Adrienne watched her husband, her eyes blazing with love and pride.

The fool will obey me. I am his Queen.

Hawk paused a whisper of a breath, not enough to break continuity, but enough to acknowledge.

And besides, you're past commanding. You're pontificating and being positively redundant. Still, well done, mortal. She is safe, you both are. I will see to it for now and always.

Hawk continued, ". . . all elements conjoined by ifs, ands, or buts, or other conjoining verbiage shall not, when seemingly in conflict, operate in exclusion or limit in any fashion but shall function conjunctive, overlapping, and allowing the broadest possible definition of the terms as used herein . . ."

The Fairy Queen sighed. *Ahhh, I see. You will not cease this drivel until I offer you assurance. Clever man. You seek my troth? I grant it. You have the sworn oath of the Fairy Queen upon the pact of the Tuatha De Danaan. T'will never be broken, lest our race vanish.*

Hawk released the scroll and it rolled shut with an audible snap. Only then did Adrienne see the tremor in his hands as he met her gaze, eyes triumphant.

"She has given us protection and fealty." His smile could have lit the Samhain bonfires. His eyes swept her from head to toe, lovingly lingering on every inch in between.

"We're safe?" Adrienne whispered, tears springing to her eyes.

I shall see to it myself, the silvery voice lilted. *Now and for always. Fool?*

Adam growled.

Since I can't seem to keep you out of trouble you have a new companion. Aine will spend the next five hundred years with you. She will endeavor to keep you in line.

Not Aine! Adam's plea was a shade away from a whine. *That snoopy little fairy has a crush on me! I could spend my time pleasing you, my Queen. Let me!*

You will please Aine, fool, or you will spend the next thousand years in the foot of a mountain by yourself. You think you're bored now?

With one last searing look at the Hawk, Adam vanished.

Now where were we? the Queen asked. Adrienne squinted hard in the direction of the voice. She could barely discern the shimmering outline of a woman hovering in the misty air behind the Hawk.

Ah, yes. The two of you were about to have a wedding on the ridge by the sea. The fool has a beastly sense of timing. I shall pick up where it was left off. I, Aoibheal, Queen of the Tuatha De Danaan, name you man and wife. Neither mortal nor immortal shall ever tear you asunder, lest they incur my eternal wrath. There. You've been wed by the Fairy Queen. None can lay claim to such a legend.

Adrienne and the Hawk were still staring at each other across a space of garden, both afraid to move even an inch.

Well? Kiss the woman, you big beautiful man! Go on.

The Hawk sucked in a harsh breath.

He'd changed, Adrienne realized. Time had rendered him even more beautiful than before. She didn't know he was thinking the same thing about her. His eyes slid over her, from her silvery-blond hair to her bare toes peeping from under a pair of strange trousers.

And then she was in his arms, folded in that strong embrace she'd dreamed about every night for the past five months as she lay in bed, her hand resting on her rounded belly, begging the heavens for just one more day with her husband.

He brushed her lips with his. "My heart."

"Your heart is . . . oh!" She lost her breath beneath his ravishing lips.

"Ahhh," the Queen marveled, for even the Tuatha De Danaan were in awe of true love. *You are worthy of what I now give you,* she whispered just before she vanished. *Consider it a wedding gift. . . .*

EPILOGUE

ADRIENNE BREATHED DEEPLY. NOTHING WOULD EVER COM-
pare to the scent of roses and spring rain, the unceasing roar
of the waves against the west cliffs and the splash of salt in
the unspoiled air. She had ducked outside to watch twilight
move in over the sea. Then she would return to Lydia and
continue making baby plans. She smothered a laugh with
her hand. Lydia had finally outright ordered the Hawk to go
away, complaining that she couldn't possibly welcome her
daughter-in-law back properly and prepare for her grand-
child if he wouldn't stop kissing her all the time. Not that
Adrienne had minded.

Like a chastened boy, the Hawk had glared.

"You have the rest of your lives together," Lydia had remarked crisply, "while we women have only a few short
months to prepare for the babe."

"A few short months?" Hawk had looked stunned. Then
worried. He'd raced off, muttering under his breath.

Now Adrienne stood on the stone stairs, head tilted back, drinking in the quiet beauty of the velvety sky. A flicker of movement on the roof caught her eye.

Grimm peered over the parapet at her and his handsome face lit with a smile. She and the Hawk had talked that afternoon and he had filled her in on what had transpired, including Grimm's part in helping to bring her back. Only hours before, Grimm had clasped his hand to his heart and on bended knee begged forgiveness for lying. She'd granted it readily.

"Hope you're not looking for a star, Grimm," she called up to him.

"Never again," he vowed fervently.

Adrienne gasped, as at precisely that moment a tiny white speck sparked and sputtered, then traced a downward spiral across the sky. "Oh my God! Grimm, look! A shooting star!" She squeezed her eyes shut and wished fiercely.

"What did you just wish?" he growled down at her, rigid with tension.

When she opened her eyes again, she said saucily, "I can't tell. It's against the rules."

"What did you just wish?" he roared.

"My, aren't we superstitious?" she teased with a smile.

He glowered down at her as she made her way back into the castle. Glancing over her shoulder, she flashed him an impish grin. "Brace yourself, Grimm. I will tell you this much—I spent my wish on *you*."

"Don't you know how dangerous it is to be throwing idle wishes about, lass!" he thundered.

"Oh, this one wasn't idle at all," she called cheerfully before the door swung closed. On the rooftop of Dalkeith, Grimm sank to his knees and stared up into the sky, desperately seeking another wishing star . . . just in case.

*   *   *

Adrienne's gown rustled as she slipped down the corridor.
Lydia had told her where she might find the Hawk and, over
tangy mint tea, had filled her in on a few things her husband
hadn't bothered to mention to her. Such as the fact that he'd
destroyed her beloved nursery, the one she'd lain awake fan-
tasizing about when she'd been stranded in the twentieth
century. So *that* was where he'd rushed off to looking so
worried about "the scant few months left." She entered the
nursery so silently, Hawk did not hear her approach.

She traced her fingers lightly and lovingly over an exquisitely carved doll and paused.

He was kneeling beside a cradle, rubbing oil into the
wood with a soft cloth. Clad only in the blues and silvers
of his kilt, his dark hair fell forward in a silky wave. The
nursery was aglow with dozens of oil globes, casting his
powerful torso a gleaming bronze. His eyes were narrowed
in concentration and the muscles in his arms flexed and
bunched as he rubbed.

Adrienne leaned against the jamb and watched him in silence, tallying the room's meager furnishings. Many of the
toys were back, but all the cradles and beds were all gone.
What phenomenal passion must have raged through him!

"I suppose I should feel flattered," she said softly.

His head jerked up guiltily.

Adrienne stepped into the room, conscious that her
breasts, made fuller by pregnancy, swayed beneath her
gown, and that the Hawk seemed fascinated by the ripeness
of her lusher curves. They'd made love that afternoon, desperately, quickly, and fiercely, scarcely making it from the
gardens to the privacy of their bedroom. Lydia had patiently

waited all of one hour before she'd knocked on the door and demanded to see her daughter-in-law.

When Adrienne had been trapped back in the twentieth century, fearing she would never be intimate with her husband again, memories of their incredible passion had cascaded through her mind with bittersweet fury, heightening her awareness of all the sensual things she'd longed to do with the Hawk, but had been denied. Those long, torturous months of desire, coupled with the demanding hormones of pregnancy, enhanced her daring now. She hungered for the slow, delicious loving she'd been afraid she might never experience again. "Hawk?"

He gazed up at her, still crouched on the floor, ready to pounce if she so much as moved an inch.

Adrienne moved—deliberately and erotically. She stooped to pick up a toy soldier, bending so that her breasts threatened to spill from her bodice. She caught her lower lip between her teeth and sent the Hawk a smoldering look from beneath lowered lashes. He was on his feet in an instant.

"Stop!" Adrienne raised a hand to hold him back.

Hawk froze mid-stride.

"What do you wish of me, Adrienne?" he whispered huskily.

"I need you," she said breathlessly. He lunged forward and she raised her hand again. "No, let me look at you," she said as she circled slowly around him. She smiled when his eyes widened. "When I was back in my time, one of the things that I really wanted to clear up was a question about Scotsmen and their kilts. . . ."

"And that question was?"

"I saw you mounting your horse one day—"

"I know you did," he said smugly. "You were in the window by the nursery."

"Oh! You *did* do it on purpose!"

Hawk laughed, mischief crinkling his eyes, and it fueled her bold resolve. If he could tease her—well, two could play that game. She'd see how well he handled such toying with his desires.

Stepping closer, Adrienne placed her hand on his muscled thigh and stared into his eyes provocatively. His nostrils flared, and his eyes darkened beneath hooded lids. With her other hand she tugged the bodice of her gown, freeing her breasts to spill over the top. She felt deliciously wicked, knowing her nipples were rosy, puckered, and begging to be kissed. When he leaned forward to do just that, she pushed him back playfully, slid her hand up his thigh, and wrapped it around his shaft, delighted by his husky groan. "Nothing beneath this plaid, just as I suspected," she observed pertly.

"Adrienne. You're *killing* me."

"I've only just begun, my love." She wrapped her fingers around his magnificent arousal and slipped her hand up and down his shaft with a velvety friction.

Hawk grabbed her hips and lowered his head to kiss her; but she moved her head and laughed when he buried his face in her breasts instead.

"Stop," she commanded.

"What?" he asked disbelieving.

"Step back," she encouraged. "Don't touch me until I ask you to. Let me touch you."

Hawk groaned loudly, but let his hands fall from her body. His eyes were fierce and wild, and Adrienne suspected he wouldn't permit her subtle torture much longer.

She leisurely unfastened his kilt and dropped it to the floor. Her husband stood nude before her, his bronze body glistening in the candlelight, his hard shaft bucking insistently. Adrienne traced a fascinated and admiring path over his shoulders and across his broad, muscled chest. She lightly brushed his lips with hers, kissed his jaw, his nipples, teased his rippled abdomen with her tongue, then sank to her knees, her mouth inches from his shaft, her hands splayed on his thighs.

"Adrienne!"

She kissed the sweetness of him, stroking her tongue up and down his hard length. Hawk buried his hands in her hair and made a raw sound deep in his throat. "Enough!" he pulled her to her feet and backed her against the ledge beneath the windows. He swept her off her feet, deposited her upon the ledge, and tossed her gown up, spreading her legs to accommodate him. *"Now*, Adrienne. I want you *now."* He kissed her deeply as he gently but insistently thrust into her beckoning wetness. Adrienne gasped with pleasure as he filled her completely. Hawk stared into her face, taking careful note of each shudder, each moan that escaped her lips, and just when she reached convulsively for the exquisite apex, just when she felt the sweet tremor begin—he stopped moving completely.

"Hawk!"

"Will you be teasing me again like this, my love?" he murmured.

"Absolutely," Adrienne replied saucily.

"You *will*?"

"Of course. Because I know my husband would *never* leave me wanting. Just as I would *never* tease him without completely satisfying his desires. So, satisfy me, my sweet highland laird. Take me to Valhalla, husband."

He laughed softly, then thrust into her carefully and gently until they came in perfect tempo. The intensity of their union, so perfect in body and soul, made Adrienne cry aloud with the wonder of it.

Later, the Hawk shut the nursery door and carried his sleepy, satisfied wife to the Peacock Room, where he held her in his arms through the night, marveling at the completeness of his life with her in it.

✴   ✴   ✴

Lydia smiled when she heard the nursery door close soundly above her. All was well at Dalkeith-Upon-the-Sea. She paused a dreamy moment imagining the wee bairns that would grace the nursery soon.

Life had never been sweeter.

But it could be even sweeter still, Lydia.

Lydia's eyes narrowed thoughtfully on Tavis Mac-Tarvitt's back as he stood pensively before the fire. A wave of guilt crashed over her as she recalled how he'd come back to her that night after talking to the Hawk, and she'd turned a cold shoulder to him, and retreated once again into the familiar safety of formality.

The strain in his patient smile was all the reproof he'd betrayed.

My love, he'd called her, and she'd felt so guilty for having love when her son had been so alone that she had refused to acknowledge it. *How much more time do you plan to waste, lass?*

Very quietly, Lydia unpinned her plaits, freeing her wavy chestnut hair. Her eyes never wavered from Travis's back. With a smile of anticipation she tossed her head upside-down, finger-combed her hair into tousled curls, then flipped it back over her head, allowing it to fall in a wild tumble down her back.

So many years!

She tugged nervously at her gown, studied his back another moment, then shrugged and unbuttoned a few pearl buttons at her collar. She took a deep, trembling breath as the butterflies took silken wing inside her belly.

"Tavis?" she called softly. Once decided, she fully committed to not wasting one more precious moment.

Tavis's back straightened and he peered briefly over his shoulder at her.

She almost laughed aloud when his eyes flew wide and he jerked completely around to face her, his gaze roving over her wild mane, her loosened collar, her parted lips.

"Lydia?"

She heard a hundred questions in his one word, and was thrilled by the knowledge that she finally had the right answer to give him. "I've been wondering a thing, you see, old man," she said patting the bench beside her. "Those hands of yours . . ." Her voice trailed off, a wicked sparkle in her eyes. Coquettishly, she wet her lower lip in an invitation older than time itself.

"Aye?" There was a hoarse catch in his voice.

"Being that they're so talented and strong . . ."

"Aye?" His brows rose. His breath snagged in his throat as Lydia made a suggestion for those hands that shocked and delighted Tavis MacTarvitt to the very seat of his soul.

*　　*　　*

When Grimm finally left the rooftop that night and entered the Great Hall, he stifled an oath and scrambled, in full retreat, right back out the door. *In the hall, of all places! Lydia! And Tavis!*

"Och! Love!" he grumbled to the stars that twinkled above him with dispassionate splendor.

✳   ✳   ✳

Three months later the healthy cry of a baby boy resounded
through the halls of Dalkeith-Upon-the-Sea.

Hawk Douglas, bursting with pride, sat at Adrienne's
side on the bed.

"Look at him, Hawk! He's perfect!" Adrienne exclaimed.

"He's not the only one," Hawk said huskily, smoothing
her hair back from her forehead.

Adrienne smiled at him. He'd held her hand through her
labor, alternating between cursing himself and cursing her
for letting him get her pregnant in the first place.

But there would be many more such times, Adrienne
thought, because she fully intended to have half a dozen babies. Hawk was just going to have to get used to the process
of bringing them into the world.

Adrienne touched his cheek wonderingly. "You're crying," she whispered.

"Happy tears. You've given me a new life, Adrienne—a
life I never dreamed I'd have."

She gazed at him adoringly, their baby snuggled between them.

Adrienne could have remained like that for hours, but
Grimm entered the Peacock Room just then, briskly order-
ing the guards about. "Place it there, by the bed."

Hawk glanced over his shoulder. "Ah, the cradle. I finished it last night. I suspect he will not be seeing much of
it for a while." Hawk possessively drew their tiny son in
his arms. "He should sleep with us for a time, don't you
think?"

"I don't think I could allow him out of my sight, could
you?"

Hawk nodded his agreement as he studied his son intently. "My jaw," he said proudly. "Just look at that fine strong angle."

Adrienne laughed. "Stubborn angle," she teased, "and he already has dark hair."

Behind them Grimm made a choked sound.

Hawk glanced over his shoulder questioningly.

"What the bloody hell . . . er, excuse me, milady," he said to Adrienne, "and pardon me, wee one," he said to the babe. "But why did you go and carve this on the cradle, Hawk?" Grimm asked. "Haven't we all had enough of the blasted Fairy?"

Hawk raised his eyebrows in confusion. "What are you talking about, Grimm?" He gently relinquished their son to Adrienne and strode to the cradle.

Flowing letters had been carved deep into the wood. The entire cradle gleamed as if it had been brushed with a sprinkling of gold dust. Hawk gazed a long moment at words he knew *he* hadn't put there. A smile curved his lip as he read aloud to Adrienne:

Remember this, mortal—you have your own kind of
forever—the immortality of love.
Blessed be the Douglas.
Aoibheal, Queen of the Fae

About the Author

KAREN MARIE MONING graduated from Purdue University with a bachelor's degree in Society & Law. Her novels have been *USA Today* bestsellers and have appeared on the *New York Times* expanded bestseller list. They have won numerous awards, including the prestigious RITA Award. She can be reached at www.karenmoning.com.

Visit our website at www.bantamdell.com.

*Don't miss the greatest
adventure in the
Highlander series*

the immortal
highlander

by

karen marie
moning

A Delacorte hardcover on sale in August

Please read on for a preview. . . .

the immortal highlander

Adam Black raked a hand through his long black hair and scowled as he stalked down the alley.

Three eternal months he'd been human. Ninety-seven horrific days to be exact. Two thousand three hundred twenty-eight interminable hours. One hundred thirty-nine thousand six hundred eighty thoroughly offensive minutes.

He'd become obsessed with increments of time. It was an embarrassingly mortal affliction. Next thing he knew, he'd be wearing a watch.

Never.

He'd been certain Aoibheal would have come for him by now. Would have staked his very essence on it; not that he had much left to stake.

But she hadn't, and he was sick of waiting. Not only were

humans allotted a ridiculously finite slice of time to exist, their bodies had requirements that consumed a great deal of that time. Sleep alone consumed a full third of it. Although he'd mastered those requirements, over the past few months, he resented being slave to his physical form. Having to eat, wash, dress, sleep, piss, shave, brush his hair and teeth, for Christ's sake! He wanted to be himself again. Not at the queen's bloody convenience, but *now*.

Hence he'd left London and journeyed to Cincinnati (the infernally long way—by plane) looking for the half-Fae son he'd sired over a millennium ago, Circenn Brodie, who'd married a twenty-first-century mortal and usually resided here with her.

Usually.

Upon arriving in Cincinnati, he'd found Circenn's residence vacant, and had no idea where to look for him next. He'd taken up residence there himself, and had been killing time since—endeavoring grimly to ignore that, for the first time in his timeless existence, time was returning the favor—waiting for Circenn to return. A half-blooded Tuatha Dé, Circenn had magic Adam no longer possessed.

Adam's scowl deepened. What paltry power the queen had left him was virtually worthless. He'd quickly discovered that she'd thought through his punishment most thoroughly. The spoll of the *féth fiada* was one of the most powerful and perception-altering that the Tuatha Dé possessed, employed to permit a Tuatha Dé full interaction with the human realm, while keeping him or her undetectable by humans. It cloaked its wearer in illusion that affected short-term memory and generated confusion in the minds of those in the immediate vicinity.

If Adam toppled a newsstand, the vendor would blithely blame an unseen wind. If he took food from a diner's plate, the person merely decided he/she must have finished. If he procured new clothing for himself at a shop, the owner would register an inventory error. If he snatched groceries from a passerby and flung the bag to the ground, his hapless victim would turn on the nearest bystander and a bitter fight would ensue (he'd done that a few times for a bit of sport). If he plucked the purse from a woman's arm and dangled it before her face, she would simply walk through both him and it (the moment he touched a thing, it, too, was sucked into the illusion cast by the *féth fiada* until he released it), then head in the opposite direction, muttering about having forgotten her purse at home.

There was nothing he could do to draw attention to himself. And he'd tried everything. To all intents and purposes, Adam Black didn't exist. Didn't even merit his own measly slice of human space.

He knew why she'd chosen this particular punishment: Because he'd sided with humans in their little disagreement, she was forcing him to taste of being human in the worst possible way. Alone and powerless, without a single distraction with which to pass the time and entertain himself.

He'd had enough of a taste to last an eternity.

Once an all-powerful being that could sift time and space, a being that could travel anywhere and anywhen in the blink of an eye, he was now limited to a single useful power: He could sift place over short distances, but no more than a few miles. It'd surprised him the queen had left him even that much power, until the first time he'd almost been run down by a careening bus in the heart of London.

She'd left him just enough magic to stay alive. Which told him two things: one, she planned to forgive him eventually, and two, it was probably going to be a long, long time. Like, probably not until the moment his mortal form was about to expire.

Fifty more years of this would drive him bloody frigging nuts.

Problem was, even when Circenn *did* return, Adam still hadn't figured out a way to communicate with him. Because of his mortal half, Circenn wouldn't be able to see past the *féth fiada* either.

All he needed, Adam brooded for the thousandth time, was one person. Just one person who could see him. A single person who could help him. He wasn't entirely without options, but he couldn't exercise a damned one of them without someone to aid him.

And that sucked too. The almighty Adam Black needed help. He could almost hear silvery laughter tinkling on the night breeze, blowing tauntingly across the realms, all the way from the shimmering silica sands of the Isle of Morar.

With a growl of caged fury, he stalked out of the alley.

*   *   *

Gabby indulged herself in a huge self-pitying sigh as she got out of her car. Normally on nights like this, when the sky was black velvet, glittering with stars and a silver-scythe moon, warm and humid and alive with the glorious scents and sounds of summer, nothing could depress her.

But not tonight. Everyone but her was out somewhere having a life, while she was scrambling to clean up after the latest fairy debacle. Again.

It seemed like all she ever did anymore.

She wondered briefly what her ex was doing tonight. Was he out at the bars? Had he already met someone new? Someone who wasn't still a virgin at twenty-four?

And *that* was the Fae's fault too.

She slammed the car door harder than she should have, and a little piece of chrome trim fell off and clattered to the pavement. It was the third bit of itself her aging Corolla had shed that week, though she was pretty sure the antenna had been assisted by bored neighborhood kids. With a snort of exasperation, she locked the car, kicked the little piece of trim beneath the car—she refused to clean up even one more thing—and turned toward the building.

And froze.

A fairy male had just stalked out of the alley and was standing by the bench in the small courtyard oasis near the entrance to her office building. As she watched, it stretched out on the bench on its back, folded its arms behind its head, and stared up at the night sky, looking as if it had no intention of moving for a long, long time.

Damn and double-damn!

She was still in such a stew over the day's events that she wasn't sure she could manage to walk by it without giving in to the overwhelming urge to *kick* it.

It.

Fairies were "its," never "hims" or "hers." Gram had taught her at a young age not to personify them. They weren't human. And it was dangerous to think of them, even in the privacy of her thoughts, as if they were.

But heavens, Gabby thought, staring, he—*it*—was certainly male.

So tall that the bench wasn't long enough for it to fully stretch out on, it had propped one leg on the back of the bench and bent the other at the knee, its legs spread in a basely masculine position. It was clad in snug-fitting, faded jeans, a black T-shirt, and black leather boots. Long, silky black hair spilled over its folded arms, falling to sweep the sidewalk. In contrast to the golden angelic ones she'd seen earlier that day, this one was dark and utterly devilish-looking.

Gold armbands adorned its muscular arms, showcasing its powerful rock-hard biceps, and a gold torque encircled its neck, gleaming richly in the amber glow of the gaslights illuming the courtyard oasis.

Royalty, she realized with a trace of breathless fascination. Only those of a royal house were entitled to wear torques of gold. She'd never seen a member of one of the Ruling Houses before.

And "royal" was certainly a good word for him, er . . . it. Its profile was sheer majesty. Chiseled features, high cheekbones, strong jaw, aquiline nose, all covered with that luscious gold-velvet fairy skin. She narrowed her eyes, absorbing details. Unshaven jaw sculpted by five-o'clock shadow. Full mouth. Lower lip decadently full. Sinfully so, really. (Gabby, quit *thinking* that!)

She inhaled slowly, exhaled softly, holding utterly still, one hand on the roof of her car, the other clutching her keys.

It exuded immense sexuality: base, raw, scorching. From this distance she should not have been able to feel the heat from its body, but she could. She should not have gotten a bit dizzy from its exotic scent, but she had. As if it were twenty times more potent than any she'd encountered before; a veritable powerhouse of a fairy.

She was never going to be able to walk past it. Just wasn't happening. Not today. There was only so much she was capable of in a given day, and Gabby O'Callaghan had exceeded her limits.

Still . . . it hadn't moved. In fact, it seemed utterly oblivious to its surroundings. It couldn't hurt to look a little longer. . . .

Besides, she reminded herself, she had a duty to surreptitiously observe as much as possible about any unknown fairy specimen. In such fashion did the O'Callaghan women protect themselves and the future of their children—by learning about their enemy. By passing down stories. By adding new information, with sketches when possible, to the multivolume *Books of the Fae,* thereby providing future generations greater odds of escaping detection.

This one didn't have the sleekly muscled body of most fairy males, she noted; this one had the body of a warrior. Shoulders much too wide to squeeze onto the bench. Arms bunched with muscle, thick forearms, strong wrists. Cut abdomen rippling beneath the fabric of its T-shirt each time it shifted position. Powerful thighs caressed by soft faded denim.

No, not a warrior, she mused, that wasn't quite it. A shadowy image was dancing in the dark recesses of her mind and she struggled to bring it into focus.

More like . . . ah, she had it! Like one of those blacksmiths of yore who'd spent their days pounding steel at a scorching forge, metal clanging, sparks flying. Possessing massive brawn, yet also capable of the delicacy necessary to craft intricately embellished blades, combining pure power with exquisite control.

There wasn't a spare ounce of flesh on it, just rock-hard male body. It had a finely honed, brutal strength that, coupled with its height and breadth, could feel overwhelming to a woman. Especially if it were stretching all that rippling muscle on top of—

Stop that, O'Callaghan! Wiping tiny beads of sweat from her forehead with the back of her hand, she drew a shaky breath, struggling desperately for objectivity. She felt as hot as the forge she could imagine him bending over, hard body glistening, pounding . . . pounding . . .

Go, Gabby, a faint inner voice warned. *Go now. Hurry.*

But her inner alarm went off too late. At that precise moment it turned its head and glanced her way.

She should have looked away. She tried to look away. She couldn't.

Its face, full-on, was a work of impossible masculine

beauty—exquisite symmetry brushed by a touch of savagery—but it was the eyes that got her all tangled up. They were ancient eyes, immortal eyes, eyes that had seen more than she could ever dream of seeing in a thousand lifetimes. Eyes full of intelligence, mockery, mischief, and—her breath caught in her throat as its gaze dropped down her body, then raked slowly back up—unchained sexuality. Black as midnight beneath slashing brows, its eyes flashed with gold sparks.

Her mouth dropped open and she gasped.

But, but, but, a part of her sputtered in protest, *it doesn't have fairy eyes! It can't be a fairy! They have iridescent eyes. Always. And if it's not a fairy, what* is *it?*

Again its gaze slid down her body, this time much more slowly, lingering on her breasts, fixing unabashedly at the juncture of her thighs. Without a shred of self-consciousness, it shifted its hips to gain play in its jeans, reached down, and blatantly adjusted itself.

Helplessly, as if mesmerized, her gaze followed, snagging on that big dark hand tugging at the faded denim. At the huge swollen bulge cupped by the soft worn fabric. For a moment it closed its hand over itself and rubbed the thick ridge, and she was horrified to feel her own hand clenching. She flushed, mouth dry, cheeks flaming.

Suddenly it went motionless and its preternatural gaze locked with hers, eyes narrowing.

"Christ," it hissed, surging up from the bench in one graceful ripple of animal strength, "you see me. You're *seeing* me!"

"No I'm not," Gabby snapped instantly. Defensively. Stupidly. *Oh, that was good, O'Callaghan, you dolt!*

Snapping her mouth shut so hard her teeth clacked, she unlocked the car door and scrambled in faster than she'd ever thought possible.

Twisting the key in the ignition, she threw the car into reverse.

And then she did another stupid thing: She glanced at it again. She couldn't help it. It simply commanded attention.

It was stalking toward her, its expression one of pure astonishment.

For a brief moment she gaped blankly back. Was a fairy *capable* of being astonished? According to O'Callaghan sources, they experienced no emotion. And how could they? They had no hearts, no souls. Only a fool would think some kind of higher conscience lurked behind those quixotic eyes. Gabby was no fool.

It was almost to the curb. Heading straight for her.

With a startled jerk she came to her senses, slammed the car into drive, and jammed the gas pedal to the floor.

*   *   *

Adam was so caught off guard that it didn't occur to him to do a series of short jumps and follow the woman, until it was too late.

By the time he'd tensed to sift, the dilapidated vehicle had sped off, and he had no idea where it had gone. He popped about in various directions for a time but was unable to pick it up again.

Shaking his head, he returned to the bench and sat down, cursing himself in half a dozen languages.

Finally, someone had *seen* him.

And what had he done? Let her get away. Undermined by his disgusting human anatomy.

It had just been made excruciatingly clear to him that the human male brain and the human male cock couldn't both sustain sufficient amounts of blood to function at the same time. It was one or the other, and the human male apparently didn't get to choose which one.

As a Tuatha Dé, he would have been in complete control of his lust. Desirous yet cool-headed, perhaps even a touch bored (it wasn't as if he could do something he hadn't done before; given a few thousand years, a Tuatha Dé got around to trying everything).

But as a human male, lust was far more intense, and his body was apparently slave to it. A simple hard-on could turn him into a bloody Neanderthal.

How *had* mankind survived this long? For that matter, how had they ever managed to crawl out of their primordial swamps to begin with?

Blowing out an exasperated breath, he rose from the bench and began pacing a stunted space of cobbled courtyard.

There he'd been, lying on his back, staring up at the stars, wondering where in the hell Circenn might have hied himself off to for so long, when suddenly he'd suffered a prickly sensation, as if he were the focus of an intense gaze.

He'd glanced over, half-expecting to see a few of his brethren laughing at him. In fact, he'd hoped to see his brethren. Laughing or not. In the past ninety-seven days he'd searched high and low for one of his race, but hadn't caught so much as a glimpse of a Tuatha Dé. He'd finally concluded that the queen must have forbidden them to spy upon him, for he could find no other explanation for their absence. He knew full well there were those of his race that would savor the sight of his suffering.

He'd seen—not his brethren—but a woman. A human woman, illumed by that which his kind didn't possess, lit from within by the soft golden glow of her immortal soul.

A young, lushly sensual woman at that, with the look of the Irish about her. Long silvery-blond hair twisted up in a clip, loose shorter strands spiking about a delicate heart-shaped face. Huge eyes uptilted at the outer corners, a pointed chin, a full lush mouth. A flash of fire in her catlike green-gold gaze, proof of that passionate Gaelic temper that always turned him on. Full round breasts, shapely legs, luscious ass.

He'd gone instantly, painfully, hard as a rock.

And for a few critical moments, his brain hadn't functioned at all. All the rest of him had. Stupendously well, in fact. Just not his brain.

Cursed by the *féth fiada,* he'd been celibate for three long, hellish months now. And his own hand didn't count.

Lying there, imagining all the things he would do to her if only he could, he'd completely failed to process that she was not only standing there looking in his general direction, but his first instinct had been right: He *was* the focus of an intense gaze. She was looking directly at him.

Seeing him.

By the time he'd managed to find his feet, to even remember that he had feet, she'd been in her car.

She'd escaped him.

But not for long, he thought, eyes narrowing. He would find her.

She'd seen him. He had no idea how or why she'd been able to, but frankly he didn't much care. She had, and now she was going to be his ticket back to Paradise.

And, he thought, lips curving in a wicked erotic grin, he was willing to bet she'd be able to *feel* him too. Logic dictated that if she was immune to one aspect of the *féth fiada,* she would be immune to them all.

For the first time since the queen had made him human, he threw back his head and laughed. The rich dark sound rolled— despite the human mouth shaping it—not entirely human, echoing in the empty street.

He turned and eyed the building behind him speculatively. He knew a great deal about humans from having walked among them for so many millennia, and he'd learned even more about them in the past few months. They were creatures of habit; like plodding little Highland sheep, they dutifully trod the same hoof-beaten paths, returning to the same pastures day after day.

Undoubtedly, there was a reason she'd come to this building this evening.

And undoubtedly, there was something in that building that would lead him to her.

The luscious little Irish was going to be his savior.

She would help him find Circenn and communicate his plight. Circenn would sift dimensions and return him to the Fae Isle of Morar, where the queen held her court. And Adam would persuade her that enough was enough already.

He knew Aoibheal wouldn't be able to look him in the eye and deny him. He merely had to get to her, see her, touch her, remind her how much she favored him and why.

Ah, yes, now that he'd found someone who could see him, he'd be his glorious immortal self again in no time at all.

In the meantime, pending Circenn's return, he now had much with which to entertain himself. He was no longer in quite the same rush to be made immortal again. Not just yet. Not now that he suddenly had the opportunity to experience sex in human form. Fae glamour wasn't nearly as sensitive as the body he currently inhabited, and—sensual to the core— he'd been doubly pissed off at Aoibheal for making him unable to explore its erotic capabilities. She could be such a bitch sometimes.

If a simple hard-on in human form could reduce him to a primitive state, what would burying himself inside a woman do? What would it feel like to come inside her?

There was no doubt in his mind that he would soon find out.

Never had the mortal woman lived and breathed who could say no to a bit of fairy tail.

Beyond the highland mist

KAREN MARIE
MONING

ONLY
$3.99

BEYOND
the
HIGHLAND
MIST

Adrienne sighed, shook her head, and ordered her muscles to relax. She had nearly succeeded, when overhead a floorboard creaked. Tension reclaimed her instantly. She dropped Moonie on a stuffed chair and eyed the ceiling intently as the creaking sound repeated.

Perhaps it was just the house settling.

She really had to get over this skittishness.

How much time had to pass until she stopped being afraid that she would turn around and see Eberhard standing there with his faintly mocking smile and gleaming gun?

Eberhard was dead. She was safe, she knew she was.

So why did she feel so horridly vulnerable? For the past few days she'd had the suffocating sensation that someone was spying on her. No matter how hard she tried to reassure herself that anyone who might wish her harm was either dead—or didn't know she was alive—she was still consumed by a morbid unease. Every instinct she possessed warned her that something was wrong—or about to go terribly wrong. Having grown up in the City of Spooks—the sultry, superstitious, magical New Orleans—Adrienne had learned to listen to her instincts. They were almost always right on target.

Her instincts had even been right about Eberhard. She'd had a bad feeling about him from the beginning, but she'd convinced herself it was her own insecurity. Eberhard was the catch of New Orleans; naturally, a woman might feel a little unsettled by such a man.

Only much later did she understand that she'd been lonely for so long, and had wanted the fairy tale so badly, she'd tried to force reality to reflect her desires instead of the other way around. She'd told herself so many white lies before finally facing the truth that Eberhard wasn't the man she'd thought he was. She'd been such a fool.

Adrienne breathed deeply of the spring air that breezed gently in the window behind her, then flinched and spun abruptly. She eyed the fluttering drapes warily. Hadn't she closed that window? She was sure of it. She'd closed all of them just before closing the French doors. Adrienne edged cautiously to the window, shut it quickly, and locked it.

It was nerves, nothing more. No face peered in the window at her, no dogs barked, no alarms sounded. What was the use of taking so many precautions if she couldn't relax? There couldn't *possibly* be anyone out there.

She forced herself to turn away from the window. As she padded across the room, her foot encountered a small object and sent it skidding across the faded Oushak rug, where it clunked to a rest against the wall.

Adrienne glanced at it and flinched. It was a piece from Eberhard's chess set, the one she'd swiped from his house in

New Orleans the night she'd fled. She'd forgotten all about it after she'd moved in. She'd tossed it in a box—one of those piled in the corner that she'd never gotten around to unpacking. Perhaps Moonie had dragged the pieces out, she mused; there were several of them scattered across the rug.

She retrieved the piece she'd kicked and rolled it gingerly between her fingers. Waves of emotion flooded her: a sea of shame and anger and humiliation, capped with a relentless fear that she still wasn't safe.

A draft of air kissed the back of her neck and she stiffened, clutching the chess piece so tightly that the crown of the black queen dug cruelly into her palm. Logic insisted that the windows behind her were shut—she *knew* they were—still, instinct told her otherwise.

The rational Adrienne *knew* there was no one in her library but herself and a lightly snoring kitten. The irrational Adrienne teetered on the brink of terror.

Laughing nervously, she berated herself for being so jumpy, then cursed Eberhard for making her this way. She would *not* succumb to paranoia.

Dropping to her knees without sparing a backward glance, she scooped the scattered chess pieces into a pile. She didn't really like to touch them. A woman couldn't spend her childhood in New Orleans—much of it at the feet of a Creole storyteller who'd lived behind the orphanage—without becoming a bit superstitious. The set was ancient, an original Viking set; an old legend claimed it was cursed, and Adrienne's life had been cursed enough. The only reason she'd pilfered the set was in case she needed quick cash. Carved of walrus ivory and ebony, it would command an exorbitant price from a collector. Besides, hadn't she earned it, after all he'd put her through?

Adrienne muttered a colorful invective about beautiful men. It wasn't morally acceptable that someone as evil as

Eberhard had been so nice to look at. Poetic justice demanded otherwise—shouldn't people's faces reflect their hearts? If Eberhard had been as ugly on the outside as she'd belatedly discovered he was on the inside, she never would have ended up at the wrong end of a gun. Of course, Adrienne had learned the hard way that any end of a gun was the wrong end.

Eberhard Darrow Garrett was a beautiful, womanizing, deceitful man—and he'd ruined her life. Clutching the black queen tightly, she made herself a firm promise. "I will never go out with a beautiful man again, so long as I live and breathe. I hate beautiful men. Hate them!"

✳   ✳   ✳

Outside the French doors at 93 Coattail Lane, a man who lacked substance, a creature manmade devices could neither detect nor contain, heard her words and smiled. His choice was made with swift certainty—Adrienne de Simone was definitely the woman he'd been searching for.

to tame a
highland warrior

It wasn't easy for Jillian to hide in her chambers all day. She wasn't the cowering sort. Nor, however, was she the foolish sort, and she knew she must have a plan before she subjected herself to the perils of her parents' nefarious scheme. As afternoon faded into evening and she'd yet to be struck by inspiration, she discovered she was feeling quite irritable. She hated being cooped up in her chambers. She wanted to play the virginal, she wanted to kick the first person she saw, she wanted to visit Zeke, she wanted to eat. She'd thought someone would appear by lunchtime, she'd been certain loyal Kaley would come check on her if she didn't arrive at dinner, but the maids didn't even appear to clean her chambers or light the fire. As the solitary hours passed, Jillian's ire increased. The angrier she became, the less objectively she considered her plight, ultimately concluding she would simply ignore the three men and go about her life as if nothing were amiss.

Food was her priority now. Shivering in the chilly evening air, she donned a light but voluminous cloak and pulled the hood snug around her face. Perhaps if she met up with one of the oversized brutes, the combination of darkness and concealing attire would grant her anonymity. It probably wouldn't fool Grimm, but the other two hadn't seen her with clothes *on* yet.

Jillian closed the door quietly and slipped into the hallway. She opted for the servants' staircase and carefully picked her way down the dimly lit, winding steps. Caithness was huge, but Jillian had played in every nook and cranny and knew the castle well; nine doors down and to the left was the kitchen, just past the buttery. She peered down the long corridor. Lit by flickering oil lamps, it was deserted, the castle silent. Where was everyone?

As she moved forward, a voice floated out of the darkness behind her. "Pardon, lass, but could you tell me where I might find the buttery? We've run short of whisky and there's not a maid about."

Jillian froze in mid-step, momentarily robbed of speech. How could all the maids disappear and that man appear the very instant she decided to sneak from her chambers?

"I asked you to leave, Grimm Roderick. What are you still doing here?" she said coolly.

"Is that you, Jillian?" He stepped closer, peering through the shadows.

"Have so many other women at Caithness demanded you depart that you're suffering confusion about my identity?" she asked sweetly, plunging her shaking hands into the folds of her cloak.

"I didn't recognize you beneath your hood until I heard

you speak, and as to the women, you know how the women around here felt about me. I assume nothing has changed."

Jillian almost choked. He was as arrogant as he'd always been. She pushed her hood back irritably. The women had fallen all over him when he'd fostered here, lured by his dark, dangerous looks, muscled body, and absolute indifference. Maids had thrown themselves at his feet, visiting ladies had offered him jewels and lodgings. It had been revolting to watch. "Well, you are older," she parried weakly. "And you know as a man gets older his good looks can suffer."

Grimm's mouth turned faintly upward as he stepped forward into the flickering light thrown off by a wall torch. Tiny lines at the corners of his eyes were whiter than his Highland-tanned face. If anything, it made him more beautiful.

"You are older too." He studied her through narrowed eyes.

"It's not nice to chide a woman about her age. I am *not* an old maid."

"I didn't say you were," he said mildly. "The years have made you a lovely woman."

"And?" Jillian demanded.

"And what?"

"Well, go ahead. Don't leave me hanging, waiting for the nasty thing you're going to say. Just say it and get it over with."

"What nasty thing?"

"Grimm Roderick, you have never said a single nice thing to me in all my life. So don't start faking it now."

Grimm's mouth twisted up at one corner, and Jillian realized that he still hated to smile. He fought it, begrudged it, and rarely did one ever break the confines of his eternal self-control. Such a waste, for he was even more handsome when he smiled, if that was possible.

He moved closer.

"Stop right there!"

Grimm ignored her command, continuing his approach.

"I said *stop*."

"Or you'll do what, Jillian?" His voice was smooth and amused. He cocked his head at a lazy angle and folded his arms across his chest.

"Why, I'll . . ." She belatedly acknowledged there wasn't much of anything she could do to prevent him from going anywhere he wished to go, in any manner he wished to go there. He was twice her size, and she'd never be his physical match. The only weapon she'd ever had against him was her sharp tongue, honed to a razor edge by years of defensive practice on this man.

He shrugged his shoulders impatiently. "Tell me, lass, what will you do?"

the highlander's touch

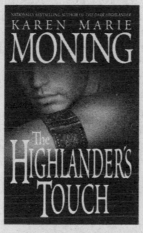

Lisa awoke abruptly, uncertain of where she was or what had awakened her. Then she heard men's voices in the hallway outside the office.

Galvanized into action, Lisa leaped to her feet and shot a panicked glance at her watch. It was 5:20 A.M.—she would lose her job! Instinctively she dropped to the floor and took a nasty blow to her temple on the corner of the desk in the process. Wincing, she crawled under the desk as she heard a key in the lock, followed by Steinmann's voice: "It's impossible to get decent help. Worthless maid didn't even lock up. All she had to do was press the button. Even a child could do it."

Lisa curled into a silent ball as the men entered the office.

"Here it is." Steinmann's spotlessly buffed shoes stopped inches from her knees.

"What amazing detail. It's beautiful." The second voice was hushed.

"Isn't it?" Steinmann agreed.

"Wait a minute, Steinmann. Where did you say this chest was found?"

"Beneath a crush of rock near a riverbank in Scotland."

"That doesn't make any sense. How did it remain untouched by the elements? Ebony is obdurate wood, but it isn't impervious to decay. This chest is in mint condition. Has it been dated yet?"

"No, but my source in Edinburgh swore by it. Can you open it, Taylor?" Steinmann said.

There was a rustle of noise. A softly murmured "Let's see . . . How do you work, you lovely little mystery?"

Lisa battled an urge to pop out from under the desk, curiosity nearly overriding her common sense and instinct for self-preservation.

There was a long pause. "Well? What is it?" Steinmann asked.

"I have no idea," Taylor said slowly. "I've neither translated tales of it nor seen sketches in my research. It doesn't look quite medieval, does it? It almost looks . . . why . . . futuristic," he said uneasily. "Frankly, I'm baffled."

"Perhaps you aren't as much of an expert as you would have me believe, Taylor."

"No one knows more about the Gaels and Picts than I do," he replied stiffly. "But some artifacts simply aren't mentioned in any records. I assure you, I will find the answers."

"And you'll have it examined?" Steinmann said.

"I'll take it with me now—"

"No. I'll call you when we're ready to release it."

There was a pause, then: "You plan to invite someone else to examine it, don't you?" Taylor said. "You question my ability."

"I simply need to get it cataloged, photographed, and logged into our files."

"And logged into someone else's collection?" Taylor said tightly.

"Put it back, Taylor." Steinmann closed his fingers around Taylor's wrist, lowering the flask back to the cloth. He slipped the tongs from Taylor's hand, closed the chest, and placed the tongs beside it.

"Fine," Taylor snapped. "But when you discover no one else knows what it is, you'll be calling me. You can't move an artifact that can't be identified. I'm the only one who can track this thing down, and you know it."

Steinmann laughed. "I'll see you out."

"I can find my own way."

"But I'll rest easier knowing I've escorted you," Steinmann said softly. "It wouldn't do to leave such a passionate antiquity worshiper as yourself wandering the museum on his own."

The shoes retreated with muffled steps across the carpet. The click of a key in the lock jarred Lisa into action. *Damn and double-damn!* Normally when she left, she depressed the button latch on the door— no lowly maid was entrusted with keys. Steinmann had bypassed the button latch and actually used a key to lock the dead bolt. She jerked upright and banged her head against the underside of the desk. "Ow!" she exclaimed softly. As she clutched the edge and drew herself upright, she paused to look at the chest.

Fascinated, she touched the cool wood. Beautifully engraved, the black wood gleamed in the low light. Bold letters were seared into the top in angry, slanted strokes. What did the chest contain that had perplexed two sophisticated purveyors of antiquities? Despite the fact that she was locked in Steinmann's office and had no doubt that he would return in moments, she was consumed by curiosity. *Futuristic?*

Gingerly, she ran her fingers over the chest, seeking the square pressure latch they'd mentioned, then paused. The strange letters on the lid seemed almost to . . . pulse. A shiver of foreboding raced up her spine.

Silly goose—open it! It can't hurt you. They *touched it.*

Resolved, she isolated the square and depressed it with her thumb. The lid swung upward with the faint popping sound she'd heard earlier. A flask lay inside, surrounded by dusty tatters of ancient fabric. The flask was fashioned of a silver metal and seemed to shimmer, as if the contents were energized. She cast a nervous glance at the door. She knew she had to get out of the office before Steinmann returned, yet she felt strangely transfixed by the flask. Her eyes drifted from door to flask and back again, but the flask beckoned. It said, *Touch me,* in the same tone all the artifacts in the museum spoke to Lisa. *Touch me while no guards are about, and I will tell you of my history and my legends. I am knowledge. . . .*

Lisa's fingertips curled around the flask.

The world shifted on its axis beneath her feet. She stumbled, and suddenly she . . .

Couldn't . . .

Stop . . .

Falling . . .

kiss of the highlander

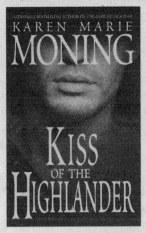

She'd fallen on a body. One that, considering she hadn't disturbed it, must be dead. *Or,* she worried, *perhaps I killed it when I fell.*

When she managed to stop screaming, she found that she'd pushed herself up and was straddling it, her palms braced on its chest. Not its chest, she realized, but *his* chest. The motionless figure beneath her was undeniably male.

Sinfully male.

She snatched her hands away and sucked in a shocked breath.

However he'd managed to get here, if he was dead, his demise had been quite recent. He was in perfect condition and—her hands crept back to his chest—warm. He had the sculpted physique of a professional football player, with wide shoulders, pumped biceps and pecs, and washboard abs. His hips beneath her were lean and powerful. Strange symbols were tattooed across his bare chest.

She took slow, deep breaths to ease the sudden tightness in her chest. Leaning cautiously forward, she peered at a face that was savagely beautiful. His was the type of dominant male virility women dreamed about in dark, erotic fantasies but knew didn't *really* exist. Black lashes swept his golden skin, beneath arched brows and a silky fall of long, black hair. His jaw was dusted with a blue-black shadow beard; his lips were pink and firm and sensually full. She brushed her finger against them, then felt mildly perverse, so she pretended she was just checking to see if he was alive and shook him, but he didn't respond. Cupping his nose with her hand, she was relieved to feel a soft puff of breath. *He isn't dead, thank God.* It made her feel better about finding him so attractive. Palm flush to his chest, she was further reassured by his strong heartbeat. Although it wasn't beating very often, at least it was. He must be deeply unconscious, perhaps in a coma, she decided. Whichever it was, he couldn't help her.

Her gaze darted back up to the hole. Even if she managed to wake him and then stood on his shoulders, she still wouldn't be near the lip of the hole. Sunshine streamed over her face, mocking her with a freedom that was so near, yet so impossibly far, and she shivered again. "Just what am I supposed to do now?" she muttered.

Despite the fact that he was unconscious and of no use, her gaze swept back down. He exuded such vitality that his condition baffled her. She couldn't decide if she was upset that he was unconscious, or relieved. With his looks he was surely a womanizer, just the kind of man she steered away from by instinct. Having grown up surrounded by scientists, she had no experience with men of his ilk. On the rare occasions she'd glimpsed a man like him sauntering out of Gold's Gym, she'd gawked surreptitiously, grateful that she was safely in her car. So much testosterone made her nervous. It couldn't possibly be healthy.

Cherry picker extraordinaire. The thought caught her off guard. Mortified, she berated herself, because he was injured and there she was, sitting on him, thinking lascivious thoughts. She pondered the possibility that she'd developed some kind of hormonal imbalance, perhaps a surfeit of perky little eggs.

She eyed the designs on the man's chest more closely, wondering if one of them concealed a wound. The strange symbols, unlike any tattoos she'd ever seen, were smeared with blood from the abrasions on her palms.

Gwen leaned back a few inches so a ray of sunshine spilled across his chest. As she studied him, a curious thing happened: the brightly colored designs blurred before her eyes, growing indistinct, as if they were fading, leaving only streaks of her blood to mar his muscled chest. But that wasn't possible. . . .

Gwen blinked as, undeniably, several symbols disappeared entirely. In a matter of moments all of them were gone, vanished as if they'd never existed.

Perplexed, she glanced up at his face and sucked in an astonished breath.

His eyes were open and he was watching her. He had remarkable eyes that glittered like shards of silver and ice, sleepy eyes that banked a touch of amusement and unmistakable masculine interest. He stretched his body beneath hers with the self-indulgent grace of a cat prolonging the pleasure of awakening, and she suspected that although he was rousing physically, his mental acuity was not fully engaged. His pupils were large and dark, as if he'd recently had his eyes dilated for an exam or taken some drug.

Oh, God, he's conscious and I'm straddling him! She could imagine what he was thinking and could hardly blame him for it. She was as intimately positioned as a woman astride her lover, knees on either side of his hips, her palms flat against his rock-hard stomach.

She tensed and tried to scramble off him, but his hands clamped around her thighs and pinned her there. He didn't speak, merely secured and regarded her, his eyes dropping to linger appreciatively on her breasts. When he slid his hands up her bare thighs, she seriously regretted having put on her short-shorts this morning. A slip of a lilac thong was all that was beneath them, and his fingers were toying with the hem of her shorts, perilously close to slipping inside. . . .

the dark highlander

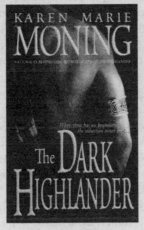

KAREN MARIE MONING

Some days Dageus felt as ancient as the evil within him.

As he hailed a cab to take him to The Cloisters to pick up a copy of one of the last tomes in New York that he needed to check, he didn't notice the fascinated glances women walking down the sidewalk turned his way. Didn't realize that, even in a metropolis that teemed with diversity, he stood out. It was nothing he said or did; to all appearances he was but another wealthy, sinfully gorgeous man. It was simply the essence of the man. The way he moved. His every gesture exuded power, something dark and . . . forbidden. He was sexual in a way that made women think of deeply repressed fantasies therapists and feminists alike would cringe to hear tell of.

But he realized none of that. His thoughts were far away,

still mulling over the nonsense penned in the Book of Leinster.

Och, what he wouldn't give for his da's library.

In lieu of it, he'd been systematically obtaining what manuscripts still existed, exhausting his present possibilities before pursuing riskier ones. Risky, like setting foot on the isles of his ancestors again, a thing fast seeming inevitable.

Thinking of risk, he made a mental note to return some of the volumes he'd "borrowed" from private collections when bribes had failed. It wouldn't do to have them lying about too long.

He glanced up at the clock above the bank. Twelve forty-five. The cocurator of The Cloisters had assured him he would have the text delivered first thing that morn, but it hadn't arrived and Dageus was weary of waiting.

He needed information, *accurate* information about the Keltar's ancient benefactors, the Tuatha Dé Danaan, those "gods and not gods," as the Book of the Dun Cow called them. They were the ones who had originally imprisoned the dark Druids in the in-between, hence it followed that there was a way to reimprison them.

It was imperative he find that way.

As he eased into the cab—a torturous fit for a man of his height and breadth—his attention was caught by a lass who was stepping from a car at the curb in front of them.

She was different, and it was that difference that drew his eye. She had none of the city's polish and was all the lovelier for it. Refreshingly tousled, delightfully free of the artifice with which modern women enhanced their faces, she was a vision.

"Wait," he growled at the driver, watching her hungrily.

His every sense heightened painfully. His hands fisted as desire, never sated, flooded him.

Somewhere in her ancestry the lass had Scots blood. It

was there in the curly waves of copper-and-blond hair that tumbled about a delicate face with a surprisingly strong jaw. It was there in the peaches-and-cream complexion and the huge aquamarine eyes—eyes that still regarded the world with wonder, he noticed with a faintly mocking smile. It was there in a fire that simmered just beneath the surface of her flawless skin. Wee, lusciously plump where it counted, with a trim waist and shapely legs hugged by a snug skirt, the lass was an exiled Highlander's dream.

He wet his lips and stared, making a noise deep in his throat that was more animal than human.

When she leaned back in through the open window of the car to say something to the driver, the back of her skirt rode up a few inches. He inhaled sharply, envisioning himself behind her. His entire body went tight with lust.

Christ, she was lovely. Lush curves that could make a dead man stir.

She leaned forward a smidgen, showing more of that sweet curve of the back of her thigh.

His mouth went ferociously dry.

No' for me, he warned himself, gritting his teeth and shifting to lessen the pressure on his suddenly painfully hard cock. He took only experienced lasses to his bed. Lasses far older in both mind and body. Not reeking, as she did, of innocence. Of bright dreams and a bonny future.

Sleek and worldly, with jaded palates and cynical hearts—they were the ones a man could tumble and leave with a bauble in the morn, no worse for the wear.

She was the kind a man kept.

"Go," he murmured to the driver, forcing his gaze away.